A Tribute to Kathleen E. Woodiwiss

"Woodiwiss made women want to read. She gave them an alternative to Westerns and hard-boiled police procedurals. When I was growing up, I saw my mother and grandmother reading and enjoying romances, and when I was old enough to read them myself, I felt as if I had been admitted into a special sisterhood of reading women."
New York Times bestselling author Julia Quinn

"Kathleen E. Woodiwiss was an innovator of genre fiction."
New York Times bestselling author Eloisa James

"I am humbled by what a tremendous debt of gratitude we all owe Kathleen E. Woodiwiss. . . . At the conclusion of *The Flame and the Flower,* she shouldn't have written 'The End,' but 'The Beginning.' "
New York Times bestselling author Teresa Medeiros

"We all owe our careers to her. She opened the world of romance to us as readers. She created a career for us to go into."
New York Times bestselling author Susan Elizabeth Phillips

"She ranks alongside Georgette Heyer as one of the greats in the field, and provided a seminal influence on my works and those of many other authors. . . . Romance, especially historical romance, would have been much diminished without the contributions of Kathleen Woodiwiss."
New York Times bestselling author Stephanie Laurens

By Kathleen E. Woodiwiss

EVERLASTING
THE RELUCTANT SUITOR
A SEASON BEYOND A KISS
FOREVER IN YOUR EMBRACE
THE ELUSIVE FLAME
PETALS ON THE RIVER
SO WORTHY MY LOVE
COME LOVE A STRANGER
A ROSE IN WINTER
ASHES IN THE WIND
SHANNA
THE WOLF AND THE DOVE
THE FLAME AND THE FLOWER

Anthology
MARRIED AT MIDNIGHT

KATHLEEN E. WOODIWISS

EVERLASTING

AVON

An Imprint of HarperCollins*Publishers*

This title was previously published in hardcover November 2007 by William Morrow, an Imprint of HarperCollins Publishers.

AVON BOOKS
An Imprint of HarperCollins*Publishers*
10 East 53rd Street
New York, New York 10022-5299

Copyright © 2007 by Kathleen E. Woodiwiss
ISBN 978-0-06-054553-6
www.avonromance.com

First Avon Books paperback printing: December 2008
First William Morrow hardcover printing: November 2007

Avon Trademark Reg. U.S. Pat. Off. and in Other Countries, Marca Registrada, Hecho en U.S.A.
HarperCollins® is a registered trademark of HarperCollins Publishers.

Printed in the U.S.A.

10 9 8 7 6 5 4 3 2 1

*In everlasting gratitude, this book is dedicated
to all of Kathleen's beloved readers*

Chapter 1

August 24, 1135

She knew his name was Raven Seabern, that he was here at Westminster Castle in the service of his king, and she was aware of something else as well, that the tall, raven-haired Scotsman was staring at her again. But she was the Lady Abrielle of Harrington, daughter of a late Saxon hero of the Crusades, stepdaughter of a Norman knight who had also gained high esteem for his brave years of service in the Holy Land, both to be honored here tonight, and she would give the man's attention the lack of regard it deserved. For here, at the court of King Henry, she was being paid the admiration of so many men. She turned away quickly and nodded to her mother's soft-spoken praise of the interior grandeur of the great hall of Westminster Castle. Two massive hearths dominated the room at each end, with flames roaring higher than a man. Tapestries kept out the chill drafts and depicted scenes of men in battle or men at the hunt. The stitches were colored in royal crimson and gold, the deepest blue of a king's robe, the startling green of dark forest. Never had Abrielle been in a castle so magnificent in its display of wealth and power. And she had been invited by the king himself.

She wanted to savor this happy occasion, as nights such as this had become sadly rare in her life since her father's death and her stepfather's recent difficulties. It was hard to be at ease, however, much less concentrate, with the Scotsman's vivid blue gaze following her with an intensity to which she was not accustomed. And as if his staring were not unsettling enough, the man seemed to possess some mysterious power over her own traitorous gaze, as time and again she found it straying in his direction, despite her resolution not to reward his attention in any way. Thus far, she'd caught herself before indulging in anything more than a swift sideways glance or guarded perusal from beneath the sweep of her long, dark lashes, but in fact she had no need to look his way simply to confirm the fact that he was watching her yet again. It was as if his keen appraisal were tangible; she could feel it, the heat and weight of it, as surely and distractingly as if he were trailing a silken feather over her skin.

He was but one of the many men who had shown interest in her in recent days. Ever since her arrival in London with her mother, Elspeth, and her stepfather, Vachel de Gerard, Abrielle had received the overwhelming regard of noblemen looking for a suitable wife. Though Vachel did not yet have a title, it was assumed that King Henry this night was ready at last to confer such honors on a man known for his heroic deeds on the great Crusade. As a title brought with it lands and income, all knew that afterward, Abrielle's dowry would increase substantially. During her short stay in London, men had come and gone from her stepfather's apartments within Westminster Castle, presenting themselves first to her parents, then to her.

Those who had done so were men of honorable intentions, which it would seem the Scotsman was not, as for all his apparent fascination with her, he kept his distance. Even now he stood beside King Henry on the other side of the great hall. Tall and powerful, decked out in bonnet and plaid, he was of an age perhaps a score and ten, mayhap two or three years beyond. But it wasn't only his height and impressive display of muscle and sinew that caused him to stand out from the rest of the noblemen gathered by the king to converse and await the announcement of dinner. There was about him an air of confidence that he wore as easily as he did his colors.

Or so it seemed to Abrielle, who could hardly judge for certain when she'd never heard him utter a single word or seen him without the distance and clamor of a crowded hall between them. Other men spoke to her of the fine evening air, or pointed out the treasures and paintings displayed beneath the light of thousands of candles, but not the Scotsman. It troubled Abrielle that his reserve caused her even a slight twinge of disappointment. She should not expect more from a stranger, a foreigner born, a man serving as emissary to King David of Scotland, one whose loyalty lay with those who had so often through the centuries ravaged the northern English lands in which she was born and bred.

He was the very last man she should be wasting her

time thinking about, especially on a momentous eve such as this. For tonight she was concerned with matters of far more import, as the king's words would seal her fate, determining whether life held for her despair or joy. Sufficient largesse toward her stepfather would bring the maiden a boon dearly sought but rarely won, gained only with a very large dowry. 'Twas the gift of choosing her husband from among the best of the land.

She turned away and back to her stepfather and mother, whose excitement suffused her with pride. So much would be happening this night—reward for Vachel, a loyal servant of the king, but also a poignant ceremony that evoked a heartrending memory for Abrielle. Recognition for Berwin of Harrington's efforts in the Crusade was scheduled to take place this very evening, and King Henry was in agreement that some esteem should be shown to her late father as well as others who had fought in that campaign. At the Norman court, many Saxons had gathered, after spending countless months striving to have some homage bestowed upon their friends and kinsmen who had fought in the Holy Land, especially since the death of Lord Berwin of Harrington. It had been their way of throwing their own gauntlet at the feet of the unsavory Norman who had gone out of his way to provoke her parent and then, upon accepting his angry challenge, humiliate him for his lack of skill in defending himself. To their regret, the Norman had deftly delivered a deathblow that had left Berwin's family and friends grieving over his loss.

Although her stepfather of three years, himself an honorable Norman knight of the realm, had escorted her and her mother to the palace for the event, Abrielle knew the honors that were to be bestowed upon her father's memory were at first tantamount to a glove being flung across Vachel's cheeks. For he had been assured by others among the knights that at last it was his turn for recognition from the king. He had spent nearly a decade defending Jerusalem and been deemed a hero by many.

Abrielle knew numerous individuals who were as deserving of the honor that was to be bestowed upon her father's memory, not just Vachel but also her late betrothed, Weldon de Marlé, another Norman who had proven himself to be among the noblest of heroes during that campaign. Shortly after his return home, he had begun building a keep, during which time he had petitioned her stepfather for her hand in marriage. Sadly, after completing his keep, he had fallen to his death the day before they were to be married, leaving her as bereft as a widow true, but without the sweet memories of love to sustain her.

Dearest Weldon could not be here to see Vachel's reward for service well done, but sadly, his only kinsman, Desmond de Marlé, had somehow managed to be present. How he had done so was difficult to fathom, as he had a repugnant air, being lecherous in the extreme, with eyes full of greed and lust within his too-round face. She could only believe that he had convinced some errant page or servant to accept a generous sum for allowing him access. Several months before they were to be married, Weldon had introduced her to his only kinsman, and thereafter the most unpleasant Desmond had been inclined to dog her heels. Since Weldon's death, the ogre's propensity to intrude into her life had increased by an alarming degree. Little had she imagined after receiving word of Weldon's accident that she would then find herself contending with his dastardly half brother on a fairly frequent basis. Although Desmond had been in dire financial straits before Weldon's death, he was now basking in the wealth her betrothed had left behind and obviously using it in order to get close to her. Now in the heat of the king's great hall, his face glistened with sweat, his overlarge eyes watched Abrielle with a fascination that unnerved her.

She knew she had much to be thankful for in the support of her lifelong friend, Cordelia of Grayson, who with her family was attending the London festivities. Cordelia, a great heiress, received her own share of attention from the men in the hall, and Abrielle hoped that together later this night they would relive the evening and discuss all the men they'd met.

Cordelia watched with great satisfaction as the men of king's court became enthralled with her truly beautiful best friend, one whose appearance was bested only by the kindness of her nature. Her very favorable translucent blue-green eyes, rosy cheeks, and swirling reddish curls made her irresistible to a goodly number of men. Although Lord Weldon had been nigh to two score and five years of age when he had asked the lady to marry him, he had nevertheless been totally smitten by her beauty and eager to wed her. Having known her friend as long and as well as she had, Cordelia was convinced that Abrielle had been genuinely pleased by their betrothal and been looking forward with eager anticipation to their wedding, only to suffer grievous remorse when news of his death had come. It was encouraging to see evidence that her companion had recovered from the tragedy enough to show some interest in other handsome men.

As a blast from a horn announced the serving of the

great feast, Abrielle and her parents and Cordelia and her parents, Lord Reginald Grayson and the Lady Isolde, moved to their table just below the king's dais. Abrielle, on display to many, felt that she looked her very best for the ceremony honoring her late father. Although the gown had originally been made for Elspeth for her wedding to Vachel a trio of years ago, after that event it had been carefully wrapped and stored in a coffer. The iridescent beads and bejeweled embroidery of deepest blue delicately adorning the gown from ornate collar to hem made no less than a stunning work of art that had taken numerous servants untold weeks to finish.

That had been when coins and servants had been fairly plentiful. However, in the family's present dire circumstances, it was a rare occasion indeed when mother and daughter could garb themselves in beautiful attire and attend elaborate functions. Prior to his death, Berwin had provided for them very well, and so had Vachel before his father, Willaume de Gerard, had broken a promise he had made to his younger son prior to accepting financial assistance from him in the form of both money and goods. Although Willaume had sworn to return such to his son at the earliest moment possible, he had obviously failed to remember from whom he had received such help, for he had left everything to his elder son, Alain, who had been responsible for his father's financial straits in the first place.

Before tonight's recognition, Vachel had been forced to consider just how dire his own family's future was going to be if he didn't recover some of the help he had also extended to his knights. Like him, they had returned to England to find many of the nobles refusing to give out honors and titles lest the kingdom be impoverished, yet whenever he saw others basking in the wealth and titles they had managed to glean from frivolous deeds, Vachel was wont to resent their refusal to give him a title. Elspeth was everything he had ever hoped to have in a wife, especially since his first one had been less than pleasant and had died in childbirth cursing his name. In view of their deepening impoverishment, he feared he would eventually lose Elspeth's love and respect. But at last tonight would come a reckoning, a reward from the king for his years of hazardous service.

Much to Abrielle's amazement, she recognized the Scotsman among the men talking and laughing with the king, at a place of honor at the head table. As they were awaiting the servant's approach with a warm bowl to wash their hands, Cordelia nudged her. "Aye, there is a man fine to look at."

Abrielle quickly looked away from the head table, feeling a flush bloom in her cheeks. "The king is too old for me to even—"

But Cordelia only laughed and slyly whispered, "You cannot fool me, my dear Abrielle. You are not the only woman looking at that handsome Scotsman, for every last one of us here by now knows that his name is Raven Seabern, and he is an emissary for his majesty, King David of Scotland, an ambassador for his country to this Norman court."

"There is a Scotsman at the head table?" Abrielle asked innocently, then gave a faint smile when Cordelia only rolled her eyes and covered her mouth against escaping mirth. "Cordelia, if there is any man not even worth thinking about, it is one such as he. King Henry may have married King David's sister, and given rise to the peace between our two kingdoms, but you and I both know the deep resentment experienced by our own kinsman in the north. Terrible deeds have been done in the name of both countries on the borderlands, and both you and I are well aware that people do not easily forget."

Cordelia cocked her head, her eyes impish with delight. "Oh, I don't know, Abrielle. Can a woman not look at a handsome man and forget where he comes from? Do not a pleasant brogue and a masculine smile make for a warm summer's evening?"

Abrielle sighed at her friend's playfulness, but inside she experienced a feeling of unease that would not go away. Would tonight's festivities be interrupted by the arguing of prideful men? She saw more than one of her father's neighbors here to honor him, yet giving the head table narrow-eyed looks of anger that could be directed only at the Scotsman.

"Cordelia, I cannot even imagine taking such light pleasure in something so serious," Abrielle said, leaning into her friend so that their parents could not hear. "Even looking at him makes me feel disloyal. There is strife enough in our land betwixt Saxon and Norman; I need not marry someone who might well add to the tension felt by many."

"Did I say anything about marriage?" Cordelia asked.

Abrielle frowned at her, then reluctantly began to laugh. "Nay, you did not. And this only goes to show you that I have been too deep in my cares. Tonight is for enjoyment."

"Then enjoy it, Abrielle," Cordelia replied softly, touching her friend's arm. "You of all women deserve it."

As the dinner was served, the two young women gaped in awe at the stuffed peacocks carried over the servants' heads as they paraded about the hall, still looking like live birds floating in a river. Every course of the meal brought such satisfaction to their mouths and stomachs. They ate more than they spoke, and Abrielle felt a nervous tension thrum through her for the rest of the evening's ceremonies. They could not be certain what would happen, and for the first time since Weldon's death, she felt full of possibilities. She glanced at her mother and stepfather, saw their own hope in the loving looks they gave each other. If Norman and Saxon could come together as they had, then she had to believe that there was a chance for her own happiness.

To her surprise, she could hear much of what went on at the high table, and Cordelia nudged her when a nobleman asked Raven Seabern how he had come by his given name. The deep, gravelly tones of the Scot's voice caused the strangest of shivers across Abrielle's flesh. She knew she should not listen in on the conversation of others, but he so openly played to the crowd that he obviously meant his story to be heard. His voice was sonorous, its rough burr evoking the fierce, wild land from which he'd sprung. She had no choice but to listen.

"When my mother was expecting me, she awoke in the middle of the night ta the sound of pecking on her window. It persisted, it did, until she got out of bed and opened the shutters. In came a raven, as bold as ye please, and cocked his head at my mother." Slipping into a deep brogue, he quoted her. " 'Saints alive,' said she, 'ye act as if ye belong here,' whereupon the bird flew out and returned a moment later with a tiny branch he had plucked from my mother's rosebush. Considering that my da hadn't returned home, she was a-frettin' he may've been thrown from his horse or waylaid by brigands. She had a servant hitch up a cart and drive her along the lane that my da usually took upon his return home. The raven flew ahead, he did, and ta my mother's surprise, he led them straight ta my da, who'd been crossing the river when the planks fell through the bridge, dropping his steed inta the chilly water and himself firmly betwixt two rocks. My da was nearly frozen from the crisp winds, but our servant pulled him free and started rubbing some life back into his limbs. Thereafter, my mother found good reason ta be thankful for ravens, and decided when I was born ta name me Raven in appreciation."

Everyone within hearing chuckled, including Abrielle, but her soft laugh caught in her throat when, as though hearing her laugh through the chorus of others, Raven suddenly swung his gaze to her and held her in its dark blue depths. Suddenly she was the captive of those fathomless midnight eyes, and while doubtless those around them went on breathing and speaking normally, Abrielle felt as if she and the Scot were alone in the world. Though 'twas most definitely not a feeling to which she was accustomed, some burgeoning feminine instinct deep within her recognized the fiery gleam in his eyes and understood that he felt the same.

"So what happened to the raven in the story?" someone called out, as from a great distance it seemed to Abrielle. Still, it was enough to break the spell.

"Oh, my mother had him cooked for her vittles the very next day," Raven replied, still holding her gaze.

Abrielle's jaw dropped in astonishment, causing Henry's hearty laughter to reverberate throughout the room. The king could not have helped noticing where Raven had been looking and she found herself the object of the royal stare. His Majesty slapped a hand upon the planks of the table. "The lad's teasing you, my lady, never fear."

Abrielle now found herself the focus of even more inquisitive stares. At her side, her mother glanced at her with interest, and her stepfather, on Elspeth's far side, gave her a frown. She knew he was distracted and wished nothing to go wrong this evening.

Abrielle could see the sudden way that Raven's smile changed from open humor to something more guarded, and she was uncertain of its meaning. Had he, too, realized that she was not one for a man such as he? He clasped a lean hand against the folds of plaid that lay across his black-garbed chest and spoke with a more cautious air. "Forgive my teasing, my lady. The raven stayed with us and was as watchful over my da as a dog over a bone. We never knew the reason for the bird's attachment, excepting my da had a twin who drowned a year earlier. He had a raven that would fly alongside his cart. In any case, the bird stayed with us until he died of old age. So ye see, with the proper incentive, even a bird of prey can be tamed."

Abrielle was relieved when he deliberately turned away from her to respond to something spoken softly by the king. But beneath her relief was an uneasiness she couldn't quite place.

At last the meal was over and the king rose to his full height, presiding over his silent hall. Hundreds of noblemen, knights, and their families waited for what the king would announce. Abrielle saw that Vachel took her mother's hand and squeezed gently, as if in support and courage.

The king spoke ringingly of the great deeds of the Saxons who fought in his name, especially honoring Berwin of Harrington, leaving Abrielle feeling proud of her late father. Her mother had tears in her eyes, and Vachel, unlike other men, showed no jealousy. He obviously loved Elspeth enough to share her with her memories. At last the king came to what affected Abrielle's new family and their future.

"There are thousands of men, both Norman and Saxon, who fought in our name against the Infidels overrunning the Holy Land. The crown extends its deepest gratitude and wishes that every man could have every reward due, but we must balance the good of several men against the good of an entire kingdom. England must remain strong, and her treasury with her. So for now our soldiers have our humblest gratitude and the reward of knowing their service was invaluable. Tonight let us celebrate their accomplishments in song and dance."

The king raised his hand and his minstrels began to play a rousing song on pipe and lute, but Abrielle sat numb, full of disbelief. The king's treasury could no longer afford to be depleted, so there would be no reward for Vachel's long years of service? Where others before tonight received wealth and titles, he would have nothing? The lump in her throat felt as if she would never swallow again, and her eyes, so strangely dry one moment, stung painfully the next. She knew others at the long trestle table were staring at them, muttering to each other, discussing her family's future. To avoid their eyes, she fixed her attention on the goblet before her, a gift from her beloved father, presented to her mere months before his untimely death. Fashioned of silver, it bore runic Saxon writing in a band encircling its center. She clasped her right hand around this family legacy, drawing comfort from the reminder of both her late parent and the noble Saxon heritage she shared with him, as well as strength. For now her thoughts could return to her mother and stepfather, and she turned her aching neck to look at them.

They still held hands, as if frozen together. Elspeth's eyes did not glisten with tears; she was too proud for that. Her chin was lifted with hauteur, and her flashing eyes dared anyone to make remarks. Vachel's grim expression said all. This was a blow he had not expected, and her grief for the man who'd saved her and her mother was intense and painful. How would he bear this new burden?

Vachel himself could barely think, so confused were his thoughts. The honor due him at last would never be; the reward he'd justly earned had gone to others, and now there was no more to be had. The king did not look at him, but he could feel the eyes of dozens of others, speculative, curious, even grimly amused, as if his woes served only to mark another tragedy that one could relate to the next gossip avid for another's misery. Though he had been at pains to keep secret the true extent of his problems, the fact that he and his small family were close to impoverishment would fairly soon be known to one and all. He would not be able to compensate his knights, nor even to afford the running of a household. Far more devastating to his pride, and to his heart, was the knowledge that his beloved Elspeth and her daughter would be forced to share the grim consequences of his misfortune, consequences that would be immediate and unavoidable. Everyone present there would realize at this moment that Abrielle would not have the great dowry formerly anticipated and the most worthy of those men seeking wives, those best able to provide the standing and security Abrielle deserved, would turn their attention elsewhere in search of a maiden who would bring wealth with her. His stepdaughter would be undeservedly forced to lower her expectations. Worse, she would be ripe for pursuit by unscrupulous men seeking to use her for her beauty, rather than treating her with the dignity a wife deserved. And it was all too possible the maiden would not find a husband at all, bringing more humiliation and heartache to both her and her mother. For who would want to marry a girl with so little to bring to the union?

How was he to stay in Westminster Castle after this? All he could think of was leaving, absorbing his own pain in peace.

Abrielle took a deep, tight breath, watching blankly as the servants cleared away the remains of the feast, dismantling the trestle tables so that the dancing could begin. Only hours ago, she had been the one men flocked to, the one treated as the great heiress. But men and fate, it seemed, were equally capricious, though men were buffeted about by fate, and she by the fate of men. First her father had died before his time, then her noble betrothed, and now the deeds and decisions of her stepfather and of King Henry himself had shaken the very ground on which she stood, taking from her the one thing that could have given her a hand in making her own future, the right to choose her husband. As she stood with her parents, the men who'd once flocked to her for a morsel of kindness now avoided even her gaze. There were true heiresses to fawn over, and she was no longer one of those. Deep inside her something shifted, and a new insecurity rose to engulf her, though she tried to thrust it away. Was there something wrong with her, that only wealth mattered in taking her to wife?

Cordelia was asked to dance by a young man who only yesterday had remained outside Abrielle's door for hours in hopes of catching a glimpse of her. Cordelia's face was a mask of misery as she glanced at Abrielle, barely holding back tears, but Abrielle did not want her to suffer. She sent her dear friend off with a brilliant smile that stabbed her own heart.

She felt her mother's hand slide into hers, and turned to the woman who bore her, who now suffered as equally for Abrielle's pain as for her own. She grieved for both husband and daughter, and Abrielle had to do what she could to alleviate her mother's suffering.

"Mama, how is my stepfather?"

Elspeth sighed and spoke over the cheerful notes of music echoing through the great hall. "He will not speak to me now, not when others can see. But I know the grief and suffering in his heart. This unfairness to him causes me great sorrow. And as for what it does to you—"

"Speak not of it, not here," Abrielle said, giving her mother a brittle smile that she feared might separate her face. "Everything will work out for the best, and this painful evening will soon be forgotten."

But Elspeth's expression was full of doubt, and Abrielle could look at her no longer without feeling the insidious threat of tears. She looked back at the crowd of dancing men and women, keeping her chin lifted as if she had not a care in the world.

And she saw Desmond de Marlé watching her with open interest that he no longer couched with simpering fawning. Nay, he was not one of those men who looked at her for her wealth; he stared with a lustfulness that sickened her to her soul. She quickly looked away lest he think her gaze an expression of interest.

Was he the only type of man she could attract now? A man who would own her like a rare tapestry and hang her about his great hall for all to view and envy?

And he wasn't the only one, she saw with a quiet feeling of growing horror. Men who skulked about the edges of the hall now moved nearer, as if they were rats after only one small piece of cheese.

Yet Vachel stood guard over her, his face impassive, his eyes watchful, and she knew a feeling of temporary relief. But how long could it last? How could he protect her, when he had so little consequence at court?

And then she saw that Cordelia, who'd been given from one dance partner to the next, was now approached by Raven. Inside, Abrielle felt a tightening she couldn't explain, but quickly asked herself why on earth she should feel slighted that the handsome Scot would choose to dance with a wonderful woman like Cordelia? And Cordelia was not just any woman, but the very one who also happened to be her oldest and dearest friend. Later, in the privacy of her chamber, she would sort out her feelings, but for now, she fashioned a dazzling smile so that no one would suspect the turmoil inside her. She also felt true concern for her friend, as Raven had not yet been introduced to Cordelia, yet approached her nonetheless; such behavior did not speak well of his intentions toward her, for he should have presented himself to her father first.

As she continued to smile and pretend to be enjoying the festivities, she realized that Cordelia and Raven were not dancing, but speaking, quietly and with great absorption, occasionally casting a furtive glance in her direction. Unless her instincts were entirely mistaken, they were discussing her, and when the two suddenly turned to look at her, Abrielle was the one caught staring as her dear friend smiled and the Scotsman frowned. Abrielle held her breath as she wondered what they were about. She had to caution her head-strong friend to be more careful as well, for the Scots-man seemed to be overly bold.

They began to move toward her through the crowd, and with each step she felt dread mixed with a strange chilling excitement that she didn't want to feel. To her horror, Cordelia was doing her the great favor of per-suading a man to dance with her, and not just any man, but one whose manner of approaching both young women was questionable. It was true a part of her would not mind a dance with the handsome Scot, only under more appropriate circumstances.

She glanced toward her parents, only to see that they were, quite understandably, speaking intently between themselves. She was obviously doing nothing to attract the Scot, but to her he came, his long stride marked with easy grace and an air of quiet power that made others instinctively move from his path. As he drew steadily closer, Abrielle could not help noting how per-fectly his traditional garb fit his frame. It stretched taut across his broad shoulders and chest, and emphasized his lean hips and long legs, as if very talented hands had stitched it with him inside.

It was not his clothes that commanded her attention as he came within a stone's throw, however. An infi-nitely more gifted artist had chiseled the man himself and she was mesmerized by the raw beauty of his countenance: full dark brows curved above alert blue-black eyes filled with awareness, a slight bump where it had once been broken only added to the appeal of an otherwise perfectly configured nose, and high, sharp cheekbones provided a thrilling hint of the fierce predator. Only his mouth, full and exquisitely shaped, added a touch of softness and . . . and then he stopped before her.

Cordelia's smile was full of a subtle nervousness that only Abrielle could see. "Abrielle, this gentleman has requested an introduction to you." Neither of the friends spoke aloud about the fact that this was not, could not be, a formal introduction, but they were indeed young women, and eager to learn more of the world, especially when the lesson involved such a devastatingly handsome, devastatingly masculine male. "May I present . . ."

Raven swept into a bow and spoke solemnly. "Raven Seabern, my lady."

Abrielle managed a curtsy. "I am Abrielle of Harrington," she said, thinking that he was even more skilled at hiding his true feelings than she was. Anyone looking on would believe Raven really had sought to dance with her, rather than being wheedled into so doing by the kindhearted Cordelia.

"And your late father is one of the braw men we honor this night?" Raven asked.

She nodded, not daring to look at Vachel, who also deserved such honor; she was relieved, as well, that her parent had other things to think about in the wake of the king's announcement. Her stepfather would be concerned that she was meeting a man whom he did not know, who had not presented himself to Vachel as custom required. Would he consider it an even deeper dishonor to have a Scot speak to his stepdaughter?

Cordelia placed a hand on her arm. "I asked if there were more like him at home, but he insists he has no brothers."

Raven smiled faintly at Cordelia. "Only my da, but

he's become set in his ways since my mother passed on. Ta be sure, lass, ye've the looks that could quicken his heart ta a loud drumbeat were he here."

Abrielle blinked in surprise, not knowing whether to feel affronted. Was Raven flirting with Cordelia brazenly in front of her? She felt greatly conforted when her friend actually giggled in response to the Scotsman's gallant words. "You must understand, sir. I wasn't necessarily asking for any particular purpose." She lifted her shoulders, offering a reason for her question. "I was merely curious."

Abrielle could have groaned at her friend's remark, but just at that moment the musicians began another dance. It was this that Abrielle was truly dreading, as Raven no doubt would feel obligated to dance with her. To refuse outright would publicly dishonor him and herself, but her fierce pride ached to do precisely that. Her fortunes may have changed in the past hour, but she refused to be the object of any man's pity and was frantically searching for a way to balance honor with pride when his deep voice intruded.

"May I have this dance, my lady?"

Abrielle lifted her chin, keeping her voice low so only he could hear. "You honor me with your request, sir, but surely you would enjoy the dance more with your first choice of partner." She gave the slightest of nods toward Cordelia, who'd been drawn into conversation with an older woman on her right.

"I couldna agree more," replied Raven. "Which is why I stand before ye, my lady, hoping beyond reason your kind heart will move ye ta take pity on a clumsy Scots oaf and keep him from appearing a total clod amongst the local talent."

Abrielle couldn't help smiling at how cleverly he'd

turned the tables, as she'd been chafing at being the object of his pity and he'd very openly and charmingly made a plea for hers. The man might not have a talent for dancing, as he claimed, but his persuasive skills were of the highest order. Clearly he'd been born to be a diplomat, and when he held out his hand to her, Abrielle couldn't have resisted if she wanted to.

The moment the beautiful young woman was in his arms, Raven Seabern knew he'd made a terrible mistake. He was leading her by the hand into the quickly forming circle as couples young and old merged together. The steps were simple enough to follow as others began to demonstrate their talents and abilities in time with the music, doing a sprightly jig or a tapping of a toe and heel as they moved around in a never-ending wheel of cavorting dancers. Henry's booming laughter evidenced the pleasure he was savoring as he watched his guests enjoying themselves. To be sure, those who had been inclined to think the banquet would be a dull, solemn occasion came quickly to the realization that it had changed into a very lively affair indeed, obviously the sort His Majesty preferred over more somber events such as the one that had just been concluded.

But rather than watching the earlier dancers, Raven had been watching Abrielle far too much this evening, for she was the most stunning creature he had ever seen. From the moment he'd first seen her tonight in the great hall, he'd found it nearly impossible to keep from openly staring. Her red-gold hair tumbled freely as a maiden's should, a shining, flaming glory to the torch that was her beauty. Her pink lips had called to him for kisses; her smooth, creamy skin, glowing beneath the softness of candlelight, had beckoned his trembling fingers to touch and caress. Never before had he felt such a response on merely seeing a maiden.

It was because he'd been watching her so intently that he'd seen the change in her. He'd seen the light of exhilaration so suddenly and utterly extinguished and how, for a fleeting moment, it was replaced with a look of total desolation. It was the sort of look that could break even the hardest heart. It had taken everything in him to avoid her after the banquet, to watch her stand between her parents with quiet courage when no young lords asked her to dance. And that was when he'd realized that her stepfather must have felt it was his time to be honored, and the king's decision had dealt him a blow, thereby affecting this sweet maiden. But how? What secrets did this small family conceal? So taken by her was he that he approached her friend and then her without having been formally introduced to either young woman.

Her young friend Cordelia of Grayson had obviously wanted to help her by presenting Raven as a dance partner. He watched her watching him as he approached and saw her every thought reflected in her translucent eyes. Interest, uncertainty, suspicion, dread. All girded with that dauntless pride of hers. She was not the sort to take pleasure in a man trammeled on her behalf and served up to her on a platter . . . not even by a friend with the best intentions. She clearly had not wanted his attention, and where with another woman he would have felt merely challenged, if he felt anything at all, Abrielle's rejection, delivered with that sweetly slashing smile, cut dangerously deep. Raven rarely encountered an unwilling woman, and rarer still were those occasions when he bothered to exert himself to change her mind. But a man like Raven Seabern got what he wanted, and dance with her he would.

And dance they had, separating as the pattern required, coming together, and joining hands repeatedly. Each time it was as if he were burned, scorched by her beauty and softness. He didn't like feeling as if his own control meant naught. At one point, he lifted her high, his big hands spanning her fragile rib cage. It was then that he saw the tinge in her face and sensed her breathing stop and felt a momentary wonder: Could she, too, be feeling the lure of deep attraction?

The dance was over too soon, and all he could do was escort her back to her parents. Her mother gave him a smile, her stepfather a simple nod, and Abrielle a deep curtsy. And then she wouldn't look at him. After that moment they'd shared on the dance floor, he was even more intrigued by her reticence. He wondered what it portended, though he doubted whether he would ever know for sure, for on the morrow he was yet again to be off in the service of his king, was not even cognizant of when he would return to his beloved highland home.

He left her with a quiet farewell and yet found himself unable to stop watching her. Though he knew her stepfather more than capable, it was obvious the man had an air of distraction this evening as he considered his own future. And unsavory men continued to watch Abrielle. One in particular, squat and overweight, approached Abrielle and bowed to her. When Vachel stepped forward to confront the man, Abrielle laid a hand on his arm and went with the stranger quietly, though it was obvious his touch distressed her. Raven would have to keep watch this evening over this one he perceived as a threat to the maiden.

The difference in dance partners was stark, Abrielle realized in dismay. Raven had moved with the gracefulness of a knight, a man used to wielding a sword as he circled an opponent. Desmond de Marlé, her late betrothed's half brother, lurched through the sweet rushes scattered over the floor. His wet, hot hand gripped hers too hard, and when the dance called for him to touch her waist, she could swear he squeezed as if he were checking the tenderness of a piece of fruit. His eyes devoured her with greed, and she would have run from him, but she did not want Vachel to feel compelled to defend her.

"I will call on you tomorrow, my lady," Desmond said in a confident voice.

"I—but you cannot, my lord," she said, scrambling for appropriate reasons. "My stepfather may have plans that he has not shared with me."

"I know what happened to him tonight," Desmond said, not bothering to lower his voice.

Abrielle cringed, wondering who could overhear his loud voice. "Please, my lord—"

"He might need the friendship of a man of influence such as me."

His insistence on pushing himself on her only served to strengthen her courage. "My lord, I must insist that you speak with my stepfather."

"Oh, believe me, girl, I will."

When the music ended, he left her on the dance floor instead of escorting her back to her parents. When she made her way to them, her mother began, "Abrielle, that horrid man—"

Vachel interrupted with a stern voice. "My lady wife, speak not a word that others may hear."

Biting her lip, Abrielle moved back into her place between them. Oh, how she wanted this evening to be over, but that would not put an end to their troubles. She would continue to see worry in her mother's eyes and cold pride in Vachel's. A hollow sickness inside Abrielle could not be appeased.

And to make matters worse, Raven was watching her again. There was no look of flirtation in his eyes as he gave so many other women, confirming her suspicion that their dance had meant nothing to him, but then, why should it have, as she was no longer worth his notice. He had focused his attention on her when all still thought she would soon have a great dowry, then made her acquaintance inappropriately once Vachel's hopes for a title had been dashed; she had to ask herself what the Scots emissary knew of her stepfather's dashed dreams. Nonetheless he had danced with her, but seemed to have judged her unworthy after having spent some time with her; truly men were beasts, for only a beast could show such interest in her, then withdraw it so cruelly after deeming her of insufficient value without property.

She tried to distract herself by watching His Majesty, who bade a servant to crisscross a pair of swords on the floor before directing the musicians to play an appropriately swift ditty on the lutes. To her surprise, Raven allowed himself to be drawn reluctantly forward. What could he be about?

After a sweeping bow to the king, he began a high-stepping dance over the swords. It was a dazzling display of footwork as Raven struck toe and heel to the floor with amazing quickness, weaving his way over and around the weapons, the clicking of shoe leather on stone its own kind of music. A clumsy Scottish oaf indeed, thought Abrielle, enthralled, and she was not alone, for the performance drew an ever growing audience, including many young maidens whose sharp, feminine gasps were interspersed with delighted giggles whenever his kilt flew dangerously high.

"My goodness, I don't think he's wearing anything underneath it," Cordelia gasped in shock as she joined Abrielle within the circle of spectators. In spite of the fact that the fair-haired woman's cheeks were evidencing a deepening blush, she was closely attentive to the swishing movements of the wool.

Abrielle backed away, allowing others to swarm in front of her, confused by the rising feeling of warmth and excitement brought on by watching him. Raven only put on a display to shock the court, not her personally. She thought Cordelia would remain near to watch the entertainment, but instead her friend drifted with her, biting her lip.

"So just tell me what is on your mind," Abrielle said patiently, recognizing Cordelia's pensiveness.

"I saw you dancing with Desmond de Marlé."

Abrielle's only answer was a shudder.

"I heard people talking about him. Do you know he's had two wives, both of whom died in childbirth?"

"Those poor women," Abrielle murmured.

"In more ways than one. It seems he received money from each wife, and then when Weldon was killed falling down the stairs of his newly finished keep, Desmond inherited his true fortune. Doesn't that seem suspicious to you?"

Abrielle searched her friend's face, feeling ill. "Do people think Desmond had anything to do with Weldon's death?"

Cordelia shrugged. "It is only speculation, but he did benefit the most."

"And I lost my future," Abrielle added with a sigh. Then she took a deep breath and straightened her shoulders. "But I cannot live in the past. A new opportunity will come, I am sure of it."

Cordelia's expression was too sympathetic, and Abrielle had to look away before tears threatened again.

At last her mother and stepfather approached with the intention of retiring. An evening that began with joyous expectations had plummeted into one of numb despair. Cordelia and her family left the castle, and even Elspeth and Abrielle found themselves alone in their chambers when Vachel expressed a need to walk off his frustrations.

Abrielle stood hugging herself as her mother sadly withdrew into the bedchamber she shared with Vachel and began to undress. Abrielle suddenly realized that she had left behind the drinking goblet given to her by her father. It had to be somewhere in the great hall. She gave no thought to her own safety in her panic at losing such a precious memento. Anxious to retrieve the item before it was forever lost to her, she dashed out of their chambers, in her haste failing to inform her mother that she would be returning to the great hall. Once she reached it, she felt relief to see the goblet where the servants had placed it when taking down the trestle tables so the attendees could dance. With it once again in her grasp, she hurried toward the stairs, not feeling the presence of another until it was too late.

CHAPTER 2

Like a wily serpent, Desmond leapt from his make-shift lair and promptly muffled Abrielle's screams beneath a sweaty palm. Dragging her writhing, kicking, and with arms flailing about in an attempt to claw him or do him some other injury, he swept her into one of the chambers off the great hall and promptly pressed her down upon the chaise. In mounting fear, Abrielle clawed at his face and tried to turn her own aside, but he dug his fingers into her jaw and, with his foul-tasting tongue, ravished the depths of her mouth.

Abrielle had never been kissed by a suitor before, not even by Lord Weldon, nor had she ever been mauled. The fact that she was being held against her will by the horrid rapscallion Desmond de Marlé was not only thoroughly frightening to her, but immensely revolting. The looming possibility that she'd soon find herself a victim of his lust caused her to fight with every measure of resolve she could muster. Clasped within his tightly confining arms, she bit, clawed, and gouged in a frantic attempt to regain her freedom.

Panic was soon joined by wild instinct as she struggled to free herself, but his sweaty weight and the swathing folds of her own skirt were against her. When at last she managed to free one leg and began to kick blindly, de Marlé didn't budge, but she dropped the goblet so precious to her and it hit the floor, the sound reverberating loudly.

Desmond immediately tightened his grip on her jaw, causing Abrielle to cry out in pain.

"Quiet, you little fool," he ordered, his tone harsh, his overbright eyes terrifying. "If you know what's good for you, you'll lie there and . . ."

His words were lost in a sudden swirl of plaid and a feral growl rent the air, and as quickly as she had been waylaid, Abrielle was freed. She had a fleeting impression of Desmond's beady eyes widening in sheer terror as his big soft body was lifted straight up from hers and swung aside as effortlessly as if he were stuffed with feathers instead of lard. It was only then that she realized who it was doing the lifting and swinging, who it was who'd caused the awful terror in his eyes, and who was even now—judging from the sounds being emitted from a cowed de Marlé—causing even worse pain.

Raven, his dark hair whirling about his shoulders, held Desmond up by the scruff of the neck with one hand while the other fist pummeled his face, actions that engendered in Abrielle feelings of both horror and blessed relief. For what seemed to the maiden an infinite amount of time, she remained unable to move, then she gathered herself enough to sit up and try to smooth her skirts, now bunched beneath her and leaving her thighs and a goodly bit of hip exposed. She managed to tug the fabric loose, but not quickly enough to escape Raven's notice.

His attention was snagged by her motion and he froze mid-pummel. As he slid his gaze from Desmond to her, the look of abject fury on his face gave way to something else, something equally dark and dangerous, but in a very different way. The sly Desmond took full advantage of his distraction and wrenched free, but Raven let him go in order to hand Abrielle an embroidered throw from a nearby chair, earning from her a murmured "Th-thank you."

Honor, both his and hers, decreed that he avert his gaze and turn away, and after a few moments more, he did so, allowing Abrielle to cover herself quickly and stand.

He turned then, reaching out with one hand, tentatively, as if wanting to prop her up, or soothe her, or touch her, but she was left to wonder which as his hand dropped back to his side.

"Are ye hurt, my lady?" Raven queried as Abrielle sought to cover her reddened breasts with the throw.

The best answer Abrielle could manage was to shake her head in denial and then she, too, fled the hallway. Racing toward the chambers in which her mother was ensconced, she dared not pause for even an instant. In her absence, Raven noticed her goblet lying upon the floor near the chaise where Desmond had dragged her. Picking it up, he made his way to the landing above the stairs, where he waited for some moments, for doubtless the frightened maiden was even now telling her parents what had just taken place and he must give them at least a bit of time to collect themselves. After a decent interval, he rapped his lean knuckles lightly upon the portal.

"Who is it?" Elspeth called out as she leaned near the door.

" 'Tis the Scotsman, Raven Seabern."

The door opened a meager degree, allowing the woman to meet his gaze. She offered him a trembling smile, grateful that he had been on hand to save her daughter from the horrible monster their entire family loathed. "I fear my daughter is unable to come to the door to thank you properly, and her father will be returning soon, but if you would kindly accept my undying gratitude, you surely have it. If not for you, I truly fear that evil man would have had his way with her."

"I found your daughter's goblet after she left," Raven murmured, holding the item where the woman could see it.

Drawing back the portal, Elspeth felt no fear as she accepted the item from the Scotsman; indeed, she even managed a small smile, for her daughter would feel relief to learn that the valued vessel had been returned to her. "I thank you truly, kind sir, for 'tis something both she and I hold quite dear. 'Twas her late father's, and that of generations of Harringtons prior to Berwin. Before his untimely death, her father gave it to her, and when Abrielle discovered that she had left it behind her, unthinking she rushed back to fetch it. Of course she had no idea that she would be set upon by that horrible man. I'm not sure just how much you know about my daughter, but she was once betrothed to Lord Weldon de Marlé. Since his lordship's death, Desmond seems inclined to follow her about."

"Ye say that ye expect your husband to return shortly, my lady? Mayhap I should keep watch out here on the landing till he does, just ta make certain ye and your daughter are safe. If ye feel a need, brace a chair against the inside of the door."

Upon realizing she was still shaking from the incident

involving her daughter, Elspeth managed a tremulously grateful smile. "I do think Abrielle and I would feel more secure if you would keep watch until my husband returns . . . just in case Desmond tries to force his way into our chambers. He seems to have his mind fixed on having my daughter, and there is no one Abrielle loathes more. But as for when he'll return, I do not know. Thank you again for your protection . . . and your kindness," she murmured as she fought back grateful tears. "You've proven a godsend tonight, not only by coming to my daughter's rescue, but for watching over us when you barely know us."

"Aye, 'tis true I hardly know ye, my lady, but I'm well acquainted with the sort of rascal who attacked your daughter. I didna think the man was ta be trusted when I first set eyes upon him. Ta be sure, my lady, I'm more inclined ta favor the ones who find themselves beset by such a man. Now I'll be saying good night ta ye. Rest yourself, if ye can."

Upon closing the door, Elspeth entered the adjoining bedchamber, where her daughter had flung herself across the bed and was still sobbing. Even a handsome individual could evoke a horrible memory were he to resort to the vile tactics the squire had just employed. In view of the rampant disdain Abrielle had felt for the man before his attack, her aversion to him had likely been compounded.

Gently stroking her daughter's back, Elspeth sought to soothe her fears. "Raven Seabern will be keeping watch outside our rooms until Vachel returns," she murmured, wondering when that would be. A long moment passed as she thought of their protector. "The Scotsman gives every indication that he is a man to be admired . . . a very handsome gentleman . . . even more so than Lord Weldon. But then, I must remember that his lordship was nearing two score and five years of age when he fell to his death."

Memories of his lordship's demise evoked a lengthy silence that neither woman seemed willing to break until Elspeth heaved a pensive sigh. "I know it isn't proper for a lady to speak of such things, but for some time now, I've been thinking . . . even more so since this latest incident, that if Desmond were threatened with violence after daring to approach you, mayhap he'd learn to keep his distance."

"I wouldn't be inclined to think so," Abrielle muttered against the coverlet. "Just leave it be, Mama. We will be leaving London soon." She almost told her mother what Cordelia had told her about the suspicion of Desmond's part in Weldon's death, but how could she further upset her? She didn't want Vachel challenging the man to a contest to the death. Her own father had died in the same senseless way. And after all, Desmond had been stopped in time. She shuddered.

OUTSIDE, A SAFE distance away, Desmond licked his wounds and made plans. After pulling free of that arrogant, meddling Scot, he'd dashed toward the nearest portal, frantic to make good his escape. The rapidity of his flight had been clearly evidenced by the sound of his clattering heels echoing back through the halls. He never halted until he had escaped from the castle and dragged himself onto his shaggy steed. Even then, he thumped his heels frantically against the animal's heaving sides. He'd been thwarted and made the fool this night, but there would be another night, and he would not forget Raven's possessiveness of Abrielle.

IT WAS LATER that night when Vachel returned to the castle and began to slowly climb the stairs to the chambers wherein his family was ensconced. He was in a foul mood, having repeatedly mulled over in his mind his limited choices for the future.

Upon nearing the landing, Vachel was taken aback when he espied the Scotsman sitting with his back braced against the far wall. "Why are you here?"

Raven pushed himself to his feet with a single, graceful movement. "Desmond de Marlé took it inta his head ta force himself on your daughter."

Vachel's heart went cold with dread. "Is she all right? Did he do anything to her?" Though reluctant to ask and have his suspicions confirmed, he had to know the truth. "Has the girl been . . . sullied?"

"She would've been had I not been there ta send the rat scurrying off ta his hole," Raven replied. "I told your wife that I'd watch till your return. Although ye'll likely be thinking 'tis none of my concern, ye need ta watch over your family whilst that filthy toad is in the area . . . just ta keep them safe."

Vachel needed no one, especially a stranger, telling him that he had seriously erred by leaving his family alone. His frustration during the evening had risen to an intolerable degree when he had seen the very same lords who had courted Abrielle now after the scent of richer quarry. His guilt for not being there to protect her caused him to wonder if he wasn't deserving of the situation in which he presently found himself. Even so, in the mood he was in, he found it difficult to accept the Scotsman's counsel. "I can take care of my family well enough without your interference."

In response to this less-than-gracious remark by Abrielle's parent, Raven only arched a dark brow, then bowed and took his leave of Vachel.

Deeply ashamed by his earlier lack of caution in seeing to the welfare of his family, Vachel turned his back and stepped through the door.

Elspeth was anxiously pacing about their chambers, awaiting his return as he stepped through the portal. Sobbing in relief, she flew into his arms. "I thought you'd never return!"

"Tell me what happened," Vachel urged, feeling her trembling against him, and she did so, her voice shaky, ending with these words: "I am so grateful the Scotsman was guarding our door until you returned, for there is no telling what Desmond might have done had he found us here alone."

"The despicable actions of that beast have clearly upset you, Elspeth, with reason, but I cannot imagine that coward Desmond being brave enough to force his way . . ."

Elspeth's ire rose. "Do you think I make too much of his assault upon my daughter?" she demanded, her eyes flashing with sudden ire. "I tell you, Vachel, that despicable man will not rest until he has violated Abrielle. Indeed, he was intent upon doing that foul deed this very evening. If not for the Scotsman's interference, he would have ravished her."

"I apologize for leaving you and Abrielle alone," Vachel replied in humble tones. "Obviously this incident would never have happened had I stayed here with you, but there's nothing I can say or do now that will rectify that matter." He heaved a laborious sigh. "If you don't mind, I've had very little sleep since I came here, and I'm very tired at the moment. Perhaps we can continue this discussion on the morrow."

Seeing vivid evidence of his dispirited dejection, Elspeth took pity on him as she rubbed his arm. "Let's not quarrel. I'm sure in time something better will come our way. We need only wait."

ABRIELLE LAY ON her bed, listening to the muted voices of her parents. She could not hear the words, but she understood the emotions, for she, too, experienced the bitter depths of them. Her trembling had finally eased, but she kept playing the terrible attack over and over in her mind, remembering the loathsome feel of Desmond's hand on her innocent flesh.

And then her feeling of grateful relief when Raven had stormed into the chamber, his face a mask of cold fury. She would be forever grateful for his timeliness in coming to her aid and forever in awe of how effortlessly he had dealt with the loathsome Desmond. But she felt something else, too, something more, and somewhere deep inside, she mistrusted her own feelings, for her gratitude felt too much like desire.

God above, every time she saw Raven Seabern, a part of her yearned for him. What was happening to her? Were despair and distress making her mind vulnerable to her basest impulses? Why could she not see Raven and feel only simple gratitude? After all, he'd only rescued her and guarded their chambers out of duty. He'd spent the evening avoiding her except when they were forced to dance, as if she were beneath his notice now that her family circumstances had changed. He was a Scot, for heaven's sake, looked on with suspicion by all she knew, and yet her treacherous body yearned for him, as a woman yearned for a man.

A MONTH HAD passed since the event honoring the Saxon heroes of the Crusades had been held at Westminster Castle. Since then, Abrielle's thoughts had returned fairly often to Raven Seabern and the troubling emotions he had awakened within her. As much as his brilliant blue eyes, leanly chiseled nose, and the charmingly wayward grin had evoked her interest, she was unable to ignore the distressing situation in which their small family presently found itself. What they were now facing would likely force her to make a decision that she would despise for the rest of her life. She couldn't blame her stepfather for the concern he had shown for his men and his father upon his return home from the tumultuous conflicts raging in foreign lands. Willaume had been the one who had gone back on his word by not returning the funds that Vachel had so kindly permitted him to use before his death or mentioning them in a statement to be read after that event. Even now, Vachel was unwilling to condemn his parent as he offered the excuse that Willaume hadn't been thinking too clearly before his death. Unfortunately, because the elder had failed to consider or remember the funds that Vachel had extended to him in an effort to restore his flagging wealth, the latter was now faced with ruin. Vachel's only chance to escape impoverishment was now in Abrielle's hands, and the decision she made would affect all of their lives, but most especially hers.

Desmond de Marlé had approached Vachel and asked for Abrielle's hand in marriage, and now she stood in her stepfather's private solar, facing the two people she loved above all else, knowing they loved her and grieved for her decision, but they let her have her peace while she paced and thought.

Desmond had offered a sizable stipend to be paid for Abrielle's hand upon the execution of the agreement, plus guarantees in writing that upon his death she would inherit most of what he owned except for another stipend to her stepfather and to Desmond's nephew. Although Desmond had been Weldon's half brother and had barely known his lordship, he had been Weldon's only heir. That fact had served to make Desmond an immensely wealthy man upon his lordship's death, so rich that he could now afford to be generous if it meant he'd be getting what he had been yearning for since first espying Abrielle in the company of her parents at Weldon's keep. Abrielle couldn't help wondering why, if there was a nephew in the family, he had not inherited anything from Weldon, who had been a generous man.

Little had Desmond realized when he had offered to buy his bride just how close Vachel was to ruin. As it stood now, all the latter had to do to replenish his coffers was to accept Desmond's request for Abrielle's hand in marriage. Unfortunately, the squire's proposition failed to assuage the rapidly mounting qualms of all three members of the family, perhaps Vachel most of all, because the girl would be giving up all hope of marrying someone she loved in order to save the family for which he was responsible. He could not be the one to take her future from her.

Elspeth's elegant brows gathered in fretting concern as she watched her husband pacing about. "Vachel, I know we are desperate . . ." she began, but the look on his face forestalled her frantic pleading. She instead approached her husband and rested a gentle hand upon his arm, caressing it unconsciously. Although she was aware that he could be obstinate at times, she had little doubt that she had made the right choice when she had accepted his proposal of marriage. As far as his tendency to make decisions contrary to her preferences and wishes, it had recently dawned on her that she preferred to be challenged by one of his manly disposition and intellect rather than to be bored to the marrow of her bones by another who might have readily complied with her smallest request. Although Berwin had considered her advice when she had offered it, he had not always followed it, as he had proven the day of his death. She had to believe there was some way out of their predicament without laying it all upon her daughter's shoulders. To burden a young woman with the likes of Desmond de Marlé as her husband seemed a cruel blow indeed.

Straightening to his full height, Vachel thrust out his meticulously bearded chin in vexation. Normally his amber eyes glowed with a mesmerizing radiance of their own, but at the moment they seemed as cold and lifeless as stone as he stared across the room. He could rally no hope for the future, knowing that his family faced nothing but bleakness unless he accepted Desmond's offer.

Elspeth knelt on the rush-covered floor beside her husband's chair and folded her hands in her lap as she looked up into his frowning face. "Vachel, if you would please consider Desmond's reputation, you would know that he isn't a suitable husband for Abrielle."

"By all that's holy, woman, what kind of a monster do you think me?" he demanded, distraught at the idea that she would think he would barter off her daughter to provide for their family. "I could never live with myself if I were to force Abrielle into such a union. That decision is entirely hers to accept or to reject, but please consider that Desmond now has all the wealth and lands that once belonged to Weldon, enough to guarantee that his offspring will never lack for riches and position. That's more than I can say for that small league of suitors who've been wont to offer themselves since all at court learned of my low standing with the king. I've seen starving hounds drool less over a meaty bone than the besotted buffoons who slaver in lusting eagerness after your daughter. But then, you witnessed that very thing yourself before we were married, so I needn't try to describe the zeal her admirers have been wont to evidence."

"Vachel, I understand how troubled you are by our dilemma," Elspeth said in a quiet voice. No less distressed than he, she sought to find some ray of hope in a painfully dark future. "Do you know of anything else we can do to alter our present unfortunate state?"

His laughter was brief and harsh. "I fear without the occurrence of some miracle, my dear, there is no hope." Noticing the pooling of tears in his wife's eyes, he heaved a sigh, quickly lamenting his callousness. "I fully understand Abrielle's aversion to Desmond," he stated. "'Tis no less than my own. Nevertheless, what he has recently offered appears to be our only hope. Although I will try to find a suitor more acceptable to all of us, I fear there is none who has as much wealth as Desmond now has. I truly wish we had some other choice."

Her mother's sudden sob of despair wrenched Abrielle's heart, and she turned aside in an effort to hide the rush of tears that quickly gathered in her own eyes. They streamed down her cheeks, forcing her to wipe them away surreptitiously. As much as she disdained Desmond, she could see no option open to her now but to accept his proposal of marriage. It was either that or see her loved ones suffer. Even so, if Desmond wanted her so much, then he would have to be willing to extend far more generous terms than he had thus far offered. If she were going to be miserable, then she would have to be generously compensated for having to endure that repugnant wretchedness.

And after all, with no dowry, there was no guarantee that she could even find a worthy man to love her. And she shuddered at the thought that, without Vachel's knights and the protection they offered, perhaps a man wouldn't even feel the need to take her to wife.

Approaching her parents, Abrielle managed a tremulous smile as she claimed her stepfather's attention. In an effort to hide the fact that her hopes for happiness and a worthy future with a man whom she loved seemed to be dying beneath the grievous weight of the situation in which they presently found themselves, she tried to speak with some semblance of enthusiasm. "The choice is mine to make, and I will do what I must to help," she stated, hating the quavering weakness that hindered her voice. "I cannot . . . will not allow our family to live in poverty . . ."

"No!" Elspeth cried, thoroughly distraught by her daughter's words. "We'll find another way! Please . . . oh, please . . . no!"

"I've decided there is nothing else that can be done," Abrielle replied, steeling herself against her mother's desperate pleading. Upon facing Vachel, whose dejected appearance evidenced a serious lack of relief, she quickly laid out her intentions. She had no real idea how Weldon had actually met his death, whether it had truly been an accident as had been supposed or if it had been carried out by design by the very one who had stood to inherit his wealth. Nevertheless, the premise seemed fairly simple to her that if Desmond wanted her so much, then he would likely be willing to pay a sizable sum . . . perhaps even a goodly portion of what had once belonged to her betrothed in order to get her. "Considering the vast riches that Weldon once had, I urge you to demand far more than Desmond may be willing to offer. I care naught for the fact that he may have been kin to Weldon. He isn't deserving of anything that once belonged to his lordship."

"And if Desmond complies with all of your demands, what then?" Vachel asked, fully agreeing with her on all counts. Even so, the idea of such a dastardly man reaping so fine a bride left him feeling more than a little nauseous. Unfortunately, at the moment there seemed to be no other way for the family to survive.

"Then I shall wed the man," Abrielle replied with a serious lack of enthusiasm.

Elspeth moaned in despair as she clasped a handkerchief over her mouth and stared at her daughter with a profusion of tears welling in her eyes.

Vachel could not ignore his wife's deepening dismay and was led to question Abrielle again as to the extent of her commitment to make such a sacrifice. "Your marriage to Desmond may be more horrible than you can imagine. I've been hearing rumors that have led me to believe that the man has been rather despicable to the serfs he recently inherited from Weldon. Once you exchange vows with him, you'll no longer be able to dismiss him from your life. He will become a part of you . . . your spouse. You'll have to conform to his way of life, his wishes, his demands, and with all seriousness, I must warn you that it may be more than you can imagine or will be able to tolerate in the future."

"As far as I'm concerned, the matter is already settled," Abrielle replied, steeling herself against the fears he had evoked. "Desmond wants me for his wife, and that is what he shall have . . . for a sizable price. If I'm going to marry him, then it will be for no less than what I demand, so refrain from giving him the idea that he can haggle for my hand. When the price is sufficiently generous and you're nearing the end of your negotiations, then you must seek my approval before the terms can be finalized, but you must not allow him to know that you intend to discuss them with me. As far as Desmond is concerned, I will have had nothing to do with the negotiations and it will be a matter that you will personally be deciding."

"Very wise," Vachel replied, pursing his lips and nodding his head in approval. Clearly Abrielle had benefited from being so close to her late father, who'd permitted her to listen as he conducted his business affairs. "Very wise indeed. You will be absolved of all blame should he begin to resent the price he paid for you."

On any other occasion Abrielle would have smiled in pleasure at her stepfather's praise, but she feared the bargain they would be making with Desmond was equivalent to forming an agreement with the devil himself, and the idea of that frightened her. "I may very well regret it all once the vows have been exchanged," she admitted, trying to subdue a shiver at the thought of allowing the loathsome man to touch her, much less be intimate with her. "And if you could spare a few prayers for me, you might begin to offer them now lest I be tempted to run away and hide."

Although Vachel knew his wife was deeply distressed over what Abrielle was planning, he couldn't help but feel overwhelmed by the girl's willingness to sacrifice her own happiness for the family's welfare. Although his men had been disposed to risk their lives to fight alongside him in numerous conflicts, the like of which even now seemed to still be raging on that same foreign soil, they had always nurtured the hope that they would all survive and be the better for it. This thing that Abrielle was willing to do to save him from impoverishment was tantamount to tying herself forever to a hateful fiend whose first and subsequent thoughts were entirely for his own gratification.

He knew what Abrielle had directed him to do was not to Elspeth's liking, and yet, with Abrielle's willingness to sacrifice her own happiness for them, he couldn't help but feel as if a heavy burden had been lifted off his chest. As anxious as he had been to find some viable escape from his poverty, her proposal was to him as refreshing as a breath of fresh air to a smothering man.

Vachel reached out and threaded his lean fingers through his wife's as he peered at her. He tried to find some reason to be hopeful about the union. "Marrying Desmond de Marlé should make Abrielle a very rich woman," he stated in a subdued tone. Receiving no encouraging response, he tried again. "Should Desmond expire, she'll be able to choose another to meet her own admirable standards. It wouldn't surprise me if a lofty title would be in the offing should she so desire it. Considering how wealthy she will likely be, she'll be able to dictate her future as few women have ever done. She'll want for nothing."

Elspeth was so disheartened by the thought of her daughter marrying the repulsive man that she could manage no better response than a meager twitch of her lips. Even so, she knew if it hadn't been for Vachel, Abrielle would have likely suffered the consequences of being uncommonly beautiful and totally bereft of the protection she would need.

Berwin's death had engendered a difficult situation wherein many of the older Norman lords had begun laying odds on the rake of their preference who, in their opinion, was handsome and charming enough to be the final victor in the growing collection of bachelors intent upon stripping away Abrielle's innocence without benefit of a betrothal or wedding vows. After all, many of them were overheard chortling, she was of Saxon lineage and without sufficient dowry, therefore suitable prey for the conquering heroes, that fine collection of youthful Normans who had been spawned well after their fathers or grandfathers had landed on English shores. Thereafter, when Abrielle had turned an eager gallant on his ear with a hotly spoken rejection, the stakes had been sharply elevated. It had proven a highly amusing game for the collection of lords wagering on the outcome, for it had evoked much laughter and deepened others' interest in the sport until many could foresee a weighty purse being divided among the winners once viable evidence of her deflowering was presented by the debaucher responsible.

To stave off the seemingly ever-increasing horde of young men vying to strip away her daughter's virtue, Elspeth had deemed it beneficial to accept Vachel de Gerard's proposal of marriage. Since then, his presence as head of the family had been sufficient to keep the lusting lords at bay and, deservedly so, to frustrate the greed of those who had been laying heavy purses on the outcome of the game they had invented.

In retrospect, Abrielle was thoroughly convinced that Vachel would have defended her to the death if it had come to that, for he had stood his ground numerous times before prominent nobles who had warned him not to interfere because of the heavy purses they had riding on the outcome. What mattered most to her was the fact that he had given every indication that he was genuinely smitten with her mother and would do almost anything to avoid seeing her distressed. Considering his deep regard for her parent and for herself, how could she not sacrifice a measure of her own happiness to help him, and in so doing help her mother?

Elspeth gazed compassionately upon her offspring. No stranger staring into those silkily lashed, bluish-green eyes would have ever guessed that underneath that softly feminine breast there beat a heart as passionately loyal to her family and to her king as any devoted knight of the realm. Sadly, it seemed those qualities were of little benefit to a young woman. Nevertheless, Abrielle was selflessly evidencing her noble spirit in her willingness to sacrifice her own happiness to assuage the tenuous position in which their small family was presently entrapped. How could a mother not be moved to tears by her gallantry?

CHAPTER 3

The wedding was only three days away, and Abrielle was grateful that she had her dear friend Cordelia with her in this time of fear and worry. She needed someone to confide in, someone to distract her from her cares. She was to wed Desmond immediately after the annual de Marlé hunt, so she had no wish for the entertainment to be over quickly.

"According to the men, the signs point to a good hunt," Abrielle remarked dismally as she and Cordelia ventured forth from de Marlé's keep.

Cordelia cast a glance awry toward the crowded courtyard whence they had just made their departure. "With so many of Lord Weldon's friends and previous participants protesting Desmond's new regulations and threatening to leave if the previous ones aren't reinstated, 'twill be surprising if there even is a hunt."

Abrielle shuddered at the thought of the wedding taking place even earlier.

Already several hunters who had been Weldon's closest friends had stalked out in an outraged huff over the new rules that Thurstan, Desmond's nephew, had presented. Among the men who had remained, many had become embroiled in angry squabbles with Desmond's cohorts, who had shown up in large number. All had been presided over by Thurstan, a haughty, cold young man who looked upon Abrielle with a distaste she found curious.

"A more insufferable group I've never met in my entire life," Cordelia remarked derisively. "I'm fairly certain they're representative of the dregs to be found mucking the bottom of a cask of wine. 'Tis always best to throw the residue out."

If only that were possible, Abrielle thought wistfully, and not for the first time. Unfortunately she had not that choice, nor any other to rid herself of Desmond and his odious associates. Her future, such as it was, as well as her family honor, rested on a successful union between them. The marriage agreement might as well be a dungeon cell without a door for all the hope she had of freeing herself.

As much as Abrielle and Cordelia had sought to remove themselves from the numerous arguments that were even now being provoked within the courtyard, they glanced knowingly at each other as several more of Weldon's friends left the structure and stalked down the length of the drawbridge, where they promptly motioned for their horses to be brought forth. In a few moments, they had taken their departure. It was just another example of the ire that Desmond, his companions, and his nephew had managed to cause since the first hunter had arrived. They had changed so many rules, from who decided the winners—once an impartial group of elders, and now merely Thurstan—to the obscene size of the purse needed to enter.

"Abrielle, you know there could be another reason that so many noblemen are leaving," Cordelia said slyly.

Abrielle winced at her friend's less-than-subtle reference to the food served at the keep under Desmond, and regretfully conceded in a small voice. "It is rather . . . plain and unappealing."

"Promise me you'll do something about this when you're the mistress here. The older cook seems especially cantankerous, and by the looks of her, I'd be willing to wager she wields a war ax as well as any brigand and eats a goodly amount of her own cooking."

Abrielle spread her hands in a helpless gesture. "Frankly, I have no idea why Desmond tolerates the cooking. For a man trying to move up in the world, he's not trying very hard to impress anyone in that area."

Indulging herself in the autumn-scented breezes wafting across the drawbridge, Abrielle sighed and paused a moment to look around. After being confined within the smoke-filled courtyard much longer than she had thought she could tolerate, the fresh air seemed especially invigorating.

She could fully understand why Weldon had chosen to build his keep in this area, for the scenery was no less than breathtaking. Some furlongs upstream, a tributary branching off from the river wound its way through thick forests before flowing beneath the drawbridge upon which they now stood. The stream not only supplied the moat surrounding the keep, but also continued on a winding path beneath the smaller bridge that led to the serfs' dwellings, easily providing the families there with an abundance of fresh water.

The keep had been well conceived by Weldon de Marlé, under whose supervision it had been meticulously constructed with the intent that it would serve him, his family, and their descendants as an impenetrable fortress well into the future. From its numerous battlements and parapets, a defensive response could be launched from a vantage point of some safety to counter any attack that came against it. Drawbridges fore and aft could be raised to provide a refuge for its inhabitants if enemies were to attack. Weldon had been not only a valiant warrior but also a man of great vision and intelligence. Providing sufficient provisions were stored within its walls before an army laid siege to it, the keep had the potential to offer protection for several months for those living within the confines of its exterior walls.

Still, as much as Abrielle could appreciate the security of the keep as well as the serenity and beauty of its surroundings, the knowledge that she would soon be residing within its stone walls with an odious husband did much to augment the melancholy that had been cruelly assailing her spirit since she had offered her freedom in exchange for her stepfather's. The fact that she was now committed to marrying such a repulsive individual was enough to bring her threateningly close to retching.

Although many of her Saxon kin had yet to arrive for the wedding, Abrielle had already sensed that those who had were maintaining a cool reserve in the midst of their less-than-genteel host and his odd assortment of vulgar companions. She could certainly understand her kinsmen's annoyance with the situation in which they found themselves. Most of Desmond's acquaintances were strongly prejudiced against Saxons, as if they were themselves notable figures with impeccable lineages instead of undisciplined rowdies lacking prestige, titles, or wealth.

Most of the elderly women had removed themselves fairly quickly from the crowded courtyard and had gathered on an upper floor of the keep near the warmth of a hearth. Along with Cordelia and some of their distant cousins, Abrielle had lent an arm to those forced to limp along on wobbly limbs or climb stairs with the aid of gnarled walking sticks. Upon reaching their destinations, a mischievous gleam had come into the eyes of the ancients as they shooed the younger women away, threatening to exchange spicy tales about them in their absence. There, in softly muted, deeply worried tones, the elders did indeed discuss the forthcoming nuptials as they offered a variety of conjectures on the questionable fate of the young bride, if she'd fare any better than the squire's previous two wives, or if, in view of her youth and quick mind, she'd actually be the one to survive him.

Cordelia glanced around as she heard ponderous footfalls on the drawbridge behind them and then mentally groaned as she espied their portly host scurrying toward them. It took no mental feat of logic to determine that Desmond de Marlé was absolutely delighted with what he had managed to arrange for himself, for he was beaming with joyful enthusiasm.

Surreptitiously Cordelia leaned near to whisper a warning. "Behold, yon lecher hastens to his beloved."

Abrielle issued a muted groan, realizing her nightmare was already coming to fruition. Dipping her head as if espying something of interest in the stream, she hurriedly pleaded beneath her breath, "Stay with me, Cordelia, please, I pray. Otherwise, I shall panic and be tempted to run away."

The flaxen-haired woman heaved a laborious sigh as if reluctant to be anywhere within close proximity to the man. "Desmond repulses me to the core of my being," she admitted in a muted tone. "Nevertheless, I've always prided myself in being a truly loyal friend, so I shan't desert you."

To say that Abrielle felt trapped by the swiftly approaching man would have definitely been an understatement. Even so, she gathered what aplomb she could muster and faced her intended with a smile that in spite of her best efforts was hopelessly strained.

Striding almost on the squire's heels was the tawny-haired nephew, Thurstan, who had earlier aroused her ire as well as the anger of many of Weldon's friends. He seemed fully aware of himself, for his nose was held at a haughty elevation as he glanced about. In spite of the fresh autumn breezes, his nostrils seemed pinched, as if he detected something foul in the air. A full head taller than the squire, he was quite lean and muscular. His clothing and accessories were stylish and well made. The neckband and sleeves of his black gown were accentuated with a woven green braid. Black suede boots were trimmed with appliqués of green leather resembling the fronds of a fern, a design that also embellished his dagger's sheath and the money pouch that hung from a belt worn at a fashionable angle over his narrow hips.

His stylish appearance contrasted sharply with the deplorable condition of the serfs who were scurrying about the keep or in the compound beyond the narrow footbridge traversing the stream. Although they had seemed clean, well fed, and very cheerful while Weldon was alive, Abrielle had seen enough serfs during her present visit to realize a sinister change had occurred since his death. There were now many thin, gaunt features and lash marks across arms and faces of a goodly number of them. Indeed, most of them seemed fearful of Desmond and his nephew.

For one purported to have inherited great wealth from his half brother, Desmond didn't seem averse to a vast number of serfs wearing filthy rags and going about their duties unwashed, to the extent that a scented handkerchief was now required to block the stench of their bodies as they came near to do some service. At least when she became mistress, there would be much she could do to remedy that situation. She might not be able to improve her own dismal lot, but she would find what happiness and satisfaction she could in helping these other wretched souls. She would insist that everyone who worked within the confines of the keep bathe and have suitable clothing with which to maintain a tidy appearance. But most important, she would see that they were all well fed, from the youngest to the oldest, regardless of their ability to work.

"My dear Lady Abrielle," Desmond gushed, holding out his pudgy hands, as if fully expecting to receive hers with equal zeal as he halted before her.

"Squire, how goes your day?" she asked, unable to ignore the quavering weakness in her voice.

"Very well indeed, my dear," Desmond responded. "But how could it not be when I see before me an exquisitely beautiful and wondrous young lady who is about to make me the happiest person alive? At such a moment, a man is wont to think everything in the world suits him."

Managing to present some semblance of a cordial smile, Abrielle grudgingly complied with his unspoken request by settling her fingers within his grasp. She found his puffy hands nauseatingly soft, strongly hinting of a slothfulness that was likely thriving since so many serfs attended his every need. In the next moment, a rising panic swept through her as Desmond clasped both her hands and, in an eager display of affection, began to cover them with moist, greedy kisses, evoking within her a shuddering revulsion that threatened to send her flying to the nearest convenience to throw up her latest meal. Far more difficult to suppress, however, was the sickening feeling in the pit of her stomach that had much to do with the realization that once they were married, she'd have no right to withhold herself from the man.

Abrielle quickly averted her gaze from the rotund squire, only to find herself confronting Thurstan's probing gaze. His eyes were a strange yellowish green, fringed with brown lashes and shadowed by thick, tawny brows. His high cheekbones, straight nose, and equally crisp chin seemed sharply chiseled, yet his mouth was overly soft and expressive, as evidenced by the sardonic smile that drew up a corner of his lips. If she could ascertain anything from his smirk, she could believe that he was also a very perceptive individual who had recognized her repugnance for what it was and seemed highly amused by it.

Resentful of the younger man's close scrutiny, Abrielle took herself mentally in hand and deliberately turned aside without acknowledging the man. Upon facing her intended, she said, "I was beginning to wonder if you were even aware that I was here, Desmond. You seemed so involved straightening out numerous details for the hunt that I was beginning to feel slighted."

Desmond chortled in amusement. "Banish such an inconceivable thought from your lovely head, my dear.

I assure you with all sincerity that I did not dismiss you from mind. Be assured that I am counting the days and hours that must pass ere we are wed. If I were able to hasten them on their way, I would surely do so."

In spite of his averred enthusiasm, Abrielle preferred to think of that event not at all. Without issuing a yea or a nay, she swept a hand about to indicate her lifelong companion. "I believe you're acquainted with the Lady Cordelia of Grayson. Lord and Lady Grayson have accepted your invitation to attend our wedding and are at this very moment visiting my parents in the chambers you have so graciously provided."

"Of course! Of course!" Desmond cheerily responded, bending his plump body forward several times in a manner that clearly evidenced his delight in being in the company of those with fine lineage. "Although this marks the first occasion of our actual introduction, my lady, I can assure you that I've been distantly acquainted with your parents for some time now."

Cordelia smiled gingerly and dared to lift a brow. "And they you, Squire."

The innuendo within her friend's reply made Abrielle wonder if she had erred by insisting that Cordelia remain beside her. Although they were in full accord with their mutual abhorrence of the squire, there were occasions when Cordelia wasn't nearly as subtle around people she disliked as caution might have dictated. But then, Abrielle reminded herself, her friend did not have the same need to be cautious.

Cordelia, unlike Abrielle, had not lost a most worthy betrothed to fate, and her beloved father to his own overabundance of stubborn pride, leaving her in a most precarious position in a world where a man's protection was not merely a luxury for a woman, but a matter of survival. It did not rest on Cordelia's pampered shoulders to save her stepfather from ruin and her mother from public humiliation. Not that Abrielle would wish any of that on her dear friend, not for a single moment. She desired only that fate had had a different future in mind for her . . . one in which she did not have to sell her heart to save the family she loved, one that did not have her destiny quite so entwined with the misfortunes of men.

Were the place where she found herself other than what it was, it wouldn't have bothered Abrielle in the least to have her friend sparring with the man, since he was no match for Cordelia intellectually, but any tiff between the pair would likely cause tensions to rise in her own family, especially since Elspeth disdained Desmond as much as Cordelia did.

It seemed excellent timing that a fish flipped into the air from the water beneath the drawbridge. Considering the fact that most drawbridges traversed moats notoriously stagnant and overgrown with an abundance of weeds, Abrielle was relieved to have something she could boast about while Desmond was in their midst. "Cordelia, did you see that? Imagine having a moat filled with fish so near at hand!"

Though another might never have discerned the subtle change in her friend's melodious tones, Cordelia readily sensed Abrielle's nervous tension. She could hardly blame her for being anxious. For some time now it had seemed that whenever Desmond was afoot, strangely perplexing events were wont to happen, not the least of which dealt with the disappearances of people strongly opposed to the man as well as the theft of jewels, paintings, silver plates, golden goblets, and other costly treasures. No evidence yet had confirmed the possibility that Desmond was guilty, but that didn't mean he was innocent of any of those deeds, only devious enough to get away with them. Lest she blunder on in her avid abhorrence of the man, Cordelia deemed it necessary for the sake of her friend to distance herself from the couple, and crossed to the far side of the bridge.

Abrielle was thankful that Cordelia was not only intelligent but also keenly perceptive in a variety of ways. It was now necessary to be wary, considering that she would soon be Desmond's wife. Weldon's death had served to make Desmond a very rich man, far more than those of his first two wives had done, but all three deaths had greatly benefited her repugnant betrothed, which often left her wondering now if their passing had been something deliberately planned by the very one who had profited from it.

Avoiding the steward's gaze, Abrielle reluctantly bestowed her attention upon Desmond and somehow managed to quell the nausea as she posed a question in sweetly muted tones. "Did you wish to speak with me about some particular matter, Desmond?"

Her use of his given name brought a smile of pleasure to his lips. "I was certainly hoping to, my dear. As you may be aware, Sir Vachel has presented the last draft of our marriage agreement for me to look over and sign. Except for several clauses here and there, I see nothing untoward to hinder the events that have thus far been planned for our wedding. Thurstan keeps my business affairs in order and is far more astute than I am in determining the practicability of such a contract. In this instance, he advises only a few minor changes ere the agreement is fully executed . . ."

"Does this mean that you're now suffering doubts

about the terms that you and my stepfather earlier agreed upon?" Abrielle asked, wishing she could rejoice, but feeling a cold dread at the thought of a future without this match. She would have to bluff her way through this. "If so, then I shall have to carry this news posthaste to my parents, since there is so little time remaining before the nuptials. We were under the impression that you were in full accord with everything that had been laid out when you finalized it with your personal seal and announced that we could be married after the hunts. It seems a poor late hour indeed to bring up other issues after the pact has been sanctioned by both parties. I can only wonder what you are now expecting."

"Actually, there are only a few minor changes that need to be made ere the wedding," Desmond hastened to assure her. Chortling, he tried to brush off any cause for concern with a casual wave of a plump hand. "I'm sure any differences your father and I may have over the actual wording of the agreement can be easily settled and another document written within the next pair of days, well in time for our wedding."

Abrielle certainly wasn't going to encourage the man by suggesting that a correction so near to that event would be easily tolerated, especially by her or her stepfather. "If you haven't already noticed, Desmond, then you should be made aware that my stepfather has become rather adamant about this matter, so if you're now of a different persuasion, then he should be informed posthaste." She risked an outright lie, hoping to force the man to back down. "I have no doubt that before Sir Vachel takes up the matter with you again, he will be speaking with several petitioners who've recently come forth to express their own interest in having me as their wife."

"Perhaps that would be wise—" Thurstan began in a gracious tone.

She felt a chill of fear that the nephew might be able to sway his uncle, leading to Vachel's ruin.

But Desmond interrupted the man with an abrupt, slashing gesture of his hand as he tossed an angry glower toward him. Forcing a smile as he turned to her again, he hastened to assure her, "There is no need for that, my dear. The terms are acceptable as is."

Abrielle barely withheld her sigh of relief. She had no way of knowing who had cautioned the squire on the generous sum the marriage agreement would require him to bestow upon her once the vows were exchanged, not to mention the sizable fortune she'd reap upon his death. She could only conclude by Thurstan's attempt to urge her to consider other proposals that he may have been the one to broach the feasibility of a less lucrative stipend, which in turn caused her to wonder what he expected to personally gain from it. As Desmond's only relative, did he want more of the wealth that was now promised to her family?

If Desmond had failed to consider all aspects of the agreement beforehand, then she could only believe that he was not as astute as a man of properties should be. After all, his wealth had come to him through the efforts of others and was nothing he had actually earned through prudent deeds or foreign ventures as a soldier of the realm. Perhaps he was wont to let wealth sift fairly quickly through his fingers.

"Uncle, may I speak with you for a moment?" Thurstan requested in a muted tone, looking gravely concerned. "I truly believe the agreement needs to be clarified for your benefit. You need to reconsider—"

"I've made up my mind," Desmond stated resolutely,

punctuating his statement with a quick, slashing gesture. "No changes will be necessary. You may go."

The lean features of the younger man stiffened noticeably as he was curtly dismissed. Beneath lowering brows, the yellow eyes seemed to shoot flinty shards at the older man. Abrielle could hardly mistake Thurstan's resentment at being brushed aside so callously.

Thurstan stalked back along the drawbridge to the inner courtyard, dismissed as if he were a servant, and his hand itched to draw his sword and be done with his uncle once and for all. How dare the man be the second de Marlé to deny Thurstan his proper inheritance! Weldon had promised such to him, and then died before having the chance to change his will. And now Desmond was freely throwing money at some chit of a girl, when it only took a real man to show a woman what she was worth. Thurstan vowed silently that he was not through manipulating his uncle.

If Desmond was aware of the younger man's exasperation, he gave no indication that he cared one way or the other, directing his attention to Abrielle. "Have I told you how sublimely lovely you are, my dear? Definitely the most winsome lady I've ever seen."

Abrielle felt her stomach convulse. "Please, Desmond, such extravagant praises embarrass me. To be sure, I feel so unworthy."

"Oh, but you are worthy, my dear. Infinitely so! In all my travels I've never seen a more beautiful woman."

Abrielle feigned a coyly skeptical laugh. "Then I shall have to question the extent of your travels, sir, for I fear the distance may have been extremely limited."

Desmond was wont to silently agree, but would never have openly admitted it. His half brother had been the clever, ambitious one in the family, venturing as a crusader far beyond his homeland, not only returning a valiant hero but also with greater wealth and fame than when he had left, no doubt the difference a devoted mother could make in the life of her offspring. From what Desmond had overheard from neighbors in his youth, Weldon's mother had been an imposing lady whose lineage had reaffirmed and strengthened the dignity and honor of her husband's house. Not so the wily chambermaid who had sought by devious methods to assuage the father's grief over his wife's mysterious death, the result of a witch's potion that had later been used again, only in smaller portions, to muddle the mind of the father.

By such schemes, his mother had brought about the birth of her bastard son and had then managed to shame the befuddled man into marriage by claiming that he had raped her during his delirium. She had even been inclined to brag on her accomplishments to her son. She had unleashed the last of her secrets as she lay dying of a vile, torturous disease.

Using the knowledge his mother had spilled that night, Desmond had learned much in the way of changing one's destiny by the use of strange, ofttimes hallucinogenic and poisonous concoctions. Thereafter, he had used the secret potions on those who had possessed what he had coveted or had unwittingly stood in his way as he strove for greater riches and gain. He could not now name how many he had poisoned throughout his lifetime. They had slipped from his memory as easily as dark shadows moving past him through the night.

And in all of this he was assisted by his half sister, Mordea, who'd been raised among the witches who had been his mother's friends. No one knew of his relationship to Mordea, and he'd been able to hire her as the castle's cook, keeping her close enough to take advantage of her knowledge—and close enough to make sure she didn't reveal any of his own secrets. She kept promising to expand her knowledge of cooking, but he had to tread lightly where she was concerned.

After being saddled with his first wife, he had been greatly relieved when he had found the right occasion to dispense a potion to relieve himself of her during childbirth and, later, after marrying his second wife, disposing of her in much the same manner, in each case making certain that he alone could claim their possessions.

He was proud of the fact that no one had yet discovered how he had been able to dispense with his half brother. A few droplets of a particular potion in Weldon's wine had allowed him to push the much taller, stronger man down the stone stairs beyond his chambers. It had amused him to watch the imposing figure tumbling down the steps, knowing if the fall didn't kill him, other measures certainly would. To ensure that he had an alternative plan in case his first attempt failed, he had carried a heavy cudgel tucked within his robe. As it turned out, it hadn't proven necessary once Weldon's head struck the stone barrier buttressing the stairs. Even now, he was wont to chuckle over how smoothly everything had gone that singular evening. It had certainly meant a new, more profitable beginning for him, and further confirmed in him the steadfast belief that he was in full control of his own destiny and would now have whatever he desired.

CHAPTER 4

"Shall we join Cordelia?" Abrielle asked Desmond as she swept a slender hand about to indicate her friend, surprised and relieved that the trepidation, nay the revulsion, she felt to her very core did not cause her to tremble. She was more than willing to allow her friend to serve as a human bulwark between them. She could only wonder who would function in that capacity after they were wed, and to hope against hope that she could continue to conceal the feelings of dread and impending doom that never ceased threatening to rise up and consume her.

Upon reaching the far side of the drawbridge, she stared down into the moat as she struggled to create an impression of serene pleasure. Tolerating a kiss on her cheek proved another test of forbearance that made her wonder what could be found to treat his horrible breath. Although she knew she had no choice but to face the fact that she was now destined to become Desmond's wife, she began to fear that her badly flawed pretense would soon be dashed asunder and she'd run sobbing in remorse to the spacious chambers that she and her parents had been given. Regrettably, the commitment she had made was dragging her down into a pit of despair whence she feared there would be no escape.

When Desmond begged a moment to go speak with a nearby servant, she gladly granted him her permission. Cordelia stood quietly while Abrielle braced an arm on a buttressing rail and settled her chin glumly upon the heel of her hand. "I wish I could look forward to the nuptials with as much enthusiasm as the men are evidencing for the upcoming hunt."

Cordelia hesitated, and then softly asked, "How can you marry a man you're unable to trust? A man whom you and all others loathe? When you wrote about the wedding, I must confess that I was shocked."

Abrielle glanced over her shoulder to make sure the squire was still well occupied. "It was either that or see my family come to ruin. Vachel has been brought to impoverishment due to his generosity to his late father and to his knights," she admitted.

Cordelia gasped. "What are you saying? That you must marry that ogre because of your stepfather's ill-considered actions?"

"The fault was not his." Abrielle hurried to explain the injustice done by Vachel's father. "Vachel was willing to face destitution rather than force me to accept Desmond's proposal. I chose to spare him, and my mother, that shame."

Cordelia clasped her friend's hand as she looked with tear-filled eyes into the blue-green orbs. "And some people think only knights have such noble traits."

"Say nothing of this to anyone," Abrielle urged. "Vachel would not take it well if people thought his father had been unfair. He'd be hurt by any criticism they'd be wont to bestow upon the elder. Considering that he was a little addled toward the end, he might not have been aware of what he was doing."

"If you would permit me, I will only speak of this to my parents, who truly have the highest regard for Vachel. 'Twill be in tribute to him that I will share this with them."

"To them and no other," Abrielle agreed. Thoughtfully she stared off into the distance as the softly wafting breezes lifted her kirtle.

"What are you thinking now?"

A doleful sigh slipped from Abrielle's lips. "Though I'm ashamed to admit my feelings after accepting Desmond's proposal of marriage, I do disdain the man more than anyone I've ever known."

Cordelia recognized her friend's loss of hope in the overly restrained way she conveyed her lack of regard for her future husband, and laid a gently consoling hand upon Abrielle's sleeve. "Ofttimes, when one approaches the unknown, circumstances may look the bleakest and most threatening. From experience, I know you have a valiant spirit and will rise above your fear. Did you not rescue me from a horrible drowning when we were children, though you were terrified of going into the icy waters after me?" Freshening tears welled within Cordelia's green eyes as she added, "If not for your valiant spirit and victory over your own qualms, I would not be here today."

Abrielle's own vision grew misty as she recalled their childhood and the frightening incident that had sent prickling shards of terror coursing through her being. Her own fear had seemed as painful as the icy slush she had been forced to tread to reach her friend. If not for the goading dread that she was about to lose her dearest companion, she might never have found the courage to go into the frigid depths after her.

"I know I must take heart," Abrielle admitted, and then heaved a dismal sigh as she considered what she would soon be facing, "but at the moment, my future looks so bleak that even drowning in an icy stream seems preferable. Truly, the horrors I'll be facing as the wife of such a despicable creature seem so overwhelming that I have to wonder if I'll be able to endure them."

Cordelia turned aside in an attempt to calm her own troubled spirit. She could only wonder what she would do in Abrielle's stead. Mulling over her companion's abhorrent plight, she did not notice the small company of mounted men approaching until they were halfway down the lane leading to the drawbridge. There were six horsemen in all, but Cordelia felt no inclination to move her gaze past the handsome gray-haired man astride the black stallion prancing in the lead. The horse's smooth-flowing gait was a perfect complement to the proud, majestic bearing of his rider, a Scottish gentleman of an age nearly threescore years. In spite of the man's maturity, Cordelia was certain she had never seen such a magnificent individual or a more admirable mount anywhere within Henry's realm.

Leaning near her companion, Cordelia urged in a hushed whisper, "Abrielle, glance behind you discreetly and tell me if you've ever seen these gentlemen before. If my opinions haven't been led astray by wagging tongues, I could almost swear your future husband detests Scots as much as he loathes our kinsmen, the Saxons. In view of that possibility, 'twould seem these men have ventured into Desmond's pilfered realm without being fully cognizant of the danger."

Abrielle swept the surrounding countryside with a leisurely gaze before honing in on the approaching retinue, and once she did so, everything inside her froze. Then, with a distinct lack of caution or subtlety, she whipped her head around toward Desmond, relieved to find him still flailing his arms as he berated the cowed servant, and it was clear to her that he had not noticed the new arrivals. "Cordelia! Quick . . . look closely at the second man in the party. Unless my sight fails me, 'tis Raven Seabern!"

Abrielle's heart was pounding so loudly she was certain it must be echoing off the castle walls for all to hear, pounding with alarm, she told herself, alarm and dread, and not at all with excitement. What was the man thinking to come galloping onto de Marlé's property as if 'twere his God-given right to be there, as if he would be welcomed with open arms? Did his brashness blind him to the fact that his very presence, not to mention the fact that he was flanked by a company of Scotsmen, was sure to rile every nobleman within miles?

Stiffening her shoulders in an effort at least to appear composed, she turned and managed to keep her gaze off Raven long enough to glance at the similarly tall, brawny Scot who'd dismounted to stand at his side. The older man took note of her interest and stared back at her with a teasing twinkle in his brilliant blue eyes. When he succeeded in causing a blush to redden her cheeks, his smile deepened into a charmingly wayward grin, revealing gleaming white teeth beneath a massive mustache, the well-groomed ends of which reached past his chin. A deeply chiseled cleft, similar to the one her erstwhile protector possessed, punctuated the elder's cleanly shaven chin. Although the man was well past a youthful age, he wasn't above looking her over in a roguish manner, starting with her slippered toes and ending at the top of her head. Upon completing his assessment, he gave her a flirtatious wink and was rewarded by her startled gasp.

Having witnessed the exchange, Cordelia ducked her head in an effort to hide her amusement from the elder. "He's a bold one, that he is. Do you think he is the elder Seabern?"

Sourly, Abrielle said, "The only difference betwixt the two seems to be their age and the color of their hair."

Continuing to grin, the Scotsman cocked a hoary brow and canted his head at an angle as he peered back at the two women as if wondering what had evoked their interest in him. Then he glanced at Raven and Abrielle felt her own gaze drawn reluctantly in the same direction. She'd managed to avoid meeting Raven's eyes directly until now, fearing not so much what she might see in them as what she herself might feel at the mercy of that intense regard she remembered so vividly, a concern that was well founded. True, with her intended close by, he did not indulge in gazing as boldly as he'd done when they met last. Rather, his mesmerizing blue eyes narrowed in a look of lingering speculation that was still more than enough to cause a heated flush to sweep over her.

A dozen questions raced through her head, all pertaining to his reason for being there, and she was forced to ask herself if the man had lost his senses entirely, or merely just his recollection of that night at the palace when he'd thwarted Desmond's forced tryst with devastating ease, and sent the cowed man scurrying into the shadows like the spineless creature he was. An even more interesting question was whether Raven had knowledge of her betrothal to Squire Spineless, a possibility that made Abrielle's throat constrict as she wondered if that might have had something to do with his sudden appearance.

She drew a deep breath and pulled sharply on the reins of her imagination. Now who was taking leave of their senses? It was one thing for Raven to be passing in the castle hallway, hear her screams and struggles, and come to her rescue; 'twould be quite another for him to travel a distance out of his way, to a place he was not wanted, in order to . . . what? Abrielle was certain of only one thing; he was not there by invitation. After the humiliation he'd delivered the squire, Raven Seabern would be the last man in all Christendom to be invited. Most likely, she decided in an effort to calm herself, he was there on a matter of import to his king. Whatever his business, it was none of hers, though she would dearly love to know why he'd seen fit to bring along his father.

Cordelia peered at her friend as a mischievous grin bowed her lips upward at the corners. "'Tis my opinion that a young lady should behave herself and not take advantage of that poor, elderly Scot. Why, he's old enough to be your grandfather, and there he is with his heart on his sleeve."

"Whose heart is upon her sleeve?" Abrielle challenged as she cast a meaningful glance askance at her friend. "'Twould seem you're far more taken with this Scotsman."

Cordelia was unable to deny the fact that the man had evoked her interest. "Well, he is very handsome . . ."

"Then perhaps you should have Raven Seabern introduce you," Abrielle said, trying for a lightheartedness she didn't feel. "The man does owe you the favor of an introduction, after all."

As the shock of Raven's sudden appearance eased, Abrielle felt a wisp of sorrow. For reasons she could not name, seeing him gave rise to thoughts she'd been valiantly struggling to avoid, thoughts of what her life might have been, what it should have been, a full and happy life with a good man and a family of her own. It was the life she'd once looked forward to sharing with the kindly Weldon de Marlé, a girlish dream that had died when he did. There was no longer a place in her life for daydreams and romantic notions, and to wish it were otherwise only added to her misery. Far better to accept that her union with Weldon's brother would be the cruel opposite to anything a young woman would hope for in her marriage, and turn her attention elsewhere. Soon she would have the mundane affairs of a squire's wife to fill her days and occupy her mind, soon, but not yet, and as hard as she resisted, she could not help wondering what it would be like to be married to a man like Raven Seabern. Though she told herself her question arose solely from intellectual curiosity, she had to concede that such a marriage would be exciting and perhaps not entirely unpleasant.

Not that Abrielle could now seriously entertain the idea of marriage to one other than Desmond, as she'd committed herself to saving her family, and she was not one to go back on her word, no matter how loathsome she found the consequences. Besides, the priests said a betrothal contract was as legally binding as a marriage, and she had to acknowledge that her grim future was set.

After they exchanged words among themselves, the new arrivals walked toward the women, leading their horses. And for all that she'd just sworn off wishing for the impossible, Abrielle found herself wishing for all she was worth that she could hitch up her skirts and run from the confrontation. She wished it nearly as much as she wished she'd never met a Scotsman with the name of a predator and the face of a fallen angel, an annoying, arrogant, enticing man with the power to make her feel nervous and feverish and sad all at the same time.

Scarcely a moment before the group of Scots reached them, Desmond suddenly appeared beside Abrielle and Cordelia. Considering how his last encounter with Raven turned out, Abrielle had expected him to be outraged when he recognized the men in the party. But although she detected a hateful gleam in his eyes, it was offset by a forced smile and a strange air of satisfaction that she could not help but think boded ill.

The elder Scot's eyes were even more vividly blue up close, and their twinkle of quick and unquenchable wit even more apparent. But he'd tethered his flirtatious charm and for the moment seemed entirely dedicated to politely claiming the squire's attention. Not so his descendant. Raven was paying no heed to his host and making no effort to hide his interest in the young women by his side. Abrielle grew warm as she became the center of his focus. She had not seen him since the night he'd rescued her, when fear and awkwardness—and the revealing state of her torn clothing—prompted her to make nearly as hasty a retreat as her attacker. Despite the fact that he had shown a most improper interest in her that evening, she knew that she had not properly expressed her gratitude to him. Her concern was how it might be received once he learned she was betrothed to the very villain from whom he'd rescued her, if he did not know already. Would he think her a fool who cared only about wealth, and that her gratitude was tainted by her greed? At the thought, Abrielle bit her lip and had to wonder what was wrong with her, for she was a betrothed woman, for pity's sake, a desperately betrothed woman. And while his opinion of her should not matter, she knew that it did, just as she knew that that must change. At her first opportunity she would thank him for his gallantry and that would be the end of it.

Raven and the older man bowed to the two maidens, then turned to face Desmond.

"Squire de Marlé," the elder Scotsman rumbled cheerily in a deeply resonating voice, revealing one more difference betwixt father and son, that Raven's parent spoke in a much heavier brogue. Laying a hand upon his chest, he inclined his bonneted head in an abbreviated bow. "Ye've truly honored us by inviting us ta your keep."

Abrielle swallowed a gasp of surprise at hearing the Scotsman say that he and his son had been invited to the keep, but then, perhaps it was not such a surprise after all. The only possible reason for Desmond to extend an invitation was so that he could have the last laugh by waving her beneath Raven's nose, for of course he would want to be certain Raven saw and understood who was the true winner in this contest. It was Desmond who'd won the prize he'd sought; he'd won full and lasting rights to her heart, her mind, and her body, Lord help her, a thought that made Abrielle feel ill inside. It mattered little that his victory had been secured with gold rather than valor or worthiness, for the agreement was duly settled and soon the deed would be done. And besides, she reminded herself, the memory like a small stab to her heart, Raven had been in no hurry to court her even when he had the chance.

Desmond was gleeful to welcome the latest arrivals, for several reasons. It never hurt to be associated with respected and influential men . . . even if they were Scots. Far more important, however, he had a score to settle. Since that unfortunate incident at the castle he'd been busily gathering information. In talking with knowledgeable people cognizant of individuals living within the northern climes of Scotland, he'd learned the elder Seabern had for years been a close confidant of Scottish royals and had, in fact, served as second-in-command of the last king's forces. As for his son, he had been serving nearly five years as an important envoy for King David.

You would think being entrusted to carry missives to and fro would have taught him not to stick his nose where it didn't belong, but such was not the case. And so Desmond himself would teach the Scot that lesson and relish every moment of it. He would parade his betrothed before Raven and his esteemed father until he'd driven home the message that he owned her, before man and God, that he alone had the right to touch her, whenever and wherever he pleased, and that no man would ever again dare challenge that right. It would be most satisfying to demonstrate to two such confident and accomplished men how little power they had to control the fate of one beautiful woman.

He could hardly keep from rubbing his hands together in anticipation as he greeted them. "'Tis you and your son who honor me this day by joining me and my guests for the hunt, Laird Seabern." Desmond spared no effort in appearing the cordial host. "I've heard there are no finer hunters in these northern climes than the pair of you. Many of my guests have come here hoping to match your best feats. Indeed, they have begun wagering on the outcome, and I've been told many generous purses have been collected, and more are being added hourly. 'Twill be rich prizes awaiting those who fell the finest stag and the largest boar. Now that you are both here, I'm sure the stakes will be raised significantly. Thus the reason for your invitation to my keep."

Abrielle barely contained a snort of derision, for she doubted if anyone could believe that.

"But I am being remiss in my duties as host," Desmond conceded, and turned briefly to Abrielle and Cordelia. "My ladies, you no doubt remember the Scots emissary from the festivities held within His Majesty's castle, but I believe you haven't yet made the acquaintance of his father, Laird Cedric Seabern."

A lopsided grin stretched across the elder's lips as he clasped Cordelia's slender fingers within his and bestowed a kiss upon the back of her hand. "I've na seen a more winsome pair of lasses in many a year," he claimed. "Ta be sure, ye've brought the beauty of the heavens down ta us mere mortals, and for that, 'tis greatly heartened I am that such splendor exists even for such as I."

Cordelia's fair cheeks warmed with a vivid blush as she smiled back at the elder. "I know the Celtic bards wove magic out of words, kind sir, and 'tis in my mind that you must have inherited the silver from their tongues."

Cedric threw back his hoary head and chortled in delight. "Aye, lass, and if I could steal more, I truly would, just ta make ye smile."

Cordelia swept a hand aside to indicate her companion. "Have you made the acquaintance of my friend Lady Abrielle?"

"Another of fine, rare beauty," Cedric claimed as he rubbed his palms together in glee. "By heavens, if the sights are so wondrously fair so near ta this keep, then I'll be moving in and making myself at home."

Abrielle laughed nervously, preferring the safety of Cedric Seabern's teasing to the unsettling and intense gaze of his son, a look that spoke of only one thing— possession. His regard evidenced the arrogance and boldess he had so clearly displayed at the banquet in London. "I must warn you, Laird, there are many Normans presently housed behind those walls. Were I you, I wouldn't enter lest you're familiar with sword and buckler."

There was an awkward pause, as all present reflected on the past hostilities between their respective countries.

He winked down at her. "Then I guess I'd better be finding some weapons for myself and my son, for 'tis there I think we'll find our chambers."

Stepping before Cordelia, Raven drew her hand to his lips and placed a light kiss upon her fingertips. "I'm pleasured ta see ye again, my lady. I am sure that my da would agree, we've not seen such beauty since we last saw ye at Henry's palace."

Cordelia smiled and swept a hand about to indicate her companion. "Mayhap you'll remember my friend the Lady Abrielle."

Abrielle wanted to wince, for she had not confided in her companion about Desmond's attack or Raven's heroic deeds. Cordelia had no way of knowing just how well Raven was sure to remember her, or why. To her relief, he gave no hint of what had transpired, responding to her friend's query with a respectful nod.

"Of course. 'Tis also a pleasure ta see ye again, Lady Abrielle. Squire de Marlé is truly a fortunate man ta have claimed such a wondrously fair bride for himself. I canna but imagine the ardent swains who'll be left languishing over their loss."

Raven sensed de Marlé's beady eyes studying him and told himself it was for that reason alone he reached for Abrielle's hand. After the briefest of hesitations, she placed it lightly atop his outstretched palm. He felt her slight tremble as he curled his fingers around hers and slowly drew her hand to his mouth.

Raven would have to have been a dullard not to know the real reason for his invitation; the squire wanted to watch Raven's reaction to seeing him with his bride-to-be, seeing him touch her, dance with her, hold her. He resolved that first he'd give the fat little cockroach something worth watching.

He bent his head to her hand and then purposely stopped with but a hairsbreadth between his mouth and her pale silken flesh. He glanced up, holding her gaze, his senses thrumming with awareness of the feel and scent of her, and the way she caught her breath even as he used his own warm breath to caress the back of her hand, delighting in the resulting gooseflesh along her slender arm. He hoped the squire was watching closely, for it took a master of the art to draw so much from a woman by doing so little, and Raven knew he was a master. He allowed the contact to stretch for another silent second, then another, and then he quickly touched her hand with his lips and let her go.

Abrielle's hand drifted bonelessly to her side as her whole body tingled, as if from hundreds of bee stings, and her head was spinning. And still she could sense the tension between Desmond and Raven. "Thank you for your generous compliments, Sir Raven," she said, hoping to strike just the right balance between cordial and reserved that would cause Desmond to cease glowering and wipe a bit of the smugness from Raven's face. "Your tongue is as gilded as the setting sun, noble sir."

"Now my da, here, can assure ye that he raised me up ta be a man of truth, my lady, and so I am. Ye can take me at my word when I say that ye and the Lady Cordelia are rare gems of great beauty. As a man, I find myself much in awe of ye both."

But not, thought Abrielle, so much in awe he'd been moved to favor her with such a kiss when it might have mattered.

Cordelia dared not admit her own appreciation of such a handsome man, yet she was quite mischievous and couldn't resist questioning him in front of de Marlé, even though she already knew the answer to her query. She would delight in having Raven's status underscored in the presence of the rotund squire, who himself was doubtless already cognizant of the Scotsman's privileged position. "How came you to be at the palace for Lord Berwin's dedication? Or should I ask such a question?"

"Alas, my lady, I am usually but a stranger ta such lofty places, except when I serve as ambassador for my own king, David of Scotland. Then I must travel hither and yon, wherever the need takes me. 'Tis not often that my duties afford me the opportunity ta indulge in the company of such winsome lasses as I see before me here."

As Cordelia had thought, the exchange greatly annoyed their host, and both she and Abrielle could readily surmise that Desmond's patience was at an end.

"Kindly make yourselves known to my steward. He will show you and your father to your chambers. Tonight we'll feast and make merry in the banquet hall. Come early morn, the men will gather for a stag hunt, and the following day, boar. Those who bring back the most impressive trophies will be honored that same evening. On the third day hence, the Lady Abrielle and I will be exchanging our wedding vows and celebrating our union with a banquet later that same evening. Of course you'll both attend as special guests of mine."

He might as well have spoken his true purpose aloud, Abrielle thought, but he was wasting his time if he hoped to get a rise from Raven. The Scotsman had never shown serious interest in her, so why would he care whom she married? It was only she who was being hurt by this cruel joke.

"Ta be sure, we'll be marking each occasion with our presence," Raven assured the man, laying a hand upon the folds of plaid across his chest as he inclined his head and retreated several steps. "We're honored ta be among your guests."

In response to the remark, Desmond nodded perfunctorily.

Straightening to his full height, Raven cast his gaze about as though admiring the scenery surrounding them, but only Abrielle had his attention. He was not surprised by the realization that he had remembered the lady in infinite detail. But then, no other woman had even come close to ensnaring his heart as she had done during their initial meeting. She was watching him, too, although he sensed a coolness about her. She was a woman betrothed, of course, but she also seemed to be taking great pains to avoid his gaze, the reason for which he could not fathom.

Desmond held forth an arm in silent invitation to his bride-to-be. It was impossible not to compare the gesture with Raven offering his hand in similar fashion only moments before. If ever she had been whisked from fantasy into harsh, morbid reality within the passage of a moment, then Abrielle was convinced such an occurrence took place the instant she laid a trembling hand upon the squire's sleeve. She loathed touching him, yet she found no viable escape and was forced to feign a smile in spite of the fact that she felt as if a ponderous weight was now crushing her heart. If only Raven hadn't accepted Desmond's spiteful invitation. She wouldn't now have to look at him and imagine herself married to someone like him, handsome and bold. Why did she always have to force herself to remember that he had had his chance, that he clearly hadn't even wanted to court her properly, to present himself to her stepfather at the apartment Vachel had taken in Westminster Castle for their stay in London? She could only assume he was looking for a wealthy bride, and in her despondence, she truly wondered if that's all a man cared about. Bitterly, she knew she was no less guilty, for it was the only reason she was marrying the squire.

Desmond preened with pride as he paraded her past the Scotsmen, nodding to each in turn before leading her away. As they entered the open courtyard, the guests occupying the area came forward to offer salutations and wishes for a joyous union. Abrielle heard only half of what was being said and, when presented a question, could only smile with a dull sense of numbness as de Marlé answered in her stead. He readily assured them that she was as anxious to wed as he, and although her silence seemed to convey a mutual accord with his claims, inwardly she felt as if she were a spiritless puppet with a fixed smile painted on its face and its strings being manipulated by the man at her side.

Continuing on by a ragged scrap of lackluster resolve, Abrielle traversed the inner courtyard with that same fake smile pasted on her face. The feeling of being emotionally empty inside was almost more than she could bear. Had there been a moment of freedom wherein she could have found a hidden niche, she would have fled to such a place and sobbed out her heart in unrelenting anguish until she had no more tears to spill. Nothing she had ever experienced before had seemed more akin to the horrors of a dark netherworld than the bleak, empty passages of time through which she was now passing, all because she was destined to become the bride of a despicable ogre. Had she been walking a stony path toward an ominous block upon which she'd be required to rest her head and awaiting her there was a hooded executioner clasping an ax, she would have felt no less dismayed.

LATE INTO THE night, Abrielle lay in rigid repose upon a narrow bed in the small room adjoining the chambers her parents were occupying. Staring fixedly at nothing more significant than the silken panels draped around the tester, she found it difficult to even breathe, much less sleep. A morbid heaviness lay over her spirit, a feeling no doubt evoked by the fact that only a few, paltry days separated her from the ceremony that would forever bind her to Desmond de Marlé. Whenever she considered what she would have to submit to in order to fulfill her wifely obligations, it seemed a prelude to another descent into a pit of despair. If not for fear of waking her parents, she would have succumbed to the overwhelming sobs that were threatening to burst free. She had committed herself to a hell on earth by giving her word, and not only would she not take it back, she could not.

Unable to bear the conflict within her, she finally tore herself free from her narrow bed and fled into the outer hall in a burgeoning quest to find absolute solitude for just a few moments so no one would hear the sobs that were threatening to break free and overwhelm her. When she finally halted, she found herself in a corridor leading to the tower stairs. Her nightgown clung to her, and her bare feet were nearly frigid against the stone floor. Her long hair tumbled in wild disarray around her shoulders and over her bosom, providing a mantle of warmth against the chill pervading the hall.

The only light came from the moon shining through a lofty turret. The leaded panes of glass cast their muted colors and reflection upon the stone floor. In spite of her mood of utter hopelessness, Abrielle took comfort in simply being alone in a place where she could cry aloud if need be, and tears were increasingly shed as her wedding day grew closer. Her peace of mind was brief; after only a few moments of solitude she had the uneasy sense that someone was nearby. Alarmed, she peered intently into the surrounding blackness and wondered who might be watching. Desmond? Since their arrival, it seemed he was always lurking about, hiding in some nook or cranny . . . that is, hiding as well as a man of his girth could hide. He was obsessed with spying upon her. 'Twas yet another in an ever-growing list of reasons she prayed God might send a miracle in time to stop the wedding.

Had Desmond followed her tonight, hoping to catch her unaware the way he had at Henry's castle? Was he so greedy for her flesh he would seek to deny her a few final hours of peace and privacy? Anger and revulsion coursed through her. Of course there was also the possibility it was someone unknown to her skulking in the shadows. It hardly bode well for her future that she could not say whom she would most detest encountering in the middle of the night in this dark isolated corner, her betrothed or a total stranger.

A scraping sound by the tower steps, like boot heel on rough stone, brought her conjecturing to a hasty halt.

"Desmond?" she called out, thankful her steady voice betrayed none of the trepidation she felt, for it would do little good to give in to her fear. Even if someone were to hear her screams, Desmond's word was law here. And it would be foolhardy to hope for a conveniently passing gallant to again come charging to her rescue, especially considering the distinct dearth of gallants in her life these days. She could honestly name only one, and even so foolhardy a Scot might be reluctant to intervene a second time.

She had but one recourse and that was to rescue herself. After all, she'd gotten herself into this predicament, hadn't she? She was convinced her stalker was Desmond, in spite of the fact that he hadn't answered when she called his name. It would be like him to remain silent just to prolong her misery. The little toad was probably hoping that if she were sufficiently frightened she would collapse in his arms with gratitude when he finally showed himself. Abrielle nearly snorted at the thought, for the odds were better that she would flap her arms and fly out of there than that she'd cozy up to him of her own free will.

She would wait him out, knowing he had to step forward eventually, and when he did she would remain calm and make him see it was to both their advantage for him to respect her family's dignity—as well as a gentleman's duty to invited guests in his home—and restrain himself until they were officially wed. If that failed, she was prepared to hoist her skirts and bolt before he could lay hands on her. God help her, she would not surrender her body to that lecher one second sooner than required by the terms of the devil's bargain they'd struck.

The silence stretched until Abrielle was certain her nerves would shatter. Finally there was the sound of footsteps, slow and deliberate, and a shadow fell across the patch of moonlight at her feet. She still could not see well enough to make out who it was and instinctively she grasped the fabric of her gown, poised to flee for her life. "Desmond?" she demanded more forcefully. "Is that you?"

The shadow moved, and a voice too deep, too masculine, and far too appealing to belong to the squire said, "Nay, Lady Abrielle. I can only pray ye're not overly disappointed."

CHAPTER 5

It was not disappointment she felt, but something else, something she could not yet name, as she realized it was Raven, the moon bathing him in shadows and a pale glow, revealing enough for Abrielle to recognize him, but not enough for her to see clearly the expression on his face. So, her intruder was neither squire nor stranger, and she knew she ought to feel relieved, but she did not.

Caution and propriety dictated she leave his presence immediately, but something else, something far less familiar, kept her rooted to the spot. It was as if the damp evening fog had seeped into her brain, making her forget everything and everyone save the handsome man who was once again watching her with bold, unguarded interest. What strange power did he hold over her that a mere glance or a small curve of his mouth could set her senses reeling this way? The very sight of him should send a betrothed woman scampering for the safety of her chamber; instead Abrielle felt more powerfully drawn to him than ever, her body reacting in the age-old way a woman responds to a man.

He shifted his weight slightly and a shaft of pearl light illuminated the loose, long-sleeved white shirt he wore with his kilt and soft leather boots. "So," he said quietly. "Are ye?"

Are ye? Abrielle frowned in consternation. *Was she . . . what*? It was no easy matter to concentrate with one's heart racing and an army of butterflies assaulting from within and she struggled to recall his words to her.

"Disappointed," he prompted before she had to ask. "Assuming, of course, it was your intended you slipped from the warm safety of your bed ta meet with in this . . ." He glanced around. "This perfectly dark and dank spot for an assignation. I freely confess ta being a poor substitute for the man ye seek, mayhap the poorest ta be found the world over. Perhaps ye've noticed how very little I have in common with the man of your dreams." When she blinked in confusion, he added, "Our gracious host."

Abrielle tossed her loosened hair over her shoulder. "I fear 'tis you who'll be disappointed, sir," she told him.

"Truly?" He ambled a few steps closer, regarding her with deliberation. "I cannot think how, when the heavens above have seen fit to reward my own nighttime rambling with a glimpse of the fairest beauty ever sent to earth."

Though she roiled inside, she feigned control, rolling her eyes in seeming humor. "Indeed you are your father's son, a Seabern through and through. But since there is no one here you seek to impress, you may as well save your pretty words. I was referring to the disappointment you will surely suffer when you realize how very wrong you are. You see, I've no assignation

planned for this evening, with our gracious host or anyone else."

He took another step, and Abrielle was very aware
that the closer he came, the softer and lower pitched his
voice became, and as he moved closer still, she felt a
frisson of velvet shivers along her spine. "Are ye so
sure ye know me well enough ta know whom it is I
seek ta impress?" he asked.

"I am sure I do not need to know you any better than
I do," she told him.

"Ah," he said, with an unmistakable trace of amusement. "In that case, my lady, I acknowledge my poor
judgment, and can only wonder what causes you ta
wander through the keep, dressed so poorly against the
chill, and at an hour most happy brides would be sound
asleep, dreaming sweet bridal dreams."

Abrielle hugged herself as if she were cold, thankful
he could not know how very warm she'd grown these
past moments. "I marvel at your intimate knowledge of
brides, sir. Speaking only for myself, I could not sleep,
and thought some crisp night air might bring those
sweet dreams you refer to. In my restlessness, I wandered farther than I intended."

Abrielle tensed as he came closer still, and reminded
herself it was past time for her to take leave of him, and
assured herself she would soon, but not just yet. She
had to ask herself what was wrong with her, for if ever
there was a time in her life when she ought to be erring
on the side of caution, it was surely now. Instead, with
so much at stake, not only for her, but for those she
loved most in the world, the troublesome reckless
streak she'd shared with her father and had thought
she'd outgrown, or at least learned to suppress, suddenly chose to make itself known.

"It is easy ta wander too far in a place such as this," he assured her, now very near, his closeness forcing her heart to beat even more rapidly than before, something she would not have thought possible.

She lifted her chin, vowing she would not let him see her fear, and forced herself to dissemble. "Yes, you're right, I find I'm much further from my chamber than I'd thought. One must cope with one's nerves as best one can, and a wedding causes so much happy anticipation . . ."

The words nearly stuck in her throat, but she would not have him know the extent of her family's desperation. She had lost much, her dear father, her first betrothed, her safety and peace of mind, even her dreams for the future, and soon even more would be taken from her, but she would not surrender the battered remnants of her pride.

Raven arched a dark brow. " 'Happy anticipation'? Forgive my impertinence, my lady, but I seem ta recall that the last time I saw ye with de Marlé, he was accosting ye. Is it that which inspires such happy anticipation? Or was my judgment also faulty that night at the palace? Mayhap ye were not in need of rescue."

Abrielle bristled, especially at the fact that he seemed to relish every moment of her discomfort. "What happened that night was a . . . misunderstanding between the squire and myself," she told him. "One since rectified."

His expression changed, becoming harsher, and his voice changed also. It was clearly full of anger, and his tone was deadly quiet, and she took a step back. "A misunderstanding, was it? The squire perhaps misunderstood that he had not yet formally presented for your hand, much less had his suit accepted by your stepfather, and that no agreement had been reached, no bond formed, nor banns published. Did he also misunderstand the fact that he had no better right ta waylay and manhandle ye, ta touch and paw ye . . ."

Abrielle determined to keep her composure, though the effort cost her dearly, and offered only a shrug and halfhearted murmur. "I believe it was more a matter of the squire simply being too eager."

She could see that the anger she'd heard building in his voice had become etched on his face, turning the already hard lines and angles to granite, as he responded to her words. "I can only hope ye don't truly believe that rubbish, or worse, have it in your head that such 'eagerness' is normal for a man. An honorable man knows what is his and what is not, and he acts accordingly . . . no matter how badly he wants—" He broke off sharply. "An honorable man understands there are things in this world worth the waiting."

For no good reason, a warm melting pleasure spread through Abrielle. Everything about him, from the stubborn set of his jaw to the fervor in his tone, revealed that Raven was such a man and she recoiled from the prospect of defending de Marlé to him. She fumbled for a response of some kind, finally settling for a halfhearted obligatory, "I trust you do not mean to imply that my betrothed is not honorable."

"It matters not at all what I think. What matters is what ye think of him."

She looked into his eyes, fully prepared for a knowing gleam and instead finding understanding, and it was too much to bear.

"Oh, for pity's sake," she exclaimed, "if you think so poorly of him, why on earth did you accept his invitation?"

"Ta be honest, I was curious."

"About his motives?"

He smiled sardonically and shook his head. "No. He's not that complicated; his motives were obvious. He wanted me here so he could flaunt his conquest of ye."

She inhaled sharply. She'd had the same thought, but Raven did not have to know that. "The castle is in near proximity to your country," she reminded him. "Perhaps he only hoped to show his goodwill to your King David."

"Then he should have invited King David," he said drily.

"Do you already so regret coming here?"

His hesitation was long, and the tension rising between them was something new and unmistakable. "Nay, my lady, for the chance ta see ye again, I would have braved far worse."

There was no one but her about to hear his pretty phrases, leaving no doubt he meant them for her alone. There was a husky intimacy in his voice that was also all new to Abrielle. Her feelings of uneasiness blossomed into yearning—followed quickly by fierce anger. Surely he knew what he was doing, tempting a woman about to be married.

"Do not speak so to me," she hissed, "or I will know who lacks honor."

She whirled about and retreated, intent on reaching the closest safety, her parents' bedchamber, and not stopping until she did.

Raven followed at a distance, then waited directly outside the heavy door until he detected the sound of the wooden bar being eased into place on the other side. Her safety mattered to him more than it ought, certainly more than was wise.

He ran his hand down his face with a soft groan. Why did he lose all sense of restraint when he was near Abrielle? He'd promised himself he would handle all dealings with her as befit a distant acquaintance.

Then he saw her standing alone in the moonlight, a fairy princess with curls the color of sunrise tumbling about her shoulders, her lithe graceful form more tempting in her soft cotton gown than any woman he'd ever seen dressed in velvet and jewels. And he'd seen his share of women, dressed and undressed; more than enough not to respond to a glimpse of pleasing curve or hint of enticing hollow like a green boy yet to steal his first kiss. Yet somehow simply looking at Abrielle robbed him of caution, and perhaps—as she suggested—a bit of the uncompromising honor he prided himself upon.

God, the woman was right about him, and he despised his weakness where she was concerned. If he were half as smart as he was proud, he would do as he'd sworn before coming and stay as far away from her as possible for the duration of his visit. If he were just a bit smarter than that, he would leave now, in plenty of time before the wedding ceremony itself, which he fully expected to be an exercise in torment. He did not need to see Abrielle before the church doors in her lace and finery to know the sight of her could make his knees want to buckle and slam his heart into his ribs so hard it hurt. Or that seeing her given to de Marlé, before man and God, would make him want to bellow an ancient war cry and steal her away at sword point.

Damn, he should leave tonight, this very moment, he thought, knowing he had no intention of following his own good advice. Leaving would be cowardly and Raven Seabern was no damn coward. Nay, he would stay and give the sniveling squire his petty satisfaction.

He would stay and do something that would take more guts than any battle or brawl or beating that went before. He was a royal emissary, trained to keep even the most riotous emotions in check, a skill that in his world could mean the difference between blessed life and certain death; he would stand in silence and watch the only woman who'd ever touched him to his very core, without so much as placing a gloved fingertip on him, marry another man.

THE NEWLY RISING sun glimmered through the lower branches of the trees lining the hills along the eastern horizon, with its rosy glow tingeing the heavily swirling mists drifting eerily over the marshy terrain that partially surrounded the keep. Within the enclosed courtyard of the well-fortified edifice, serfs with lackluster eyes and cheeks noticeably sunken scurried about in anxious haste as they laid heavily laden trenchers before the hunters. When the trays were whisked away, many of the serfs were seen hurriedly cramming whatever meager scraps were left into their mouths.

More than a score of hunting hounds were creating an underlying cacophony of pleading whines and snarls as they sought to keep close to their masters. A well-placed boot or the heavy end of a sturdy staff evoked sudden yelps and usually sent the dogs scurrying off in every direction, whence they soon ventured forth again to lick up whatever scraps of meat had fallen from overflowing platters being borne by hastening serfs.

Sitting among those whose greed set their minds aflame with various schemes to seize whatever prizes they could pilfer were men of quieter, subtler natures who took the hunt seriously and were confident of their own abilities. Leaving others to their wily wrangling and overloud boasting of past pursuits, these men silently inspected the straightness of their spears and arrows. The pair of Scotsmen was firmly a part of this latter group.

Raven casually honed several spears to a sharper point in preparation for the boar hunt on the morrow. The fact that he and his father knew no one in attendance had been expected. In spite of the fact that his friends in the highlands had been wont to question his rationale for accepting an invitation to attend the nuptials of one who would likely prove a treacherous enemy, Raven hadn't been able to forget the bonny lass he had rescued, nor could he ignore the fierce desire he felt to possess her. She seemed to him a delicate flower whose beauty was beyond measure. To mature into a full-fledged woman, she would have to be gently nurtured, and there was scant chance of that happening in the hands of a fiend like de Marlé. Raven feared she would not long survive under his abuse.

Cedric pursed his mustached lips as he contemplated the blade he had been honing and then elevated his gaze to meet his son's. "We hadn't a chance ta talk of this earlier, so I'll be asking ye now. I warned ye that de Marlé might be craving revenge, and now that I've seen the look in his eyes, I believe it even more so."

Raven glanced at his father. "Ye don't find his sudden camaraderie convincing?"

Cedric snorted. "Lad, would ye mind telling your old da why ye insisted upon venturing inta this trap like some blind beggar?"

Raven bestowed a wry grin upon his parent. "I know ye've na been a widower so long that ye canna admire a pretty face right along with the rest of us, Da. Ye've seen for yourself how bonny the lass is."

"Please tell me ye mean the Lady Cordelia."

"Nay, 'tis Abrielle who's struck her arrow deep in my heart."

Cedric sighed and shook his head. "I was afraid of just that when I saw the keen way you looked at her yesterday, and that's before I took note of the way the lady was looking back. Didna I hear some wild rumor whirling about on the winds that the lass is spoken for? Was that not our reasoning for venturing ta this here keep, ta attend the nuptials betwixt de Marlé and his lady fair?"

The younger man shrugged. "If ye'll remember, Da, I didna ask ta be invited. The good squire did that on his own. It's true I would have preferred the poor lass not be tied ta such a man, but the contract's been signed and I have to accept it." Even as he said it, everything in him roiled in protest. To distract himself as much as his father, he turned to a different subject. "Of course it does make me wonder even more what he's about. It might be far-fetched ta suppose he means ta do us both ill, but then again, 'twould prove interesting. Might be I could add some excitement ta the occasion."

"I'm not sure Abrielle would consider violence breaking out in the middle of her wedding 'interesting.'" Cedric slowly waggled his gray head. "Aye, ta be sure, lad, ye'd then have a right ta defend yourself. Still, taking inta account the poor man's nearly twice your age and weight and no taller than your shoulders, any altercation ye'd be starting betwixt the two of ye wouldna seem entirely fair ta that brood of vipers he calls his friends."

"Oh, I dinna intend ta invite it, Da," Raven assured

his sire. "And the lady has made it obvious she wants no help from the likes of me. Yet I feel . . . guilty."

"There be no need for that, lad. Ye dinna even ken the reasons she chose such a man."

"Desperation, Da, what else could it be?"

"Whatever it is, 'tis not our concern."

Raven made a noncommittal sound, thinking those words weren't any more convincing coming from his father than they had been when he said them to himself.

ABRIELLE SPENT THE first day of the hunt with the women. They'd all gathered to see off the men, cheering and shouting and waving tokens of their affection. She could not help but notice that wherever the two Scotsmen rode, the crowd quieted, as if they did not want to encourage the enemy. Desmond's cohorts took to jeering in a most dishonorable manner, and Abrielle did not want the celebration of her marriage to turn ugly and have someone hurt. When at last Desmond looked at her, she gave him an appealing glance, and with a wave of his hand, he quieted his raucous men. The two Scotsmen rode forth in dignity, but Abrielle knew the uneasy quiet did not bode well. And she saw Desmond glance at her again, his small eyes narrowed.

That night, when the hunters brought back their spoils, it was obvious that Cedric had claimed the honor of bagging the largest and most majestic stag, and would win the first purse. So large was the stag that even Thurstan could not claim another the winner, though Abrielle thought he hesitated enough over the carcasses.

At supper, no one wanted to share the trestle table

with Raven and his father. The two men ate heartily as if they had no concerns, but how could they miss the tense resentment from both Saxon and Norman alike? Cordelia and Abrielle exchanged a worried look.

"It is most unseemly that guests are treated so," Abrielle murmured to her friend.

Hesitantly, Cordelia said, "You are not yet the mistress of this keep."

"I know, but these men are behaving as if the Seaberns personally attacked our lands in times past. They're Highlanders, not the men from just over the border. And if a melee breaks out, will that not ruin everything?"

"If it delays the wedding, will you not be grateful?"

"Cordelia!" Lady Grayson gasped, looking around, but no one had overheard them.

"I do not want to delay the wedding," Abrielle said firmly, wishing her stepfather didn't look so despondent as he hunched over his tankard of ale. "But if this will soon be my home, Desmond's friends must understand common decency. Now they are like a pack of dogs, allowing themselves to be all riled up. And if fighting breaks out, do you not think our fathers will feel forced to become involved?"

As Cordelia blanched, Elspeth leaned toward her daughter. "Abrielle, you are correct in your concerns. You and I both know how men can behave when they're past thought. Remember how your late father felt compelled to accept that challenge that took him from us forever."

Abrielle shuddered. "I cannot let that happen again." She rose gracefully to her feet and began to walk across the great hall, stepping through rushes that had not been swept out in months.

Raven stopped eating when he saw Abrielle moving through the raucous crowd. She was like the proud bow of a boat, leaving ripples of quiet in her wake. Such was her beauty that men stopped eating to stare at her, and Raven knew he was no different.

"Close your mouth, lad," his father said with amusement. "Och, soon ye'll be catching flies that way."

Abrielle stopped at table after table, her smile sweet, her melodious voice soothing. They could not hear what she said, but more than one guest gave a last glance at the Scotsmen and sank back onto their benches.

"What is she doing?" Raven murmured, frustrated that he could only watch and wonder.

"Calming her guests," Cedric ventured.

As intent as he was on Abrielle, Raven made a point of also watching de Marlé's reaction. At first, when it seemed Abrielle was coming to join him, the squire's expression was full of pleasure, but as she stopped at more tables along the way, he began glancing at Raven's table with increasing displeasure. Raven did his best to ignore what was going on, but it wasn't easy when he was so captivated by the woman's slightest movement and every hint of emotion that flickered across her face. He couldn't stop looking at her, and every time he did, he wanted to touch her, to hold that wondrous body against his and assuage his need with her softness. He had been unable to wipe her from his mind this last month, and now being in the same keep with her only made his desire stronger. At that moment he was very grateful for the diplomatic experience that enabled him to sit there expressionless, revealing none of the thoughts and feelings rioting inside. De Marlé might seem like an ignorant man, but he was no fool. His cunning was of the malicious sort, and Raven knew that if the other man's glare were a sword, his head would have rolled clear across the hall by now.

To Raven's great relief, Abrielle did not come to his table, but went instead to her betrothed and gave him her sweetest smile. Raven wished he were free to challenge the man for the right to stare into those lovely blue-green eyes. As if sensing his restlessness, his father touched his thigh briefly in warning, and Raven, still as restless, went back to pretending to concentrate on his meal.

Desmond gladly took the hand of his beautiful betrothed and held it high before planting a kiss on it. There were good-natured calls now about the wedding night, and he saw Abrielle's face redden in a virgin's blush.

But he could not forget the way she'd calmed his guests, all for the Scotsmen. His plan to avenge himself against Raven Seabern by parading his bride before him wasn't turning out as he'd planned. True, he knew the Scot still burned for her, but so did every man here, and Raven was doing better than most at keeping his desire submerged.

Worst of all, he saw how deliberately Abrielle kept her gaze from Raven, as if she was afraid to look too close, afraid of what she might feel.

And Desmond could not stand for that. His plans would have to be altered. His nephew Thurstan had men held in reserve in case a show of strength was necessary. It was time to call them into action. An attack by thieves would be more believable than having two healthy men suddenly succumb to poison.

DUSK WAS NIGH as Raven and his father reined their mounts along the far bank of the meandering river some distance from the keep, very near the place where the fast-flowing water rippled over rocky shallows. On this, the second day of the hunt, father and son had glimpsed several boars, none of which had seemed worthy of being pursued, although Cedric had commented that any fresh boar would only improve the castle's menu. With the number of huntsmen wandering hither and yon, in the process making enough noise to send a variety of animals scurrying off to hidden niches, the more commendable game had been difficult to find.

Raven and his father had decided to venture farther afield in the opposite direction, not only to seek their quarry in an area to which others would unwittingly drive theirs, but also, hopefully, to stay out of harm's way from errant arrows and spears. The combination of hilly terrain and fast-flowing streams posed no difficulty for those nurtured throughout their lives within the highlands of Scotland. 'Twas not long before those who trailed in their wake desisted in their attempt and retreated to a more level area of ground closer to the keep.

The sun was sinking beyond the uppermost pinnacles of the lofty trees when father and son found themselves on the trail of a boar that promised to challenge another record. Moments earlier they had descended to an area near a fast-flowing stream where Raven espied the animal scurrying off into a thicket deeply shaded by towering trees. Silently gesturing to his father, he brought Cedric's attention to bear upon the animal's tracks and a freshly broken branch near the base of a larch. Raven leaned from the saddle and, with his spear, brushed aside the lower boughs to reveal an enormous boar, complete with massive curved tusks, taking shelter near the trunk. Immediately an angry squealing rent the silence as the quarry raced forth, leaving the lower fronds swaying wildly in its wake. As the boughs raked his bristly hide, the animal danced aside and thrust about with his tusks in an effort to find his phantom foe.

Very much in a temper, the boar squealed as it charged into the clearing. At its approach, Raven touched his spurs lightly against his stallion's flanks, turning the steed to allow him to face the smaller animal directly. The boar fixed its eyes upon this menacing presence looming before it and snorted threateningly as it began tearing up the ground with its tusks, hurling thick tufts of grass helter-skelter. Then, thrusting back upon its hind legs, it launched itself in a forceful race toward the stallion.

Raven promptly reined his mount aside, allowing the prey to race on past. A moment later, the boar ended its furious charge beneath the wide-spreading boughs of another larch no more than a stone's throw beyond the place where Raven had halted. The lower branches of the towering tree swayed wildly to and fro as the animal tore through them in a vicious temper.

Upon emerging from the lower boughs, the boar rushed forward, only to find the man awaiting him with lance held at the ready. With a mighty thrust Raven sent the spear toward its target, promptly skewering the boar on its shaft. Squealing in agony, the animal twisted this way and that in a frantic attempt to free itself. Gradually its movements slowed and became awkward as it staggered haphazardly in retreat. There, the animal collapsed upon its short legs.

Raven rose in his stirrups, intending to dismount, but from out of nowhere a spear whizzed past, opening a tiny gash on one cheek. Blood drops flew without his notice. Instinct and knowledge gained from his father's relentless tutoring over the years took over and he followed the path of the weapon to where its jagged point lodged in the trunk of a tree. From behind came the splashing sound of riders crossing the stream and he quickly reined his stallion about to face them, eager to do battle with an enemy who attacked without warning or provocation.

Raven looked from the riders back toward the tree and with a quick nudge of his spurs sent his stallion racing in that direction. Without slowing, he grasped the weathered shaft of the brigand's spear and jerked it from the trunk, tossed it briefly into the air to claim a better grip on it, and with its shank firmly in hand, again reined his steed around. His sire turned as well and together they faced the pair of cloaked, helmeted riders spurring their huge, shaggy steeds toward them.

Their thundering hoofbeats seemed to echo through the forest glade as one of them reached behind his back and drew forth a heavy battle-ax. Its bearer lifted the weapon high above his head, and though his dark eyes were barely visible beneath the visor of his crude, battered helm, they fixed unswervingly upon the younger Scotsman.

Drawing the spear back over his shoulder, Raven bided his time, closely eyeing the pair advancing toward him. Cedric sent his own steed racing forward as he sought to intercept them before they could do harm to his son. Upon espying him, the nearest brigand wheeled his warhorse about and dispatched the animal in a straight line toward the elder. Glimmering through the eyeholes of the mask, the gray eyes never strayed from the older man, the brigard's widening, black-toothed grin conveying a grim promise of death beneath the crudely finished headgear as he slowly swung the heavy mace he clasped to and fro.

The elder's gleaming claymore sang richly as it was drawn forth from its scabbard. Facing the oncoming charge squarely, Cedric touched his spurs to his stallion's flanks. Clods of greensward and leaf-matted turf flew helter-skelter as both steeds raced toward each other across the narrow expanse of land separating them. Raising a war cry that widened the eyes of his adversary, Cedric swung his claymore in a circular motion high above his head as he guided his mount merely by the pressure of his knees. The two steeds met, the smaller one easily whisking alongside the huge warhorse as the elder rose in his stirrups. In the next instant, the claymore rang with a note of deathly clarity as it whipped about with a deft stroke, clanging briefly against the crude helmet before separating the brigand's head from his cloaked form.

The heavy mace plummeted from a lifeless hand, but Cedric took no notice of the decapitated body's tumbling descent as he whirled his steed about to see what further assistance he could be to his son. Another moment more, and he would have failed to witness the skewering of the stranger on Raven's spear.

Cedric eyed his offspring for any evidence of injury and, upon seeing none, rumbled in the chiding tones of a parent, "It took ye long enough ta finish off that brigand, lad. Didna I always tell ye ta be punctual in the face of danger?"

Cocking a dubious brow at his sire, Raven gave as good as got. "I was averse ta shaming ye by finishing off the man afore ye took care of the one ye went after. Besides, if ye'll remember, I had ta retrieve the brigand's weapon afore I could enter the fray."

"Fine excuse ye're giving me," Cedric chided. Though conveying a lighthearted mood, this most recent attempt upon his son's life left him seething with a burning hatred for the man who had invited them for such a diabolical purpose. "Might ye be knowing the names of these beggarly souls we've just killed, laddie? And might ye be explaining your thinking as to the man behind them?"

Dismounting, Raven tied the two shaggy warhorses to a pair of trees, proceeded to remove the helmet from the man he'd killed, then shook his head and shrugged. "I'm guessing they're simple soldiers. Who put them up ta this foul deed is what we'll have ta determine . . . should there mayhap be a wee chance the culprit is someone other than Squire de Marlé."

Cedric shook his head sadly as he surveyed the carnage. "Betwixt the two of us, lad, I'd say there's no mistaking the wily toad who put this pair up ta killing ye. De Marlé had no reason for inviting us, except ta serve us up as meat for his dogs."

"Aye, that and his preening arrogance." Raven's gaze narrowed. "Still, it's hard to believe even a sorry excuse for a man like de Marlé would be contemplating murder only a day before he's to exchange wedding vows with a woman as fair and winsome as Abrielle."

"Ye shamed him, lad, that ye did, not only by saving the bonny lass from his foul purposes, but by showing him ta be a coward his own mother wouldna own up ta birthing."

Raven smiled. "I canna think it helped him warm ta me when he saw how his betrothed went ta the trouble of quieting an entire hall in our defense at the banquet last eve."

"I saw the look he gave ye and I didn't like it," admitted Cedric.

"But does he question the lass's loyalty so much that he would kill?"

"I'd be more likely to question her eyesight," his father retorted. "The thought of the bonny lass about ta marry that man would make a stone weep."

"So now ye agree she'd have ta be desperate ta make such a choice? If, indeed, he was her choice. I think there's more ta the arrangement than anyone knows, something so dire Vachel had no choice but ta agree ta the match."

"So what do ye intend, seeing as how we're guests of the murdering rascal?" Cedric asked, peering at his offspring speculatively. He waved a hand about to indicate the gory scene around them. "If we stay, we'll be facing more of what we've just encountered."

"And it'll end the same. I speak only for myself, Da, I'll be staying, and past the nuptials as well. If something should go awry, the lass will be needing protection."

"That doesn't mean it has to be your protection," Cedric pointed out.

Raven squashed any further protest with a sideways glance. "I'm staying."

"Ye can be sure de Marlé willna be waiting long ta find another ta kill ye," Cedric warned. "Once we bring back these men, he'll be even more set ta see ta your death."

Raven canted his head thoughtfully for a long moment before meeting his father's gaze. "Whatever comes, I mean ta deliver these men ta the keep ta let him know 'twill take more than two soldiers ta dispense with us. Mayhap the sight of these poor beggars will sour his gut or cause him ta fear for his life. After that, I'll be biding me time, but one way or the other, I'll be having it out with the man. What's between him and his lady may not be my business," he said with another quick glance at the dead men, "but this surely is."

Cedric whisked a knuckle beneath his bushy mustache. "Mayhap the toad'll have a seizure when he sees what we've bagged for ourselves."

Raven snorted in contempt. "I wish he would . . . a permanent one ta lay him inta his grave. Then the Lady Abrielle would be free."

"Free ta be choosing another, ye mean?" Cedric responded, cocking a brow curiously as he peered at his son.

Raven slowly grinned as he met the elder's blue eyes. "Ye know, Da, ye've always been so clever at reading me thoughts, making me wonder at times why I even bother voicing them."

"Mayhap ye'll be having the same canny sense of your own in a few more years." Cedric harrumphed, as if trying to clear his throat. "Till then, just follow my lead if ye think the matter is worthy, otherwise see ta yourself."

"I intend ta," Raven said, his amusement fading.

CHAPTER 6

Upon arriving at the far end of the drawbridge, Raven dismounted and, with a casual wave of his hand, bade his parent to wait beside the shaggy destriers bearing the remains of the two culprits and the boar. Several guests espied the tightly bound carcasses and immediately came rushing out to see what had happened. Raven ignored them. There was only one man with whom he was interested in discussing the matter. And should that discussion turn into something more vigorous, he thought, clenching his fists as he strode across the keep, so much the better.

Soon after being circumvented by Raven, Sir Colbert, a young man of Norman lineage, stalked down the length of the drawbridge as if he were the lord high sheriff of the area. He had already been conveying an attitude of authority among his friends in view of the fact that he was a distant relative of the squire. He had also been evidencing a strong disdain for anyone who wasn't of Norman lineage, the only exception being the young bride, whom he eagerly declared was the most beautiful Saxon he had ever seen. Having been nurtured from youth by parents who had encouraged friends and family alike to disdain the Scottish clans who had fought against their kinsmen, he stepped before the elder and promptly ordered him to lay the slain men out on the drawbridge where they could be seen.

"We shall have a look at what you bloody Scots have trussed up like so much grain. If your victims prove to be our friends, then we'll teach you the folly of your murdering ways. To be sure, ere the day is out your Scottish heads may well be adorning a pair of pikes."

"Aye, that's telling him, Colbert!" another young man shouted, beckoning for their companions to join them. "Let's give this bloody Scot a harsh lesson in manners right here and now."

Cedric's hand settled almost casually upon the hilt of his claymore as he directed a question toward the youth who had suggested the like of such tutoring. "And who do ye think will be helping ye, laddie? I'll be warning ye kindly, 'twill take more than ye and your young friends ta best this old man."

The second young man lifted his chin in haughty arrogance as he gave the elder a chilly stare. He glanced around at the score or more of his acquaintances and kinsmen who had gathered close around him. "Surely Colbert and I are not the only ones outraged by this unprovoked slaughter of innocents. What say you, lads? Are there not among you a goodly number who disdain these loathsome Scots as much as we do? Let's deal with them as they rightly deserve! The same as they dealt with this pair they murdered."

Having been the first to confront Cedric, Colbert assumed authority as he demanded, "What do you have to say about this matter?"

The elder cocked a dubious brow as he scoffed, "Naught ta you, I'll wager, nor ta these young bumpkins collecting like a bunch of goats behind ye."

"You will answer for your crimes," Colbert railed threateningly, "or, by heavens, we'll see the pair of your heads stuck on pikes right here and now!"

Summoning the full force of his companions with a wave of his arm, Colbert smirked in pleasure as they surged forward to do his bidding. He could easily foresee the lot of them serving the aging man his just due long before the younger Scot returned from the courtyard.

This time the heavy claymore sang a different steely song as it was slowly unsheathed. Indeed, the elder seemed to take his own time clasping the hilt and settling into a fighting stance as he braced his legs firmly apart. His broadening grin evidenced an unswerving confidence in his own abilities as he arched a hoary brow and challenged his youthful adversaries to a contest of arms. "Now, who's ta be the first ta feel this blade?"

His audience of hotheaded young men glanced at one another warily. The more astute among their group were fairly quick to comprehend that this was a warrior who loved a battle, whereas the best the lot of them had ever achieved was to joust in an open tourney with thick pads protecting them from tip of toe to top of head. Whatever expectations they had briefly savored of teaching the Scot a harsh lesson faltered as quickly as their flagging courage. Of a sudden they were of a mind to retreat before this threat.

"Take heart and stand fast!" Colbert railed at his companions in mounting frustration as they began to sidle away, much like lapdogs facing a savage wolf. "If we stand together against this old man, surely he won't be able to defeat us all!"

"I wouldn't be too sure about that" came a reply from the second young man, who was already scurrying toward the courtyard. By the time he reached the outer doors of the keep, he was nearly breathless and didn't bother closing them behind him as he rushed in. Upon espying the younger Scot, who had been followed by several curious youths, he pressed back against the outer curved wall, where, with a modicum of safety, he could watch what transpired between Raven and the rabble.

Thurstan had been seated with several older men at a trestle table when Raven pushed his way through the gathering. Upon settling his yellowish eyes blandly upon the Scotsman, Thurstan lifted a brow, leaned back on his elbows, and stretched out his legs. "Were you looking for me?"

Raven halted directly in front of him. "Nay, I was looking for your uncle, but ye'll do." The mere sight of de Marlé's nephew made his hackles rise, and the look of smug disdain on the young cur's face all but proved his suspicions were on the mark. The urge to lash out with tongue or sword or both was strong, but he was a master at keeping them tethered until the moment was right.

"My da and I brought back two dead men," he said simply, his tone level. "They're tied onta the back of their mounts at the far end of the drawbridge, if ye care te take a look."

"And why would I want to do that?"

"For appearances?" Raven suggested with only the barest hint of sarcasm. "It occurs ta me your uncle might want ta at least feign concern that a couple of henchmen took it inta their heads ta kill his invited guests."

"Why should the squire care about the doings of two thieves?" Thurstan asked coldly.

Raven's dark brows lifted. "Did someone mention thieves? These men were equipped as soldiers, not thieves."

Thurstan shrugged. "So, what you're saying is some of my uncle's men took it upon themselves to attack guests?"

Without taking his gaze from Thurstan's face, Raven swung out hard with one boot and knocked the younger man's negligently crossed ankles apart so forcefully he had to scramble to hold his seat. "Do try ta listen more closely. What I am doing here is distinctly not saying it." Why should he, Raven thought, when the words a man didn't speak could be so much more effective?

The penetrating coldness in Thurstan's expression continued to convey his loathing for the Scotsman. As much as he would've enjoyed ordering the pair to bury what they had killed, he suddenly realized he ought to maintain a proper decorum with the eyes of so many respected guests upon him. "I will see them."

Raven casually followed Thurstan as he stalked outside to the drawbridge, then bent down to begin untying the bodies.

Desmond shouldered his way through those who had paused near the end of the drawbridge and, upon arriving at the fore of a youthful audience, found himself facing the Scotsmen. He had realized that they would be hard to kill. Even so, these soldiers had been chosen on Thurstan's promise of their cunning—and the threat to murder their families if they didn't comply.

The Scotsmen returned Desmond's slack-jawed astonishment with unwavering stares as he made a desperate effort to reclaim his aplomb. He failed to a great degree before he turned his attention to his nephew. A harsh frown drew Desmond's bushy brows sharply together.

"What's the meaning of this commotion?" he demanded, and then, upon espying the slain men tied to the backs of their huge steed, he whirled upon Cedric. "What have you done?"

The laird's chortle was seriously lacking in humor. "I was just going ta ask ye the very same question, Squire. Do ye ken these men who tried ta murder us whilst we were out hunting?"

"Did you provoke them?" Desmond asked curtly.

"Only with our presence," Cedric said. "Ta be sure, we had na ken they were even in the area till they charged across the stream with weapons drawn."

"My wedding is on the morrow," Desmond cried, "and you've brought the brumes of gloom down upon us with this senseless killing."

Raven scoffed. "Senseless? I dinna ken about that. Where I'm from, when faced with a man who's got it in his head ta kill ye, it makes perfect sense ta separate that head from his body before he has the chance. This pair were clearly of a mind ta kill us. With that settled, all that's left to discover is their motive. Since me da and I knew them not at all," he continued, his tone becoming cold and speculative, "we thought ye be knowing what reason they had ta seek us out?"

"The promise of a fat purse, perhaps," Thurstan said drily. "I still say they're thieves."

Over the squire's shoulder, Raven espied Abrielle, Cordelia, and their mothers venturing out onto the drawbridge. Upon facing Desmond again, he warned in a muted voice, "Your guests are approaching."

Promptly turning, Desmond scurried toward the four as he advised them, "My ladies, I must urge you to return to your chambers. There has been some trouble . . . the Scotsmen have brought back two bodies, and though I'm reluctant to frighten you, I'd be remiss in my duties if I failed to think of your safety before looking into this matter more thoroughly. I must urge you to return to the security of your chambers and to stay there until we've managed to make some sense of this dreadful matter."

Abrielle had had a terrible feeling all day, and now she could see the anger from Desmond's cohorts directed at the Scotsmen. Raven and his father had been forced to kill two men? She could only believe it was because they were attacked first, but then, she didn't know him very well. She could not let a handsome face mislead her into assuming he was honorable. But Raven was watching her now, standing at his father's side. There was no appeal in his expression, as if he would never beg her to believe him.

"But who has been killed?" she asked Desmond, noticing too late that he'd been watching her when she'd been thinking about Raven. What had her expression revealed? she wondered, feeling a chill of mounting concern. She had to be more careful.

"I cannot yet explain how this tragedy happened," Desmond said, "only that two men are now dead. So I must urge you to retire to your chambers until this dreadful matter has been looked into more thoroughly."

Though she wanted to resist being ordered about so, Abrielle inclined her head slightly in assent to placate Desmond. "Then we shall leave you to deal with this problem as well as you can." She laid a hand briefly upon her friend's arm and then touched the older women's as she turned back toward the keep. "Come, ladies. Let us return and allow the men to deal with this horrible tragedy." She would find out the details later, when she was not so on display.

Thurstan faced Raven as the Scotsman drew near. "Perhaps I should have a look at the slain men to determine if they're known hereabouts. Then I would suggest that we remove them from sight lest some of the other ladies venture out and espy them."

"And you should have a look, too, Squire," Cedric said, motioning to the man.

Beyond the end of the drawbridge, Raven and Cedric laid out the two carcasses in the midst of the tufts of dried grass. More men had come forth from the keep, including Vachel and Reginald, who watched the proceedings with stern frowns.

When the severed head was placed within close proximity of its former body, Thurstan said, "I have never seen these men before, neither here in my uncle's home nor at my own manor several leagues away."

"And I haven't either," Desmond insisted, looking away from the bodies quickly.

Cedric questioned several older serfs who had gathered around them. "We'd be obliged ta know if any of ye recognize these men and can tell us where they belong."

While Thurstan and Desmond were there watching the proceedings, the small group seemed wary. None admitted that the two had come from the squire's lands, and they continued to shake their heads at nearly every question presented to them, frustrating the Scotsmen's attempts to find out exactly where the dead men had come from. Finally Cedric waved them away, allowing them to return to their duties.

"So your contention is that they're merely thieves," Raven said slowly, "who happened ta intrude on your hunt and randomly decide ta kill two well-armed men."

"Are you suggesting there could be another reason?" Desmond demanded, puffing out his chest like a rooster.

"Should I?" Raven queried in return, the dead calm of his demeanor more threatening than any display of choler.

"And do you have proof of any accusations you might make?"

"Nay, Squire."

"Then just bury these men and be done with it before their deaths ruin the festivities that have been planned," Desmond said, trying to sound reasonable. "If they were trying to kill anyone, then they've paid for the deed with their lives."

"Very well," Raven said, "but in case they have kinsmen here, 'tis only fair ta let them know what has befallen these two."

Thurstan scowled. "Neither my uncle nor I recognize them, but if you will not be satisfied with that, then lay out the bodies in the midst of the serfs' huts. If no one claims them, then at least they've been seen. After that, I'll have men see to their burial."

Sensing victory, Desmond could not let it go, but threatened more by Raven than by his parent, he addressed his remarks to the father. "I seriously doubt more will be discovered, considering that you have managed to kill the only two who could have adequately appeased your desire to know why they sought to kill you . . . if that is what they did. Of course we have only your word for that, yours and your son's."

"I dinna lie," Cedric rumbled, settling his hand once again upon the hilt of his claymore as his brilliant eyes flashed with a flaming fury.

Desmond flung up a hand, conveying his disinterest in the elder's declaration. Upon turning about, he stalked back to the keep. It incensed him beyond measure that the two fools had failed so miserably to accomplish his directive. Because of their bungling efforts to comport themselves as warriors, he would now have to find another who would be more competent at the task of dispensing with the Scotsmen. No doubt he would have to promise a lucrative fee, but if it would mean that he could forget the pair thereafter, he would be willing to placate the assassin . . . at least until the deed was done.

After witnessing their host's departure, Vachel returned to the keep to abide by his earlier promise that he would tell his family everything that had transpired. He was certain both would be extremely distressed over this latest occurrence and fearful that Desmond was somehow involved. If he could, he had to placate their qualms and reassure them that Abrielle's betrothed couldn't have been involved in this attempt on the Scotsmen's lives. Even so, it was the strange, intensifying coldness around his own heart, a feeling that had served him well throughout his efforts in the Crusades, that was warning him to be extremely leery of the squire. He hated to lay the whole ugly burden on Abrielle, for he knew she was far too fine and noble for the likes of Desmond de Marlé. But the betrothal contract was signed and binding, and he knew that man could not sever it, and he doubted God would.

REACHING UP WITH trembling fingers, Abrielle closed and latched the stained-glass window overlooking the drawbridge where the Scotsmen had briefly lingered after Thurstan's departure. She was grateful that the younger firebrands had dispersed to prepare for the event to honor the hunters. No doubt many would be lamenting the fact that the highland pair had captured both trophies, leaving none for the rest of them to garner.

And then her thoughts returned to what she had trouble facing: Could Desmond really have made an attempt on the Scotsmen's lives? Was she legally bound to a man who could murder to get what he wanted? She would be spending the rest of her life treading delicately for fear of upsetting such a man.

Abrielle was worried about the continued well-being of the Scotsmen. It was beyond her ability to understand their reasoning for daring to remain in the area, for she could only believe they were inviting similar attempts by staying.

Oblivious to the colorful aura created by the lowering sun glimmering through the leaded panes of stained glass, Abrielle stared across the room at nothing in particular as she tried to imagine herself going through the wedding ceremony as if nothing untoward had happened. At the moment it seemed an impossible feat. Indeed, had she fallen into a dark pit of despair whence there would be no escape, she would have felt no less miserable than she did now.

A light rapping on the outer door of the chambers evoked a sharp gasp from her, for she couldn't help but be fearful that Desmond had come for a visit. Dutifully progressing to the portal, she paused in an effort to collect her wits. If it were he, then she would have to give the excuse that she wasn't feeling well, and that would be no lie. Merely the possibility of having to entertain the man would make that premise a matter of fact.

Leaning near the barrier, Abrielle asked in a muted voice, "Who is it?"

"Cordelia," came the softly murmured response.

Greatly relieved, Abrielle swung open the heavy door before hurriedly motioning her friend into her parents' chambers. Cordelia cast a cautious glance up and down the hall before complying, and then closed the portal securely behind her before following her friend into the sitting room. Although Abrielle took a seat upon the chaise and patted the cushions to invite her to do the same, Cordelia chose instead to claim her full attention by placing a small bench directly in front of her.

"So do you think that Desmond had something to do with the attack on the Scotsmen?" Cordelia asked in a low voice.

"I don't want to believe it of a man I am soon to marry. I know there is little proof, but it seems as if no one else has a motive. Who else would bother?"

"There is Thurstan."

"I think Thurstan is angry because my family and I are to receive most of Desmond's fortune, one way or another. But that has nothing to do with the Seaberns." She gave a heavy sigh. "This is all my fault. Little did I imagine when Raven Seabern rescued me that night from Desmond's vile intentions that his life would thereafter be in serious peril."

Cordelia canted her head curiously. "Mayhap you'd care to appease my curiosity by telling me about that occurrence. Thus far, you've failed to mention anything that happened after we left you that night. What prompted Desmond to resort to such despicable measures?"

"After you and your parents left for home, he sought to have his way with me in the palace, but Raven heard our scuffling and intervened before Desmond could accomplish his objective. Desmond managed to escape before being harmed, so 'twould seem he's angry because Raven intruded on his plans to ravish me. 'Twould be better by far if the pair returned to their homeland this very hour rather than attend the festivities marking the end of the hunt. If they delay much longer, they may well be killed in their beds."

"And that was the whole reason he extended them an invitation to the wedding? How cruel!"

"I'm not certain that Desmond meant to have them killed at first. I assumed when the Scotsmen first arrived that Desmond only invited them to show Raven that Desmond had won me in the end."

Cordelia tapped her forefinger thoughtfully against her chin. "If Desmond is truly intent on dispensing with the Scots, it probably doesn't matter who is killed as long as he gets his way in the end. Obviously, he's of the opinion that simple soldiers are to obey his every command, even if it's to murder another individual he despises. Could he think that Raven somehow means to have you for his own?"

"But we have a betrothal contract! It cannot be put asunder. His jealousy has no purpose."

"You must remember, 'tis Desmond of whom we speak."

Abrielle sighed. "There has to be some way to prove to him that Raven is not interested in me. Then Desmond's jealousy—murderous or not—might be appeased. Mayhap if Raven were shown to be interested in someone else . . . you, perhaps?"

Cordelia straightened. "You mean to make him pursue me somehow?"

"Nay, but if he were shown to be flirting with you, that might soothe Desmond's suspicions."

"And how would we convince him to flirt with me?"

"Why . . . you'd initiate it, of course, tonight at the banquet. He is entrusted with the business of kings, Cordelia, so I'm certain he would realize the purpose soon enough."

"Shouldn't you explain to him—"

"No!" Abrielle protested too forcefully. "I cannot risk being alone with him."

"Do you not trust yourself?" Cordelia asked slyly.

Abrielle gasped. "You make light of what could mean death for both Scotsmen, and others, should the blood of young men run too hot, as too oft is the case."

Cordelia laid a hand on her shoulder. "My dearest companion, I only mean to ease your concerns, to somehow lighten the load you bear. Do not mistake my teasing for anything but that. You know I will do anything to help you, and that you can rely upon me to distract Desmond where Raven is concerned."

Abrielle hugged the other woman fervently.

"'Tis a noble thing you're doing, saving your family in this way, though dear indeed is the price for doing so," Cordelia told her with heartfelt sympathy. "I certainly don't envy you. Truly, 'tis far more reasonable to imagine Raven Seabern as your suitor than that contemptible beast of a man you're pledged to marry."

"For pity's sake, Cordelia," said Abrielle. "Neither of us truly knows Raven. Desmond is fully revealed in his face and form, but the Scotsman has looks, grace, and charm that may indeed be only weapons he uses to get what he wants. In spite of his gallantry, and the intensity of his gaze when turned toward me, I cannot forget that he did not attempt to court me before my betrothal to Desmond, that he never even sought from my stepfather a proper introduction to me. It sorrows me to confess this thought to you, but I believe that he is seeking a wife with a rich dowry, with property to offer him, that he would but dally with a woman of my circumstances. I alone, without riches to accompany me, am not enough." Here, in spite of her strongest efforts, her eyes filled with tears. "Oh, Cordelia," she cried. "Why am I not enough?"

CHAPTER 7

Most of the hunters entered the great hall that evening with their wives, relatives, or in the company of long-established companions or newly found friends. Shortly after settling themselves at the garland-bedecked tables, guests were served goblets of wine or tankards of ale, depending on their individual preferences. A table placed within close proximity of the head table was held in reserve for the champions of the hunt.

Although most of the hunters were arrogant and greatly resented being bested by a pair of Scots, there were a rare few with more gracious dispositions who readily paid tribute to the laird and his son immediately upon their entry into the hall. Rising to their feet, two hunters lifted aloft their tankards of ale in a rousing toast. When no one else around them followed suit, the embarrassed men quickly sank back onto their benches.

These two toasts greeted Desmond much like a slap across the face as he strode into the great hall, garbed in clothing as costly as any great lord of the realm might have worn. Jealousy as foul as his black heart made him lament his failure thus far to dispense with the Scots. Throughout the evening, he found it impossible to think of anything but savoring his revenge upon the pair.

Thus, when Desmond espied both of the Scotsmen being escorted to their designated table, his animosity intensified to an even greater degree. He was plagued by the rather bizarre notion that they had somehow connived to claim those seats merely to taunt and irritate him with their presence.

An appreciative murmur arose from the guests seated at the far end of the hall. Espying the group of ladies progressing ahead of their male escorts through the aisle, Desmond was taken aback by their beauty. Admiration promptly replaced anger, and he found himself smiling in appreciation. When the younger two inclined their heads graciously to acknowledge his presence, his buoyant mood was promptly restored. He was certain he had never seen a pair as fair.

In continuing on toward the squire's table, Abrielle, her parents, and their close friends Lord and Lady Grayson and their daughter, Cordelia, claimed the unswerving attention of those in attendance. The younger gallants evidenced a rapidly burgeoning awe of the maidens, yet, in all truth, Elspeth and Isolde drew as many stares from the older men, a fact which seemed to tweak the ire of their husbands until Cordelia urged the pair to consider the stares as a compliment to their own refined tastes.

Abrielle's gown had been created by combining numerous layers of a translucent golden fabric, trimmed with delicately bejeweled ribbons, as if she were clothed in a cloud that flowed in shimmering waves around her slender body. Its beauty had most of the women staring agog with envy, whereas the men were more wont to gape at the lady who wore it.

Softly shimmering layers of creamy-hued silk flowed in mesmerizing waves around Elspeth's slender form, causing at least one who had earlier held aspirations of marrying the comely widow to lament the fact that she had chosen another. If anything, he was even more envious of Vachel de Gerard than he had been before.

With her blond hair and bright, pale blue eyes, Cordelia looked very much like her mother, the Lady Isolde. Clothed in garments as beautiful as those of the other members of their party, they drew almost as many admiring stares as the bride. From Lord Reginald Grayson's broad smile, it was apparent he was very proud of his small family.

When Desmond caught sight of his intended bride, she was strolling beside Cordelia, slightly ahead of their parents. Much in a manner of one stricken dumb, he leaned back in his chair and gaped at them. A full moment passed before he realized his own slack-jawed astonishment and, in some discomfiture, cleared his constricted throat. Upon sweeping a surreptitious glance about the hall, he realized to his relief that most of the men were now staring at the four women in much the same manner.

Raven was no less awed by Abrielle's beauty than any other man in the hall; he was simply more skilled at hiding it. Unfortunately he was not nearly as good at concealing his feelings from himself. To be sure, his pounding heart readily affirmed his deepening infatuation. His desire to have Abrielle for his own was so great he was not at all deterred by thoughts of the havoc he'd create were he to follow his gut impulse to sweep the lady into his arms and abscond with her to the highlands of Scotland. Given the slightest sweet look of encouragement, he would be on his feet and by her side before de Marlé had wedged himself from his gilded chair. But her blue-green eyes never turned his way.

Approaching his future bride with an arm outstretched in invitation, Desmond smiled as the young beauty settled a slender hand upon his sleeve. "You're far more ravishing than any lady I've ever beheld, my dear," he assured her. "I can only consider the depth and breadth of my good fortune. Once I take you as my bride and the bonds between us are secure, no man will be as privileged as I."

Abrielle shuddered to think of those precise moments. Unable to make a befitting response, she turned silently and allowed him to lead her to the trestle table where he had been sitting. As much as she doubted her ability to manage even an evanescent smile for Desmond and his guests, she made every effort to force her lips into compliance.

As the feast was served, Abrielle could see the sagging shoulders and depressed miens of men and women who could not even look forward to a true feast. Once again, the food was of the plainest sort, and all one could say about it was that it was edible. If there was one thing she was looking forward to, it was finding a superior cook so that the people of the castle would be better served.

Upon the conclusion of the meal, the trenchers were taken away, and Desmond rose to his feet, raising both his arms to claim the attention of his guests. He had decided to evoke some animosity toward the Scottish pair and was eager to progress toward that goal. "Normans and Saxons alike, give heed to my words. As all subjects of King Henry know by now, he chose his daughter, Maud, to become rightful heiress of the kingdom he rules after the tragic drowning death of his son many years ago in the White Ship disaster."

Though his words seemed badly slurred to his guests, Desmond was convinced he would have given the best orator in the king's service cause to stand in silent awe. By now, he thought, the Scotsmen would likely be expecting a boring discourse on the royals.

"Should our liege lord expire in the years to come, the Empress Matilda—or Maud, as some of her subjects have been wont to call her—shall claim the throne. So far, all his nobles have signed pledges of fealty to support her should his majesty be laid to rest. Considering his age, one has to consider that he will not live forever. It has also been acknowledged that her uncle King David of Scotland has given his oath to uphold her as divine ruler of this land should His Majesty pass on. By Henry's edicts, we should all pledge her our troths and be bound in unity after his death. Of late, however, I've been wont to wonder if recent rumors being bandied about are actually true, that King David has been secretly nurturing aspirations of seizing England's throne for himself rather than allowing his niece to succeed her father."

Many of the guests nodded and spoke in murmurs to one another, eyeing the Scots dubiously.

Raven rose to his feet, claiming the attention of those within the hall. "I've no knowledge of my sovereign lord ever coveting the English throne," he stated forthrightly, sensing the squire's ploy to evoke ill will toward the Scottish clans and their king. "For what it's worth, 'tis my belief that King David intends ta assist the empress in whatever capacity she may require during her reign and ta bestow as much homage upon her as he has thus far extended ta King Henry. After all, Malcolm Canmore was her grandfather, a man much beloved and respected in our country. The Scots could do no better than ta swear allegiance ta her. And if ye do indeed sense any undermining of the empress's sovereign right ta claim the throne, then mayhap ye should look closer ta home for such culprits rather than condemn the clansmen of Scotland as treasonous. 'Tis fallacy ta think we'd go against her."

"Are you actually claiming that you would remain loyal to the Empress Maud once she claims Henry's throne?" Desmond prodded with a distasteful sneer.

"My loyalty will always be ta Scotland," Raven stated without hesitation. "Much remains ta be seen, but I dinna anticipate havoc for our clans coming from Empress Maud. We've always considered her one of us."

"You Scots have your own way of lending careful regard to a notion and, when the time pleases you, turning your backs upon the very ones you've previously claimed to admire."

"Scots usually speak their minds whether you and your sort are able ta or not," Raven retorted.

"Are you calling me a liar?" Desmond railed, making an effort to rise from his chair in spite of the fact that at present the whole hall seemed to be dipping and swaying unnaturally around him. Clasping a nearby tankard, he tried to bring it to his mouth, but alas, it promptly slipped from his hand and went reeling across the trestle table, showering those sitting to his right before they could scurry out of its path.

Desmond was incognizant of the christening he had

given many of his guests. He was far more interested in bestowing a glower upon the younger Scotsman. Even in that effort, he fell short of his objective. Having consumed more wine and ale than most of his guests, he was hampered by the very disturbing possibility that there were now two of his adversary, whereas a moment earlier there had been only one irksome rogue by the name of Raven Seabern.

"Did you jus . . . call me . . . a liar?" Desmond demanded again thickly.

Raven replied simply, "If the name fits, Squire, then I'd advise ye ta call it your very own."

"Call . . . what . . . my own . . . ?"

Repulsed by the squire's drunken state, Raven rose to his feet and was promptly joined by his father, who spoke for himself and his son. "If ye'll excuse us, Squire, we woke early this morning, and have become increasingly weary as the day has progressed. Mayhap ye'll allow us ta finish this discussion at a later time."

Chortling, Desmond sought to make light of the pair's inability to endure the rigors of a hunt with the same depth of stamina as his other guests had. If he had cared to join in the sport, he was certain he would've shown the two up as poor comparisons to his unwavering endurance. Mimicking Cedric's Scottish burr, he chided, "Ye have a son who dinna seem ver-ry robust. Have these frosty English climes chilled your luster?"

The elder just ignored Desmon's drunken taunts, and Raven smiled blandly, refraining from the temptation to enlighten the overstuffed squire as to his early-morning baths in an icy stream flowing near his family home in Scotland. "Ye should remember, Squire, I'm from the highlands. There, every morning would chill the luster of a stranger, whether it be a Norman or

Saxon, who's ventured inta our frigid climes without due caution. Or mayhap ye've no ken that we're straight north of ye."

Deliberately avoiding further comment, Raven turned crisply on a heel and followed his father in striding from the hall. The wedding guests stared after them in tense silence for a long moment.

"Wait!" came a sudden cry.

Abrielle realized too late that Cordelia had jumped to her feet and was following the two Scotsmen. What was she about? Did she not realize their plan to deceive Desmond could no longer work?

"What is she doing?" Lady Grayson demanded of Abrielle in a whisper as she watched her daughter come abreast of the Seaberns and begin to speak with them.

Abrielle groaned and put her face in her hands. At last she said, "We had made plans to . . . distract Desmond from his obsession with the Scots. But this evening has ended so badly, it should never have gone forward. I never thought she'd—"

"Abrielle," her mother scolded, "you should never have tried to put yourself between the two men."

"But, Mama, don't you see, I already am? At least in Desmond's mind," she added glumly.

"And in your mind?" Vachel asked quietly.

Abrielle looked at him somberly. "In my mind my duty is as clear as ever."

Dismay flashed over his features, until he replaced it with an impassive mask. Elspeth put her hand on his and he allowed it, but Abrielle guessed his thoughts were of the past, and what he might have done differently. She grieved for him so much that she, too, placed her hand on his, beside her mother's.

At the same time she watched Cordelia closely. Her

friend spoke brightly to the two men, evoking their eventual smiles and the restoration of their good humor. At last she curtsied as they left her to depart the great hall. Abrielle slanted a glance at Desmond, hoping their plan had worked after all, but to her dismay, he was so busy eating and drinking, he hadn't even noticed Cordelia with the Scotsmen.

Cordelia returned to their table and began to eat her dessert as if nothing had happened.

Into the uneasy silence of both their families, she said, "Hmm, this isn't half bad."

"It's hard to ruin fresh fruit," Abrielle answered dourly.

Reginald rolled his eyes at his daughter's antics and hushed his wife, who began to speak with Elspeth.

Abrielle leaned toward her friend and whispered, "You shouldn't have gone, but since you did, what did Raven say?"

"He was a gentleman, of course, but I really wasn't flirting with him. That father of his is hard to resist."

Abrielle groaned and closed her eyes.

"But I made it look as if I had been flirting with Raven, didn't I?"

"Aye, you did," Abrielle responded grudgingly. "My thanks for your efforts."

"Though Raven smiled at my words to his father, I received the impression that he wasn't so happy with our plan."

"Of course not," countered Abrielle. "He's the sort of man who believes he's invincible and can confront alone any circumstance that presents itself. My only hope is that his father will be able to talk some sense into him, and make him see that he is vastly outnumbered and 'tis time for them to go."

Cordelia smiled broadly. "Having made his father's acquaintance, I can only say that what you desire most likely will not occur, for both men are proud, and clearly fierce fighters in the way of their Celtic ancestors."

IT CAUSED ABRIELLE a great deal of consternation that it took a very long time before she was able to stop fretting about all the ways Raven might come to harm, and drift off to sleep. A great part of her discomfort about her thoughts arose from something she could not understand. As she had told Cordelia, his action in not courting her before her betrothal evidenced his lack of interest in taking her to wife, a view she strongly felt was due to her inability to provide a large dowry; why then, did she worry about him so? And once sweet sleep had finally embraced her, she had no respite, for her dreams were filled with Raven . . . the look and feel and fresh-air smell of him when he was close . . . things she should not know and would be better off forgetting and wanted to remember for the rest of her life. She tossed and turned upon her pillow, smiling when her dream Raven brushed a stray curl from her face and sighing when the back of his fingers stroked her cheek, and then going from hot to cold to hot again when she realized that dream Raven was the man himself. Raven Seabern was leaning over her bed, lit only by moonlight, and her hand was curled around the back of his neck, his smooth and very warm neck, as if . . . as if . . .

Her eyes went wide and her gasp of pure, abject shock ended before it began when he covered her mouth with his big hand and shook his head. His callused palm was pleasantly rough against her soft lips, sending a shiver dancing along her spine.

"Speak in the softest tones, my lady, unless ye wish ta bring the whole household down on us."

When at last he freed her mouth, she jerked her hand away and sat up, pulling the coverlet to her chin. "How dare you invade my chamber, sir! And on the night before my wedding!"

He sat back on his heels beside her bed to look solemnly at her. "I dared because ye dared this evening ta try and help me—ye and Lady Cordelia. I wanted ta return the favor by warning ye na ta risk so much again."

"I did not do it for you!" she countered quickly, too quickly, she knew. "An outbreak of violence will make matters worse for everyone. I could not just sit back and see you and your father at the mercy of Desmond when the numbers and advantages are all his."

"So ye came to my rescue this time."

She shrugged and looked away. "I simply did not want your pigheadedness and spilled blood to ruin my wedding day."

One corner of his mouth lifted as he pressed his hand over his heart. "I am deeply touched, my lady."

"Don't be," Abrielle snapped. "And do not underestimate Desmond . . . he is far too jealous a man to trifle with."

"Aye, and he's done much ta prove it these past days," Raven added.

Abrielle thought of the dead bodies tied to the horses. "I am so sorry you and your father were attacked. When I think of how badly you might have been injured, or . . . worse . . ."

"'Twas only two men," he said, his tone matter-of-fact.

"Against two men."

He grinned. "I'd gladly square off against two dozen ta see that soft look in your eyes."

"You need to leave."

"I am in no danger. Me da is watching outside in the corridor."

"I mean leave my room . . . and the castle! Tomorrow . . . or tonight . . . Now! Before anything worse happens!"

"Do ye want me ta go, lass?"

Rather than moving to leave, he leaned closer. His voice was soft and guttural, a rumbling that made something primitive stir deep inside her. She wanted to immediately affirm her wishes, but found the words wouldn't leave her throat. She kept looking at him all bathed in the white glow of the moon, his dark hair shining, his blue eyes full of a peace she had not known in so long. Why was he doing this? Was there some reason he was trying to help her?

She forced herself to remember what was at stake. "Aye, go," she said coldly. "I do not want your death on my conscience."

"Nor do I," he assured her. "I am, however, less concerned with how your conscience will deal with this."

Without warning or hesitation, he bent his head and brushed her parted lips with his own. Abrielle's mind went blank and then exploded with sensation. His kiss was slow, hot, sweet, thick honey pulling her under, to someplace far away and deep inside, someplace new and exciting.

He didn't rush or push or force. When the tip of his

tongue touched hers, her lips opened a little more without any direction from her or urging from him. Some part of her that needed no direction or urging wanted more, but Raven simply let his mouth linger a few heartbeats longer and then pulled away, gently disengaging the hands she hadn't realized were gripping his shoulders.

He rose to his feet, towering over her in the small chamber. "I'll go now, lass, but I willna be leaving tomorrow. 'Tis a matter of pride now."

Abrielle, her senses still spinning, wasn't sure which bothered her more . . . that he dared to kiss her or that he seemed so unaffected by it.

"Pride or arrogance? You dare too much, sir. I could scream and—"

He cut in. "Ye could, but ye havena. And ye won't. Ye might take a moment—before returning ta whatever sweet dream I interrupted—ta ask yourself why that is."

He bowed and left her chamber. It would serve his reckless soul right if he got caught, she thought, even as she held her breath until she knew he was safely through her parents' sitting room and into the corridor. Only then did she release a loud sigh and flounce backward, staring up at the wooden ceiling and hoping he had left her dreams as well as her chamber.

YEARS AGO, THE heavily embroidered, mauve gunna had regally clothed Elspeth for her first wedding; now it would serve her daughter in that same capacity. The fact that it fit so wonderfully well, as if it had been made especially for the younger woman, would surely have brought pleasure to the parent had the groom been a gentleman worthy of her daughter. As it was, Elspeth could only heave a deep sigh of lament as she imagined her only offspring trapped in Desmond's arms. The fact that she had come to suspect that the man was as evil as a poisonous viper disheartened her for the task ahead.

All the necessary preparations had been done to present the bride at her best. The reddish, hip-length hair had been gathered at the nape of Abrielle's neck and then braided with a wealth of narrow ribbons of the same hue as her gown. Upon her head lay a finely wrought golden crescent from which flowed a shimmering mauve veil, the delicately embroidered hem of which fell softly around her slender shoulders and down her back. The fact that the bride's cheeks were unusually pale and her slender fingers shook uncontrollably escaped everyone but her mother's attention.

New tears welled within Elspeth's eyes and were nigh to overflowing as she considered her daughter's valiant efforts to appear calm. It amounted to an impossible feat for both of them. "I pray for a miracle," she whispered to her only offspring as she made a pretense of adjusting the veil. "I cannot bear the thought of you in Desmond's arms, and yet I have no idea what can be done at this late hour to save you from that horrible wretch. Vachel hopes you'll be happy once you realize the extent of your wealth, but I fear that will mean little to you while you're married to Desmond."

"Mama, please don't cry," Abrielle whispered softly as a gathering wetness blurred her own vision. "If I see you weeping, I shan't be able to endure this evening without succumbing to my own tears. We must both try to be brave and calm."

Sensing the approach of their friends, Elspeth swept

a handkerchief hurriedly across her cheeks and offered the other women a trembling smile.

"Please take heart," Isolde urged in a softly compassionate tone as she laid an arm about her friend's shoulders. "The day is not over, Elspeth, and, as you well know, on rare occasions miracles have been known to occur. I pray that you and Abrielle will be able to enjoy God's mercy in this matter, but whether it comes swiftly or takes years, I've no doubt that you will both be able to endure what comes and revel in a miracle of mercy whenever it should happen."

Elspeth smiled in spite of her misery. She had never before realized that her closest companion could be so optimistic. "I know I must try to take heart, my dearest, dearest friend, but with so little time remaining ere the wedding vows are exchanged, 'tis difficult to believe a reprieve will come in time. As much as Vachel may need what Desmond is offering, I loathe the idea of that ogre claiming my daughter as his bride. He's so despicable!"

"I'll be fine, Mama. Truly, I will be," Abrielle stated valiantly as she clasped her mother's slender hand against her cheek and feigned a smile. "There is really no need for you to fret so much. I'm sure Desmond will treat me kindly."

Elspeth bestowed a trembling smile upon her daughter, but failed to find any strength in her voice. She could only whisper, "'Twould seem the time has now come for us to join the others."

Isolde laid a gentle hand upon her friend's arm. "Cordelia and I will go ahead. Reginald is awaiting us in the chapel."

Elspeth squeezed her hand. "We'll be there shortly."

Isolde swept her arms briefly around each of them

and then waited as Cordelia did the same. Tossing back meager smiles over their shoulders, the pair wiped away the tears that streamed down their cheeks and sadly took their leave.

Vachel was awaiting Elspeth and Abrielle in the adjoining room and, upon seeing his wife's face, had cause to wonder if he had been wise in allowing his stepdaughter to make such a sacrifice for the family.

"You're looking very lovely, my dear," he said softly, clasping Abrielle's hand within his.

"Desmond is no doubt wondering where we are," she murmured, trying to convey some semblance of enthusiasm. She kept her voice firm, her body from trembling, for she knew how this day was hurting her stepfather.

Vachel glanced aside at his wife in time to see her press a lace-trimmed handkerchief to her trembling mouth. If ever in his life he had felt like a beast, then surely this was that moment. Yet he knew what his small family would suffer in poverty; their lives would be unbearable, with consequences far more grievous than even her marriage to Desmond promised to be.

What was he to do? What could he do? He felt as if his back was to a stone wall and a knife was pressing into his throat, waiting to drain him of his life's blood. The joyful union he had come to savor with all of his heart would likely never again be the same, with his wife pining away in misery for her daughter.

Elspeth touched his sleeve as she reminded him, "We should go now, Vachel. Desmond is waiting for us."

Vachel heaved a despondent sigh. At the moment the squire was the last person he wanted to see. "I have no doubt."

CHAPTER 8

Abrielle suppressed the overwhelming urge to run screaming from the chapel in rising panic. She knew that to all but a handful of onlookers, she appeared calm and elegantly regal, and that was as it must be. The miracle she'd prayed would stop the wedding had not arrived, but she counted it a minor miracle of sorts that she had managed to repeat the vows that would bind her now and forever to the grotesque man at her side.

At last, and far too soon, the priest pronounced them man and wife. Abrielle laid her hand upon her groom's arm. Even that scant intimacy made her want to recoil and she wondered how she would make it through the coming hours, much less the dreaded night that would follow. A small, tight knot formed in the pit of her stomach and remained as she and her new husband traversed the banquet hall to greet their guests. Lords and ladies alike rose to their feet and toasted the occasion with uplifted cups and a wealth of good wishes intermingled with hearty banter. Abrielle concentrated on maintaining an appearance of happiness and was successful until she happened to turn her head and caught a glimpse of a man all but hidden within a shadowed corner of the stairs. Instantly the knot in her belly became tighter, and bigger.

Raven stood with arms folded across his broad chest, watching the proceedings with a hard, somber expression. Nothing in his face indicated the path of his thoughts, yet Abrielle felt the weight of his unrelenting gaze as surely as if it were a hand upon her shoulder. She told herself it was only natural that being stared at in such a dogged manner should pull her gaze back in that direction, again and again, no matter how diligently she steered it elsewhere. She assured herself it had nothing at all to do with how magnificent Raven looked in his black plaid, the impeccable white of his shirt a flattering contrast to his long dark locks. Nor did it have to do with what had transpired the night before or the buzzing in her head and tingling of her bottom lip whenever she thought about the way his dark head had slowly bent and . . .

She would not think about that. Not tonight, not ever again. What was done, was done. But she was a married woman now, she reminded herself, ignoring an inner shudder; she was honor bound to act accordingly . . . and see to it that Raven did the same.

To that end she put her back to where he stood. She forced a smile and lingered in mindless conversation and counted to one hundred before allowing herself a fleeting glance beyond the gathered revelers to find him still watching. Abrielle looked away, smiled at comments she barely heard from people she didn't know, and looked back to find his attention just as rapt. And inscrutable. Really, what was the man thinking?

And what was she thinking to allow his audacious behavior to distract her on this of all nights.

There was much toasting of the bride and groom throughout the wedding feast, and with each tankard of ale or goblet of wine he emptied, Desmond grew increasingly inebriated and less and less bearable to his young bride. On numerous occasions, Abrielle's costly raiment received a liberal dousing, causing her bridegroom to chortle in amusement as he wiped vigorously at the spills that dotted her breasts and lap. Sitting dutifully quiescent beside him proved almost more than Abrielle could bear. It was even more difficult to tolerate his sticky lips brushing her cheek and his teeth nibbling at her throat. His attentions reminded her of some evil serpent searching for a place to begin his meal.

Once she was in the master's bedchamber, Abrielle tried to subdue the violent tremors that beset her as she sought to prepare herself mentally for that moment when her bridegroom would arrive at their chamber door. She found herself reassuring her mother, when her mother was trying to console her.

Elspeth's lips trembled as she wavered on the verge of fresh tears, but upon taking in a deep breath, she forbade herself to cry any more than she had already, knowing that if she started sobbing, it would benefit no one. Seeking to discipline herself, she straightened her trim back and lifted her chin. Even so, it was a lengthy moment before she could trust herself to speak without her voice faltering.

"I never once dreamt that by accepting Vachel's proposal of marriage I would also be ushering you into a union with Desmond de Marlé. I'm so very, very sorry, my dear. When I chose to follow my own heart, I failed to consider the arduous trials that you might be facing because of my selfish actions."

Slipping her arms around her mother, Abrielle held her closely, fighting back encroaching tears as she met her parent's gaze. "You've always told me to look ahead with hope toward the morrow, Mama, and that's what I must do now . . . trust that some good will come from my marriage to Desmond." Though her heart was heavier than she seemed able to bear, Abrielle forced a smile, feeble though it was. "I shall pray that in time our union may prove beneficial. Now find your bed, Mama, I'll be fine."

No more than a half hour later, Abrielle's qualms were magnified tenfold as Desmond staggered drunkenly through the anteroom into the bedchamber where she awaited him. His bloodshot eyes seemed to protrude even more than usual from his pudgy face as he stared at her lying upon his bed clothed in nothing more than a gossamer gown. As if he were already savoring a luscious sweetmeat, his tongue flicked slowly over his lips.

In spite of her ongoing efforts to assure herself that she could tolerate whatever happened during her initiation into wedlock, Abrielle hardly imagined that her bridegroom would throw himself upon her, and she screamed in sudden fright. Fear reached spiraling heights as he tore open the lace bodice of her nightgown and thrust a hand inside, evoking a pained whimper as he seized her breast. She bit into her bottom lip to keep from screaming and promptly tasted blood.

She feared she wouldn't be able to survive the night, much less their first conjugal mating. Considering Desmond's cruelty thus far, she could only wonder what further harm she'd be subjected to if she were to stay with her besotted bridegroom one moment longer. The way he was progressing, the threat of being cruelly raped seemed very, very real. Abrielle knew she would have to flee from the man for the sake of her own sanity, if not for her very life.

Loosening his grip on her, Desmond began throwing aside the coverlets. Recognizing that this would likely be her only chance to escape, Abrielle hurriedly rolled away from her drunken bridegroom and leapt from the bed. At first she had no real destination in mind, only a goading desire to flee to a place of safety.

Desmond's furious bellow lent wings to her bare feet, and in rising panic, she raced toward the antechamber, snatching up her dressing gown from the chair where she had left it as she passed. Flinging wide the door, she dashed into the corridor in spite of the fact that she was still having difficulty dragging on her robe. She glanced to the left, whence she could foresee no help emerging, for there were no other chambers along the corridor. Promptly she whirled in the opposite direction, knowing the passageway would lead her fairly quickly to the stairs to the lower floor where her parents' chambers were located. It seemed the only place she could seek refuge.

She heard uneven footsteps on the floor, readily affirming the fact that Desmond was giving chase. Abrielle dared not even consider what he would do to her if he managed to catch her. Indeed, her life might well be forfeited if she allowed him that advantage.

Racing down the passageway with a zeal born of desperation, she gave no heed to the hazards of trying to find her way in a poorly lit and totally unfamiliar corridor. She chanced a brief glance over her shoulder and was relieved to find her bridegroom panting heavily as he stumbled through the hallway behind her, at times momentarily running a hand along the stone wall as if seeking much-needed support. She prayed fervently that he wouldn't have the endurance to follow her to her parents' chambers or, if he did, that her stepfather would be far more worried about displeasing her mother than his host. In view of Desmond's drunken condition, that premise was not at all far-fetched. Vachel was not known to have much patience with those who imbibed beyond acceptable limits.

"Abrielle, come back here!"

To her surprise, his voice was soft, as if even in his inebriated state, he realized that being discovered chasing his bride would make him look the fool.

"If you don't stop, then by heavens I'll see you locked away in the depths of this keep. Then you can be assured I will make you pay for what you're doing. Believe me, your back won't look so fine and lovely after a cat-o'-nine-tails has marred it! Once you've had a taste of its wicked tongues, you'll beg for mercy and come crawling to me on your hands and knees."

His warning sent icy shards of dread shivering through every fiber of her being. In spite of the fact that she believed her bridegroom to be completely capable of beating her senseless or even worse, she could not bring herself to yield to his demands. If she halted, she had no doubt that she'd have to endure the forced consummation of their marriage, and that act seemed far more heinous to her than any painful torture or horrible beatings.

Abrielle chanced a glance behind her in an effort to gauge the distance between herself and her besotted groom. In the next instant, a cry of pain escaped her as she stubbed her bare toe on an uneven stone. Stumbling awkwardly about as she tried to regain her balance, she careened into the wall, nearly knocking herself senseless.

Desmond sprang forward, much faster than Abrielle would have imagined for one so roundly proportioned and well into his cups. The realization that she was in danger penetrated the enveloping fog in which she found herself, causing her heart to leap in sudden fear. The horrible dread of being trapped again in her groom's malevolent clutches quickly prodded her to her senses, and she whirled away, frantically trying to avoid his outstretched hand. His fingers caught in her long, loosely swirling hair, but in a desperate quest for freedom she snatched free, in the process sacrificing more than a few meager strands to his unrelenting grasp. She raced onward with frantically beating heart, all too keenly aware that her life was in serious peril.

The way of escape was barely visible just ahead, softly illuminated by the moonlight streaming downward through the narrow windows in the lofty turret high above the stone steps. If she could manage to make her descent to the lower level without Desmond actually gaining on her, perhaps she'd be able to reach her parents' rooms before he could catch her. Vachel might even be able to reason with the squire and convince him to be patient with his new bride.

Abrielle chanced a glance over her shoulder in a quest to see how far away her besotted groom was. To her dismay, he was much closer than she had dared to imagine, barely leaving her enough time to swing around the newel. Unless she laid out a ploy to lure him beyond the stairs or to confuse him, her flight would be in serious jeopardy. She was afraid he would then take malicious delight in locking his stubby fingers into her hair again, especially since her scalp was already throbbing. But if it meant escaping her besotted bridegroom, she'd just have to take that chance.

Forcing every fiber of strength she was capable of mustering into her limbs in a desperate attempt to lengthen the distance between herself and her groom, she raced onward through the passageway and then, upon reaching the end of it, whirled to face the besotted ogre.

"Yu'll never be able to escape me now, Abrielle," Desmond boasted confidently in spite of his thickly slurred words and wheezing efforts to breathe. "The wall is to yur back, an' yu've only one path ye can go . . . and that is past me."

Sweat dappled her bridegroom's brow and ran in heavy runnels down his flushed cheeks. He pressed a hand to the side of his distended belly, as if trying to ease the pain of exerting himself, and then smirked confidently as he waddled toward her.

She tensed as she awaited the arrival of the moment when she might be able to flit past him. Her nerves seemed to stand on end as he sauntered toward her with all the confidence of a tyrant. The closer he came, she reasoned nervously, the better her chances of slipping past him. If too much space were left between them, he'd have enough time to realize what she was about and block her path.

Desmond was no more than an arm's length away when she shot through the opening as if her very life depended on it. Her bridegroom flung out an arm in an effort to catch her, but to no avail, for she spun about like a whirling dervish, easily avoiding his grasp. A foul curse exploded from Desmond's lips.

Racing toward the stairs, she forced every measure of strength she possessed into her limbs. The threat of being caught by her drunken bridegroom proved a very strong incentive indeed.

"I'll catch yu yet," Desmond wheezed irately as he stumbled along behind her, "an' when I do, be assured, I'll teach yu to run from me."

The wan glow of moonlight streaming in from the turret allowed her to see the stairs that were just ahead. She was greatly encouraged to have had her ploy work as well as it had, but she knew she was far from safe. She could hear the plodding footfalls of the oaf behind her, slower than before, but nevertheless persistent.

An instant after facing forward again, Abrielle ran full force into a wall, a tall, warm, firmly muscled wall. She stumbled backward, her senses reeling, and then strong hands caught her up by her elbows, gently steadying her. Befuddled, she lifted her head and found herself staring into a pair of all-too-familiar blue eyes.

She gasped and tried to pull away. "Oh, Raven, nay, get thee gone from here. You must not interfere!"

"Yu vile, dastardly cur! Take yur hands off my wife!" Desmond de Marlé snarled. He was wheezing heavily, having exerted himself well beyond the limits of his usual slothfulness, and in the gloom, his sweaty, reddened face seemed far more bloated than usual. "Yu impu-dent Scot-tish rogue," Desmond slurred thickly, his words now liberally punctuated by hiccups. He shook a balled-up fist threateningly beneath the noble nose of the taller man and continued his tirade. "Yu've intruded . . . far too often . . . in my affairs . . . An' this time . . . yu've gone . . . too far. I'll have yu thrashed . . . till yur bones show! This is my wife . . . my keep . . . filled with my friends . . . an' countless men . . . who owe their allegiance to me."

Raven easily knocked aside the pudgy fist with the back of his forearm. There was a dangerous edge of contempt in his soft laugh. "Men ye send out ta do your foul deeds, like the last two who lost their lives, and for what? A promise of a mere pittance as their reward? Or is it true that this allegiance ye brag of is secured not with coin but threats, vile threats against not just their lives but those of innocent wives and children as well. Was that the payment that awaited those men if they didna kill me?"

"That's no business of yurs," mumbled Desmond, his drunken smirk growing as he thought of something that would more adequately appease his deepening desire for retribution. "Truth be, yu bloody Scotsman, I'd enjoy seeing yur severed head stuck upon a pike beyond the drawbridge of this very keep! Then every time I'd ride past yur putrefying skull, I'd be able to laugh at the memory of yur futile efforts to seize Abrielle for yurself."

"If ye believe ye can do better than those poor men ye sent ta die upon my sword, I canna think of one more prone ta idiocy than ye."

The taunt caused Desmond's bulging eyes to flare, vividly attesting to his mounting rage.

Abrielle stood at a loss, despairing of this confrontation ending well. For now, at least Desmond was distracted from her, but she couldn't leave Raven here to take the brunt of Desmond's foul temper. Raven was setting himself up to be murdered, what with all of Desmond's friends still housed within the keep, ready to kill any Scotsman.

An amused half smile curved Raven's lips as he

further taunted, "Still, if ye should be of a mind ta try ta kill me yourself, then I'll gladly give ye leave ta choose the weapons we'd be using. Or is it your wont ta murder me in me sleep whilst no one is around ta see your deeds? Ye're like a fat old rat what comes out of his hole at night, skittering here and there ta see what foul mischief he can get inta whilst others are sleeping. But I've ways of dealing with the likes of such vermin. Feeding their carcasses ta the cats would surely save burying them."

"Yu filthy Scot-tish beggar! I'll show yu who's lame-witted!" Desmond railed. "Mark my words, 'twill be yur remains the cats'll be feasting on this very night!"

"If ye're set on accomplishing that feat yourself, Squire, then ye'd best bear in mind what your men failed ta consider. Afore I ever became an emissary, I was trained ta be a warrior, so 'tis a rare occasion that I dinna fight back. But then, I expect ye'll be remembering that from our encounter in His Majesty's palace. Ye ran off then with your tail tucked betwixt your buttocks. Had ye any courage ta claim, ye'd have led your men inta the forest yourself instead of merely telling them where me da and I could be found."

The taunt was too much for Desmond to bear with any degree of calm prudence. Whatever logic he had been able to lay claim to prior to the wedding had for the most part flown after guzzling copious tankards of ale. He was thoroughly incensed, goaded beyond the core of reason, which at the moment was most fragile.

A foul, guttural oath issued forth as Desmond lunged toward the taller man with fingers curled into claws. Come what may, he intended to tighten them around his adversary's throat until he was thrashing about on the floor in the throes of death. A second before Desmond reached his antagonist, the Scotsman stepped deftly aside, allowing the squire an open path to plow on past.

A sharp, fearful gasp was promptly snatched from Desmond's throat as he saw before him the stone stairs down which he had deliberately pushed his half brother to his death months ago. Desperately he strove to untangle his stumbling feet and dig in his heels, but to no avail. A thumping heartbeat later he was teetering on the brink of that very same precipice whereon his lordship had wavered, experiencing firsthand the sudden stark terror that he had once fantasized his elder brother would feel prior to setting into motion his murderous deed. His short arms flailed wildly about in a frenetic attempt to halt his forward momentum. Alas, he couldn't recover his equilibrium, no matter how desperately he strove to stop himself from falling.

His wildly thumping heart pounded in his ears and against the inner wall of his chest. In an expanse of time that spanned the chasm between life and death, an eternity flashed before his mind's eye. Precipitous views, perhaps comparable or mayhap totally dissimilar to those his elder half brother had glimpsed in the swiftly fleeting moments prior to plunging to his death, filled Desmond's mind with a swiftly burgeoning dread. His breath caught again in a ragged gasp as terror cauterized his very being with his own expanding visions of what seemed his hellish doom. There was only darkness at the bottom of the stairs, yet he had sat through enough burial services for those he had killed to have committed to memory many of the dire warnings in those messages. All too vividly he recalled the tormented ravings of his own mother who had writhed in abject terror of what her delirium had created. Like her, Desmond felt as if he could see demons writhing beneath him in a twisted, indistinct mass and, in the midst of their agony, lifting their arms in plaintive appeal for some sublime angel of mercy to release them from their torment. Other specters from that dark, foul abyss seemed to beckon to him and await his presence with evil, leering grins, as if they were the doomed gaolers of that despicable place. Then, as if the horror he was experiencing weren't enough to cauterize his very being with terror, whitish vapors seemed to pass before his mind's eye, forming an image that reminded him of his half brother. Shaking his head sadly, the ghostly apparition pointed downward toward the dark chasm opening up beneath him.

"I never meant to push you down the stairs, Weldon," Desmond blubbered as drool dribbled unheeded down his chin. "It was an accident! You have to believe me, brother! I adjure you not to take revenge upon me for what happened that night! You must have mercy! You must let me live! Please have pity!"

Raven and Abrielle both experienced a strange tingling along their napes as they looked at each other. Never before had they heard so much terror evident in the cries of a person facing death as they were now hearing in Desmond's desperate pleading.

Desmond tried mightily to find something to hang on to to halt the momentum that was swiftly building. Briefly, in passing, he braced his forearm against the buttressing stone wall, but his flabby muscles could not sustain his weight for even a fleeting moment. Of a sudden, he was plummeting head over heels in an awkward, flopping descent of the stairs, during the course of which muffled grunts escaped his throat. Then his head slammed into the wall, knocking it strangely askew his neck. Though his tumbling descent continued on unchecked, no further sound issued forth from his flabby throat. Finally his rotund form came to rest beside the newel post on the lower level, and there he lay, his limbs sprawled wide, his mouth gaping open, his eyes staring vacantly upward.

It seemed an uncommonly long passage of time that he lay sprawled at the bottom of the stairs where he had come to rest after flopping face up on the stone floor. Only a wan glow from flickering candles cast from some distance away lent a vague hint of where Desmond's body lay. From where they stood on the landing, neither Raven nor Abrielle could see into the murky gloom well enough to determine if he had been knocked unconscious by the fall or if his silence was merely a ploy to draw them near, much like a spider waits for its victims to become entangled in its web before pouncing on them and inserting its deadly venom. If the situation was indeed the latter case, then surely Desmond intended to exact harsh revenge, if not on both of them, then surely on his young bride, ere the night had passed.

The night had exacted a heavy toll upon Abrielle's composure, to the degree that she was now shaking uncontrollably. She remembered Desmond calling out his brother's name . . .

Had he seen Weldon's ghost? Or had that merely been his past murder haunting him?

Even as Abrielle crept cautiously down the stairs behind Raven, her trembling legs seemed so unreliable that she feared any moment they would collapse beneath her and send her tumbling headlong down the stairs into her bridegroom's arms. It didn't matter whether Desmond was alive or dead. The thought of that possibility raised nettling hackles on the back of her neck, the like of which she was sure she would never forget.

"Please be careful," she urged Raven shakily, noticing the lower half of Desmond's right arm was hidden beneath him. Rampant distrust of the man spurred her trepidations to an even higher level. "He may have a dagger hidden within his clothing and is merely waiting for you to draw near. He will surely kill you if he can."

Wary of deception, Raven paused on the step just above the squire and, with the toe of his boot, nudged the elder's hip in an effort to evoke some reaction. There was none, not even a groan, only a rippling effect of his body, much like a dead asp being wiggled by its tail.

Stepping across the grotesquely sprawled form, Raven went down on a knee and pressed two fingers against the flabby throat in an effort to find a throbbing beat. After a moment he decided his search was futile, for if the man had been alive, he certainly wouldn't have been able to hold his breath long enough to continue any kind of ploy. Yet Raven was wont to consider the many ramifications that Desmond's death would likely provoke and how best to protect the lady from ugly suspicions being cast her way.

Sitting back upon his haunches, he lifted his head and peered up at Abrielle. "If I'm na mistaken, my lady," he said in a softly muted tone, "ye've naught else ta fear from the squire. I'm thinking his neck may've been broken during the fall."

A shocked gasp escaped Abrielle as she clutched a trembling hand over her mouth and sank against the stone wall, sliding bonelessly until she was sitting inches from Raven. Not only was she shaking to the very core of her being, but her heart was hammering so wildly that she couldn't seem to breathe, much less think.

"What am I to do?" she queried in a desperate whisper. All she could think of was the financial agreement that would leave her a very rich woman and, at the same time, cast all manner of suspicions upon her as well as on her stepfather.

"What am I to do?" she repeated, a dozen or more discordant thoughts streaking through her brain. "What will I say happened?" She pressed her clenched hands to her breast. "Surely Desmond's friends will think I am somehow to blame . . . how can they not when he only just joined me in our chambers and now we are out here . . . with him lying dead on the stairs? What if someone saw me running away from him through the halls? How will I ever be able to explain?"

"Ye'll explain nothing," Raven replied.

Seeing her in such distress tore at his heart, but not so much that he had not already assessed the situation fully. It was unlikely anyone had witnessed what had just transpired. Desmond's nephew Thurstan had shut himself up in his quarters, as if sulking in protest over the squire's marriage or mayhap merely biding his time until he could turn the two Scots out on their ears. All the other guests had either left or withdrawn to their own chambers. Raven was in a position to know that since he'd meandered through the halls, seeking to release some of his bitterness after watching the innocent Abrielle pledge to love and honor de Marlé. Her sweet innocence and utter vulnerability had been driven home to him last night when he'd make the mistake of kissing her and he hadn't been able to sleep knowing how she would be spending this night. It was no accident he had been close by to hear her cries.

"Explain nothing? How can I not explain?" demanded Abrielle, deeply distraught. She hugged herself tightly, blinking through a blur of tears. "I must think on what to do."

Raven reached for her clasped hands and held them in the warm haven of his own as he dragged her to her feet. "Do not think. Just listen. You will return ta the squire's chambers and remain there till someone brings ye news of his demise."

"But . . ."

He squeezed her hands. "Shh. Just listen . . . and trust me." He saw the way she bit her lower lip and added, "At least trust me for this one night. Considering the squire's lengthy delay in making his way ta ye, 'twould na be unreasonable for anyone ta suppose ye'd fallen asleep waiting for him ta join ye. Just be assured, my lady, ye've done nothing for which ye should feel any shame. De Marlé's own drunkenness and his hatred of me led ta his death, nothing more. Ye're innocent of any wrongdoing. Can ye believe what I'm telling ye?"

She was nearly frantic with fear of what might happen should the circumstances surrounding Desmond's death be found out. "But I ran from him. I couldn't bear to be with him. I was afraid . . ."

"Ye had good reason ta be fearful, my lady. The man was despicable, caring nary a whit for anyone but himself. He sent out men ta kill us, though they lacked the skill ta appease his murderous bent. What did he care if they didna return alive? All he wanted was my death, and he didna care if they lived or died, as long as the blame was cast elsewhere. He could as easily have killed ye in a fit of temper had ye na fled his chambers. As for that, didna he threaten ta do ye harm whilst he was chasing ye? Who knows what injuries might've happened ta ye had ye stayed with the man. By the way he called Lord Weldon's name, perhaps in the end he cried out in guilt for his part in the man's death."

His words made sense, and she latched on to them with relief. Yet in that frozen moment, she truly considered Raven. Why had he been roaming the halls on her wedding night? He now knew the terrible deed she'd instigated by running away from her lawful husband—would Raven want something in exchange for his silence? She remembered the way he'd flirted with her even though he knew she was almost a married woman. Worse, she remembered his kiss and her own weak protest, and her stomach tightened in worry and shame until she felt truly ill.

"But what of you? What will you do?" she queried. "Who will you tell?"

"No one." He held her gaze through the shadowy gloom. "I'll be doing the very same . . . returning ta me own chambers and awaiting the dawning of a new day. Now go."

Abrielle turned and hurried toward her late bridegroom's chambers, feeling as if a thousand eyes watched her from every dark corner. Raven's words about the dawning of a new day echoed in her head with each step she took. She was as cold as the death that Desmond had just descended to. She was going to keep her silence to protect herself from suspicion. She hadn't done anything wrong, so why did such guilt fill her? She should be relieved, for she was free of Desmond de Marlé. Yet she still didn't know how the castle guests would take the discovery of the body—and what they would suspect her of.

And what was she to do about Raven Seabern? She wished he would depart, that when the new day he spoke of dawned, he would simply be gone, taking his knowledge of this dreadful secret with him. At least part of her wished it. For all the good wishing was likely to do. For better or worse, she knew enough of the man to suspect he would not be so easily dispensed with.

CHAPTER 9

A frantic tapping on the chamber door snatched Abrielle abruptly awake after a fretful night of tossing and turning. In light of the many trepidations to which she had mentally subjected herself after her panic-stricken flight through the halls of the keep and, perhaps more acutely, after forcing herself to occupy her bridegroom's chambers, she had reason to wonder if she had closed her eyes for longer than a moment. Throughout the torturous night, the frightening reenactment of Desmond's fall had kept running over and over in her mind, plaguing her mercilessly. When she considered the consequences she would suffer if anyone had witnessed her desperate flight or, later, her terrifying confrontation with Desmond in the hallway, she could foresee a trial of demonic proportions taking place in the very near future.

She'd have no viable defense against the accusations that could be hurled against her. With the possible exception of her mother, Cordelia, and other close friends, everyone in the keep would likely be of the opinion that as a new bride, she should have submitted herself dutifully to her bridegroom, no matter how loathsome and vile she had found him to be.

But if she had merely dreamt that her bridegroom had been killed tumbling headlong down the stairs, then her torment would surely begin anew. Better she die now by some merciful stroke of fate than be constantly subjected to Desmond's mental and physical abuse the rest of her life. That would indeed be an earthly hell whence there'd be no escape, at least until one of them died.

Even as far-fetched as it was for her to fear that Desmond was still alive after Raven had pronounced him dead, she was plagued by images of the man stumbling through the chamber door with blood trickling down the side of his face. She would not find any reprieve, of that she was sure, for he would then be intent upon beating her senseless for having run away from him.

Such ominous thoughts sent shards of prickling dread shivering down her spine. Thus, when a frantic rapping of knuckles actually sounded upon the portal, Abrielle was so startled that her heart nearly leapt from her breast. It wasn't difficult to imagine why she had trouble finding her voice in the following moments.

"Yes, who is it?" she finally called out in an unusually high-pitched squeak, the best she could manage under the circumstances.

"M'lady, m' name is Nedda. I was brought here ta the keep yesterday ta be yer maidservant, but alas, I fear I've come this mornin' bearin' grave news. Do I have permission ta enter yer chambers, m'lady?"

Abrielle slumped back upon the pillows as her heightening tensions began to wane to a more tolerable level. Grave news could only mean one thing: affirmation that Desmond was dead. As much as she might have been appalled by her own callousness weeks ago, she felt as if an enormous weight had just been lifted from her mind. Indeed, she likened the announcement to a reprieve from a sentence of death. Who but her own mother could have possibly understood the overwhelming relief she was presently feeling at the realization that Desmond was now dead and that she would not have to submit herself to his hateful dictates or, perhaps more important, to his brutal husbandly attentions?

"Yes, Nedda, of course. Please come in," Abrielle replied, thankful she had had the presence of mind not to place the wooden bar across the portal to secure her privacy. The maidservant would have considered it strange indeed had she bolted the door while awaiting her bridegroom.

After scurrying through the antechamber, an older woman as much as twoscore and five or so years of age, garbed in a black gown and a wimple, entered the bedchamber and approached the canopied bed wherein her new mistress reclined against several pillows. Having tugged a sheet beneath her chin, Abrielle peered at the servant warily, wondering whether she'd prove a friend or a foe. The gentle empathy evident in the soft hazel eyes and smile readily assuaged Abrielle's brewing fears. Indeed, if the compassion the maidservant evidenced counted for something, then she could believe she was a very kindly individual.

"M'lady, 'tis sad I am ta have ta bring ye such news so soon after yer weddin' vows, but I fear the brumes o' gloom were wont ta visit this keep durin' the night," the older woman announced in a soft, solemn voice.

"No sooner were ye wed than yer poor husband was taken . . ."

"My poor husband?" Abrielle hated falsehoods, but knew it was needful to cast suspicion away from herself as well as from others. She was shaking uncontrollably as she clasped a trembling hand to her throat and stared at the elder. In spite of the lengthy moment in which she sought to find the nerve to trust her voice, she finally managed to ask, "Dear Nedda, what are you trying to tell me?"

The servant heaved a forlorn sigh, collecting her wits for the task the steward had given her. "M'lady, sometime durin' the night, likely whilst he was makin' his way ta these very chambers, yer bridegroom . . . Squire de Marlé . . . took a dreadful tumble down the stairs. There he was, poor man, decked out in his wedding finery, lying knotted up near the bottom step. The ones what discovered him say he likely tripped and struck his head against the stone wall afore tumblin' ta the bottom, seeing as how there was blood smeared on the stones higher up and his temple had a horrible-lookin' bruise and an open gash . . ."

Abrielle had the presence of mind to throw back the covers and swing her legs over the side of the bed as she sought to leave it. "Then, by all means, Nedda, we must see to the squire's wounds."

Holding up a thin, wrinkled hand to forestall her mistress, Nedda solemnly shook her head and looked at her compassionately. "Nay, m'lady, I fear there be no need for haste now."

Pausing in response, Abrielle managed to convey a perplexed frown as she searched the elder's face. "But why not?"

" 'Tis terribly grieved I am ta be the one ta tell ye,

mistress, but Sir Thurstan gave me no other choice. It seems when Squire de Marlé ... fell, he not only struck his head on the stone but, mayhap at the same time, broke his poor neck. From what I've been able ta glean from the rumors making their way about the keep this early morningtide, he died in much the same manner as his lordship did months ago. The serfs are sayin' Lord Weldon was found in the very same spot, all crumpled up at the bottom of the stairs early in the mornin'."

Abrielle's hackles rose as she recalled Desmond crying out his brother's name. Had that only been his mind evoking haunting memories of his murderous deeds? Or should she believe that there was a chance that the ghost of Weldon de Marlé had finally taken revenge?

"Cruel as it may seem ta a new bride," Nedda continued, "there's naught else that can be done for the poor squire but ta bury him. I fear 'tis the black of mournin' yer pretty self 'll be wearin' in the days ta come, mistress. Ye're no longer a bride but a widow."

There, it had been said, and simple though the words might be, Abrielle said them again and again silently to herself: "no longer a bride but a widow." 'Twas no dream or nightmare or any other flight of fancy, but the truth of what had been wrought over the course of her wedding night.

In spite of her best efforts, Abrielle could not summon forth a single tear with which to feign even a meager amount of sorrow. Desmond was dead and she was free and the best pretense she could convey was to clasp her hands over her face and pass a lengthy moment in silence, which she truly hoped Nedda would accept as a suitable response for a young widow.

"My parents must be told," she stated at long last, and heaved a trembling sigh as she lowered her hands into her lap. She dared not glance up, for fear the woman would detect her lack of remorse.

"After learnin' of Squire de Marlé's fate, I took it upon meself ta inform yer parents afore bringin' ye the tragic news. I thought ye'd be needin' their comfort as soon as they could get dressed. They should be comin' any moment now ta offer ye solace."

"Thank you, dear Nedda, for your thoughtfulness and concern," Abrielle murmured, carefully avoiding the servant's gaze. Though innocent of any wrongdoing, she felt as if she were guilty of the most diabolical subterfuge known to man and had to wonder if her conscience would ever be cleansed of that dark stain. "'Twas very considerate of you."

No sooner had the servant given her a dressing gown in which to meet her parents than a soft rap of knuckles sounded upon the portal. Without waiting for a verbal response, her mother called through the oaken door, "Abrielle, my dearest child, Vachel and I have come to be with you in this difficult hour. Are you able to see us now?"

"I pray but a moment more to make myself presentable, Mama," Abrielle replied, and hurriedly wrapped her robe about herself as she left the bed. While smoothing her hair into some reasonable order, she had cause to wince as she was painfully reminded of the patch of hair that Desmond had torn from her scalp. Though the wound was extremely tender, it seemed a small price to pay to be free of that brutish monster. It definitely made her grateful that she had fairly thick hair, for she wouldn't have to worry about hiding the spot. "You may come in now, Mama."

Elspeth's tears were ones of joy as she folded her daughter in her arms, and Abrielle shuddered and gave herself up to her mother's comfort. "Oh, Abrielle, Abrielle," was all Elspeth could manage.

Abrielle did feel some of the relief her mother felt, but in the back of her mind lingered thoughts of Raven, the man who knew her secret. How would she feel when she saw him by the light of day? For just a moment she considered relieving her burden by telling her parents everything. But she did not want them to bear the guilty secret. No one should have to suffer the pangs of conscience but herself. And if someone had seen her—planned to accuse her? How could she allow her parents to be implicated?

If anyone had been saddened by the news of de Marlé's demise, Abrielle knew that her stepfather was not among them. If anything, Vachel appeared to have some difficulty curbing his delight over the way things had turned out. After all, he had been instrumental in arranging the fortune she would now be inheriting as Desmond's widow. No doubt he had also gained concessions for himself that would likely put him in the league of other wealthy men.

Abrielle was far too relieved to have escaped Desmond's amorous attentions to consider making much of a bereavement that was nonexistent. On the other hand, she had little difficulty appearing solemn and respectful toward the dead or even dressing the part of a widow. The main impediment with which she was forced to contend centered mainly on the hauntingly persistent memory of Desmond's body thumping down the stone steps and the spine-tingling cries for mercy he had made while confronting his brother's apparition. Though she tried to banish that frightening recollection from her mind, she could not long escape its frequent repetition, for its memory proved persistent.

THE WINDING SHEET in which Desmond had been wrapped for burial readily evidenced his short, portly form as the serfs lowered his body into the grave. Standing with her family and the Graysons beside the open grave, Abrielle watched as one transfixed. Her last morbid view of her bridegroom prior to his body being wrapped for burial seemed permanently scored into her brain. As much as she sought to banish the memory of his milk-white face, the wrinkled brow strangely elongated by a hairline evidencing a purplish bruise on his temple, and his clawlike fingernails that no amount of scrubbing had been able to whiten, she knew she would not be able to banish such sights overnight. Being a virginal widow, she had been loath to view his maleness and had been grateful when Vachel had discreetly bade the priest to leave the lower half of Desmond's body covered for her benefit. Staring down at her bridegroom with something approaching paralyzing horror, she knew she could not have calmly borne the sight of his nakedness. Even covered by a sheet, his figure had appeared oddly grotesque, for his large belly had protruded much like an oversize mushroom beneath the shroud.

In a gesture of farewell, Abrielle tossed upon Desmond's breast a single rose from a bush that a kindly servant had carefully nurtured throughout the cooler months and, in quiet empathy for a newly widowed bride, had presented to her with softly murmured condolences. Staring at the bloodred petals lying scattered upon the white bindings swaddling Desmond's form,

Abrielle was inundated once again with persistent visions of his falling to his death and the horror and fear she had experienced after Raven announced the squire's death.

Hardly a moment had been allowed to pass after the priest had cast a symbolic handful of dirt into the grave and murmured the words "Ashes to ashes, and dust to dust," than Abrielle found herself barraged by a bevy of bachelors and widowers conveying their condolences for her loss. Still very much in a stupor, she listened as they offered to assist her in whatever capacity she might require or desire either now or in the near future. She thanked them graciously, but assured them that their services wouldn't be needed since her stepfather would likely be helping her to sort out her affairs.

Beyond assuring her that she had his deepest empathy and respect, Raven maintained a discreet distance, as did his father. Yet bluish-green eyes were wont to meet those of deep blue fairly often, and Abrielle tried to look stoic and strong. Some deep part of her mind protested her concern that, now she was an extremely wealthy widow, Raven might well try to press his advantage. She knew she had to remember the very words of caution she had so recently uttered to Cordelia: What did she truly know of him beyond a handsome face and smooth words?

To alleviate the possibility of any unkind soul becoming suspicious, Abrielle deemed it prudent for all concerned to lend her attention primarily to the other guests. In a solemn yet gracious manner, she listened to the condolences offered by her kinsmen and the hunters and their families, many of whom had felt no more liking for Desmond than she had. The rowdy rabble that had attached themselves to the squire in an effort to enjoy their share of the fortune he had inherited had obviously seen no further profit in remaining at the keep in the midst of the bride's Saxon friends and relatives and the Normans who had disdained them. To the relief of many, they soon took to the path down the road.

Throughout the solemn service, her parents, Cordelia, Lord Reginald, and Lady Isolde remained near her side. Their nurturing presence proved more of a comfort to her than the vast majority of guests. Most of the men had only come for the hunt and were naught but strangers to her. Even so, many of the bachelors were wont to leave mementos and beg assurances that she would not forget them, promising to visit her in the near future. Though she smiled as if to convey her consent, she soon realized how benumbed her poor beleaguered mind truly was, for in the space of a few moments she had trouble distinguishing one keepsake from the next or the face of one young gallant from all the others who had stepped near.

Shivering inwardly from the gruesome recollections that were wont to prey upon her mind, Abrielle decided that she must find a new way to view the life that she would now lead. In so doing, she realized that as mistress of the keep, she now had the authority to correct some very irksome situations she had become privy to shortly after the death of the two men who'd attacked the Seaberns. Having acquired full possession of the keep and the lands upon which it had been built through the agreement Vachel had insisted Desmond sign in his quest to have her, she could now set aright many wrongs that had been done to the serfs.

Graciously she invited the guests who had been wont to stay beyond the graveside service to dine with her in the main hall later that evening. Upon assuring the Graysons, Cordelia, and her own parents and relatives that she'd be seeing them later at sup, she begged their indulgence to allow her to take care of some pressing matters. As people drifted back toward the castle, talking together in twos and threes, she saw Raven standing as still and tall as an oak, watching her. A skittering of nervousness and something else moved up her spine. She wished she could shoo him away, make him stop watching her. If only he didn't know what had happened last night—yet she tried to imagine what she would have done had he not appeared to distract Desmond from his pursuit of her. She was torn in her feelings about him, from gratitude to suspicion. But he was not her main concern today.

Upon approaching Thurstan, who had remained at the grave site to direct the serfs laboring to fill in the hole, she halted beside him and then waited a lengthy moment before he deigned to meet her gaze. The coldness in his eyes surprised her, and she was taken aback that on the day of his uncle's funeral, he could spare her so much animosity. She began to wonder when he would return to his own lands, but could not imagine cruelly asking him to leave.

"I apologize for interrupting you, Thurstan, but could you possibly spare me your attention at this present time?" she queried in a pleasant tone. "I understand that you greatly assisted your uncle in the management of the castle. If I am wrong, I can always seek out the steward . . ."

He folded his arms over his chest. "You may speak freely to me."

"Thank you, Thurstan. I do have some matters that have been plaguing me for several days now, yet, until now, I've had no authority to do anything about them. Since circumstances have taken an unexpected change by the squire's death, 'tis my desire to remedy various problems that have become evident to me."

He said nothing, just continued to watch her in a way that made her uncomfortable. The more bothered she was by his lack of graciousness, the more firm she became in her convictions.

"I shall be initiating new standards to which those with any authority here must abide. The new principles are to benefit those who have no voice, and as for the timing of these initiatives, I mean to set them into motion this very day."

"What vexing matters are those, my lady?"

She sensed sarcasm in his tone and clenched her jaw. She should have gone directly to the steward, for she knew Thurstan was no friend. She remembered how he had advised his uncle to change the terms of the betrothal contract. He certainly must resent that the contract had given her so much. In fact she began to wonder, by his barely subdued animosity, if he would receive much at all in his uncle's will. But that was not her concern.

She swept a hand about to casually indicate the direction in which she desired to go. "I will be touring the area where the serfs' huts are located. Since you seem to know your uncle's concerns, I'm giving you the opportunity to join me. If not, I can always go to the steward."

His pale brows came together in a fleeting frown. "That will not be necessary. I can assist you as I did the squire."

Without further comment, Abrielle lifted the hem of her black gown as she led the way across the secondary bridge traversing the stream, on the far side of which stood the serfs' hovels, which had been built fairly close together in a wide circle, in the center of which large stones surrounded a glowing bed of coals whence a few meager flames flickered upward. As Abrielle halted beside the dwindling fire, Thurstan peered at her questioningly.

"Would you please call out the serfs who are here," she asked. "I wish to speak with them directly."

"My lady, if you would only tell me what this is about, I will have your wishes carried out."

Abrielle inclined her head graciously. "Thank you, Thurstan, but my wish is to speak with the serfs directly and explain what I will be expecting from them henceforth as their new mistress. If in the future they should have any complaints, then they'll suffer no uncertainty that I am the one who issued the directives."

Without another word, Thurstan crossed to a large metal disk which hung from a sturdy wood frame on the far side of the fire. Dangling beside it was a hide-covered metal disk attached to a heavy wooden handle, with which he applied three strokes to the gong. Returning to Abrielle's side, he clasped his hands behind his back and stood tall and rigidly aloof. As they waited, she could not help but notice that Raven had followed them from the grave site, and now stood silently near the trees, as if he'd appointed himself her bodyguard. She frowned at him, but could do nothing more, because the serfs came scurrying out of their dwellings, causing Abrielle to groan inwardly at the sight of them. She had never seen so many frail-looking human beings with thin, gaunt faces and lusterless eyes peering back at her from the half circle that they had hurriedly formed on the far side of the fire. A sudden breeze made her aware of the inadequacy of their paltry garments, for she saw many huddling together as if seeking to escape its sharp talons. She could only believe that many of them would die ere winter was full upon them, for they would not likely have the stamina to withstand the maladies and diseases the season seemed to spawn. In spite of the fact that Weldon had cared for them with as much compassion as a loving father, it was obvious that Desmond hadn't cared how many lived or died as long as there were enough to see to his personal needs.

"I am Lady Abrielle, your new mistress," she stated as she began to stroll in a wide circle around the fire. As she came closer to the serfs, she was surprised that Thurstan did not stay near her, but only waited, as if he didn't care what happened to her desperate people.

As a whole, the serfs seemed utterly frightened of what lay in store for them. Nevertheless she progressed within the perimeter they had formed and, with a warm smile lighting her eyes, was wont to reach out a hand and, in a compassionate manner, lay it upon an elder's arm, smooth a child's tousled curls, or squeeze a young mother's hand as she paused beside them. There were precious few who didn't evidence an abject dread of Thurstan and were hesitant about peering upward even when she halted before them. Though she slipped a hand beneath the chins of several and compelled them to meet her gaze directly, it was always toward Thurstan they first glanced, in so doing displaying a kind of frenetic fear of the man.

Upon facing them again, Abrielle found many of them readily lending her their attention. "As you may be aware, I visited the keep fairly often while Lord de Marlé was alive. Yesterday, I exchanged wedding vows with his lordship's brother, Desmond de Marlé. Early this morning, he was found dead. Henceforth, as the new mistress of this keep, I shall be setting forth some favorable changes, which you will likely welcome. You will be expected to learn skills to help support this keep and provide for new structures that will soon be built to house you." She knew Thurstan was openly scowling, but she ignored him. "New skills will also be taught to enlist your services in other tasks that may well prove lucrative, such as the carding of wool shorn from sheep on these lands as well as in the use of spinning wheels and the making of furniture. You'll start off by making your own clothing and tanning leather for your shoes and other items. Until you become proficient at such crafts, sufficient clothing will be provided to keep you warm and in good health through the approaching winter."

A thin, barefoot toddler garbed in loose sacking waddled toward her on wobbly limbs, evoking a smile from her as she threaded her slender fingers through his matted hair. His mother rushed forward, anxiously pleading for her forgiveness and then, with a quick curtsy, whisked the babe up into her arms.

And suddenly Abrielle imagined herself as the poor girl, with no way to feed her child. She turned to Thurstan, so incensed that she could barely keep her voice from shaking with anger. "From what I am seeing here in this place, 'tis apparent these serfs have not been given adequate provisions since Lord Weldon's death. That may well have been Squire Desmond's mode of doing things, but he is now dead and buried. Thus, commencing this very day, whatever it takes to feed, clothe, and warmly house these serfs, it will be done or I shall know the reason why. Do you understand what

I'm telling you, Thurstan? You and I will speak to the steward together so that he understands my intentions. I or someone I trust shall be inspecting this area on a regular basis. I will be expecting to see evidence of much progress being made."

She suspected he was much in collusion with his uncle in causing the condition of these poor people, and she was appalled. She could not look upon him for another moment, so after giving a warm smile to the people she now considered her responsibility, she strode toward the bridge—and found Raven Seabern blocking her path.

Her response to his closeness was as unwanted as it was lightning quick. She felt a hot pull of attraction deep inside that could not lead to any good, for now, knowing the truth of Desmond's death, he was more dangerous to her than ever.

She sidestepped him with a nod and kept walking, not the least bit surprised when he turned gracefully and fell into step beside her.

"Lady de Marlé, might I have a moment of your time?"

His use of her wedded name made Abrielle flinch.

"Of course," she replied, then lowered her tone to a whisper to add, "Speak quickly, for it would not look well should we be seen together as we approach the castle."

"And why not?" he asked, his expression quizzical.

"You know why," she retorted.

"I know your husband is gone. And that I am hardly the first man ta speak with ye this day. I'd have been blind not ta see the many tokens of affection ye've already received from men who want your consideration."

"Is that your purpose in waylaying me, sir? Do you seek to present me with your own token of affection?"

"I believe I already have," he countered. "But if m'lady desires, I am more than willing to . . ."

Even if he hadn't moved dangerously closer, she would have understood the "token" he had in mind and her cheeks heated. She stopped walking and faced him. "The lady most definitely does not desire anything of the sort."

"Really?" He tilted his head and regarded her intently. "Because I've some small experience in the matter and it did seem to me that—"

"Enough," she interrupted, and glanced around cautiously. "What exactly is your goal, sir?" she demanded, unable to banish her fears of discovery. "You have no reason to be here now and I believe it would be best for all that you leave. You are no longer in danger, and no longer is Desmond trying to prove himself the winner over you."

"Then ye knew why he invited us."

Abrielle shrugged and resumed walking. "'Twas not something I was told, but what I surmised."

"Then surely ye must also be clever enough ta deduce why it is that I canna leave. Why I willna." His voice had gone low and deep, almost hoarse. "Since the first moment I saw ye, I've yearned to have ye as my very own."

She gasped, feeling hot and cold all at the same time, and looked about her in fear. They were at the bridge now and she leaned over the rail as if fascinated by the stream below. She wished she could stare him in the eyes, but knew she would be unable to control her heated emotions. How could he just lie to her so blithely, when the truth was that he had not even tried to court her when she was penniless?

"How dare you, sir!" she cried softly, feeling the pain of knowing that he had deemed her unworthy until now, when she was wealthy beyond most others. Raven Seabern was no different from any man lured by money. Her disappointment should not shock her, but somehow it did, and deeply. Again, she felt the pangs of a woman who did not know if any man could love her just for herself. "You did not vie for my hand before I was betrothed." The full force of the emotions roiling within her now burst out, and she was full of pain and anger. "You are no different, sir, from any other man who ever claimed to want me, including Desmond de Marlé. Just stay away from me."

Raven watched her go in silence, his warrior instincts stirred by the depth of his passion for her, his desire to possess her now stronger than ever. The battle to win Abrielle might well turn out to be the fiercest of his life, but win her he would, no matter the cost.

CHAPTER 10

During the midday meal, the mood in the hall was far more subdued and cordial after the burial of their late host, especially since the squire's rather questionable cohorts had promptly taken their leave after the funeral, swigging down ale as they went.

Although many of the hunters had left prior to the wedding, those who had stayed over for the banquet and the nuptials had brought along their wives or other family members. Now that the squire was no longer there to vent his outrage, in particular upon the pair of Scotsmen and, to a lesser degree, upon the Saxons whom he loathed, the guests as a whole proved to be in far better spirits and lingered with members of their families to converse with the new mistress and her relatives. The Scotsmen still found themselves regarded suspiciously by the various lords and landowners in attendance, but all seemed to be following a truce of peace for the new widow. Upon making their departure, many of the guests extended their sympathies to the erstwhile bride and were wont to assure her surreptitiously that she would likely find a finer gentleman to marry in the months or years to come, one with whom she'd have more in common.

Cordelia approached Abrielle as the latter left the trestle table where she had been sitting with her parents. "I'm afraid Papa's not feeling very well," she explained. "The food here has been difficult for him to tolerate. I suppose once we're at home, it will be curds and whey for him or something just as tasteless until he's feeling better. In any case, he is wanting to return home and retire to his own bedchamber, where he can lie abed during his misery."

"Thank you for remaining as long as you have," Abrielle replied, squeezing her friend's fingers. "I couldn't have borne these last few days if you hadn't been here to listen to my complaints and allowed me to express my frustration so freely. You've always proven to be a dear, dear friend, especially when I'm in dire distress."

"When I return, my visit will likely be for a much longer period of time," Cordelia assured her. "Until then, my dearest friend, take special care of yourself. You will need to, especially after what has just come to pass."

"I shall surely miss not living close to you and your family," Abrielle assured her. " 'Twould now be a goodly jaunt to reach your home, but what is that distance between close friends?"

"Unfortunately, I fear such a visit will have to be seriously delayed now that you're lady of this keep," Cordelia replied as she heaved a sigh of lament. "As mistress of those bone-thin serfs, you must remain here until you have set into motion your rules for governing this place. Only then will you be able to leave and feel confident of doing so." Eyeing her companion, she continued, "I needn't remind you that you're no longer under the authority of your stepfather. You are capable of setting the problems aright and extending authority to those who will closely adhere to your directives. I shall be expecting great changes to occur during my absence . . . which, of course, doesn't give you much time, considering I shall likely be visiting you ere you even think of leaving here."

Abrielle laughed. "I'll try not to disappoint you."

"I suffer no doubt that you have the fortitude to succeed in whatever task you undertake," Cordelia stated confidently, and then heaved a sigh of lament. "I do wish Laird Cedric didn't live so far away. 'Twould be nice if he lived close enough to visit us, too."

"For shame, Cordelia," Abrielle scolded in laughing amusement. "Why, the man is old enough to be your grandfather."

The young woman raised her nose in the air and tossed her head, giving no heed to her friend's reproof. "Me grandfather never looked half as handsome as himself. And there I be, talking like the man. Ta be sure, not even me own da looks as fit, fine, and trim as the old laird, Cedric Seabern." In her normal voice, Cordelia continued softly, "And then there's the son. He's as handsome as his sire. 'Tis plain to see they both came from fine stock."

Abrielle looked away in discomfort. "He is not a man I give much thought to."

Cordelia frowned at her in surprise. "Nay? He does seem to be watching you rather closely."

Abrielle could only shrug. "Far too many men are watching me closely today. He is just one of many. And he's a Scotsman, too. Do you see how my kinsmen and neighbors regard him with suspicion? I've asked him to leave, and I hope he will do so soon."

"Abrielle, I do not understand why you would do so, why you would act in a seemingly discourteous manner, for I have never seen you be other than kind and thoughtful," Cordelia said slowly. "And if I but had time to question you . . ."

"There's no reason for that," Abrielle said, giving her friend a smile. "Do not worry for me. The life I thought of as bleak has surely taken a turn for the better."

IN SPITE OF the necessity of being ensconced henceforth in her late bridegroom's spacious chambers, Abrielle made a concerted effort to thrust aside the haunting memories of the previous night and find some genuine peace for her weary mind as she burrowed deep beneath the covers. She had no real reason to fear her future—except for her next marriage, for marry she must, and soon. It was obvious to her that men would be vying for her and her fortune, a strange twist of fate for a woman who was all but ignored at court only months ago. But Abrielle was determined that this time, she'd earned the right to control her own fate. But how would her stepfather react to such a thing? He would want to see her safely with a man of whom he approved. Now that she had most of Desmond's wealth in her possession, Vachel would likely seek to find her a spouse with a lofty title. It was what most fathers wanted for their daughters. In his case, she could imagine that, if truly motivated in that direction, such a desire might have arisen from his own frustration after his requests for a title had been rejected.

Still, if Vachel's ambitions could be realized by the

very thing he had earlier been seeking for himself, that being a worthy title for his own exceptional achievements, then he would likely be content. Vachel was an honorable knight who had served valiantly during foreign campaigns and, for that reason, was rightfully deserving of recognition from his king. Lord de Marlé had been honored by Henry for his heroism after returning home. As a reward, he had been given the vast area of land upon which to build this very keep. So might Vachel be honored if she were to remind His Majesty of her stepfather's bravery and daring feats during those years he had loyally served beneath the king's banner. The king just needed to be reminded that there was still a knight whose daring feats had long been forgotten. And now that Vachel had wealth of his own again, the title was more important than taking more money from the treasury.

Abrielle's heart began to sink as she realized she might offend Henry if she were to plead for a few moments of his time to suggest the possibility of bestowing a worthy title upon her stepfather. But perhaps her newfound wealth would bring her more royal notice.

Glumly she stared at the flickering flames dancing atop the stout candles nestled within the heavy sconces, wondering if she should attempt to approach any of the lesser lords with her request. No, with so difficult a task, she'd have to find an individual who was permitted fairly often within His Majesty's presence . . .

Of a sudden, Abrielle gasped and sat upright in bed as the realization dawned on her. In spite of her needless fretting, she was well acquainted with one who could perform such a feat without evoking the king's ire. He was none other than Raven Seabern! It would be a fairly simple matter for the Scotsman to carry her missive to

Henry when he was once again called upon to deliver a message to His Majesty from his own King David.

And how better to rid her own keep of the Scotsman's presence, for he would not dare to return after she'd made clear he was no longer required. All these churning emotions in her breast would depart with him, and she would be able to logically think of who would make the best husband.

Snuggling back into the downy pillows, Abrielle smiled in satisfaction as she folded her hands atop the coverlet and stared at the embroidered scene on the canopy above her head. On the morrow, she would begin the day by composing a letter to His Majesty. Truly, if Vachel were given a title and lands as a reward for his own notable achievements, perhaps he would then feel satisfied with what he had managed to accomplish during his lifetime rather than be wont to find a nobleman who'd be interested in taking his wealthy stepdaughter to wife.

AFTER MASS AND breaking her fast, Abrielle went to the lady's solar, her own private chamber. A weaving loom stood in one corner, and a long trestle table was laid out with servants' livery in various stages of being cut and sewn. She sent the maidservants away and waited for Nedda to bring Raven to her. She'd been over and over her little plan, searching for flaws, and found none. It was most clever, if she did say so herself, and she truly did not see how it could fail. She would rid herself of the Scot's very disturbing presence and lessen her stepfather's need for a noble son-in-law at one and the same time. So delighted was she that she was smiling when the maidservant announced Raven.

He stood just inside the door wearing what could only be a mask of composure, for which she could hardly blame him after their last meeting. When Nedda curtsied and withdrew, closing the door behind her, his surprise was obvious.

As Abrielle stood cool and composed, he nodded politely. "Ye sent for me, my lady?"

"I did, sir. I desire your help with a personal matter. 'Tis a delicate task I have in mind, one to which you are perfectly suited."

"You need but tell me what it is, my lady," he said, walking toward her, "and it is done."

Abrielle held up her hand, hoping she hid the alarm she felt as he drew nearer. "You need come no closer."

"There are needs, and then there are needs," he said softly, still moving, not stopping until he was but two feet from her. "What is this task with which I am so favored?"

She extended her arm between them as if she were gripping a metal shield rather than a parchment missive, rolled and tied with a ribbon and sealed with the wax imprint of the de Marlé house. "When next you have business with King Henry, please give this to him for me."

He didn't reach for it. "I have na idea when next I will be in London—or Normandy, for I think that is where your king resides for now."

She frowned, for this was hardly the response she'd expected. "Surely you will need to be dispatched soon for King David."

"Nay, he does not require me at present. I will be staying here."

"But this missive must reach the king," she countered, frustrated to find there was a flaw in her plan after all, namely that its success rested entirely on Raven's acting as she'd thought he would.

"Then so it shall," he declared, moving another half step closer to take it from her with a smile that belied the refusal to accede to her full desire that was expressed in his eyes.

Managing to squelch a sigh of relief, Abrielle offered a simple smile of appreciation. "Thank you."

"One of my men is an excellent courier, as trustworthy as they come. I will send him forth without delay." He watched her smile fade. "Or is my word na good enough for ye?"

"I know not how good your word is. I know nothing of you." This time she realized her words were not reasonable, for she indeed knew he was a trusted royal courier, but his response to her plan had thrown her off course.

"Know this, and never doubt it," he said solemnly, holding her gaze with the intensity of his own. "My word is my bond, and I pledge it ta ye. You can rest assured your missive is as good as in the king's hand this very instant."

"Thank you," she said with resignation, wishing she could think of a legitimate way to force him to take the letter personally. It was hard to think clearly with him so close, looming over her, so big and male in this small chamber used only by women.

"And how do ye fare, Lady Abrielle?"

Distractedly, she said, "What do you mean?"

"Ye're newly a widow, with many decisions ta make. I imagine the responsibilities are vast."

"Truth be told, only one person dares to threaten me at the moment," she said pointedly, her hands on her hips, leaving him no doubt to whom she referred.

"Since it is nowhere in me ta threaten a woman, I can only think it must be your peace of mind I threaten."

"Perhaps intimidation is a better word. Do you seek to intimidate me, Scotsman?"

"So ye feel intimidated, Abrielle?"

"Please do not call me by my Christian name alone, and no, I do not feel the least bit intimidated by you," she lied.

"Good. I prefer a fair contest." She wasn't aware of him leaning toward her until he straightened and it was suddenly easier to breathe. "If ever I do make ye feel threatened or intimidated, ye can be certain ye are misunderstanding my concern for your welfare."

"You are too concerned, sir, you and every other man who thinks to win a quick fortune."

"And a beauteous bride," he added, his smile quick and disarming. "I canna speak for any other, but 'tis the only prize I seek."

His honeyed words elicited an exasperated groan from her, and she pointed to the door. "Please excuse me now. I'm sure you can well understand how pressed I am in light of recent events."

She turned her back on him, not wanting one more smile or head tilt or glimpse of his overwhelming male presence to complicate her already muddled feelings. She assumed he would leave, but suddenly she felt his breath caress the back of her neck, causing gooseflesh to prickle along her skin. Before she could move away, his warm hands curled over her shoulders, gentling her in place.

"I lie not when I say I was captivated by your beauty from the moment I saw ye," he whispered, his lips dangerously close to her ear.

Abrielle refused to turn around, refused to look into his eyes and be swayed by what he wanted her to feel.

"But beauty alone—even beauty such as yours, beauty that blinds a man to reason and steals his soul away forever—beauty alone would never be enough ta challenge my own code of honor. That happened when I saw your courage and the way ye held yourself when your stepfather was denied his rightful reward for his service in the Crusades. Had I taken my leave beforehand, I would have carried away the memory of your loveliness. But it was that instant when your true beauty was branded onto my heart and I knew there was no other, and no turning back."

Lies, all lies, she told herself, childishly wanting to cover her ears against this seduction that was proving too potent. "You have said your piece. Please leave."

She felt a chill when he moved to do as she bid, but only when she heard the door close did she sag into a chair. She'd barely caught her breath when the door suddenly opened again, and she whirled about, only to see her mother peering at her with curiosity.

"Abrielle?" Elspeth began as she closed the door. "Was that Raven Seabern I saw leaving this chamber?"

"It was."

Elspeth put a hand on her daughter's shoulder. "And you met with him . . . alone?"

"It is not what you think, Mama," Abrielle said, already tired of the renewal of the husband hunt, when she'd only been a widow for a day.

"And what should I think, daughter? There are many young men within this keep who would like to be alone in a chamber with you, to press their advantage."

"That is not what Raven was doing."

"Then why does he not leave?"

Abrielle opened her mouth, but she didn't know how much to reveal. "He . . . declared himself to me," she said softly.

Elspeth's eyebrows rose. "I cannot say I am surprised, considering the way he has looked at you."

Abrielle groaned and shoved to her feet, not wanting her mother to see the anguish in her expression. "It is only the way they all look at me," she said, waving a hand to encompass the entire keep. "I am only the newest prize to be won."

"You are more than that, my dear."

"I am so tired of it, Mama," she whispered, surprised at how close to tears she was. "Yet I know it is my duty to find a man worthy of the responsibilities he will take on when he weds me."

"Should he not be worthy of you, rather than the responsibilities?"

"How can I think of that when there is so much at stake? I will have to make a decision based on many reasons, not just whether the man appeals to me."

"And does Raven appeal to you?"

"He's a Scot," Abrielle said forcefully. "Do you not see how Englishmen, both Saxon and Norman alike, mistrust his people?"

"And is that a reason to mistrust an honorable man, one who has rescued you without thought to himself?"

Abrielle bit her lip, knowing she had plenty of private reasons to mistrust Raven. "I will keep an open mind, Mama, but he is only one man among many."

THAT NIGHT AT dinner, Abrielle was surprised to find Thurstan seated at the head table with her family. He was conversing with Vachel, and she could detect not even a hint of a sneer. When he saw her and her mother approach, he rose to his feet with the other men in the great hall and gave her a small bow. Throughout the meal, he was solicitous about her first day's experiences as mistress of the great keep. He told her some of the duties he'd had the steward begin to oversee in the serfs' training. Abrielle could not understand why he was suddenly being kind to her, when all along he'd treated her as almost a rival for his uncle's attention. Unless . . . it was what all the men were concerned with now—her wealth and the power it brought.

After supper, he approached her where she sat before the massive hearth with her parents. "My lady, might I have a private word with you?"

Elspeth and Vachel exchanged a glance, and as if reading Abrielle's mind, Vachel said, "There is no need for you to leave your comfortable place, Abrielle. Your mother and I will leave you both alone."

She nodded to her parents gratefully, and then waited until they had moved away. She could not help noticing that several of the young bachelors were watching her, as if waiting their turn. Raven was speaking with his father, but he made no move to join the others. He settled for an occasional glance, regarding her with that calm confidence she found irritating and slightly ominous and, she had to admit, more than a bit intriguing. Was he really so confident he could win out over all these other decent Englishmen? Or was it that he felt that knowing her darkest secrets gave him the upper hand?

Thurstan took the bench her mother had been using, and she forced herself to concentrate on him.

"My lady, it strikes me that the terrible tragedy of my uncle's death does not have to be the end of the relationship between our two families."

She blinked at him in surprise. "This keep is now my home, Thurstan, and you live not far away."

"That is not what I mean," he said, with a hint of impatience in his voice. "You were married to my uncle; does it not make sense to keep the connection by marrying me?"

She barely kept her mouth from dropping open in shock, so much did he surprise her. "Thurstan . . . are you proposing to me?"

"I think the marriage would solve all the problems caused by my uncle's sudden death. I have been assisting him in the management of this keep since he inherited it. I could continue to do the same."

"And that is enough reason to marry?" she responded incredulously. "I have been under the distinct impression that your feelings for me were not fond."

To her rising disgust, he looked down her body. "I could not allow myself to feel anything for you when you were to become my uncle's wife. And the most important thing to bring to a marriage is respect."

"Respect?" She heard her voice rise, knew she should stop herself, but his gall proved too much. "Sir, you admit you were involved in the management of the keep and all its surrounding lands. Did I not just see the terrible condition of the people who were entrusted into your care?"

His mouth tightened. "My uncle—"

"Aye, I know, it was his land, his serfs. But you should have seen to those poor people who depended on you. I had no choice in marrying your uncle, but I would never willingly tie myself to your family again, after having seen how you treat fragile human beings."

Those yellowish-green eyes flashed at her, revealing the seething hatred he had kept banked inside him.

"Then keep your virgin marriage vows," he said angrily.

She was grateful that there were so many people about, or she would have been terribly afraid of what she heard in his voice. As it was, she forced herself to meet his gaze with cool composure.

"But understand that Desmond de Marlé had monetary agreements that preceded your marriage contract," he continued.

"What agreements, sir? Are you saying that the contract, which was examined by advisers to both parties, was entered into falsely?"

"He did not honor the agreements made by Weldon to me, agreements that Desmond vowed he would finish in his brother's place."

"You mean a larger inheritance than what he has put in writing?"

Thurstan seemed furious and upset, as if he expected her to surrender to his anger. But Abrielle was tired of being a pawn in other people's games.

"He meant to—"

"I care little what you say he meant to do," Abrielle interrupted coldly. "It is only your word, if nothing is in writing."

"And do you doubt my word?" he demanded, his voice beginning to rise.

"I am sorry that you feel entitled to more than—"

"I do not want your pity!" he said, loudly enough that several heads turned at tables scattered through the hall. "Understand that your position is tenuous here, my lady," he said through gritted teeth.

"I am the Lady Abrielle de Marlé." She emphasized her late husband's name, then continued, "My position here is not 'tenuous' at all."

"'Tis only a note of caution. If you do not have my protection—"

"I have the protection of my stepfather, his men, and the soldiers of my dead husband. Are you saying even they are not loyal?"

But Thurstan did not go so far, only meeting her accusation with silence.

"As far as I'm concerned, sir," she said, "we've settled this matter, and that is the way it shall stand until I'm shown viable proof that would lead me to decide differently. Whatever my husband inherited from his half brother months ago does not rightfully belong to any of Desmond's kinsmen, including you. My husband never once addressed any issue pertaining to his having heirs, especially anyone who should be duly considered now that he is dead. 'Tis a well-known fact that Desmond's previous wives died without issue. If you or any other men have an argument with the legality of the agreement Desmond signed of his own free will, then I would suggest that you cease your efforts to frighten me and take up this matter forthwith with my stepfather. Vachel de Gerard can convince you of the validity of the documents that he drew up with Desmond. I should further explain that if anything happens to cause my death, whether accidental or deliberate, all the wealth, holdings, and possessions that I am to inherit shall be transferred to my kinsmen without due recourse, that being my mother and stepfather. I'm sure if there are any threats made against them that Vachel shall be able to gather a force of men to protect them."

Thurstan rose to his feet. "You speak of murder as if our discussion threatened such a thing. It is not so."

The fact that he was backing down should have

appeased her, but he reminded her of a snake biding his time before striking.

"I only seek to give you the facts, Sir Thurstan, so that we understand each other."

"'Twas my purpose as well, my lady."

They were so intent on staring at each other, neither realized someone had approached until a voice spoke. "Lady Abrielle, do ye wish assistance?"

Raven stood nearby, hands clasped behind his back, looking as if he merely wanted to join in on their conversation. Abrielle was annoyed that he felt he had to help her, and she watched as the evil flame died within Thurstan's eyes.

Thurstan bowed to her. "Have a good evening, my lady."

Only when Desmond's nephew had ascended the stairs to find his chamber did Raven turn back to her. "That didna seem a pleasant conversation."

"You did not need to interrupt us. Will you always be playing my bodyguard now?"

He smiled. "If 'tis necessary." His eyes grew watchful. "Was it with him?"

"Nay, I handled our disagreement. Please do not interrupt me again."

When she rose to her feet, she heard him whisper, "Ah, but ye like my attention, lass."

Inside her, something trembled, and she despised her weakness where he was concerned. "I think not. Good evening."

CHAPTER 11

Although Abrielle felt as if she'd made Thurstan understand her position, she still took the steward of the keep with her as a precaution when she visited the serfs' village the next morning to see how the work had begun. It was wonderful to see how much more lively the people already were with food in their bellies.

Her fears were also eased when her new maid, Nedda, suggested that her parents might ease her loneliness by moving into the spacious chambers next to her own. Abrielle and her mother were delighted with the idea. As for Vachel, he was more than willing to satisfy every wish his stepdaughter might have now that she was a widow, especially if it meant getting back into the good graces of his wife. To a great degree, Elspeth had shared the trauma her offspring had recently suffered and, as a parent, wished to provide whatever succor she could offer in an attempt to alleviate any lingering fears Abrielle might have still been suffering after her abbreviated union to Desmond de Marlé.

It was while she was enjoying a private dinner with her parents that Abrielle broached a subject that Desmond's demise had forced her to consider. "Now that I've become a wealthy widow, 'twould seem that what my mother and I once confronted shortly after my father's death is happening again . . . but with definite differences, bachelors looking for a rich wife to marry, rather than seeking to strip me of my virtue to amuse wagering lords. I'd rather not have to confront any of them, no matter the title or fortune they may have."

Laying aside his knife, Vachel peered at her with a troubled frown. "I believe you have suffered much for our family's sake, Abrielle, and for that, I must apologize . . . and, at the same time, thank you for what you did for us. I was in deep despair prior to your marriage to Desmond, wondering how my family would survive. Because of your willingness to sacrifice your own happiness, I feel as if I've been immeasurably blessed by your compassion. I doubt I can ever repay you for what you've done."

Abrielle met his gaze and smiled. "By some merciful stroke of providence, I escaped that abhorrent marriage. Considering that I am now wealthy and there'll likely be many who'll be appreciative of that fact and eager to assuage their own greed, I suggest that if you wish me to consider anyone, present him to me first, and then I shall tell you whether he pleases me or not. I will bear in mind any marriage proposals you may receive from prospective suitors, but I also must tell you that no amount of cajoling will sway me if I don't care for the man. Desmond became a nightmare. I don't ever want to wed another of similar bent."

She did not want to worry them by mentioning Thurstan's strange proposal, so she kept silent, hoping that Thurstan would not be so foolish as to challenge her again.

An amused smile tugged at Elspeth's lips as she peered askance at her husband. "I think your match-making credentials have now been thoroughly singed."

Vachel waggled his head, as if reluctant to admit having that flaw, but a moment later a soft chuckle escaped him. "At least the marriage was short-lived. What about that young Raven Seabern?" he ventured, cocking a quizzical brow at her as he met her unswerving gaze.

"A Scotsman?" Abrielle said, pretending shock, for not even to her own parents would she admit how frequently her thoughts turned to this particular Scotsman. Knowing, as she did, that he was not a suitable choice for husband made it even more perplexing that his should be the first face her gaze sought when she entered a room, though truly it did not need to do so, as her ears had become so sensitive to his rough-edged tone she could find him without looking. It made no sense at all, and if she couldn't understand it herself, how could she hope to explain her tumultuous feelings to anyone else?

Softly, Elspeth said to her husband, "We have already spoken about this matter, my dear. He is not a man she is considering."

Abrielle did not like how her stepfather studied her too closely.

"You are now one of the richest women in all of Christendom," he continued. "Soon you may have a whole league of suitors vying for your hand."

She arched a brow. "Perhaps I have no interest in them."

"But you are pleased to be a wealthy widow now,

are you not?" Vachel queried, elevating a handsome brow as he awaited her answer. "Now be honest and tell me truly."

"Were I given a choice between poverty while married to a man I can love and honor, and wealth while being miserable with someone as despicable as Desmond, I can assure you that I'd rather be poor and wed to a man I can love. If you haven't realized it yet, Sir Vachel, wealth is a pitifully poor replacement for genuine love and simple contentment."

"My dear, you've never known true poverty if you haven't gone to bed hungry or been bereft of clothing to keep you warm," he countered. Although her valiant assertions were what he would've expected from one so young and innocent, he was nevertheless irked by her declarations. No one who had ever experienced weeks of hunger could lightly sweep those memories from mind. Even now he was prone to wake in the dead of night with disturbing memories still fresh in his mind. To be sure, the years he had fought against the Turks and others had left a lasting mark on his memory.

Meeting his gaze directly, Abrielle dared to challenge, "Can you honestly declare that during your lifetime you've experienced a serious dearth of those things you mentioned?"

Vachel leaned back in his chair and was silent a long moment as he pondered whether to recount the hardships he had experienced or keep them to himself. Finally he decided the truth needed to be told. "If I've seemed eager for wealth, Abrielle, then perhaps I've had just cause. There were times when I experienced great hardships. I have fought here in this country for my king as well as confronting infidels in foreign lands. During those times, I was forced to sleep on a cold, hard ground without even a cloak to warm me and with my belly so empty that it refused to stop gnawing at me. Aye, there have been times when I've yearned desperately for a few coins to buy some small bit of sustenance to assuage my hunger, but alas, they never came during those desperate hours of need, and I was forced to bear it as well as I could. As you can see for yourself, I survived those difficult trials, but not without becoming more appreciative of a full stomach, a bed upon which I can sleep, and a weighty purse that I can call my own."

Elspeth looked at him in some bemusement. "Vachel, why is it that you've never cared to discuss those arduous experiences with me directly? If I hadn't overheard you at your father's funeral telling your cousins of your experiences, I would never have known how deeply you had suffered."

His wide shoulders lifted briefly in a casual shrug. "I didn't think you would find them interesting, my dear. I only talk about them when I'm asked how difficult a campaign it had been over there. Few women enjoy hearing such tales."

"Oh, but they are interesting," Elspeth insisted. "At least to me. From what I've been able to ascertain from those who went with you on the Crusades, you won the respect of even your worst enemies. As to your valor, I even overheard your cousin say that you had earned the name Stalwart Vachel because you never retreated before the enemy, though you stood facing death time and time again. The scars you bear on your body clearly evidence the battles you fought, and yet I know very little of what you actually endured during those campaigns. I know you were held captive for a time and starved until your men rescued you, but again, I only learned that much from your cousin. Why have you been so reluctant to tell me of your experiences?"

"Those events weren't as glorious as my cousin obviously made them out to be, my love," Vachel replied. "Those were desperate times, and my men and I had little choice. It was either stand firm against our adversaries or be cut down by their charging horsemen. We chose to fight, and fight we did, nigh to our last breath. Rather than cutting us down as they could have so easily done, the enemy offered us a salute for our bravery in facing greater odds and gave us quarter by riding off the field of battle. I wouldn't be here today if they hadn't shown us mercy." Vachel reached across the table and squeezed his wife's hand affectionately. "How can I remember those times of danger and desperate need when I find myself in your charming presence, my dear? You make me feel like a wealthy prince upon whom rich blessings are continually being bestowed."

Abrielle glanced between them and realized that she had never noticed such a look of adoration on her mother's face before, not even during her first marriage. Perhaps, after Abrielle's own detested nuptials and subsequent widowhood, some benefits had actually been imparted to the older couple, for it was now apparent that Elspeth was very much in love with Vachel, more than Abrielle had previously supposed. Indeed, when Abrielle noticed how her mother's fingers intertwined with Vachel's in a loving manner, she could believe they were very devoted to each other. She found that idea rather amazing, for she had been under the impression after her father had been killed that her mother had accepted Vachel's proposal merely to quell the attempts of unscrupulous lords and their sons to win their wagers at the cost of Abrielle's virginity.

Elspeth glanced at her daughter and blushed as she stated haltingly, "I have . . . an important announcement to make . . . to both of you."

Abrielle exchanged a curious glance with Vachel, who seemed equally bemused. In unison they peered at Elspeth and waited expectantly as she sought to clear her throat. Then, in what could only have been construed as overwhelming embarrassment, she lifted her slender shoulders in a girlish shrug and said simply, "I am with child."

Thoroughly astonished by her revelation, Vachel leaned back in his chair with his handsome jaw hanging slack. "Are you . . . certain . . . ? Do you have any doubts?"

Smiling radiantly, Elspeth reached across the space between them and rested a slender hand upon his. "At least three months certain."

"But why didn't you tell us before now?" Abrielle insisted, thrilled by the news . . . and yet a little anxious for her mother's welfare. After so much time had elapsed since her own birth, she couldn't help but worry about her parent's having difficulties in the months to come or in the final birthing process. Although Abrielle had always wanted a sibling, she certainly didn't want one at the expense of her mother's life. "Is everything all right with you? You haven't been experiencing any problems?"

"Elspeth, please tell us you are well!" Vachel insisted, turning his hand to clasp hers more firmly. "You must know by now that I wouldn't be able to bear it if I were to lose you. I never knew what love was until you came into my life."

"I honestly feel fine. Truly, I do," her mother assured them with a radiant smile. "I only wanted to make certain of my condition before saying anything to either of you. After such a lengthy passage of time since Abrielle's birth, having another child seemed nothing more than a futile hope. However, within these past two months, everything has seemed to confirm that I am with child. Just within this past fortnight, I started feeling the movements of the babe, and they are now becoming quite strong . . . so I am fairly confident that my prayers will be answered approximately six months from now."

"Although this was the last thing I was expecting, the news is by far the best I've heard in some time," Abrielle declared happily. Promptly leaving her chair, she hastened around the table to embrace her mother. "You must know from all the pleading I did as a child that I've always wanted a sister."

"A son would be nice," Vachel murmured with a lopsided grin. "In truth, it wouldn't matter what we had as long as the babe is perfect in every way." Clasping his wife's hand within his, he brought it to his lips for a gentle kiss and then smiled at her with all the devotion his warmly glowing eyes could convey. "My dear, you must know how much I treasure you, so you must take care of yourself. I wouldn't be able to bear it if anything were to happen to you or to the babe. As I'm not getting any younger, your announcement has come as a complete shock to me, for it was the last thing I was expecting."

Elspeth laughed in girlish delight and peered at him with shining eyes. "I was a bit taken aback myself when I learned I was with child. I thought I was past that time."

Vachel caressed her cheek as he grinned at her. "I shall have to watch over you very carefully in the coming months."

"I'll do whatever I can to keep her from exerting herself," Abrielle assured him, her radiant smile evidencing her own joy. "Now that there'll be another child in the family, this will give me an opportunity to fret over my mother for a change. She has been doing enough of that, watching over me all these years."

"Please! I must protest!" Elspeth laughingly declared, holding both hands up as if that would put a halt to their ambitious intentions. "I can assure you that I'm not an invalid and that I am quite capable of taking care of myself. After all, I've been through this before."

"Aye, that you have, my love, but if you'll kindly consider the fact that you were much younger then, perhaps you would allow us to coddle you through the next five or six months," Vachel urged, and then smiled. "Believe me, my dear, if you're not getting any older, I certainly am, and I need to know that you'll be there to watch after me when I'm a doddering old man."

Elspeth patted his arm. "Do not fret yourself, husband. I'll be there beside you when that time comes . . . if it ever does."

Vachel raised his silver goblet in tribute to his beautiful wife. "To our growing family, my dear. May we enjoy peace and contentment throughout all the years of our lives. And as we age, may we also become wiser and take time to enjoy the simple blessings we've been given. I doubt I would have experienced such happiness had I not been blessed with you as my own sweet and noble lady."

"And may you both live to be at least a hundred!" Abrielle eagerly added, and, in more prayerful thoughts, begged that such a request might be granted. Vachel's fear had instilled within her some of the same feelings of anxiety. She didn't know what she would do if she were to lose her mother. Elspeth had always been such an important person in her life, more so than her father, whom she had dearly loved, but had never really understood, especially when he had allowed himself to be drawn into a deadly confrontation for the sake of his pride. If anything of a tragic nature happened to her mother, she had no doubt the pain and void she would feel would be infinitely greater. Indeed, they thought so much alike that it would be the same as losing a part of herself.

THAT SAME AFTERNOON, Abrielle entered the kitchen to determine what vittles remained after the majority of the guests had taken sustenance and departed. Though she had put the steward in charge of feeding the serfs, she wanted to make certain that enough was being done. In her mind, she could still see that frail toddler trying to learn to walk when so weak from hunger.

Shortly after viewing the food that remained from the meal, Abrielle realized that there were more than enough provisions to appease the hunger of the pitiful group living across the stream. In that quest, she bade several servants working in the kitchen to put whatever food had been left into crocks, kettles, and baskets and load the containers into a wheelbarrow that she had bidden a slender youth to bring around to the outer door. From there, the cart could be easily wheeled across the bridge to the area where the serfs were housed.

However, upon hearing her instructions, an old grouch of a woman with long, streaming black hair and strange eyes sauntered forward, giving every evidence of being overstuffed with herself and fully in charge of the kitchen. The other servants hurriedly retreated. The woman sniffed as she flicked her beady eyes over the food that had already been loaded. Then, peering aside at her mistress, she tugged broodingly on her hairy chin.

"Ever since I came here ta cook for him, Squire de Marlé made it a rule that I could take whate'er food was left and feed it ta m' swine," the hag stated with something approaching a derisive smirk. "He ne'er once told me I had ta share any portion of it with them lazy beggars across the brook."

Considering the amount of food that had been left, Abrielle could only imagine the enormous waste if a sizable portion of it was diverted to feed the swine rather than to relieve the hunger of the serfs. Flicking a brief glance over the rotund cook, she could imagine where some of it would go . . . no doubt down the woman's gullet. Arching a brow, she questioned, "Good woman, what is your name?"

"Mordea," she replied, and then proceeded to spit a stream of vile-looking juices into a nearby pail.

Abrielle promptly turned her face aside, seeking to control her sudden nausea. Upon recovering her aplomb, she asked, "As far as doling out such food, are you saying that Squire de Marlé never made any exceptions?"

"'Twas always his rule from the first," the cook stated arrogantly. "I oversee the cookin', and whate'er's left is mine ta take afore e'en his own swine got theirs."

"Just how much do you intend to take?" Abrielle asked curiously.

Sweeping an arm about, the woman smirked. "All of it."

From the wary glances several of the kitchen staff

were casting toward the elder, it was evident she was not one to be trifled with. This very moment the cook would learn that it didn't matter what assurances Desmond may have given her, circumstances had definitely changed.

"Squire de Marlé is no longer among the living, and I am mistress of this keep now. Therefore I shall be setting down my own rules for the serfs to follow, the first of which shall be that no single person has the right to establish any regulations that I haven't personally authorized, or claim anything that I haven't permitted them to take." Gesturing to the other kitchen staff, she indicated the food in question. "Now, if you would, please be good enough to do as I've instructed."

"Naw ye don't!" the hag railed, flying at her young mistress with wrinkled fingers curled into claws. "'Tis mine! All mine!"

If she had never had an occasion to see a witch in flight, Abrielle was certain she was seeing one now. Although she easily sidestepped the termagant, she felt her hackles rise as she likened the elder to some demonic fiend whose hatred of others had driven her into a frenzy. Obviously the other servants thought so, too, for they stared after the clumsily stumbling woman with mouths agape.

Though the shrew's arms flailed wildly about in an attempt to halt her forward momentum, the farther she progressed across the kitchen, the lower her head descended. A moment later, she was scrubbing the stone floor with her nose and the side of her face.

"What is going on in here?" Thurstan barked upon stalking into the oversize room.

Blood was now gushing profusely from the woman's nose and mouth, prompting him to snatch a towel from a nearby table and press it tightly against the nose that had been scraped raw and even now bore a dark purplish hue.

"Who did this to you, Mordea?"

Raising a flabby arm, the cook pointed toward Abrielle accusingly. "'Twas that haughty bitch. She laid me low, that she did."

Thurstan glanced around with a thunderous scowl and found himself gazing into the pointed stare of the keep's new mistress. "My lady, I—"

"Never mind what you may have to say about this matter," Abrielle interrupted. "I want that woman gone from here ere the hour is out."

Thurstan spared Mordea a scowl before he looked back to Abrielle.

"My lady, the squire brought her here shortly after acquiring the keep. She is the best cook we have on the premises."

Abrielle was wont to challenge that particular statement. "Nevertheless, I want her gone. I will not be attacked by a hireling in my own keep." She flung out an arm to indicate the nearest door. "You've been given orders. Now comply with my command and send Mordea on her way."

"But she's an old woman," Thurstan protested. "How will she manage if you cast her out?"

"No doubt by forcing her dictates upon others as she has obviously been doing for some time here in this kitchen, and tried to do with me this very afternoon. I will not allow her to continue to vex and torment those who are susceptible to her edicts one day longer than necessary. Perhaps she can beg mercy from the people she's been deliberately neglecting."

In a sharp manner of dismissal, Abrielle turned to face the other servants, bidding them to carry out her earlier directive by loading the cart and taking the food across the bridge for the other serfs. They seemed eager to comply and were wont to nudge one another and grin as they gathered up the fare. It was not unlikely that Mordea had made their labors in the kitchen one very long and grievous ordeal.

Upon glancing over her shoulder, Abrielle was surprised to find Thurstan helping Mordea from the kitchen. As Abrielle overheard the crone chiding him, she realized Mordea knew more about him than any of the other servants who had recently been living under his authority, and she was struck with suspicion.

"If me poor mother were alive, she wouldna have stood for this foul abuse. She'd have struck that chit down with nary a thought ta the cost. Ta be sure, she'd've bloodied this whole keep from end ta end so they'd long remember her."

"Shh," Thurstan urged impatiently.

"Whot, ye don't want that bitch knowin' how ye're almost kin to me?"

Thurstan met Abrielle's shocked gaze.

"Mordea, do not—"

"Aye, Desmond de Marlé be me own brother," the old woman wailed. "But for different mothers, ye, too, could have been me nephew, Thurstan de Marlé, so don't ye be thinkin' ye're mightier than me."

When they had left the kitchen, Abrielle felt a chill, knowing that the sister of Desmond, a man suspected of so many murders, had been feeding them. She went out into the autumn sunshine, trying to wipe away the feeling of so much evil.

CHAPTER 12

Some moments later, upon joining the kitchen staff that she had sent across the creek to deliver the food to the serfs' compound, Abrielle suffered something of a shock when she found Raven there also.

He was standing with a group of men, all the way to the far side of the large room, and yet, as if drawn by some power far greater than her will, her gaze instantly honed in on him among all others. She ought be accustomed to it by now, but still her heart clenched and quickened at the sight of his broad shoulders and proud bearing. For once, his full attention appeared riveted elsewhere, and in spite of how pleasing he was to look upon, Abrielle found herself curious to see what, besides her, he found so entertaining.

She followed his gaze to where Cedric, the laird, held a toddler upon his knee as he told a fanciful story of a hungry fox chasing after a rabbit and being tricked at every turn. Other children surrounded him on all sides and the elder's clever wit easily evoked delighted giggles from his young audience. They were clearly enthralled with the voices of his various characters, for which he seemed to have a rare talent. It soon became obvious to Abrielle that the witty laird took as much pleasure in the children and their responses as they relished the storyteller and his humorous tales. Much to everyone's delight, the rabbit escaped the fox, and the latter had to content himself catching a stringy old rat for sustenance.

The serfs were now less hesitant about coming forward to greet her. Indeed, they seemed eager to express their appreciation for what she was doing as the new mistress of the keep. Remembering how wary the young mother had seemed in Thurstan's presence, Abrielle was wont to suspect that the change in their behavior had much to do with his absence.

From his carefully chosen vantage point opposite the entrance, Raven was aware of Abrielle the instant she arrived. Since she'd so oft protested his watching her, he decided to appear not to take notice this time and see if she liked that better. 'Twas not an easy ruse to execute. He kept busy pitching in wherever he saw a need, hoisting a heavy crock or carrying away baskets which were emptied almost before they were taken off the cart. As fiercely as he longed to be near Abrielle, on this day he found a special pleasure in watching her from afar, and truthfully was more deeply moved by the sight of her rising to her new status as mistress of the keep than ever he'd been watching her twirl around the dance floor in her lace and baubles.

With her sleeves pushed high and curls pinned back, she worked alongside the kitchen staff to distribute the trenchers of food which, he knew, she'd personally gone to some trouble to have sent there. As a whole, the serfs eagerly accepted all that was offered, expressing their gratitude time and again. Abrielle met their effusive thanks with a smile so warm and joyful one would think they were the ones doing her the favor. Raven saw tears flow as grateful parents watched their offspring satisfy their hunger rather than being forced to endure a gnawing burning in their stomachs so intense that even sleep failed to provide them with an escape from the torment.

He'd noted the serfs' sorry lot right away. Now here they were, being nurtured by someone whose empathy toward them became obvious as soon as she assumed authority. It was no wonder their eyes grew misty and they sought to squeeze or kiss their mistress's hand as they offered their fervent gratitude for what she was doing for them. It lifted his heart to see those who had been obliged to bear the brunt of the squire's insensitivity and stingy authority for so long being treated with such kindness and generosity. And it filled him with pride, pride that was, to be fair, not yet his to claim, that Abrielle was the woman responsible.

Raven could be a patient man, especially when patience was part of a campaign that would lead to victory, oft to the frustration of those with whom he dealt as an emissary to King David. They would prefer he act recklessly or on impulse and thus give them an advantage. But that reputation was being sorely tested there in the serfs' compound, and very shortly after they'd appeased their hunger, he found an opportunity to approach the lady of the keep. She sat by the fire with a few of the younger children, and it did not please him to see her winsome smile give way to a look of wariness and resignation at his approach. Though it be a matter of pride, he wasn't used to a woman so distrusting him. He'd dared to hope his assistance the night of her husband's death would forge a bond between them; instead it seemed to have pushed the two of them even further apart.

He sat down beside her, focused on not making any sudden moves. As ridiculous as it sounded, there was no denying that the slow, gentling approach worked miracles with skittish animals all the time.

"'Tis a good thing ye're doing with these people," he told her quietly.

Her smile was reserved for the little girl in her lap, who was nestled to her bosom, contentedly sucking her thumb. "'Tis the right thing, therefore easy to do."

"Ye seem to be a born leader. Is that because ye're your mother's only child?"

She nodded, seemed about to speak, and then simply pressed her lips together. Abrielle was upset with herself that she'd almost shared Elspeth's good news as if Raven were a friend.

"I am my father's only child as well," he continued. "So that is something we have in common."

She slanted him a polite look and shrugged her delicate shoulders.

"Yes, indeed. He taught me everything I know, from sword fighting ta diplomacy. And taught me well."

"I can see that; so well you still travel with him as if you need a keeper."

He winced, glad the children couldn't detect her sarcasm. "Ye've pierced me, lass."

"Forgive me," she begged with feigned dismay. "I'd no idea the truth would be so painful for you."

Their gazes collided with an impact that made her eyes widen and brought a look of shock and panic to her face. Raven knew exactly what caused her to react so; she'd suddenly remembered the "truth" only the two of them shared about their role in the squire's death. And just as swiftly and surely he understood why instead of binding them together, that night figured strongly in her suspicion and distrust of him.

Softly, he tried to reassure her. " 'Tis true enough that some truths would only spread pain were they known by all. Ye have me word, my lady, honor bound, I would never speak them." He rose without another word and walked away, the knowledge he'd gained in this skirmish of value in his campaign to win her, for win her he would.

AFTER MAKING HER departure from the compound, Abrielle had already begun crossing the narrow bridge over the stream when she caught sight of Thurstan escorting Mordea to a horse-drawn cart an elderly serf had pulled to a halt before the drawbridge of the keep. A troop of at least twenty mounted men waited nearby. After Thurstan tossed a large sack of the woman's belongings into the back of the conveyance, Mordea bent down to pick up a rock from the ground and drop it into her apron pocket. Only then did she accept Thurstan's assistance onto the driver's bench.

Mordea slowly reined the animal about and then lifted an arm in farewell as she spoke to Thurstan in a foreign tongue. Then, upon settling her gaze upon the mistress of the keep, she gave a gleeful cackle and whipped the shaggy steed into a lively trot along the lane. Thurstan turned around in surprise as he discovered who was watching. As the conveyance passed near the spot where Abrielle had paused on the bridge, Mordea quickly retrieved the stone she had dropped into her pocket and flung it toward her erstwhile mistress.

Before Abrielle could even attempt to duck, Raven clasped an arm about her waist, sweeping her off her feet and whirling her abruptly about. She was clinging hard to his chest, her head tipped back so that she was looking into his eyes when she heard the well-aimed rock strike his back. He never flinched at the contact, and his hold on her never wavered. Trembling, she managed to give him a nod of thanks, knowing she could have been badly hurt but for him. She wanted nothing more than to rest her head on his strong chest and let him go on buffering her from the world for a few more moments or hours or forever, but the possibility that he was the biggest threat of all to her safety forced her to step away as quickly as possible from his body, too full of warmth and comfort.

Mordea snatched up the whip and elicited a sprightly trot from the steed in her haste to leave. Her fiendish laughter floated back to them, raising the hairs on the back of Abrielle's neck. She shook a threatening fist. "Mark me words, when ye're least expectin' it, ye'll be seein' me again. I'll slice yer gullets from ear ta ear, and then I'll be rippin' yer hearts out and roastin' 'em for me supper! That much I promise the lot of ye!"

Upon making that declaration, Mordea immediately launched into the language that she had earlier spewed, and although most of it was hardly discernible above the rattling of the cart's wheels as she drove it away, Cedric listened keenly to every word. Although Abrielle was not familiar with the tongue, she was convinced that it was no sacred blessing the hag had bestowed upon them.

"If ye were ta ask me, lass, I think the old crone meant ta lay ye low in your grave," Cedric said to Abrielle as he arrived on the bridge.

Thurstan made no move to join them, only took the reins of his horse from one of his men as he said, "I hope you were not injured, my lady."

"'Tis only by luck that she was not," Raven said darkly.

Abrielle saw the way the two men eyed each other with animosity, and quickly said, "Thurstan, you will see that she never returns to this keep again."

He nodded. "And I will see that your property, namely the horse and cart, are returned to you by the morrow." He took a deep breath, as if it pained him to say the next words. "My thanks, Sir Raven, for protecting Lady Abrielle from Mordea's foolish misjudgment."

"Misjudgment?" Raven echoed with contempt.

Again Abrielle spoke before the two men could do worse to each other. "Thurstan, you are taking your leave without even the courtesy of giving me notice?"

"I did not think you wished me to stay."

If he thought she would correct that impression, he was wrong.

"Good day, my lady," he said stiffly before mounting and riding off with his men.

Abrielle, Raven, and Cedric stood quietly for several moments, watching the troop ride away behind Mordea's cart.

"Lass," Cedric began, "why was Thurstan de Marlé escorting such a woman?"

She sighed. "She is not related to Thurstan, who is the son of Desmond's eldest late brother. But Mordea and Desmond shared the same mother, so perhaps Thurstan feels he owes her loyalty."

"Then 'tis good riddance to them both," Cedric said with finality.

But Abrielle couldn't help wondering if she'd truly seen the last of the pair.

AT SUPPER THAT evening, Arielle's suitors began to grow bolder. She was whisked from one to the next, whether it be for a dance or a conversation consisting mainly of one-sided boasting, and, as always, she could count on Raven being nearby. Even if his eyes were not on her every moment, she was more certain than ever that his awareness of her was absolute. He was like a big tiger stretched out in the sun, she thought, all sleepy and content, but God help the poor fool who tried to slip past and steal the treasure he guarded. That last thought brought her up short, and she was forced to ask herself, was she the treasure Raven guarded? There was something appealing about the notion, as it had been so long since she'd felt truly safe and protected. But there was also the frightening possibility that his only reason for protecting her was so he would be in a position to grab what she had to offer for himself when the time was right. She found it to be all so endlessly confusing and exhausting; if he wouldn't go away, Abrielle wished he could at least be less enticing so she could simply ignore him. How much easier her life would be if he were to grow horns, or awaken with a potbelly, or at least stop bathing.

At last she was able to plead exhaustion and escape the great hall. But before she could reach her door, she was approached by Sir Colbert, one of the Norman knights who yet lingered, hoping to win her favor.

"Lady Abrielle," he called, gasping as if he'd been breathing hard.

"Sir Colbert, what is it?"

"I was out walking this evening . . . and I heard . . . crying by the serfs' cottages."

"Crying?"

"One of the children . . . is ill. Do you know . . . the art of healing?"

"I do. Just let me get my cache of herbs."

Though he opened his mouth to speak, she had already hurried down the corridor. When Nedda had moved her to the master's chambers, she had transferred all of Abrielle's things, and it was easy enough to find the little leather bag.

She ran back into the corridor to find Sir Colbert looking both ways, then giving a start and nodding at her with encouragement.

"Come, my lady, I know the door that leads out through the lady's garden. It will be much quicker to reach the village."

Abrielle followed him gratefully, already worried about which little child could be ill. They were all in such a weakened state from lack of nourishment. She wasn't paying attention to which corridors Sir Colbert took, but at last she heard him unbolt a door, and smelled the fresh, wet earthiness of the garden.

She rushed out ahead of him, taking the garden paths quickly, her only goal to get beyond the half-wall fence, past the high walls of the castle, and over to the bridge leading across the moat. Several soldiers on guard watched her curiously, but none interceded.

She was almost to the stream when Sir Colbert cried, "My lady!"

When she turned to face him, she found him suddenly too close. He bent over and scooped her stomach-first onto his shoulder. She cried out in surprise and then was jarred awkwardly as he began to run.

"Put me down!"

"My horse is right here, my lady. We will reach the village much faster."

His shoulder slammed hard into her stomach, knocking the wind from her.

Abrielle knew he had no intention of heading to the village. He'd lied simply to get her away—to get her alone, where she'd be helpless against him. And all it would take was one night of rape, and she'd be forced to marry him, regardless of his cruelty. It was her worst nightmare coming true.

When she kicked him, he held her legs down; when she slapped and punched his back, he accepted it as if she could do him no harm. She opened her mouth for a loud shriek only to hear him say, "Do not scream, or my man will be forced to harm your maidservant."

Nedda? she thought wildly. Had they taken her from Abrielle's bedchamber so she wouldn't alert the keep about her mistress's disappearance?

"Is this the man ye refer to?" inquired a calm, deep voice that Abrielle recognized instantly.

Raven was rescuing her once again, eliciting two warring feelings from her, as she wanted both to cry and to cheer.

Sir Colbert stumbled to a halt and she heard the faint cry of another man who she surmised was lying at Raven's feet.

"I fear this man willna be of much help," Raven continued, his amusement obvious and oddly reassuring. "'Tis a shame ye didna think this through more carefully. I want the lass at least as much as ye do, so why would I let her out of my sight?"

Colbert suddenly made his move, flinging Abrielle

off so that she landed in a heap in Raven's arms. As she struggled to untangle herself, Colbert grabbed up his friend and practically tossed him over the horse's back and vaulted up behind him. The sound of hoofbeats faded away.

At last Abrielle straightened and pushed away from Raven a bit too forcefully.

He only smiled. "Ye're welcome."

"You have my thanks." She added, "Again," and as he looked down at her in the moonlight, his smile faded, and the intensity in his eyes took her by surprise.

"Ye look touched by fairy dust, lass," he whispered hoarsely.

Unable to face the dangerous weakness he inspired in her, she turned and hurried back the way she'd come. She heard him chuckle, knew he followed her, but she didn't stop until she was all the way back in the corridor outside her own bedchamber. She peeked inside and, to her relief, saw Nedda dozing in a chair by the fire, reassuring herself that at least Colbert had lied about that. She then returned to the corridor and knocked on her parents' door.

Raven waited patiently as it was answered by Vachel, who stared at Abrielle, and then at the Scotsman, in surprise. She strode past her stepfather and shut the door in Raven's face.

"Abrielle!" her mother cried with disapproval, coming forward as she tightened her robe.

"'Tis fine, he understands," Abrielle said wearily, sinking onto a stool. And then she told them everything that had happened. What she did not say was how empty and sick she felt inside, knowing that Sir Colbert hadn't even bothered to converse with her, to court her in the usual way, as if she weren't even worth the attempt.

"We thought you had gone to bed," Vachel later said as he paced, his stride long with anger.

Elspeth hugged her. "Oh, Abrielle, how frightening for you!"

"I didn't have much time to be frightened," she said glumly. "As usual, Raven had been following me."

"Thank God!" her mother said earnestly, an expression of relief that made Abrielle feel even worse, for it meant that she could not ever hope to control her own fate. Surely the look on the maiden's face conveyed her sorrow to her parents, but her stepfather's words evidenced that, indeed, her destiny did not lie in her own hands, but in the hands of others, the hands of men.

"I cannot allow this to go on," Vachel finally said, coming to a stop and giving them both a somber frown. "Colbert may not have meant to actually harm you, but the next cur might be desperate, should you refuse him. Abrielle, you have to marry soon, or you will remain in danger."

"But, Vachel, I have met no one who appeals to me. You know I wish to choose my own husband."

"And she certainly doesn't want to live with an armed escort everywhere she goes," Elspeth added.

"Why do we not just send every eligible man away?" Abrielle said brightly. "I could live in peace, for at least a while."

"And have eager swains besieging the castle?" Vachel demanded. "I think not. I have conceived of an idea to have this all done quickly. We will host a tournament, where all the noble young men gather to show off their skills and to win your favor."

"But we've just sent many of them away," Abrielle said plaintively. "Now we want them all back?"

"We do, but only the right men, of course. The tournament participants will be here for several days, and at the end of it, you will have met enough men to make your decision."

"Several days?" Elspeth said.

"We'll invite the families of these young men as well. You'll have more recommendations than you'll know what to do with. You'll be able to discover the character of every man you're considering."

Abrielle sighed. "I agree. This needs to be finished."

Vachel rubbed his hands together. "It'll begin in three days."

"Three days?" Elspeth echoed, already imagining trying to find a new cook on such short notice.

"Three days?" Abrielle echoed, wondering if her stepfather had gone mad. "How will we accomplish this?"

"We'll send out heralds today. Keeping the tournament so close will encourage only northern lords to attend. You certainly do not want a husband who's only lived on the Channel, with no idea how to deal with the Scots."

"And speaking of the Scots . . ." Elspeth began, looking at her daughter.

Abrielle slumped back on the bed. "Raven will compete for me, as hard as any of them. He'll win another purse, just as he did in the hunt."

"Perhaps we should offer more than a purse to the winner," her stepfather said, with a crafty look in his eye. "It will encourage competition."

Abrielle winced. "I am afraid to ask your meaning."

"Perhaps the knight will win . . . a kiss."

COLBERT RODE HARD through the night and was met with the welcome he'd anticipated. Thurstan de Marlé opened his gates to the young man, sheltering him—and nurturing Colbert's hatred of the Scot who'd foiled his perfect plan to win Abrielle.

CHAPTER 13

Over the next three days, Abrielle managed to stay so busy that she rarely spoke to Raven, except at meals. She knew he still kept watch over her, but she ignored him as best she could, and tried to enjoy an event in her honor. She was free of the cloud of gloom with Desmond de Marlé's passing, and she told herself that with the freedom to pick her own husband, she had more than most other maidens.

She kept her maidservants company making banners and armbands to identify both teams competing in the tournament. She spent hours every day in the kitchen with her mother, where they learned that Weldon's cooks had not left, but had been forced to serve beneath Mordea the last several months. The women were grateful to have back the freedom to exercise their creativity, and the menus they all planned together would surely soothe the appetite of everyone in attendance.

In the surrounding countryside, colorful pavilions began to spring up to house the many combatants. The castle would be overflowing with their families, parents, and siblings, all the northern lords who wished a day of excitement. Pavilions were set up throughout the wooded course to be used as refuges during the melee itself, so that knights could rest or rearm themselves.

On the day before the tournament, the surrounding roads were filled with traveling companies approaching the castle. Children of visiting families raced through the courtyard, chased by nurses, and Abrielle dared to imagine a day when they would be her children. And she found within herself the strength to dare to dream that somewhere within these walls she would at last find the man who would be a true husband to her, with whom she would share a love everlasting.

The only thing that worried her was the attention Raven and his father received. There was a marked increase in surliness from the Norman and Saxon lords, even more so than when many of them had been present not a sennight before. Had they expected Raven and Cedric to be gone, and their very presence was proving too much provocation? The border had been enjoying an uneasy peace for several years; there was no reason for such animosity, especially toward a man who had the notice of the king. Abrielle didn't need angry men entering a tournament and turning it into a real battle. They used their own weapons, not the blunted weapons using by youths in training. In such tense situations, too many men inevitably died.

In the great hall that night, a feast was served that surpassed the expectations of everyone in attendance. Abrielle and her parents sat at the head table, raised on a dais. She could see her guests breaking open the fine white loaves of bread, proving that no expense had been spared. They'd roasted an oxen whole in the kitchen yard, and served larks'-tongue pie, a great delicacy. The last fresh vegetables of autumn were served in the salad, dressed with oil and verjuice. There was minced mutton with herbs and bread crumbs, cheeses served on heaping platters, and at last, a selection of tarts and pies that had everyone patting their full stomachs and sighing.

Elspeth shared a triumphant smile with her daughter, who was caught up in the excitement and energy of a large, happy crowd. After the meal, Abrielle found herself the focus of many of the knights, all of whom wanted a token of hers to take into the melee on the morrow. She could not show such favoritism as the hostess, so she encouraged the men to seek out the other maidens in attendance.

More than one man proved bold enough to ask Vachel why the Scot was being allowed to compete, and Vachel told the same story over and over again: Raven was an emissary of the King of Scotland and had found favor at King Henry's court. Why should Vachel insult either king by dismissing him?

Abrielle was dancing with a pleasant young man, who kept stepping on her toes in his eagerness, when the great double doors to the hall were thrown back. A gust of wind shivered the candle flames, and silence spread as all turned to see who was making such a late entrance.

Thurstan de Marlé led a contingent of knights a score strong from his own manor. Abrielle excused herself from her disappointed partner to go in search of her stepfather, whom she found sharing tankards of ale before the hearth with Cedric Seabern.

Cedric bowed to her even as her stepfather searched her face and demanded, "What is wrong, Abrielle?"

"Did you not see who has just arrived?" she asked, sweeping a hand toward Thurstan.

Vachel grimaced. "I did. But I could not bar his entrance, not when he was Desmond's nephew, and well respected throughout the north. He has every right to be here."

"He asked my hand in marriage," she said shortly, folding her arms over her chest in an almost protective gesture that she didn't recognize.

Vachel frowned at her in surprise. "He came to you instead of me?"

"He feels the inheritance should be his, not mine, and sought access to it through me."

"You did not tell me this," Vachel began slowly.

"Would telling you have forestalled his appearance here tonight?"

"Nay," he conceded. "Likely it would not."

"I thought as much." She sighed. "I'd hoped this tournament would be a step toward simplifying my life, but it's barely begun and already there is another man I must do my best to avoid."

"Not ta intrude where I oughtn't," said Cedric, a sparkle of amusement in his his blue eyes, "but if ye're half as deft at shunning this new arrival as ye are my son, I'd say yer worries are few."

Coming from anyone else, Abrielle might have taken umbrage, but it was difficult to feel offended when Cedric's smile and his tone were so gently teasing. Still, she felt her cheeks warm. Teasing or not, she did not owe any man her notice; perhaps the best way to get that message to Raven was through his father.

"I assure you, dear sir, I only ignore your brave son as an act of kindness."

"And I in turn assure ye, lass, it's not as a kindness he's taking it."

"Naturally. You see, this kindness is directed toward the countless other eligible ladies in the land. I wouldn't dream of monopolizing the time of a man who legend has it has turned more pretty heads than there are fish in the sea."

The Scotsman threw back his head and laughed richly. "By God, the lad's met his match in ye," he told her, looking quite pleased it was the case. "I can't argue he's turned his share of heads, and now he's havin' ta struggle ta turn the only one that matters. Don't ye worry, m'lady, he's a quick study and it will all work out right in the end."

"I'm not sure exactly what you mean by 'right,'" countered Abrielle. "I fear you may be disappointed in the outcome. There is much between our peoples that would prove insurmountable, Laird Cedric."

"And that be your only reason for na including Raven on whatever private list ye're compiling?" His mouth curved beneath his mustache. "That and, of course, your generous regard for the rest of womanhood?"

She shook her head, firmly, since the laird was proving as difficult to discourage as his offspring. "Nay, there are other reasons. I will say only that we would not suit, and I do beg your pardon if that offends you."

"Not at all, lass. Ye have ta know your own mind."

But he winked at her over his bushy mustache, as if he was privy to her thoughts, and it seemed obvious he assumed she secretly favored Raven. *Ye have ta know your own mind,* he said. Raven himself had insisted it was her opinion of the man she was to marry which mattered, and no one else's, though it would be much easier to determine what she was thinking if everyone would stop telling her what she should think. Not that she needed to devote more time to pondering Raven's place in her life, for there wasn't one. She had to find a man in whose love she could believe, someone without a royal emissary's skill at dissembling. It was clear that her fate was to be in the hands of men, but at least she could chose that man. She would seize this time to find him; he must be here this night, just waiting for her notice.

As she moved back among her guests, smiling and nodding, she saw a disheartening sight: Sir Colbert had arrived with Thurstan, and was even now standing at his side. When Colbert saw that he had attracted her notice, he gave an exaggerated bow, grinning at her. He said something to Thurstan, and both began to laugh in an ugly manner, surely at her expense. She turned away, adding another man to her list of men to avoid during the tournament. She would have to make sure she never walked about alone.

She almost ran into Raven in her haste to stay away from Thurstan. The place was overrun by men she'd prefer to avoid, she thought as he caught her by her elbows. He used the advantage of height to look over her head as he imagined her pain, knowing that a man who'd tried to kidnap and rape her was bold enough to attend her tournament. It came as no surprise that, in her usual fashion, she was putting on a brave front, looking from Raven's face, to his hands on her arms, and back to his face again. He released her, giving an unapologetic grin even as his admiration deepened.

"My lady, ye're the center of attention for every man present—whether ye want ta be or no."

She rolled her eyes. "At present, I'd be ridiculously

content if only you did not make me your center of attention. Surely there are beautiful maidens here for you to peruse."

"But none shines as brightly as ye," he murmured, his gaze softening without losing any of its wry amusement. He watched her blush and was thankful for her smooth fair skin. The color in her cheeks, or sudden loss of it, along with whatever shone or flickered in her sweet eyes, provided some insight into her true feelings, allowing him to see that she was not at all indifferent to him, no matter what she tried to make him, and herself, believe.

"Forgive me, I must see to my other guests," she said, moving past him.

"I understand," he murmured with a scant bow. "I know I'm but one of many awaiting your notice."

He'd spoken more loudly than he'd intended, and saw he had the notice of others besides Abrielle. Never before had he felt the animosity of so many people, all directed at him because of the country where he was born. He was more trusted in King Henry's Norman court, where he was given free access to the king. Now he stood his ground and cocked a dark eyebrow at them, daring them to challenge him.

But Vachel was calling for attention from his place before the hearth, and although Raven turned his head, he knew it was not wise to present his back to such dishonorable enemies.

"Honored guests, daring knights, it is now time to choose teams for tomorrow's tournament. I have in this leather bag a collection of stones, painted either red or green, with armbands and banners to match, courtesy of the ladies of the castle."

There were huzzahs and raised tankards of ale toward

the head table, and Raven saw Abrielle and her mother smile at each other.

Vachel hefted the bag. "Please come forward and draw your stone."

As one by one each knight pulled out a stone, there were good-natured cheers or jeers, and much slapping on backs. But when it was Raven's turn to pick, the hall turned silent, but for the whispers of the ladies. Raven met Abrielle's cool gaze, and she only lifted her chin. He drew out a red stone, and he understood that the resulting cheers were from men on the opposite team. Those on his own team only muttered to one another. Ah well, it was truly an individual sport, after all, and he was certain that by the end, he would succeed in helping his own team to win.

"Besides the horses and armor you capture," Vachel continued, and a shout went up, "there will also be a sizable purse to the knight who performs the best. We well-seasoned knights will make that decision." He looked among several graying and balding men, who all nodded knowingly. "And lastly, to this champion knight will be awarded an even greater gift, a kiss from your hostess, Lady Abrielle."

The cheers and applause were deafening, and Raven lifted his goblet in toast to her, as did every other man in the hall. A kiss from Abrielle was in truth the only prize he wanted; he alone of all the men in the hall knew the precise softness of her lips and the sweetness of her warm breath on his skin. Aye, it made him want her more, made him want her madly, made him burn for her. And it made him more determined than ever that this was a prize he would share with no man.

In response to the cheers, Abrielle smiled and her cheeks colored. She was by far the most beauteous woman in attendance. Though she was newly a widow, and still clothed in black, the somber color only served as the setting for the riotous beauty of her copper tresses, and the shining light of her blue-green eyes. Raven knew in that moment that every eligible bachelor in the hall was determined to win her kiss—and her hand. They were, one and all, bound for disappointment, for they would have to defeat him for the honor; he had never approached an event wanting to win more than he did now. He had yet to impress her, so perhaps a feat of arms would at least draw her attention.

Abrielle felt hot with embarrassment and pleasure as she looked out over the sea of men cheering her. She was trying to pretend that it was for her alone these men lusted, rather than her wealth, and for the most part she succeeded, determined to enjoy the tournament.

As the minstrels began to play again, Vachel came to stand beside her and Elspeth.

"I think the tournament was a wonderful idea, my dear," Elspeth said to her husband.

"Only if it helps Abrielle," he reminded her.

Abrielle slid her hand into his arm and gave him a gentle squeeze. "Your help is all I could ask for."

"'Tis a shame that Raven Seabern will have no help."

"What do you mean?" she asked, her gaze finding him in the crowd, where he stood alone with his father.

"His position is precarious. You saw the reaction of those on his own team to his presence. They will not willingly defend him. It'll be as if he competes alone, a team of one."

"Then perhaps he should not have entered," she murmured.

Vachel gave her a sardonic look. "And did you think he'd just give up in his quest for you? He is a proud, determined man."

"You sound as if you approve of him."

"I do not necessarily approve of him as your husband. And neither would most of the people in attendance. I have heard that Thurstan has been whispering in many ears, fomenting hatred of the Scots. If war should break out, and you were married to Raven, I know you would be torn in your loyalties."

"Although your first loyalty is always to your husband," Elspeth added.

Abrielle said nothing, for she had no plans to ever face such a dilemma. Yet always, if she wasn't concentrating, her gaze would wander to Raven. She didn't want to have to worry about him on the morrow. She had not thought that he might be attacked by men fighting for the same team. But as he stood smiling and talking to his father, he looked so at ease, so confident. He probably wanted the purse more than he wanted her, for he was impressed with wealth. She would not worry, she told herself, for his foolish need to enter was not her concern.

When Abrielle was escorted away for another dance, Vachel looked down at his wife and frowned. "She protests far too much where Raven is concerned."

"I know," Elspeth murmured as she slid her hand into his. "I think she is frightened to give her heart to any man."

"I am to blame," Vachel said heavily. "If it weren't for me, she never would have felt she had to marry Desmond de Marlé. I think even the betrothal scarred her."

"And the fear of what she would face. God granted her freedom from such a nightmare, but I'm worried she'll never find peace."

Vachel squeezed her hand. "God has been looking after our Abrielle. Trust in Him."

BY MIDMORNING, WHEN the sun peeked out of an overcast sky, Abrielle shaded her eyes and found herself looking again for Raven. She sat in stands built for the occasion, running along the main field of the melee. But since there were no boundaries, only some of the battles were fought before her, while others were chased through the countryside only to disappear within woodland.

She could still hear the hoarse war cries at the opening horn as the two opposing teams had ridden hard at each other. The clash of their weapons had been fierce, and more than one knight had been unhorsed and taken captive almost immediately. Throughout the morning, several men had been carried to the healers' tent, but she had heard of no deaths, thank God.

Of Raven, she had seen little. She was almost embarrassed to admit to herself that she had marked the shape of his helmet in her mind, as well as the attacking raven emblazoned on his shield, so that she would know him when she saw him again. He had knocked an opponent from his saddle at the opening horn, but after grabbing the reins of the other man's horse, he'd galloped away with his prize into the trees, probably searching for his team's pavilion. As he did so, Elspeth sat down beside her.

"And how are you feeling, Mama?" Abrielle asked.

Elspeth was pale, but she nodded. "Fine, my dear. I was able to eat some bread, so I am much improved. Have you seen—"

When she broke off, Abrielle lifted a brow. "Raven? Not very subtle, Mama."

"I only ask because your stepfather is concerned that he is a vulnerable target."

"Not all that vulnerable," Vachel said, coming to sit beside them. "I just heard that he's unhorsed five men, and his team's pavilion is filling up with his prizes. In fact, isn't that him now?"

Abrielle tried to pretend disinterest, but watched avidly as several horsemen came thundering out of the trees. Raven was in the lead, but then Abrielle realized that he was being chased by four knights. Others blocked his path, and as he wheeled his horse about, one knight's lance struck him a glancing blow across his hauberk, flinging him from the saddle. The crowd gasped and rose as one, and Abrielle knew many were hoping to see Raven captured, his tournament at an end. But he rolled to his feet and unsheathed his sword in one motion. While mounted knights milled around him, he fought savagely, parrying their sword thrusts, slashing toward their horses until they were forced to retreat one at a time or risk losing their mounts—or their own legs. At last one knight fell as he attempted to escape Raven's sword, and Raven snatched up the man's reins and vaulted into the saddle. To Abrielle's surprise there were people in the stands who cheered his triumph and display of courage.

Without thinking, she was on her feet, laughing and cheering with them. She told herself it was simply good manners; if she did not participate wholeheartedly in her own tournament, how could she expect anyone else to? Admiring Raven's skill on the field was not the same as approving of him. No matter what the swift and too frantic beating of her foolish heart might suggest.

"Have you seen Thurstan?" she asked her stepfather when the combatants had again disappeared into the trees.

Vachel hadn't, but later in the afternoon, when the sun began to set, and the knights were close to exhaustion, Thurstan and several of his men rode onto the field, their helms undented, no blood seeping from beneath their chain mail.

"Vachel," Abrielle said, "do they look refreshed to you? Perhaps they have been taking advantage of a refuge to rest."

Vachel shook his head. "It is a trick some use in tournaments, to wait until most of the field is spent, and then gallop on and defeat your opponents. It is a legal maneuver, but not very honorable."

"Thurstan and his men are targeting Raven," Elspeth said, clutching Abrielle's sleeve.

Raven had been riding away, leading a captured knight from the field, when Thurstan and his men surrounded him. Raven proceeded to defend his captive from being taken, all while unhorsing several of Thurstan's men. Though Thurstan himself struck several blows across Raven's shield and helm, he did not make the attempt to challenge Raven alone. One knight raced at Raven from behind, and the crowd gasped and rose to its feet when the knight's sword was raised high. At the last moment Raven sensed the attack and met it with his shield. The knight fell hard from his horse and lay still, heaped awkwardly on the trampled earth.

At that moment the horn sounded an end to the tournament. From her place in the stands, Abrielle was not conscious of how frantically worried she had been that something would happen to Raven until that instant, when the breath she'd been holding whooshed out of her and she felt her palms sting where the nails of her clenched fingers had dug small half-moons.

Someone brought a healer onto the field and the knights withdrew to count their winnings. Only Raven remained, standing with shoulders squared, his long hair waving about his shoulders like a victory flag as he waited to see how his opponent had fared. At last they carried the fallen knight off the field, removing his helm as they did, and Abrielle saw it was Sir Colbert. As they passed before her, she could see him stir and was relieved. In spite of the fact that he had attacked Raven from behind and then fallen, she knew the melee could have degenerated into a real battle if he'd died.

In the stands, Vachel and the older men gathered together and spoke in quiet tones, deciding the champion of the tournament. It wasn't long before he nodded, turned to face the crowd, and lifted his hands for the attention of the spectators. Knights walked or limped or helped one another as they assembled to hear Vachel speak. "Good people, we give thanks that no one was killed today, nor were there any injuries more serious than broken bones. My fellow judges and I have given much thought to our selection for the best knight of the tournament, but in the end, our decision was almost unanimous. For taking twelve men hostage, defending them against others, and generously sharing his winnings with his teammates, we award the top purse to Raven Seabern."

Abrielle was not at all surprised—or sorry—to hear Raven proclaimed the victor. He deserved the honor. She was a bit surprised, however, when several dozen people cheered him and she assumed it was due to his unexpected generosity. Whether he was buying their goodwill or attempting to ease hard feelings, it didn't matter. She searched the crowd and found him with his father. As the laird helped remove his chain-mail hauberk, she saw bloodstains on the padded gambeson he wore beneath and winced silently. The blows he took must have been powerful indeed to do such damage. And when he lifted his head, she saw a gash streaming blood on his cheek, where his visor must have cut him. Once free of the heavy mail, he stood, and judging from the exhaustion evident in his slow movements, she realized he was being driven by fierce pride alone. As he came forward for his purse, he did not limp or falter.

Vachel grinned as he handed over a clinking purse, and there was some polite applause as well as the usual angry murmurs. Then, one by one, people began to look expectantly at Abrielle, and she remembered that she, too, played a part in his reward.

How could she have forgotten about the kiss, and how could she have ever agreed to it in the first place? Too late she realized that she ought to have known Raven would be the winner and that it would come down to this moment. She needed to think and to endeavor to gather her wits about her; she needed to steady her pulse and steel her heart. She needed time, and she had none. That was made dangerously clear when Raven stopped before her and executed a sweeping bow that somehow managed to be chivalrous and mocking at once.

"My lady," he said.

Abrielle bowed her head. If he wanted to play at being gracious, she would oblige. "Sir. Your performance today was spectacular, your skill with a sword and as a horseman no less than dazzling. Would that I could offer a prize more befitting your deeds."

"Would that I could pluck the stars from the sky ta rival your beauty," he replied, his voice pitched low. "'Twould be the only deed near deserving of the prize ye do offer."

To her chagrin, Abrielle found she was unable to speak or breathe or look away. Damn him for the way he could so easily turn her composure to melted butter. It was unnerving enough when they were not being watched by scores of chuckling onlookers; this was impossible.

And then, as quickly as he'd rattled her, he saved her. It was another thing at which the man had proven himself to be so very irritatingly adept.

"Truth, 'tis this very prize that sustained me these long hours, and I would not rush the claiming, or subject ye ta the dirt and stench I carried from the field. I beg your indulgence; allow me ta bathe and change, for I wouldna want ta converse with ye under these conditions."

"Converse?" someone called, while others laughed.

Abrielle nodded agreement, grateful for any delay. But even as she began to relax, she could not stop looking at the ugly cut high on his cheek. It was still oozing blood, and without thinking she blurted, "Sir Raven, allow me to stitch the wound on your face. You may accompany me to the lady's solar."

"I should bathe—"

"Think you I have not smelled a man who's done a day's work?"

People around them laughed.

"The wound needs to be cleansed," she finished.

To her surprise, he offered, "I could go ta the healers' tent."

Vachel smiled and put an arm around his shoulders. "And wait to be attended when you are our champion? Nonsense. Abrielle is a skilled healer herself."

And so Abrielle found herself walking up to the castle at Raven's side. She could feel the heat of his exertions still steaming from his body. His face ran with perspiration, and his dark hair was wet with it. She thought she detected him favoring his right leg, but said nothing, her woman's instinct warning that he was far too proud to admit to it, especially to her. The knowledge of his fierce pride and strength warmed her in a deep and unfamiliar manner.

The great hall was bare but for servants preparing for the evening's feast, yet even their eyes were upon the two who walked silently through their midst. Abrielle was grateful at last to be in the dark, torchlit corridors of the keep. When she led him into her solar, she was taken aback to find her maidservants nowhere in sight; then she realized that they were, of course, still in the crowd outside. Which meant that she and Raven would be alone, in a room that suddenly felt very small indeed, while she tended his wounds.

She glanced around worriedly, uselessly hoping a stray servant might suddenly come forth from some nook or cranny. When none did, she was forced to accept the truth, that she would simply have to take care of him on her own. To that end, she squared her shoulders, drew a deep breath, and reminded herself that she was a healer and her sole reason for being there was to use her skills to do what she'd been trained to do, the same as she would for any man, woman, or child in need of her help. The fact that it was Raven Seabern in need, and that they were alone, mattered naught.

Then he closed the door and put his back to it, his face bloodied, his dark warrior's gaze seeking hers across the deserted room, and suddenly the fact that he was Raven Seabern and they were alone were the only things that did, indeed, matter.

CHAPTER 14

"Where would ye like me ta sit?" Raven asked.

Abrielle did not answer immediately. She did not need to stare at the sweat-damp fabric clinging to every sinew and bulge on his broad chest to know that being alone with him was worse than unwise, it was dangerous. Yet her imprudent gaze refused to be steered in any other direction. She was seldom as certain of anything as she was that she would live to regret it if she did not that very instant announce that she was very sorry, but there was no need for him to sit at all since she had changed her mind and he would have to have his wounds tended elsewhere. But the blood on his face was now dripping onto his very distracting chest, and more dried blood was visible through the numerous rips and tears, and regardless of the danger she might be in, she could not in good conscience let his injury fester.

"You may sit on the bench by the fire," she told him finally, using her most no-nonsense tone. "And, if it doesn't pain you too much, you might swing the cauldron over the flames. There is already water inside."

He did as she asked, and then began to unlace his gambeson.

"What are you doing?" she demanded.

He peered at her over the collar, his dark brows raised. "Did ye na say ye would treat my wounds?" She nodded at him, somewhat confused by his question.

"Ye would prefer ta tend them through my garments?" he inquired, eyeing her soberly, as if that were a perfectly acceptable choice.

"Nay, I only . . . I thought . . . I'm sorry, of course you must remove your garment."

He began to do so and winced.

"You need help," she observed, starting toward him without pausing to think.

"Mayhap," he agreed. "I could send for my squire. I can manage the unlacing, but the thing is stiff with blood in places and difficult ta lift over my head."

Abrielle bit her lip and weighed the awkwardness of undressing him against the risk of spending more time alone with him, sweaty and half dressed, as they waited for his squire to be summoned and arrive.

"No need," she said, deciding in favor of haste in the matter. "Since I'm already here, I can help in your squire's stead." She endeavored to sound brusque and efficient, rather than reveal her true state, which was one of fear, apprehension, and, she had to admit to herself, excitement. She didn't want to be alone with him like this, helping him disrobe, feeling all shaky and strange inside.

She moved only close enough to touch him with outstretched arms, but he swung around, cutting that cautious distance in half, as he lifted his arms over his head. Grasping the bottom edge of the loosened gambeson, she tugged upward.

"Ouch." It was far more bark than whimper, but more than enough to cause Abrielle to stop the moment the word was uttered.

"I think," he said, sidling even closer, close enough for her to feel his breath on her neck when he gazed up at her, "that 'tis best we do this very, very slowly."

As innocent as she was, Abrielle was woman enough to deduce that the sudden heaviness of his breathing was not due to pain alone. He was as disturbed by their nearness as she was; she heard it in his rough-edged burr and saw it in the heat in his eyes.

"That is one approach," she acknowledged, swaying toward him just long enough to secure her grip on the garment. "But I am of the mind 'tis best to rip it off in one motion. Like this," she added, doing so.

"God's soul, woman," he muttered.

"I'm sorry to have caused you pain, but it really is best over and done with." She eyed him worriedly. "Did I hurt you overmuch?"

His attempt to scoff ebbed into a cough. "Just a wee bit, lass. And 'tis grateful I am for your care, no matter the cost. 'Tis an angel of mercy ye are."

He was left with only a linen shirt and the leggings worn beneath his chain mail. The shirt had a dark patch of blood across his ribs, and it stuck to his skin when he moved. He loosened the laces and was about to pull the shirt off when Abrielle stopped him. After dipping a cloth in the warm water, she gently pressed it over the wounded area, moistening the shirt until she was satisfied she could pull it away from his skin easily.

"Stand up," she said. He obeyed and Abrielle took

the open front of his shirt in her hands. "I promise it won't hurt this time."

Slowly, her touch whisper-soft, she floated the shirt away from his body, leaving him standing before her naked from the waist up. She had to close her eyes until she remembered how to breathe. Though there was a wide scrape across his ribs that even now continued to bleed slowly, she could only see the width of his chest and the smooth, curving slopes of his muscles. She knew he was looking down at her, but she did not dare meet his gaze.

It was when a drop of blood from his face splashed onto his chest that she was brought back to herself. "You may sit now," she told him, her own knees feeling weak, and when she, too, was seated, she dipped a clean cloth into the heated water and pressed it gently to his face.

"Hold this here while I see to your ribs. I do not think the wound there is so deep."

"Aye, I took a blow from a lance. More of a scrape than anything. The bruise will be bonny."

"It already is," she said drily. She decided to pretend he was simply any other man, one of many she'd treated in the past, but the ruse just did not work. Touching his skin made her feel things she was sure no decent maiden should feel. She could hear his breathing as if it were her own, smell the tang of his smooth skin, and see the pulse beating in the intriguing hollow of his throat.

She quickly stepped away and opened her cache of herbs. Grinding several together, she made a paste and spread it across the wound, before winding long strips of fresh linen about his torso to keep the area clean.

"You can don your shirt," she said with great relief when it was done.

"Over my face?" he asked, the bloody towel still pressed to his cheek.

She felt foolish and knew her own face was afire. "My apologies. I'm so tired that I cannot keep my mind on the task at hand."

"Ah. Then 'tis but fatigue I feel when I'm near ye and every other thought and care turn ta naught?" he asked softly.

"How should I know what it is you feel?" she snapped, and though she tried to scowl as she reached for the towel in his hand, her touch was gentle. She carefully pulled it away from his face and washed the wound, troubled to see that it still bled freely. "I fear I'll need to stitch this closed."

"Or burn it," he suggested matter-of-factly, shrugging when she looked aghast. "I've had that done before."

"It has not been done by me, and not on your face."

"So, ye dinna want ta ruin my handsome looks?"

"You flatter yourself," she retorted. "Have you considered that I do not want to be the cause of making you even more frightening to animals and small children?"

"Needle and thread, it is," he agreed.

She was thankful for the rare lighthearted moment, hoping to hide the effect he truly had on her. Something had changed between them, or mayhap something had changed inside her. 'Twould take more thought to sort it out than she could hope to muster with the double distraction of his body that she'd just watched perform feats of strength and daring, and the expression of undisguised interest on his darkly handsome face. It would be easy to let herself be carried away at moments such as this, if not for the fact that his easy charm was a reminder of the time he hadn't bothered to be nearly so amiable to her. Say what he might in defense of his treatment of her on their first meeting, of his refusal to court her when he could have, a woman in her position needed to be certain of a man, and she could never be certain about Raven. She could not allow herself to forget that only now was he choosing to use his charm on her, that he'd not deemed her worthy before.

"This will hurt," she said as she settled near him with the threaded needle in hand.

"I'll manage, lass," he replied, his tone warmly reassuring.

The only way she could comfortably work on his face was to stand above him. But he was so large that even with him seated on the bench, she barely had to bend over to work on him. She was hesitant when first she had to push the needle into his flesh, but he didn't even flinch, so she quickly pulled it through the other side.

His eyes were so blue as he looked at her, his lashes so dark and long, she simply had to force herself to think about something else; she decided to comment on the tournament, saying, "My stepfather tells me that Thurstan's attack on you was a legal maneuver."

He waited until she was pulling on the thread to say, "'Twas, therefore I knew ta be prepared, especially with one such as he."

"But the rest of the field had been competing all day. To just wait until the end like that . . ."

"But he didna win that way, because he couldna collect enough captives."

"I don't think he cared about winning as much as attacking you."

"Concerned about me, lass?" His low voice rumbled through him, through her hands that rested on his face.

"I'm concerned about fairness," she answered primly.

"Och, there's nothing fair in war."

"But this wasn't war!" she remarked hotly.

"It's always war ta men like Colbert. All part of the game, ye know."

She held the needle back to study him. "How can you take this all so blithely, when you could have been killed?"

"And would ye have grieved for me?"

"As I would for any fallen champion," she told him. "There. 'Tis done. And with your handsome face more or less unaltered."

He laughed softly as she looked about quizzically. "Shears . . . shears," she murmured to herself. "I know you're here somewhere."

"Use your teeth," urged Raven.

She rolled her eyes. "It would tug on your stitches."

"I can bear it . . . can ye?"

There was a dangerous gleam in his eyes and Abrielle knew he was thinking about how close she would have to get to him to do as he was daring. She wanted to curse the blood of the bold Berwin of Harrington that coursed through her veins, rendering her so often incapable of tamping down the desire, indeed, the need, to meet a challenge offered. As if in slow motion, she bent forward, gripping the knot with her fingers to keep the tension away from his face, then bit the thread in two. His moist breath on her neck was hot and thrilling. She felt his arms come around her hips and stiffened, pushing against his shoulders.

"What are you doing?" she demanded, bothered by how breathless her voice sounded.

"I'm about my prize now."

"But it should be given in public, where all can see that I fulfilled my part of the bargain."

"Worry not, lass, they'll assume I took my kiss in private."

Swooping an arm around her shoulders, he lifted her up and laid her across his lap as his open mouth plummeted down upon hers. Overcome and overwhelmed, answering his kiss with all the passion she was capable of exhibiting, Abrielle yielded to the intrusion of his tongue, welcoming it tentatively with her own before their passions intensified to a flaming fire that burned within them. She became as hungry for him as he was for her and found herself clinging to him as if they were the only couple in the world. She felt compelled to press close against him as her exploring fingers stroked over his back.

Raven had known that she would be passionate; his fear was that after all her denials, she would not be capable of feeling it for him. She tasted of the sweetest strawberries, all warm and moist, making him think of pressing for more than just a kiss.

Suddenly Abrielle gasped and scrambled off his lap, her breasts rising and falling as she struggled to breathe. "That was . . . that was . . . cruel and unfair."

"How so?" he countered. "Ye freely offered a kiss ta the winner, and I always win." His blue eyes were now darker than ever, the color seemingly taken from the most tempestuous of ocean waters.

She cursed herself for having fallen, however briefly, under his spell. "'Twould serve you well to remember that 'always' is a long time. You'd be wise not to take my lapse in good sense here today as a sign. I will never marry you, for I cannot trust you. Count yourself fortunate to have won the tournament purse, because you'll never have my possessions, you'll never have me." This last she spat out, her blue-green eyes flashing, her wrath that of an outraged lioness.

She turned her back on him and ran, wishing she could closet herself in her own bedchamber, but knowing she had to play the hostess at the final feast of the tournament. Throughout the evening, she smiled and said all the correct things, but she felt like a puppet, as if someone else were telling her what to say. It took every effort not to look at Raven, not to burst into tears of sorrow and anger. She should be choosing among her suitors, but their faces blurred together, their smiles seemed false, and she could not think what to ask to learn about each of them. She felt like a failure, and knew by her mother's troubled frown that her parents were worried about her.

OVER THE NEXT two days, the castle once again emptied of visitors, and Abrielle avoided the question of choosing her husband. She knew her mother and Vachel were being patient with her, a kindness she truly appreciated. She made lists of names, and wrote down the reasons each man would make a good husband, but every time she thought of exchanging a wedding kiss, she saw herself in Raven's arms.

Sleep came with difficulty, and on the third night, she thought she would be exhausted enough to finally sleep until dawn, but in the wee hours of the morning she came slowly awake, hearing a muted weeping, interspersed with cries of pain, drifting from the corridor just outside her chambers.

A sudden fear that some sort of tragedy had happened and that her mother was at her door, needing to speak with her, sent a cold chill shivering down her spine. Desmond's fall down the stairs was too fresh in her mind to imagine that such a thing couldn't happen again, perhaps even to one she fervently loved.

Frantic to learn who was weeping and what had prompted it, she struck sparks against a flint to light several tapers in the candelabrum beside her bed before slipping a robe over her nightgown. Upon snatching up the fixture, she held it aloft to light her way as she hurried into the antechamber. For the sake of caution, she pressed an ear against the door, but all seemed quiet, at least at the moment.

"Who is out there?" she queried.

"M'lady, don't ope . . . !"

Recognizing her maidservant's voice, she set aside the candleholder and then paused as she heard what sounded like a slap, followed by a muted groan. Abrielle's hackles stood up, for it seemed evident that some brutish knave was cuffing Nedda about.

Appalled, she lifted the oak plank from its niches and, after hurriedly setting it aside, snatched the portal open. Her eyes immediately fell on Nedda, who was garbed in a robe and nightgown. At the moment the woman was lying on her side on the floor. Blood trickled from the corner of her mouth and across her cheek. Standing behind the woman was an enormous oaf whose face was badly scarred and heavily bearded. A voluminous bush of gray-streaked black hair flowed around his massive shoulders.

An intensely foul odor drew her gaze askance. A startled gasp was wrenched from her as she espied a shorter, somewhat wider version of the huge lummox who towered over Nedda pressed against the wall beside her door. Like his companion, his gray-streaked hair was so wild and woolly that it was impossible to tell where his hair ended and his facial bush began. For barely an instant he grinned at her with rotting teeth fully in evidence, and then, as she whirled about in a frantic effort to return to her chambers, he leapt forward to seize her.

Retreating with a startled gasp, Abrielle sought to slam the door in the brigand's face, but he pushed it inward with such force that she was sent stumbling across the antechamber. Crashing into a chest near her bedchamber door, she experienced a sudden, sharp pain as her head hit the stone wall behind it, nearly knocking her senseless. Stunned, she slithered over the top of the chest, past its decorated doors, and finally came to rest on the rug. From there, she peered as if through a long tunnel at the short, rotund beast who sauntered near.

Leaning his head aslant to align his face with hers, the man grinned at her in obvious amusement. "Me name's Fordon, if 'n ye be a-wonderin'." He threw a thumb over his shoulder to indicate the larger oaf standing over Nedda. "That's Dunstan."

"What do you want?" Abrielle mumbled, making every effort to clear her befuddled senses as she pushed herself upright against the decorative chest. It was a piece that Lord Weldon had brought back from the Crusades. She had never realized before how hard and solid it was until forced to confront it head-on.

In the hall beyond the open doorway, she saw the

taller oaf, Dunstan, grasp Nedda by her nightcap-covered hair and, with one hand, haul her to the tips of her toes. With an amused chortle, he sent the servant whirling into the antechamber, where, after several rotations, she fell into her mistress. Abrielle had been making every effort to get to her feet in spite of the fact that her senses had been knocked badly askew. Once again she was sent sprawling, this time in a crumpled heap beneath Nedda.

Frustrated, bruised, and seething with rage, Abrielle waited as the servant extricated herself and finally reclaimed some measure of her sorely bruised wits as she sat upright against the chest again, whence she glared at the two brutes who grinned back at them. Abrielle was definitely in a mood to serve vengeance upon the obnoxious pair, but hadn't yet figured out how she could manage that. At the same time she was wont to wonder how they would enjoy being buried piecemeal in the decorated chest that had recently caused her so many bruises.

Abrielle extricated her hand from her tangled clothing and wiped the back of it across her bruised mouth, but paused at the moisture she felt. Glancing down, she found her knuckles smeared with blood.

Nedda readily tore a strip from the hem of her own nightgown and folded it over several times. In spite of being badly bruised from the beating she had received at the hands of Dunstan, she pressed it firmly against her mistress's lip in an effort to stem the bleeding. Tossing a glare toward the oafs, the servant curled her lips in rampant disdain as she gave the men a scathing perusal. "Ye vile brutes! Ye both aught ta be hanged!"

Fordon chortled. "Instead, we're bein' paid ta take ye both for a little ride."

Abrielle and Nedda looked at each other warily, evoking another laugh from Fordon, who was obviously enjoying their subjugation.

Softly murmuring her appreciation for Nedda's care without averting the glare she bestowed upon the hairy oafs, Abrielle correctly sized them up as slovenly bullies. "Had I a broom, I'd be dusting your fat backsides good and proper," she muttered in a low, contemptuous tone. "You both smell as putrid as you act. 'Tis certain once you take your leave, these chambers will have to be aired out for at least a fortnight."

"Aye, m'lady," Nedda agreed, admiring the younger woman's spirit. Glowering at the men, she curled her upper lip in a sneer. "Though I'm thinkin' 'twill be at least six months afore their stench is gone."

"What do you want from us?" Abrielle demanded abruptly.

"Ye'll find out soon enough," Fordon replied with a black-toothed smirk.

The candles cast ominously huge shadows of the pair on the walls and ceiling. If possible, Dunstan's appearance was more unsightly than his shorter companion. An ugly scar slanted across his pudgy face, puckering one eyelid nearly closed before sweeping downward to draw his upper lip into a perpetual sneer. Unlike Fordon, he was so tall and muscular that she had cause to feel like a tiny bird perched on a twig before a monstrous man.

Fordon leaned down to smirk at Abrielle. "Now ye'd best be mindin' yer manners, m'liedy, or else I'll be clobberin' ye real hard. And who's ta say one as grand as yerself will be survivin' such a beatin'?" Chuckling malevolently, he shrugged his fat, sloping shoulders. "I'm thinkin' maybe not."

Lowering eyelids disdainfully over a stony stare, Abrielle warned, "If you kill me, you can be assured the villain who sent you will never get his hands on what he's seeking, 'Tis a simple fact, not a frivolous threat."

Fordon smirked again. "What be he seekin', m'liedy?"

"If you have no idea, then I shan't be enlightening you. I only suggest that you consider the consequences to yourself and your companion should you kill us. You'll likely be risking your own death by enraging those who sent you."

Abrielle was convinced that Thurstan was behind this intrusion into her life, no doubt to force her to renounce all claims to Desmond's wealth, or perhaps even to marry her still. As for her smelly captors, they seemed rather lame-witted, too much so for her to believe them capable of planning this abduction. She trusted them no further than she could outdistance a wild boar, but she trusted Thurstan even less.

Chortling at her chary look, the cloddish fellow retreated several steps and then abruptly whipped a long dagger from the sheath he wore at his side, snatching startled gasps from both women.

He sniggered. "Scared ye, didn't I!"

Abrielle had little trouble mistaking the pleasure Fordon was deriving by tormenting them, making her wish she had the ability to bring him up short with a double-fisted poke in the nose. At times such as these, she could understand why her father had sought restitution from his enemies, even at the cost of his life.

Having endured the brigand's mischievous humor, Abrielle was wont to bestow a deliberately bland gaze upon him. "May we be permitted to know what you intend to do with us?"

Badly decayed teeth came into view again as the burly man grinned back at her. "We're gonna take ye ta a place far from here, where ye'll have time ta think about what ye care for most, yer life or the riches ye wheedled from the squire."

"I wheedled nothing from the squire," she retorted sharply. Although at first she had thought the filthy brigands to be ignorant of what Thurstan was after, Fordon had obviously been playing her along, possibly hoping to learn how much wealth was at stake. "I never wanted to marry Desmond de Marlé, and for that reason, you can be assured I took no part in drafting the marriage agreement or any discussion involving his wealth."

"That don't matter none now, seein' as how he's dead, and ye gots the bloomin' treasure he was a-hoardin'. Problem for ye is, there be those what's considerin' all of it theirs! Right down ta the last bloody coin."

"By your reference to the last bloody coin, I must assume you intend to kill me in order to get it," she accused acidly. "Well, you can tell Thurstan and the other culprits with whom he's in league 'twill be impossible for them to get their hands on what they're wanting if I am slain."

"Ye jes' don't understands what I'm tellin' ye, do ye?" the oaf chided, shaking his head as if lamenting that fact.

Leaning forward again, he pushed his huge face close in front of hers as he displayed his black, rotting teeth in a leering sneer. "If 'n ye don't do what he wants, he's gonna let me start carvin' ye up inta tiny pieces.

Then, if ye still refuse, he's gonna let me have the pleasure of killin' yer mother slow and painful like right in front of yer eyes. That's what I do best."

With that ominous boast, the ogre straightened and, holding up the oversize blade, thoughtfully examined it in an all-too-obvious effort to intimidate her. Although Abrielle had trouble subduing the cold dread that had settled around her heart at his threat to harm her mother, she refused to allow them the pleasure of seeing her fear. Surely Thurstan was merely trying to make her so frightened that she would willingly agree to marry him.

Casting a glance toward his companion, Fordon jerked his head to indicate Abrielle. "Tie this one up good and proper. The maid can tote their belongin's ta the cart. If needs be, we'll cut off her fingers and send 'em back as a warnin' ta this one's folks." Having evoked a startled gasp from the servant, he leered down at her and then promptly threw her upon the bed. "Her kin'll likely be eager ta stop us afore we hack the rest of the hag inta tiny pieces."

Dunstan laughed. "That'll scare 'em, all right."

"I'm goin' down now ta see if'n m'liedy's carriage is awaitin' her," Fordon announced with a chortle.

In Fordon's absence, Abrielle found herself facing the towering boor. At his approach, she kicked at him and struggled frantically.

"If'n ye wants ta go on breathin', m'liedy, ye'll be needin' ta behave yerself," he snarled, thrusting a pillow over her face and holding it down until she was forced to give up her struggles. "That's more like a liedy should be behavin' herself. Now do what I says or I'll be layin' me fist so hard inta yer face, ye'll be seein' only the backs o' yer eyelids for some time ta come."

Abrielle found herself shoved facedown upon the bed and her wrists clasped in an oversize hand. She sought to thwart the man's efforts, but he braced a heavy knee in the middle of her back and held her down as he bound her wrists and ankles. At last he caught her arm and hauled her to her feet. Tied as tightly as she was, she had little choice but to stand submissively as he wrapped a quilt about her and pushed a dirty rag in her mouth. Leather cords were then wound several times around the quilt, securing it over her torso.

Trussed up much in the manner of a plucked goose for a roasting, Abrielle was tossed back upon the bed, where she was forced to wait in apprehension. However, it wasn't long before she realized her bonds weren't nearly as tight as the man had likely meant them to be, giving her some reason to hope.

Dunstan leaned toward Nedda as he displayed black rotting teeth in a sinister grin. A lock of his long, frizzy hair fell forward over his shoulder, swinging past the servant's nose, causing her to wrinkle it in rampant distaste before turning aside. "We'll soon be takin' ye and yer mistress for a long ride, and should the two o' ye misbehave even a mite . . . well, I'm here ta make sure ye both regrets it." For added emphasis, he held the sharp blade up close in front of Nedda's face until her eyes were fastened on the instrument. Then he twisted it, lending emphasis to the movement with an impromptu sound through the gaps between his teeth. Nedda understood only too well that she'd be killed if she caused him any trouble. Reluctant to allow the brutish man further satisfaction in his quest to frighten her, she nodded once, no more, and gave him a level stare for good measure.

Nedda was instructed to pack a small satchel of warm clothing, slippers, and necessities for her mistress and another for herself. In spite of the heavy muck clinging to the worn soles of his boots, he stretched himself out upon the counterpane. Taking no notice of its fine needlework, he crossed his ankles as he watched her pack. Casually, he plied the point of his blade beneath his nails. Abrielle was sure his only intent was to keep their eyes fastened on the shiny blade, as if to lend emphasis to the threat the weapon might pose to them.

Upon Fordon's return, Abrielle was swept from the bed and flung over the brawny shoulder of the taller brigand. Nedda followed closely behind, forced to carry the satchels.

Abrielle was carried ever deeper into the nether regions of the keep. Torches had recently been lit to provide illumination along the stone passageways, evidencing the fact that their abduction had been planned well in advance, perhaps according to Thurstan's instructions.

The iron door at the rear entrance of the keep had been made to withstand any siege an enemy brought against it. Lord Weldon had insisted upon its strength and durability during the planning and building of the stone structure. However, that premise would succeed only when such forces came from outside, not from within the keep itself.

Abrielle was rudely dumped onto a pile of quilts across the corridor from the rear portal. Though she peered intently to see some hint of the moon or the stars beyond the opening, there were none to be seen. Yet, prior to slipping into bed, she had sat for a time within the cushioned cubicle near her bedchamber windows, gazing through the protective iron grille at the wealth of stars visible in the night sky.

A few moments passed before it dawned on her that a black shroud was hanging over the doorway, no doubt in an attempt to prevent anyone outside from espying the light. The presence of a lantern would have likely seemed strange in that area of the keep, which seemed to lend viable support to the idea that her kidnapping had been planned well in advance. Had Thurstan been preparing for this event, even as he ate her food and competed in her tournament?

The candles in the lanterns were snuffed prior to the covering being lifted from the doorway. Immediately moonlight filtered into the lower depths of the keep, lending a silver gleam to the bearded faces of her captors. Upon being swept over Dunstan's shoulder once again, Abrielle was carried through the portal and then dumped into a cart that awaited them, causing her to wince in pain in spite of the quilt that had been tied around her. Her displeasure was not the only one evidenced during that moment, for the shaggy, short-legged steed that had been harnessed to the cart had evidently been dozing until startled awake by the sudden jolt of her weight. He leapt forward, testing the length of his tether.

Feeling decidedly bruised, Abrielle glared after the huge oaf, who gave her no further heed as he strode back through the opening. Next, Nedda emerged and was instructed to toss their satchels of clothing into the cart before climbing in. Then she was bound and gagged in much the same manner as her mistress.

Dunstan and Fordon returned briefly to the interior to retrieve the tallow lanterns and, upon emerging from the keep, tucked them into the end of the cart, whereupon they mounted a pair of shaggy steeds. A third man emerged from the postern door with a pair of pillows and quilts that he tossed into the cart before closing the door. He proved solicitous enough to tuck the pillows beneath the women's heads before covering them with a quilt. Upon freeing the horse, he climbed into the driver's seat and slapped the reins, setting the cart into motion. As his two companions set off down the narrow lane meandering away from the keep, he followed.

Abrielle grimly wondered if she would ever see her family again. She tried to find comfort in picturing their faces and reminding herself how worried they would be when they discovered her gone and how they would spare nothing to find her and bring her home safely. But as time passed and the uncomfortable journey wound on and on, their beloved images faded to make room for another, this one with deep blue eyes, high, sharp cheekbones, and a haunting smile. He would not be smiling when he heard the news of her abduction. Imagining how he would react made her shiver and gave her courage. Whatever else he was, at this blackest of moments, Raven was a strong, unwavering gleam of hope for her to cling to in the darkness.

CHAPTER 15

Gathering clouds drifted over the moon and the stars, leaving Abrielle much perplexed by the direction in which they were journeying. What vexed her even more was the potential brevity of their lives should they fail to find a way to escape. Considering the several layers in which she was now bound, it was difficult to imagine they would be able to escape their captors before they reached their destination.

She wondered if by now her mother realized she was gone and was raising up a hue and cry. She could imagine the hectic scene as Vachel prepared to lead a party in search of her. Then, unbidden, her thoughts turned to Raven; something told her he would eschew waiting around to be part of any organized search, for he was far too stubborn and independent. In the hours past she'd envisioned him riding to her rescue, black hair flying behind him as he leaned forward in the saddle, pushing his stallion to the limit. A welcome sight he was, even in her dreams, and even if another rescue by him would make her further obligated to the man. At that moment, with her muscles cramping and throat parched, she didn't care who found them, as long as she and Nedda were safe.

Though it required an equal measure of unrelenting persistence and stubborn tenacity, Abrielle and Nedda finally managed to slip their wrists out of their cords, making them both grateful for the carelessness of the huge oaf who had tied them. Abrielle wiggled around to face her servant and pressed a single finger across her own cloth-bound lips, warning her companion to remain silent.

A nod sufficed as assurance that Nedda understood. Abrielle then slid her arms within her enveloping quilt and, upon grasping her nightgown, drew it up until she could reach the hem, whereupon she began tearing off narrow strips from the bottom. The blanket sufficed to muffle the rending of the cloth, but when the driver peered over his shoulder and canted his head in some bemusement, as if trying to determine what he was hearing, Nedda began to feign low snores underneath the edge of the quilt. Issuing a contemptuous snort, the man faced forward again.

Moments later, the first, lace-trimmed scrap fluttered over the side of the cart. Another plainer piece, supplied by Nedda, was tossed out a short time later. Hopefully their rescuers would realize the tattered pieces were being left as a guide to their destination.

Several more scraps were flung out fairly close together as they swept past adjoining lanes leading to distant cottages, awash in silvery moonlight. When the way proved fairly straight again, lengthy intervals passed before other remnants fluttered out, except when the driver turned the cart onto another road and the path needed to be marked fairly quickly. Night turned into day, and open fields and pasture were left behind for forest growing close to the road.

By the time the cart was drawn to a halt in front of a ramshackle cottage at midday, both women's nightgowns had been shortened well above their ankles, yet their robes would be long enough to hide their newly tattered condition. Abrielle and Nedda quickly bound each other's wrists. The men seemed oblivious to the trail that had been left, for the women were laid over the shoulders of their original captors and carried forthwith into the decrepit structure.

Sometime in the past, the cottage's tiny windows had been boarded up by wooden slats, most of which now hung askew, allowing wedges of light from the midday sun to penetrate the narrow cracks. The last vestiges of stiff animal hides hung from nails driven into the upper corners. It seemed doubtful they would suffice to keep out the cold breezes that were even now whipping around the cottage.

Carried into the adjoining room, Abrielle and Nedda were dumped in turn upon two narrow, rough-hewn beds upon which rank-smelling, straw-filled pallets lay partially askew on the stiff, aged webbing that years ago had been woven in and out between the bed frames. After being supplied with their bundles of clothing, the women were released from their restraints and told to remain in the room until later. Otherwise, if any unusual movement were detected, leading their captors to suspect that they were trying to escape, they would be tied to their beds.

"What if we have ta go ta the privy?" Nedda was either bold or desperate enough to ask. As Dunstan faced her with a snarl on his lips, the servant clasped the quilt about her shoulders as if it were some impenetrable armor capable of withstanding his fiercest blow, unswerving before his menacing glare. The eyes of the two combatants dueled for a lengthy moment until Nedda found the audacity to raise her chin to an imperious level as she persisted with her inquiry. "I asked ye what we should—"

"I heard ye!" the brigand barked sharply.

If Dunstan had meant to frighten the servant, he was disappointed, for Nedda remained undaunted and persistent. She raised a brow as if she were no less than a queen making a demand of her subject. "Then if ye'd kindly oblige us by answering my question, my mistress and I would be most grateful."

For one astounded moment, the man stared agog at the spunky woman, as if unable to believe her tenacity. Raising an arm, he pointed to a crude chamber pot in the corner. "If'n ye or yer liedyship has a need, ye'd best be quiet about movin' 'round or else me or one of the other lads here will be comin' in here ta sees what mischief ye're about."

"And what mischief do you intend while we're asleep?" Abrielle demanded, seeking to match Nedda's fortitude. "If you think you can come in here and sport with us, then let me assure you that—"

Dunstan snarled and strode toward her until she was forced to tilt her face upward to meet his blazing gaze. "Ye'll be doin' what, m'liedy?"

Thoroughly shaken, Abrielle had difficulty standing her ground and had to resist the urge to gulp in trepidation, but having just viewed a fine example of stalwart courage, she copied Nedda's manner and elevated her own chin imperiously. "I shall most definitely scream until you and your companions are forced to flee this hovel to save your hearing."

Chortling at her claim, Dunstan settled his beefy fists upon his voluminous waist and met her gaze. "Ye've got spunk, m'liedy, I'll give ye that. Our orders are ta leaves the two of ye be till the one what hired us arrives . . . unless, of course, ye gets it inta yer head ta escape. Then we can deals with ye as rough as we wants. So, as long as the two of ye behaves yerselves right nice like, then Fordon and the rest of us'll be leavin' ye alone. Do ye ken what I'm sayin' ta ya, m'liedy?"

"In spite of your badly mauled diction, I understand completely," Abrielle retorted. Lifting a slender hand, she flicked her fingers as she shooed the oaf toward the adjoining room. "If you don't mind, we would like some privacy now. And be sure to close the door behind you as you take your leave."

The brigand glared as his mouth sagged slowly open at her audacity to order him about. In spite of his assurances that he wouldn't harm them unless they tried to escape, he raised a clenched fist as if seriously tempted to clobber her.

Abrielle merely lifted her finely boned chin to a higher level and looked at him with what she hoped was a bland expression. It would not have been to her advantage to let the man see just how much he frightened her. "I thought you said you weren't supposed to harm us unless we attempted an escape," she dared to remind him. "Let me assure you that if you do injure me, I shall complain most stridently of your abuse, so be warned."

"Who are ye ta be warnin' me?" Dunstan demanded incredulously. He bent toward her again and narrowed his beady eyes into an angry squint. "Ye'd best consider just who's bein' held against their will, m'liedy."

"Obviously, for the time being, I am your captive. However, should you forget yourself and dispense with me ere you've completed the task you were given, I can assure you that everything I personally inherited from Squire de Marlé will be added to the coffers of my parents. Sir Vachel has numerous knights who will rally to his aid posthaste if you seek to intimidate him. And if you should kill us, whether you intend to or not, the brute who hired you will likely send out more capable men to dispense with you."

Though the oaf glowered at her as if considering the pleasure he'd derive from throttling her, her threat apparently caused him to ponder the precariousness of his situation, for he finally retreated to a safe distance.

"You'd better leave us before you do something you'll likely regret," she advised. "My servant and I are extremely exhausted after being rudely awakened, not to mention what we suffered being jounced about in a rickety old cart. We'd appreciate some privacy." Raising a slender hand, she shooed him toward the door. "Now be gone with you before I start screaming."

For a moment the hulking man could only gape at her incredulously, and then he stomped through the door in a decidedly vexed manner and joined his companions in the next room.

Although Abrielle knew that she and her servant lacked the strength and stamina to defeat their captors' evil purposes and win the day against such overwhelming odds, she refused to yield the battle without a show of resistance. Upon dragging a ragged quilt from one of the narrow cots, she stuffed it tightly against the bottom of the door as a temporary barrier should the men be tempted to invade their quarters.

"What do ye think they'll be doing ta us, mistress?" Nedda asked in obvious concern.

Abrielle heaved a quavering sigh. "Thurstan de Marlé is far more interested in obtaining the wealth and treasures the squire possessed. He might try to accomplish that through forcing me into marriage." She shuddered to think what would happen if she refused to comply. "Therefore I suggest that we try to escape before his arrival. I have no doubt he's desperate enough to use whatever form of coercion is needed to get what he wants."

"But how can we defeat these clobber-headed rogues? They're brutes, m'lady. We wouldn't have any kind of chance of survivin' their blows if they start beatin' on us. And if they intend ta guard us day and night, we'll never be able ta escape."

Abrielle had to agree with her servant on all counts, yet she was wont to be more hopeful of the outcome. "'Twill only be a matter of time ere my mother realizes that I'm gone and will urge my stepfather to set out in search of me. If he finds the trail we left, then he will certainly hasten to our rescue along with those he'll rally to accompany him. If no one notices the scraps of clothing we threw out to mark our trail, then we'll likely be left to our own defenses."

"But we've no weapons or cudgels with which ta attack these oafs or ta use in defense of ourselves, m'lady. And even if we had some club ta use ta knock their noggins askew, we're only two women. How would we be able ta get the upper hand whilst battlin' the likes of such men?"

"'Tis obvious we must improvise as well as we can

with what is available to us, Nedda," Abrielle stated. "The poker iron would certainly serve as a weapon for one of us. As for the other . . ."

Abrielle glanced around the cramped room, searching for anything that would give them some sort of advantage over their captors. She directed Nedda toward the fireplace, then settled her eyes on the narrow beds, and for a thoughtful moment she considered their crude, wooden frames. Then she turned over the nearest one, spilling the filthy bedding to the dirt floor. Wedged fairly close together within the wooden frame were slats, one of which came out after a great deal of determination and tugging.

Clasping the makeshift truncheon in hand, Abrielle considered the piece with some measure of pride. "This should give those dim-witted buffoons their just due." Glancing aside at her companion, she grinned. "Perhaps considerably more than they'll be expecting from a pair of properly mannered women."

Nedda, now standing near the fireplace, chortled in sudden glee as she contemplated the poker iron's potential. "Now and then throughout m' lifetime, I've been tempted ta crack a few manly noggins. This will be the best chance I'll ever have."

Abrielle laughed. "Aye, to be sure, Nedda. No villains seem more deserving of a severe chastening than the ones who abducted us . . . with the possible exception of the culprit who hired them."

"So what be ye plannin', m'lady?"

"First, we may be better off waiting for my stepfather to arrive rather than trying to initiate our own escape. These brutes are capable of killing us with nothing more than a backward swat of a hand."

"If these three are soon joined by more of the same,

we'll have less of a chance ta escape this hovel alive. 'Twould seem ta me that it would be far better were we ta do somethin' now rather than merely foldin' our hands and waitin' for yer pa."

"Then we should commence with our attempt to escape while there are only three close at hand. Better that than the two of us trying to hold off a small army of villains."

"How should we go about takin' these brigands by surprise, m'lady?"

"Let me tell you my plan," Abrielle said softly.

Sometime later, the door creaked as Abrielle pulled it slowly inward, the sound claiming the attention of those who were ravenously appeasing their hunger at the rough-hewn table. In the hearth behind them, a warm fire now blazed, and on the floor beside it lay several pieces of firewood that had recently been brought in from outside. Obviously intent upon their own comforts, the men had not seen fit to lend any degree of consideration to the comfort of their captives. Even so, as they glanced toward her, they began to nudge one another as if only now realizing how young and uncommonly beautiful the lady was.

"What be yer wants, m'liedy?" Fordon asked.

Abrielle cleared her throat nervously. "I'm very thirsty, and I would like some water to drink. Shall I come out there to fetch it, or am I to remain a prisoner in this room?"

Dunstan rose from the stool at the far end of the table, where he had been gorging himself. After dipping a tin cup into a nearby bucket of water and loudly slurping from it, he ambled toward her with his black-toothed grin. Abrielle realized how easily the task of looking frightened could be accomplished, for she was nearly shaking in her skin. With eyes wide and fearful, she appeared to stumble backward haphazardly. Knowing that she and her servant could be bludgeoned to death if their captives were riled, she had no need to pretend that she was wary of the approaching man. Indeed, for a frightening moment, her legs seemed to lose their stability as she retreated farther into the room.

Upon reaching the portal, the brutish oaf shouldered the rough-hewn door aside, causing it to bump Nedda, who was standing close behind it. The movement of the plank as it rebounded on its leather hinges seemed so natural that the brigand never even looked back as he reached behind him to push the barrier closed.

In the adjoining room, the men exchanged humorous quips about their companion's intentions that dissolved into loud guffaws. As they did, Nedda lifted the poker high above her head and brought it down with brutal force upon the burly man's pate, rendering him totally unconscious even before his legs began to buckle beneath him. Between the combined efforts of both women, they managed to lower his huge, slithering form to the dirt floor, where he lay completely oblivious to the world and those within it. Between the two of them, they managed to drag the unconscious man behind the bed at the far end of the room. Together they lifted the cot and placed it over his sprawled form, taking care to adjust the filthy quilts in such a manner as to hide the oaf from those who might be inclined to follow him.

Abrielle took a deep breath, feeling as frightened as she had been on her wedding night while awaiting Desmond's entrance into his chambers. Nevertheless, she braced a heavy bed slat against the wall, where it would be easily accessible should she be required to act in Nedda's defense or perhaps her own.

Launching into her performance, Abrielle cried out with as much emotion as she could muster. "Oh, please! Please, don't hurt me!" She ripped her sleeve and then feigned a frightened scream as she ran to the door. Snatching it open, she thrust out a hand as if in desperate appeal and began pleading with the pair who were still ravenously filling their gullets at the table. "Oh, please! Please! You must help me! My family will pay handsomely for my safe return."

The driver of the cart chortled as he pushed himself to his feet. "I'll help ye, m'liedy."

Swaggering arrogantly across the room, he began rolling up his sleeves as if readying himself for a fight with his companion. Shouldering aside the door, he strolled into the room. Once again Nedda gave the rough wooden barrier a gentle push, sending it swinging closed behind him. In the next instant, the maidservant lifted the heavy poker high above her head and brought it down with mean intent upon yet another manly noggin. The driver's eyes rolled back into his head as his knees gave way beneath him. In total oblivion, he sprawled facedown.

Nedda hit the wall with the poker iron and then sailed a small chair across the room as Abrielle watched in amazement. After creating scuffling sounds with her slippered feet, the imaginative maid collapsed upon the bed with a frail cry. Just as quickly she rose again with a loud snort and began to thump the thin mattress repeatedly with the weighty iron.

"Pritchard? Dunstan?" Fordon called out from the adjoining room as he pushed himself hurriedly to his feet, in his haste overturning the heavy bench upon which he had been sitting. "What's happenin' in there? Ye'd best not be scufflin' over m'liedy."

"Oh, no, please! Stop your fighting!" Abrielle cried, doing her best to feign hysteria. She decided a scream would be of timely benefit and promptly released one that made Nedda clasp her hands over her ears and roll her eyes heavenward as if praying for some divine reprieve. Abrielle snatched open the door and, from there, pleaded as if in fretful anguish, "Stop them! Please! You must do something! They're killing each other!"

Her ploy proved convincing enough to bring the rotund Fordon scurrying toward her. Breathing heavily, he waddled across the threshold and then, once inside, paused in sudden confusion as he glanced around for his companions. In the next instant, Nedda delivered the lummox his just due, much as she had done his two cohorts. As he fell, he turned toward her in disbelief, his eyes glazing over, his huge body too close. He fell forward much like a gigantic tree after a sizable wedge had been chopped away from its massive trunk, landing on Nedda. Abrielle screamed as her maid fell beneath the man and lay still.

"Nedda!"

But the dear woman didn't stir. From the chest down, she was beneath Fordon's unmoving bulk. Abrielle fell to her knees and tried to push the body away, but she could not move it.

"Nedda, Nedda, wake up!" She would never forgive herself if her plan to rescue them had caused the woman's injury.

To her horror, she heard the outer door slam open in the next chamber. Had Thurstan finally arrived?

"Abrielle!" called a blessedly familiar voice.

She stumbled from the inner room shakily and espied Raven striding into the hovel with sword clasped in hand; her relief made her weak in both her knees and her senses. Advancing in reverse upon his heels, Cedric Seabern wielded a double-edged ax with proficient ease as he glanced from side to side, wary of any foe who might have been lurking nearby. Considering the various weapons tucked within their belts, it was obvious the pair had come prepared to do battle with a small army of miscreants.

"Oh, thank God!" she cried. "Nedda has been hurt. Please come help me."

Raven followed her while his father remained on guard at the door. Abrielle fell to her knees and pushed while Raven pulled Fordon off of Nedda. The maidservant groaned, and her eyelids fluttered.

"Water, please!" Abrielle said over her shoulder.

A moment later Raven pressed a tin cup into her hand, and she placed it at Nedda's lips. Some dribbled down her chin, but then she began to swallow heartily.

Abrielle's relief was almost overpowering. "Nedda? Dear Nedda, what ails you?"

The woman groaned. "My leg, m'lady. It hurts somethin' fierce."

"It might be broken," Raven said solemnly. "Ye need the services of a healer."

"Ye must get m'lady back to the keep," the servant said between grimly pressed lips. "I'll only slow yer progress."

"Nedda, we cannot leave you alone!" Abrielle cried. Turning to Raven, she asked, "Have you men?"

"They're on the way with your stepfather, but for now, 'tis just us."

Cedric appeared in the doorway. "You need ta get the women away, lad." He kicked one of the captors, who didn't move. "Who knows when these ones will awaken? Is this all there are?"

"The brigands were waiting for someone else to arrive, no doubt the man who enlisted their services," Abrielle said, allowing Nedda to squeeze her hand. "Although I have no proof as yet, Thurstan may well be the culprit. 'Tis my belief that he resented the fact that my agreement with Desmond left me the keep and most if not all the wealth that once belonged to Lord Weldon."

"But we canna ken that for sure," Cedric said. "Any number of young bucks could've taken it inta their heads ta have ye for himself. To that end, I'll remain behind and hide myself well in the forest. When I know the identity of the men behind this terrible deed, I'll meet with Sir Vachel and come to the keep, bringing these villains with me."

"And I'll remain with ye, Laird Cedric," Nedda said faintly.

"But you need healing," Abrielle cried.

"And ye need to be safe, m'lady. I not be in mortal danger; I can wait a few hours."

"And I'll make her a comfortable litter while we wait," Cedric offered.

"Let those villains ride in the bumpy cart," Nedda said, with a faint show of determination. "I have enough bruises from that."

"Are you certain?" Abrielle said, looking between her maidservant and the two men.

" 'Tis the best way, m'lady," Nedda said kindly.

"We'd best be getting these brigands inta the cart, lad," Cedric suggested. "Otherwise, there'll be the devil ta pay should we be caught by those yet ta come."

After binding and gagging all three men, Cedric

lifted one over his shoulder as his son hefted another in the same manner. Leading the way into the adjoining room, he was wont to chortle. "Raven, me lad, should I ever forget what I've seen here today, kindly remind your ol' da na ta get inta a row with these here lasses. I'm thinking me poor pate wouldna be able ta stand the abuse."

Nedda cast a glance toward the elder and spoke stiffly. "Ye needn't worry, m'lord. 'Tis only brutish culprits I'm inclined ta lay low."

"Then I'll be thanking me good fortune ye didna mistake us as part of that vermin," the laird said with amusement as Abrielle ran ahead to open the front portal for the men. Over his shoulder, Cedric advised, "Take this as a warning, lad. Treat the women kindly or they'll be of a mind ta raise a crop of lumps on your pate."

Abrielle wrung her hands in agitation, knowing the men were only trying to ease her spirits. But all she could think of was her maid's safety, for after all, the woman wouldn't be in such grave peril if not for her mistress.

Once all three villains were in the cart, Raven hid the conveyance behind a tumbledown shed where it would be easily accessible to Vachel and his knights. After erasing the tracks with a branch, he joined his father in improvising a litter with the quilts and a bed frame. Having often traveled with his father in service to their king, Raven was reluctant to leave Cedric behind. His parent had always been a noble warrior, but since the death three summers past of the beauty he had taken to wife more than twoscore years ago, he had seemed inclined to take unnecessary chances with his life. Raven decided his da would likely be heartened by the premise that he hadn't yet lost his appeal when it came to the fairer gender, and be more careful for his own life.

Seeing that Abrielle was feeding her maidservant a bit of cheese, Raven said to his father, "I overheard the Lady Cordelia saying some fine things about ye ta a cousin of hers at the squire's funeral."

Cedric elevated a hoary brow as he peered at him in wonder. "About me?"

"I'm thinking the lady has set her heart on having ye, Da."

The elder scrubbed a hand across his mustached mouth, as if making an earnest attempt to wipe away a widening grin. "'Tis true what ye say? Ye wouldna be up ta some mischief?"

"Were ye ta take yourself so young a bride, 'tis sure I'd be finding myself with a whole new brood of brothers and sisters. Why, I can just see them now, swarming 'round my knees, wanting me ta mend their broken dolls or horses."

Cedric harrumphed as he cocked a quizzical brow at his son. "Ye wouldna resent them?"

"Mayhap a few . . . at the very beginning," his son teased, "but they're sure ta grow on me after a time."

The elder laughed. "Aye, they could grow on me, too. Your mother, she never was able ta have more'n ye, lad, but ye can be sure I was always true ta her. She was me only love."

"Take care, Da," Raven urged in a moment of sincerity. "I want ta see ye at the keep after this is over. Should I be blessed with bairns of my own, they'll be wanting a grandfather ta read ta them."

Cedric cocked a brow toward Abrielle. "Dinna be

counting your chicks before they're hatched, lad. That one dinna seem too partial ta ye."

Raven smiled. "Give her time."

At last the litter was done and Nedda was settled into it. Cedric swept an arm about, urging them to leave. "Now mount up and be gone from here afore those miscreants catch us unawares. If I'm going ta fight, I'd rather be assured ye're safely away afore I start bloodying those devils." He grinned. "Otherwise, Lady Abrielle be inclined ta think me a ruthless savage."

Abrielle smiled at him after she tucked the quilt up around Nedda's chin. "I think you my heroic rescuer."

Raven straightened with pride. "And me, my lady?"

She shrugged. "I'm grateful you came to keep your father company."

He winced and staggered as if she'd wounded him, but Abrielle did not relax into a smile. Sighing, he mounted his black stallion and patted the animal's neck fondly to keep him from shying away as his father lifted Abrielle up behind him. Settling astride the steed, she adjusted the skirts of her robe and nightgown for a moment before she lifted her gaze and found Raven peering over his shoulder.

"Are ye ready, lass?"

Though she nodded, it only just dawned on her that she and Raven would be traveling alone. She would have no choice but to depend upon him for her survival.

Chapter 16

As the horse began walking down a lane into the
forest, Abrielle looked back at Cedric, who pulled
Nedda's litter down a different path near the cottage
and disappeared. She found herself wishing she could
have stayed behind. Instead she was sharing a too-small
saddle with Raven Seabern. Straddling his body with
her legs, she felt indecently close to him. To keep their
touching as minimal as possible, she was trying not to
hold on to him, but she found herself swaying with the
movement of the horse, and the awkwardness of the
two of them together.

Raven looked over his shoulder at her. "If ye dinna
hold on, ye'll find yourself on your backside in the dirt."

Gritting her teeth, she clutched the folds of his cloak
in her fists.

"That's better, lass."

She could still hear the amusement in his voice, and
she hated being the source of his humor. She needed a
distraction from this strange tension. "How did you
find us so quickly?"

"A serf named Siward alerted Sir Vachel after he saw a cart being loaded with quilts and pillows near the back entrance of the keep. He watched ta see what they were putting in it, thinking mayhap Mordea was stealing from ye again. Then he saw your maid come out afore being tied up and thrown inta the cart. He began ta suspect what was in the quilt they'd loaded earlier, and told Sir Vachel what he'd just seen."

"I shall personally offer my gratitude and a suitable reward to him for raising up a hue and cry," Abrielle avouched. "Nedda and I were afraid no one would even notice we were gone until the morning."

"Siward claimed ye'd likely saved his son's life by providing better vittles for the children. The lad was barely surviving, but when ye started sending over food, he took ta eating again. Siward said even if the brigands killed him, he couldna keep quiet on the chance that ye'd been taken."

"But what about my stepfather and his knights?" Abrielle asked.

"After Siward's news, Sir Vachel found traces of blood on the floor outside your chambers and within. He sent out riders ta bid the knights who were living fairly close ta come in haste ta the keep. Since it promised ta be a goodly wait afore they arrived, my da and I decided ta ride out ta find the brigands' trail and mark it for Sir Vachel. 'Twould seem ye did that well enough with the scraps ye left. They gave us hope we'd find ye alive."

"I am glad," she said softly, trying to think of Nedda's safety, rather than Raven's broad back and warm thighs.

"So how were ye able ta subdue three large men? Surely ye had help."

"Just Nedda and I and our clever minds," she said with faint sarcasm.

Over his shoulder, his blue eyes touched her. "I never said ye weren't clever, lass."

She frowned, tempted to say that he seemed concerned only with having a wealthy, beautiful bride until she remembered he was escorting her safely home and she was grateful. Instead she told him of their successful overthrow of their captors.

"I am quite impressed," he said afterward. "Ye certainly made things easier on us poor men who thought we were facing danger to rescue ye."

She could not suppress the small smile that turned up a corner of her mouth. For a while they rode in silence, the forest masking the setting sun and a chill beginning to seep upward from the ground. Suddenly she noticed the path they were taking. "We are not traveling the same way that our captors took us."

"Nay," he replied. "In case their leader—"

She could not help but interrupt, eager to know who had done this terrible thing to her, to Nedda, to her family. "Thurstan?" she asked.

He took a moment to reply. "Perhaps. But in case he knew to follow the same roads as his henchmen, ye and I should travel another way."

She nodded with comprehension, and found that simply closing her eyes gave her a start, as if she'd fall off the horse. Raven's voice spoke softly in her ear. "Ye didna sleep much," he said. "Hardly a surprise, considering the circumstances." His voice became even softer. "Sleep now."

She gave a little snort. "And how should I be doing that?"

"I willna let ye fall, lass. Rest yourself against me

and sleep." It was so tempting, as the rocking of the horse's gait lulled her, and although she resisted, at last she found her body easing against his, her arms creeping around his waist. What harm could it do to trust him just this once? He was large and warm and so very soothing.

He put a hand on her forearm. "See? I'll keep ye upright."

Her eyes closed for the last time and she drifted off.

Raven knew he would have no such problem, although he had not slept the previous night in his search for her. How could he even grow drowsy when Abrielle was resting warm against his back, her soft breasts encouraging the agony of denying his passion? He was between her thighs, where he longed to be—although he'd prefer them both naked and in a bed, he thought with wry humor.

Several hours after sunset, rain began to fall, awakening Abrielle and slowing their journey with the hiding of the moon. Raven had her snuggle beneath his cloak, yet still they both grew wet. She shivered against him, and at last he gave up the idea of continuing on. He found a sheltering copse of trees, and he lit a small fire to warm them both. She had little to say to him and kept a careful distance, although she did gratefully share his meal of cheese and twice-baked bread. Her wariness of him stung all the more after the sweetness of riding with her head on his shoulder and her body pressed to his. The rain finally eased, so he spread a dry blanket near the fire and bade her sleep.

He kept the fire going and watched over her, wondering how long it was going to take to break through her mistrust of him. If it took forever—and after spending the day dampening his body's eager response to hers, he prayed to God it did not—he would make her see she had naught to fear, that he would rip off his own arms and chain himself to the gates of hell before he would do her harm in any way. The sheer pleasure of watching her sleep was marred by her shivering, sometimes so fiercely he'd swear he heard her teeth chatter.

Finally he had all he could take of seeing her suffer so. He had no other blanket, and he would not let illness overtake her in this weakened state. Before he could think better of it, he carefully lifted her blanket and slid in behind her, chest to her back, his thighs hugging hers, giving of his warmth. It was just for a while, he told himself. Just until his body heat seeped into her and let her go into the deep sleep she needed. If he was lucky he could slip away before she opened her eyes in the morn and she'd never need know. He would not allow himself to think of his desire or dwell on the feel of her breasts against his back or her delicate hands curled around his arms. The last thing he wanted was to give her more reason to be suspicious of him. For this night he wanted only to see to her comfort. There would be other days to press his suit. With a grateful sigh, Abrielle relaxed deeper into sleep, and he did the same.

ABRIELLE CAME AWAKE with a start, wondering what had awoken her from the delicious warmth that eased all along her back. In confusion, she blinked her eyes open to see several dozen men on horseback grouped before her. Her first thought was that Thurstan's men had tracked them there and now had them surrounded. Raven. She raised up on her elbow to see where he was.

When her gaze fell on the lead rider, the visage of her stepfather sent a wave of relief through her. She sagged forward, thanking God in the silence of her prayers, and noticed Vachel was not smiling. Something moved behind her and it was then she realized it was not, as she'd assumed, the sound of hoofbeats that woke her, but the sudden movement of Raven Seabern, who, for reasons she could not begin to fathom, was lying at her back. He stood, and as he did, her sleep-fogged brain slowly began to clear. She had spent the night alone with him, aye, because he'd rescued her. But what was he doing sleeping so close and with his arms wrapped all around her? She had not given him permission for anything of the sort, nor had he sought it, but evidently . . .

A cold shiver of understanding and dread settled into her chest. She came stiffly to her feet, ignoring Raven's outstretched hand and its offer of help—too late, all too late. Oh, why had she ever let her guard down around this man? She noticed that Vachel was watching her with somber eyes, and she saw behind him several of his knights whispering together. They were loyal to him and would not dare to smirk openly at his stepdaughter, but their silent, sordid suspicions were as clear to Abrielle as if they had.

And what else should she expect? After all, they'd found her in Raven's arms, squashed together under a single blanket as if . . . as if . . . A thought began to dawn on her as she pondered how this had come to pass. Her thoughts a jumble of confusion and betrayal and sadness, she turned to Raven and met a steadfast gaze. In a forthright manner he told her, "Ye were so cold in your sleep, lass. I couldna just let ye catch your death."

Her stepfather looked between them. "What has become of Cedric and Nedda?" he asked.

Raven responded, "My father remained behind ta learn the identity of the man who paid the brigands ta kidnap Lady Abrielle. Nedda is injured, so she stayed with him so that I could return Lady Abrielle more quickly ta the safety of the keep." His words echoed hollowly now, for of course he had not kept her safe. "When my father and I first arrived, Lady Abrielle and her maidservant had already knocked their three captors unconscious."

Although Vachel's lips quirked slightly with amusement, he straightened in the saddle and spoke coolly. "And whose idea was it for him to remain behind, leaving my stepdaughter unchaperoned?"

"'Twas Cedric's idea," Abrielle whispered in surprise.

Raven stood so close beside her that she felt him stiffening, heard the affront in his voice as he said, "My father knew you would need to know the identity of the man threatening Abrielle."

"Yet it was his idea to leave the two of you alone," Vachel pointed out.

Into the silence, they heard someone whisper, "The Scots planned it."

Abrielle wished she were anywhere but in this gloomy forest just after dawn. But she found her gaze drawn to Raven, and she saw his anger and bitter pride.

"Someone dares to slight my own father before me?" he demanded.

Uneasy rumbles were heard among the knights, but no one spoke up.

Abrielle found it interesting that Raven seemed angrier that people would accuse his father than himself alone. She knew father and son were close. Was it possible, she had to wonder bitterly, they had planned this entire escapade? Certainly others would be quick to suspect the Scotsmen of hiring the brigands in the first place. She pondered the notion briefly and dismissed it, believing they had too much honor for such a dastardly deed. She was less quick to discount the possibility they had deliberately taken advantage of the situation once it fell into their laps. She had been so overwhelmed it had not occurred to her how Raven's rescue of her would look to others. Perhaps Raven's true anger was due to the discovery of his own part in the ruse. She felt sick thinking such a thing, and could not even look toward the uncertainty of her future.

"Come, Abrielle," Vachel said heavily. "This is not the place for a discussion of such import. And your mother needs to know you're safe. We will talk later."

A discussion of such import. The ominous words echoed inside Abrielle's head. Of course, what could be of greater import than the rest of her life and the decision as to whom she would spend it with. Was that still a decision for her to make? Or had fate and Raven Seabern conspired to at last land her in a mess she could not get herself out of?

Vachel dealt quickly with his men, sending a half-dozen knights back the way Raven indicated, in support of Cedric and Nedda, and then he reached down to his stepdaughter.

Abrielle gratefully let her stepfather pull her up behind him, and she didn't look at Raven as the troop of knights rode off, leaving him behind.

THE SUN HAD passed midday by a pair of hours when serfs working near the far end of the drawbridge espied the approach of a retinue of mounted knights. Sir Vachel's banner was immediately recognizable, and since the long, reddish hair flying out behind the lady sitting behind him was the same hue as that of their mistress, servants readily raced from the courtyard and moved across the drawbridge to have a closer look. Upon confirming that it was indeed the Lady Abrielle seated behind her stepfather, several serfs rushed about to spread the welcome news from one end of the stone edifice to the other, assuring everyone that their mistress had returned safely to the keep. The news did indeed bring Elspeth flying out of her chambers in her eagerness to be reunited with her daughter. Never slackening her pace, she was nearly breathless as she swept into the courtyard.

"Oh, thank the merciful heavens you're all safe!" she cried in teary relief as she waited anxiously for Vachel. After sweeping a long leg over the stallion's neck, he slid to the ground and lifted Abrielle down beside him.

Elspeth made no effort to halt the profusion of grateful tears coursing down her cheeks as she encompassed her daughter within the circle of her arms. "I was so fearful of what those brigands intended to do with you!" she wept with joy. "I've been nearly beside myself, not knowing if Vachel would find you alive or dead or in what condition you'd be in. An endless eternity has passed since we were told you had been abducted. My greatest fear, of course, was that you and Nedda would be killed. 'Tis now apparent that we owe a debt of gratitude to all of my husband's men for finding where you had been taken and bringing you and Nedda back to us."

"We suffered no harm, Mama," Abrielle assured her

parent as she stood back within the circle of the older woman's arms. She knew that Vachel was waiting somberly, but now was not the time for such discussions. She did not want to think about anything but her relief at being home—and somehow this keep had become such to her. "You'll be pleased to hear that Nedda and I laid enough on the dull-witted oafs who abducted us to leave their heads lolling on their shoulders."

Elspeth clasped her daughter's cheeks between her palms and gazed with tear-filled eyes into the face of her only offspring before bestowing a motherly kiss upon her brow. "I am so very, very relieved to have you back, my dearest. I would never have been able to bear your loss if they had found you dead. Who did this to you?"

"As of yet, we know not who hired such fiends." Abrielle found herself glancing back at the Scotsman, who'd ridden in the rear of their party. "Laird Cedric stayed behind to discover the man's identity while in hiding with dear Nedda, who was injured on my behalf."

"Oh heavens!" Elspeth cried. "Such a good, loyal woman." A troubled frown gathered her brows. "When we had no wealth of our own, there were no threats on your life, certainly none from the men vying for your hand. I don't suppose this new threat will be entirely erased until the men responsible for your capture are caught or killed."

Vachel put an arm around his wife. "The villain may be Thurstan de Marlé, or it may not. We will have to wait and see."

Elspeth nodded and turned back to her daughter. "You must be freezing, child! Come inside where it's warm, and then we'll talk more of this matter."

Abrielle went along with her mother, bathing and

changing into dry, clean garments, but her uneasiness about the day yet lingered, and she did not want to leave the great hall to fester with rumors for too long. As it was, when she emerged for supper, she saw that it was too late to stop the gossip, for word had obviously spread of her sojourn with Raven. Heads leaned together, wide eyes looked between her and Raven, who sat alone. Abrielle winced, wishing that Cedric and Nedda had returned, but knowing there was nothing to do, for Vachel's men had been dispatched for assistance.

At the head table, her mother waited for her, not bothering to hide her concern. "Abrielle, your stepfather has informed me what transpired last evening and into this morning," she said softly, reproachfully. "Why did you not tell me of your time with Raven?"

Abrielle sighed. "There is nothing to discuss, Mama. And if there were, I would not want it to be here."

"But there is much to discuss," Vachel said somberly. "You must be prepared for that, my dear. Even now, there is talk, and too much of it. Other suitors will hear of it."

She stiffened. "I have done nothing wrong. I am innocent."

"I know that you are," Vachel said, "but that does not excuse what others will believe. Your reputation has been harmed, Abrielle, though we all wish it were not so. You must prepare yourself for the thought of marriage to young Raven."

With the words said aloud at last, Abrielle felt her heart shatter, and her eyes sting with tears she could not shed in so public a place. If they were alone, she would fly into a rage, giving every excuse why she would not marry such a man. But perhaps Vachel had deliberately chosen such a location for his speech, knowing that she could only protest softly and listen. Elspeth put her hand gently on her arm, but Abrielle was in no mood for her mother's comfort.

She had wanted to choose her own husband, and now her stepfather was saying that yet another man would be forced on her. True, he was no Desmond de Marlé, but his fine face and form hid a man who had only showed his devotion once she had wealth. He had flirted with her when she was betrothed, another mark against him. And he was a Scot, disliked by all her neighbors for the sins of his countrymen. She wondered if she refused to marry him, would he at last hold her accountable for the secrets they shared the night of Desmond's death? She felt humiliated and hopeless. How had this happened to her? She thought she'd been safe from the clutches of one vile man, only to find herself trapped with another.

She could not look at Raven, did not want to wonder whether triumph was banked within his eyes, hidden for now, but there nonetheless.

She was saved from having to speak more of it by the arrival of the rest of Vachel's knights, Cedric, and Nedda. With a glad cry, Abrielle flew to the litter that carried her maidservant. "Nedda, how fare you?" she asked with true worry.

But the woman's color was good, and she smiled, although lines of pain had formed about her mouth. "Well, m'lady. The leg might not even be broken."

Abrielle looked up at Cedric, felt a flash of disappointment, but could not allow herself to think of what would soon come. As Nedda was taken away to be seen by a healer, all gathered around to hear Cedric's story. He told of a small group of mounted men who'd gathered at the cottage, after their failure to find the women and the three men who had captured them. Cedric had cautiously crept to the window in a quest to see if he would be able to recognize any of them. After hiding behind a stack of split firewood that over the years had deteriorated to little more than a pile of pulp, he had peered through a crack between the two shutters that had been nailed shut over a cottage window. In spite of his efforts, the best he had been able to see of the miscreants were their shadows, and only then when they stood in front of the lantern that had been lit behind them. Nevertheless he had overheard their bickering and recognized at least two familiar voices, Thurstan's and Mordea's. Two of the five culprits had been in favor of terminating what had thus far proven to be a fruitless quest and strongly argued their recommendations be accepted, but Thurstan would have none of it. Since this plan seemed to have failed, he would conceive of another to win Abrielle. The culprits had ridden off together in the same direction whence they had come.

Though only an hour had elapsed between the departure of the miscreants and the arrival of Vachel's knights, a sudden heavy downpour washed away all evidence of the trail that Thurstan might have left. Several men had ridden in ever-widening circles around the area in an effort to find some indication of the direction the brigands had taken, but their attempt proved futile after the deluge of rain.

Vachel sighed. "It is not as if we could have done much against Thurstan."

"What are you saying?" Elspeth demanded.

"He is a knight of property, my dear," Vachel explained patiently. "And although he wishes a rich bride, he chose a course that many men have used before him. Possession of the woman until she's forced to marry him."

Raven felt every eye turn to him, and the fact that they all equated him with Thurstan made his blood boil, for he was a man of honor, but he knew there was little he could do to counter the thoughts of those around him. He saw his father give him a wide-eyed glance, and knew the elder was curious, but Raven would have to explain later. For now, all Raven could do was look at Abrielle, who cast him in the same light as men such as Thurstan and Colbert, men who had no honor. He felt anger, nay rage, rising up within him.

One of the knights spoke up. "And the only proof we have that Thurstan is the culprit comes from a Scot." Heads nodded and voices murmured. Raven clenched his fists, but before he could speak in defense of his father, Vachel said, "Enough! Laird Cedric is a valued man in his country. He and his son are both spoken of highly by our own King Henry. I will not hear another slur against a valued guest in my stepdaughter's home." Mere moments later, Vachel approached Raven. "We need to speak in private."

Raven glanced at Abrielle and found her looking at him with true worry. Her expression briefly changed into one of bitterness, but she looked away and did not look back. Raven followed Vachel to the man's private solar. When they were alone within, Vachel paced, as if he didn't know where to begin. At last, he said, "You have presented me with a grave dilemma, Raven Seabern."

"I did not mean ta," Raven answered, hands clasped behind his back. "I but wanted ta see your daughter ta safety. Circumstances conspired ta keep me alone with her."

"And circumstances conspired to have her sleeping in your embrace?" Vachel said dourly.

"Ye have my word that I only thought I was keeping her warm. I did not attempt ta touch her in any other way."

Vachel knew the Scotsman to be a proud and noble warrior, a man who'd earned the confidence of kings. It was dangerous to question the honor of such a man. He decided not to do so and said quietly, "You know you'll have to marry the girl."

Raven stood before Vachel and nodded. "Ye know I will. I'll see your daughter protected from Thurstan and his brigands. Keep her property and possessions hers by right alone."

Vachel gaped at him, wondering about the depths to the man that Abrielle would soon be linked to. "You want none of it for yourself?"

"Be assured, I dinna need nor covet any of what she inherited," Raven replied without hesitation. "Had she come ta me in beggar's rags, I would've wanted her just the same. Were she ta give her consent, I'd take her ta me home in Scotland, where she'd be safe, but I wouldna want ye ta have ta endure her absence until the shock of her being taken has eased. As for her riches, 'tis hers ta do with as she pleases. I only have one request."

Vachel narrowed his eyes. "Go on."

"That ye dinna tell her about this agreement between us."

"You don't want her to know that you've refused her dowry?" Vachel thought he could not be any more surprised, but Raven Seabern was an enigma.

"I don't expect ye ta lie, but if it doesna come up, then nay, tell her not. She believes I only want her wealth, instead of the woman that she is. I want her ta come ta know for herself the kind of man I am and ta trust in me."

Vachel took a deep breath and then held out his hand. "You've eased my mind, Raven." They shook hands. "I cannot guarantee that Abrielle won't hold this marriage against you for a long time."

Raven spoke firmly. "I trust I will win her over."

"If any man can prove himself to her, you can. You have my blessing. But as for the blessing of her mother . . ."

With a grim smile, Raven said, "Lady Elspeth will be just as difficult ta win over as her daughter. But I intend ta succeed."

CHAPTER 17

Cedric sat in the great hall after supper, awaiting Raven's return from Vachel's solar. Having heard of the dilemma his son faced, he was hoping for the best, and as he knew his son well, he did not doubt that he would approach the situation with determination and aplomb. He'd heard the talk around the keep this day, the rumors and the speculation swirling among serfs and knights alike, and he'd learned long ago to let most of what was said in ignorance roll off his broad shoulders. He took pride knowing his son's back was strong enough to do the same.

Raven finally appeared, his expression resolute, as Cedric had anticipated it would be. He put a hand on Raven's shoulder. "Care ta walk the courtyard with me, son? 'Tis a fine, cool night."

Raven nodded, and when they were outside, they could hear the distant sounds of soldiers settling into their barracks, of horses nickering, and the chirping of insects. It was a peaceful moment, but Cedric understood that Raven felt anything but peace and knew to wait for his son to speak in his own time and on his own terms.

At last he spoke, and Cedric felt pride at the resolution in his voice. "I have won her at last, though not in the way I would have anticipated. I must state now that she and hers have attacked our honor, and though what they claim is not true, I have indeed now won her in name. But do not doubt that I will win her completely, body and soul. I swear it, she will be truly mine."

ABRIELLE HAD DRESSED for bed when she heard a knock at her door. Surprised, she went through the antechamber, wondering if it was her mother, come to offer her support once again. She didn't want to turn her away, but there was nothing Elspeth could do and talking about it only stirred Abrielle's feelings of anger and resentment, which in turn upset her mother even more. "Who is it?" she called.

"Raven" came the abrupt reply. So much for holding her feelings in check, she thought, then she closed her eyes and inhaled deeply, struggling against a wave of anger and uncertainty and despair. As much as she did not want her misery to add to her mother's distress, she wanted even less to give Raven the satisfaction of seeing her thus. "Go away," she said without opening the door.

"I need ta speak with ye, lass," he remonstrated.

"'Tis not proper."

"'Tis too late ta worry about what's proper."

Sorely piqued, she swung the door open so hard it hit the wall. "Yes, it is, and all thanks to you!"

He nodded solemnly. "Ye've every right ta be angry. And so do I."

"Ooh! I am so much more than angry." She grabbed his sleeve and drew him inside, shutting the door behind him.

For a moment they simply stared at each other. It was as if now that they stood on the cusp of a very different future than either of them had planned, neither knew what to say. At last Raven squared his shoulders and cleared his throat. "I spoke with your stepfather tonight."

Abrielle folded her arms over her chest and glared. "I saw."

"Surely ye ken what we discussed." She said nothing, for if he thought she would ease his path, he was as mistaken as he was devious. The muscles in his jaw clenched tightly, banishing any trace of softness from his too-handsome face, and when he spoke, the softness in his voice was far from soothing. "It has been decided—we are ta wed."

He knew her pride, her courage, and was a fair way to going down on bent knee to propose formally to her when she tossed back the shimmering curtain of her hair and through gritted teeth said, "I will marry you, but I will never respect you. I told you I would never marry you, and so you made certain that I had no choice."

"And I am telling you that I did not betray my honor, nor that of my family." His voice contained an edge she had never heard before, and suddenly, despite her legacy of the Harrington impetuosity, she knew she had to tread carefully; he was a dangerous man.

"I have conditions you must meet," she said simply. "You must promise that a large portion of money will be used to improve the plight of the serfs. The small stone cottages with hearths and thatched roofs which some of them are living in readily evidence the fact that Lord Weldon had meant to provide the same for all his serfs. Unfortunately, he was killed before he could complete that dream. 'Tis my hope to see them erected in the near future."

"'Tis good as done! Ye know I've grieved for the plight of your people."

She studied him, as if looking for a visible lie. "You're from another country, and now my marriage to you will ever keep me between those people and yours."

"Abrielle," he countered, his mien softer now, "your mother is a Saxon, her husband a Norman. Your Norman king is married ta the sister of my own King David."

His words were those of reason, but she was not prepared to listen to such calming talk and threw up her hands. "Just go! Leave me in peace!"

He would let her have her pride and exited the chamber into the corridor. There the next door opened, and Raven saw Vachel peer out and Abrielle's parent only asked, "'Tis done?"

Raven nodded. "Aye. She has agreed that we will wed."

Vachel seemed to deflate with a sigh. "Thank God." Elspeth ducked past her husband, gave Raven a frown, and went into her daughter's chamber.

"The ceremony will be in the great hall before the midday meal," Vachel continued. "Then we can 'celebrate' with a generous feast for the people."

"Ye will forgo the reading of the banns?"

Vachel winced. "There will be enough witnesses to make the marriage valid. After we break our fast in the morning, you and I will negotiate a marriage contract."

Raven nodded.

"Have a restful night, Raven. I think it might be your last for some time," Vachel concluded.

AFTER MASS, THE announcement of the impending wedding ceremony was greeted without surprise. While both Abrielle and Raven looked solemn and subdued, rather than facing the day with excitement, Vachel proclaimed the day a cause for celebration, a union between Scotland's royal emissary and England's wealthiest widow. He spoke of goodwill between neighbors on the border, both within England and Scotland. But not many seemed interested in his optimism. There were angry murmurs among Abrielle's remaining suitors, and more than one man departed the keep in outraged haste. The consensus seemed to be that Norman wealth was going through a Saxon girl to line a Scotsman's coffers. There would be no peace between neighbors, Vachel realized sadly. Nor between husband and wife, of either generation, he thought ruefully, for Elspeth, while not exactly angry at her husband, was upset on behalf of her daughter, and that strained Vachel's marriage.

And then there were Raven and Abrielle, seated side by side at a trestle table, both barely eating, not even speaking. Vachel told himself that in due time Abrielle would understand this marriage was far superior to her brief one to Desmond de Marlé. But right now she was too angry to see or to care about the depth of the passion her warrior husband so clearly felt for her.

Abrielle heaved a weary sigh as she watched Raven and Vachel retreat once again to Vachel's solar. Then, noting her mother's look of apprehension, she forced a smile. There was no need to stress her mother unduly, not in her sensitive condition.

"Abrielle, child, come, let us prepare for the ceremony."

"Again," Abrielle murmured, rising and following her mother. "What do you suggest I wear, Mama? I think my black mourning gown would be perfect." When Elspeth gaped at her, Abrielle hastened to say, " 'Twas but a jest, Mama, and a poor one I can see."

Elspeth settled herself and gave her daughter a brisk look. "I suggest that gown that you wore to King Henry's court. 'Tis the one that first caught Raven's eye."

Abrielle barely withheld a groan as she followed her mother upstairs to dress and once again bit her tongue for the sake of her mother's peace of mind. Elspeth was determined to be cheerful, and Abrielle knew it was because her mother was grateful not to be giving her away to a man like Desmond de Marlé. She would not steal that from her by revealing what weighed so heavily on her own mind.

As wretched as Desmond had been and as loath as she'd been to marry him, she feared and dreaded this union with Raven even more. With Desmond she knew to be ever on guard, so there was no trick to keeping her feelings in check, no need for a protective wall around her heart. It was a very different matter with Raven, in every way, for when she was near him she didn't know where she stood, or what the truth was, or how she was supposed to feel. As much as she distrusted the man right down to his little fingernail, there was no denying or escaping the fact that he would make her feel things she ought not to want to feel, and feel them far too easily to be safe, so easily that she feared there was no wall in the world high and solid enough to protect her heart from him.

The last time she had dressed for her own wedding, the fear utmost in her mind was for the night ahead; this time she feared the lifetime of nights to follow. She was deathly afraid that if she let her guard slip for even a sliver of time, Raven would slip in and steal her heart and soul, and make her need him, and leave her bereft in the end.

THE MARRIAGE CEREMONY was held before the remaining guests, small in number though they were, and a large contingent of serfs and servants, all of whom seemed glad for their mistress. But Abrielle's dear friend Cordelia could not attend, making Abrielle even angrier with Raven, because this haste was necessitated by him.

The same priest who'd performed her first marriage ceremony—was it only a fortnight ago?—was there to attend her once again. Raven and Abrielle pledged their troths with subdued voices, and if the lady's tone was trembling, no one would remark on it. Raven used his father's wedding ring, knowing it would be far too large for Abrielle, but it had long descended through his family, and had meaning for him.

Abrielle couldn't even look at Raven as he spoke the words, "With this ring I thee wed, and with my body I thee honor."

Her own ring to him had been her father's, which Elspeth had insisted she use. It seemed obscene to use it for this farce of a marriage, but she had not wanted to hurt her mother's feelings. She spoke the same words back to Raven in a toneless voice.

And then the priest pronounced them married. If Abrielle thought too long on the fact that she had had two unwanted marriages in such a short time, she would run from the hall sobbing. Instead she accepted the good wishes of people through the midday meal. Vachel had surprised her by arranging for minstrels to play in the afternoon. They even held a tables tournament to pass the time, and she found herself hoping that Raven would lead the men away from the board game and out to the tiltyard, anything so she wouldn't have to look upon him.

But no, he played the doting bridegroom to the hilt, remaining at her side, even challenging her to a game of tables. She could have sworn he let her win, but he assured her that it was not so.

But always, thoughts of her wedding night were not far away. Once, as the hour grew late, she even found herself thinking that mayhap she did dread this wedding night even more than her first, and that almost made her giggle with rising hysteria. What woman would not want to take Raven Seabern to bed? She had always thought him a handsome rogue and his practiced charm and words of lovemaking, even when they'd angered her, had seemed to melt her very bones.

But a wedding night meant a giving of self, and she did not want to give the most precious thing she had to offer, the gift of herself, to a man she did not trust, a thought that resulted in her feeling only sorrow for this union. How could she surrender to him what he seemed to have schemed to win? So she decided then and there that Raven would not have his manly pleasures this night. He would have to earn the right to her by more than simply compromising her.

But at last her mother left her alone in her bed-chamber, wearing a diaphanous nightgown that Elspeth had hastily sewn together just that day. Only when her mother was gone did Abrielle draw on her robe as if donning armor for a battle.

Not long after that, Raven came to her, closing the door behind him and leaning against it. He had not expected her to be waiting in bed for him, and she was not. She sat in a cushioned chair before the fire, staring at it as if in contemplation.

Yet the sight of her nearly took his breath away. From a heavily carved wooden candelabrum, stout tapers cast their flickering radiance upon the long, coppery-red hair that tumbled in soft, glorious disarray around her slender shoulders, creating a vision of beauty beyond compare. His eyes swept over her in a lingering caress, evoking a blush that left the lady's cheeks nearly as rosy as her soft lips. Her dressing gown of burgundy velvet only made him ache to see what it concealed.

Coming forward, he said, "I almost thought ye would pretend ta be asleep."

Slowly she turned her head to him. "I considered it, but I would not start our marriage with a lie—at least not on my part."

His face hardened, and his voice was low and intense. "I havena lied ta ye." She said nothing, knowing again that she was goading him too much, that he was a man of pride.

"And how do ye intend ta begin our marriage?" he asked.

"By telling you that you have not earned my trust," she said firmly, rising to stand before him, hands on her hips like an avenging angel, "and that you will not take me to bed." All of a sudden he took her arm in a firm grip, having moved pantherlike, startling her. Her wide eyes met his.

"But until then," he echoed softly, "ye're still my wife. I will have no man suggest we are na legally married."

"What are you saying?" she demanded, and feelings she could not describe coursed through her. To her growing fear, his hands loosened the robe at her neck, parting it though she tried to stop him. She saw his eyes flare with heat when they took in the pale silk gown, its simplicity framing her body for him almost like a gift, clinging to her at breast and thigh. She held her breath when his hand touched her cheek, then moved slowly downward, cupping her neck for but a moment, drifting down over collarbone and between her breasts. She could not move nor cry out nor stop him. It was as if the world had narrowed and was only the stillness of their heavy breathing, the promise and heat of his touch. With one hand, he cupped her breast, startling a gasp from her, even as her frantic eyes met his. He watched her face as he lifted her, weighed the fullness of her. "Nay," she whimpered, "please stop."

Those blue eyes softened. "I canna, Abrielle. Fight me not, for I've wanted ye from the first moment I saw ye."

His burr had thickened erotically. As if the veneer of the civilized man was falling away, exposing the real man beneath, a man of flesh and blood, of honest instinct and desire, a man who did not hide what he was and what he wanted. If only she could be sure this was the true and real Raven who wanted her so desperately.

Then his fingers found her nipple, teasing and stroking, and for the first time, she understood the true depth of her vulnerability to him, for the heated sensations such a simple touch raised all but swamped her own determination. She tried desperately to pull away, but he only drew her closer, still continuing the stroking of her delicate flesh.

And then his mouth came down on hers, bending her head back even as his tongue slid within to find her own. She was as helpless to the rising desire consuming her as she had been when first they'd kissed. He tasted of wine, and it drugged her senses. His hand on her breast caressed with more pressure, while his other hand slid down her back to cup her backside and pull her harder against him. "Abrielle," he murmured against her mouth, "Abrielle, kiss me back."

But she wouldn't, only turned her face away when she could. But she had too much pride to run from him, so when he stepped back and pulled his long tunic over his head, she stood frozen and watched. His shirt was next, then his shoes and hose. All that kept him from nakedness were his braies, the low-slung garment that covered his loins. But even that he dispensed with, and she found herself backing away from the threatening manliness of him.

Yet she could not deny that his face and form were thrilling, that the evidence of his desire for her made her wonder how much he truly wanted her. She came up hard against the bed, and felt like she'd been herded there, which only made her anger flare. But then he was upon her, pushing her back onto the soft quilts, laying his long, heated, well-muscled body over hers. He kissed her again, hard and deep, and she felt the first draft of cool air on her legs as he pulled her nightgown up and off.

"I will have naught between us this night," he whispered against her throat.

She was being pressured from all sides, as if her traitorous body were no longer her own. Then her hips and thighs were bare and he settled himself between, all heat and hardness. She gasped and squirmed, but he did not force himself into her, only held her still with his lower body while pulling her robe down her arms. Effortlessly he lifted her up to slide it off her, and even though she struggled against him, he at last pulled her gown over her head.

And then they were naked against each other, flesh to flesh. She went still, feeling his arousal at the very gates of her womanhood. But instead of pressing home, he murmured unintelligible words against her neck, and then lower, until his mouth closed over her breast. The hot flame of heat enveloped her, made her no longer herself, but his. She moaned against the exquisite torture, undulated her hips against his because she could not keep still. At last he slid home, to the very core of her, stretching her through pain until it was done. "Easy now, lass," he murmured against her lips, then took her mouth with another overwhelming kiss.

Raven knew she was a virgin, but he was beyond himself, could only give in to the need to move, to sink deeper into her and pull away. Her cries were of pleasure, not pain, and he let himself go, thrusting over and over until he felt the tautness of her, then her trembling release. He barely lasted another moment, the climax sweeping over him with a power he had thought unimaginable.

When at last his passion eased, when he could remember how to breathe, he lifted himself up on his elbows and looked down at Abrielle, who was flushed and perspiring and staring at him. "Ye are mine now," he told her, and at his words she burst into tears.

With a groan, Raven rolled off of her and tried to gather her close, but she would not have his comfort. She felt betrayed by her own body, for the pleasure it had taken from Raven had not been under her control. He had won this first battle. She rolled away from him, her slender shoulders quivering, the quiet sobs hiccuping through her body.

Raven stared at the ceiling and wondered if he'd made a terrible mistake marrying a woman who didn't trust him, who didn't want to trust him. Had lust overcome his good sense? Had he thought he could make this marriage work? But then he reminded himself that this was only the first night, with a lifetime more of them to come, and he resolved that one thought would guide his marriage from that time onward, that he would not give up on his bride.

CHAPTER 18

As Abrielle slowly opened her eyes as the rays of the morning sun fell upon her, something seemed wrong, but she couldn't remember what, until she realized to her horror and consternation that she was naked. With a gasp, she sat up, holding the quilt to her chest, but she was alone. The clothing that had been dropped haphazardly was now folded in a neat pile on the chair. With a groan, she fell back on the pillow. She was a married woman, no longer a virgin. But he had taken that last choice from her.

She threw back the bedding, and was only angered more at the spot of blood on the sheets. After foolishly covering it back up, she drew on her robe and paced. What was she to do? How was she to face Raven? He was truly her husband now, in every way; he had made sure of that.

But she could not spew her wrath at him. What would that accomplish but misery for all involved, including her parents? Nay, the deed was done, and she would have to live with it. Many women married men they had not chosen. She was just another one. She would smile and pretend to others that everything was fine. That would not extend to her bedchamber, of course, but she would face that when necessary. There was a hesitant knock on the door, and since Abrielle knew her bold husband would probably swagger right in as the new master, she called for the person to enter.

Nedda peered in. "M'lady?" Abrielle greeted her with a smile, and the servant relaxed as she came in.

"Sir Raven said ta let ye sleep," Nedda said, "but I heard ye movin' about. Would ye like a bath?"

"Oh, please, that would be wonderful," Abrielle said. She knew that Nedda continued to watch her almost suspiciously, but Abrielle remembered her vow to act like a normal wife.

As a normal wife, she bathed and dressed, and then went down to the great hall. Again, she hated her feeling of relief when she did not see Raven. The trestle tables were being folded against the wall after the morning meal, and Abrielle found Elspeth speaking with the servants.

On spying her, her mother hurried over and gave her a hug, then searched her face with trepidation. "Abrielle? Do you fare well this morn?"

She was a normal wife, Abrielle reminded herself, and forcing a smile on her face, she said to her parent, "Aye, Mama, I am well. I am simply a wife now, which is nothing unusual."

"Hmm" was all her mother said in reply, for she knew her daughter well, and readily surmised that indeed she did not fare well, regardless of her claim.

A bit too brightly, Abrielle looked about the hall. "I see I have slept through the meal. Forgive me for not being here."

"Nonsense. Yesterday had to be trying for you." Unspoken was the query asking if the same could be said for the wedding night, but Abrielle pretended ignorance. Elspeth sighed. "I'll have someone fetch bread and pottage for you."

"Nay, I'll go to the kitchens myself." Clearly her daughter was not herself, though understandably so.

"You do not ask where your husband is," Elspeth said slowly.

"I assume he is about somewhere, enjoying his status as the new master of the keep." Abrielle winced as her bitterness peered through her masquerade. "Forgive me, Mama," she said before her mother could speak. "I will become better at my new role, I promise."

Elspeth put a hand on her arm. "Every woman must learn the role of wife, my dear. The adjustments are not easy even when you're deeply in love with your husband."

"But what happens when you cannot respect him?" Abrielle said softly, feeling once again the sting of silly tears. She dashed a hand across her face and forced a smile. "It is only the first morning. Things will be better," she assured her mother, though she could not foresee how that could be so when she neither trusted nor respected the man whose ring weighed as heavily on her hand as their marriage weighed on her heart.

Abrielle spoke to the kitchen staff, consulting on the meals for the day, leaving her mother in charge of examining the food stored in the undercroft for the coming winter. She decided to show her people that this transition to having a new lord could go smoothly, so she toured the castle, speaking to the servants, learning of their lives and their work. By the time she reached the courtyard, her people's cheerfulness had her feeling a little better. She examined the harvesting in the kitchen garden, watched the dairymaids at work, and spoke with the grooms in the stable.

At last she was drawn to the sounds of clashing metal, and followed it to the rear of the keep until she reached the tiltyard, where the soldiers and knights practiced their warcraft. It was there that she found Raven and her stepfather. But it was to Raven that her eyes were reluctantly drawn. He was wearing a sleeveless leather jerkin that fell to his midthigh; his bare, muscled arms gleamed with sweat in the sun. He was speaking to a group of men, all of whom carried swords. Then Raven began to demonstrate as he spoke, sparring with Vachel, who comported himself as well as any younger man.

There seemed to be no animosity here among warriors, and for that Abrielle was grateful. The knights looked upon Raven with respect, and she saw more than one man nodding in approval at whatever maneuver he had performed. Raven may have caused dissent in the countryside, but at least here among men he must command, he was respected.

Yet only yesterday, these same men had smirked at Raven when he'd been found alone with Abrielle. Did marriage so easily satisfy their sense of honor? Would that she could be so easily reconciled to her fate. But then, they were not the ones who'd been deceived and used and had what was their choice to freely make stolen away, and a tarnished substitute forced on them instead.

Suddenly Raven's gaze fell upon her, and the smoldering intensity there froze her. He came striding toward her, still carrying his sword, and she couldn't move, couldn't even dream of escape. All she could think about were the things he'd done to her in the dark of the night, and the pleasure she hadn't wanted to feel sweeping over her. Even now, her traitorous body grew warm as her blush spread to every part of her skin.

To her shock, he slid one arm about her and pulled her to him. Her hands landed on his chest, but she couldn't push him away, not before all the men he would command. Then his mouth took hers in a searing kiss that was too sensual for such public display. She felt helpless and aroused and angry with both herself and him, especially when she heard the cheers of the men echo on the tiltyard.

When at last he lifted his head, she whispered, "You brute! How dare you handle me like this!"

He only arched a dark brow and grinned. "Ye can no longer play the outraged virgin, lass." She would have retorted with a scathing comment, but she saw Vachel coming toward them. So she donned her false smile and, in an overly sweet voice, said, "You are still embarrassing me before your men."

"Our men. And I think they're cheered by the obvious success of our marriage."

"Success—?" But then Vachel was too close and she turned to face him, conveniently stepping away from Raven to kiss her stepfather's cheek. "A good morning to you, Vachel."

He blinked at her display of affection, then warily said, "And to you, my dear. You look radiant this morn." As if a night in Raven's bed was supposed to change her for the better? she thought darkly.

"I see the two of you have wasted no time in getting back to work after the festivities."

" 'Twas necessary," Raven said, his face sobering. "I

needed ta see what months under the dubious command of Desmond de Marlé had done to the keep's fighting force."

"And 'tis not good," Vachel added.

Abrielle forgot her own concerns. "What is it?"

"Many of those men arrived with us," Vachel said, "and four with Raven. The rest have allowed themselves to grow lazy, for Desmond was more concerned about spending his newly found wealth on himself than on his soldiers. What incentive is there to train when the pay is irregular at best?"

"How terrible." Abrielle's gaze returned to the tiltyard, where the men began to spar with blunted swords.

"But now they understand what is required of them," Raven said.

"And the rewards they'll receive," Vachel added. "Your new husband has been generous."

With my money, she thought with bitterness, then chastised herself. Raven was doing his duty to her castle and her people, nothing more. If only for their sake she had to stop ascribing base motives to everything he did.

"The stores set away in case of a siege are seriously depleted," Raven said. "Much will have ta be done."

"Of course," she said, "my thanks for seeing to it."

"And why wouldna I?" Wearing his best charming grin, he put an arm around her shoulders and squeezed. "I will do everything in my power ta protect ye and our people."

She patted his chest and again managed to step away. "Then I shall see you both for dinner." Yet when the midday meal was being served, Abrielle received word that Raven, Cedric, and Vachel had been called away to a nearby manor, and though the servants seemed to be trying to protect her, she heard the whispered fears of "invasion" and "Scots."

Throughout the day, she told herself that if there were any truth to such rumors, Raven never would have left the castle gates open, with the soldiers continuing their training rather than manning their positions. But nighttime fell, and still he didn't return. On this, the second night of her marriage, she finally went to bed alone. She would have felt relieved at the peacefulness of sleeping in the big bed, except her fate and future were now tied to her husband's. What if something worse was happening? Should she have sent a contingent of men in support? Surely Raven would have sent word if he needed assistance.

It seemed as if she had barely fallen asleep when dawn's light woke her and she stirred, feeling herself suddenly trapped. She realized that Raven was there, and they were entwined together, her head pillowed on his shoulder, the broad, naked expanse of his chest before her. Thankfully, she had worn a nightgown to bed. His hand rested familiarly on her back, and to her horror, her knee rode his. She was planning the best way to escape without waking him when she glanced up and saw him watching her with amused eyes.

"What a wonderful way ta wake ta the day," he rumbled, coming up on his elbow, rising above her with too much threat.

She quickly slid out of his arms and out of the bed. "I am glad to see that you returned safely. I have so much to do, and I'm certain you do, too, what with the . . . lazy soldiers," she finished lamely.

He fell back on the pillows, folding one arm behind his head, the better to watch her. He saw how flustered she was to find a man in her bed, and, remembering her tears, had decided to allow her to escape—for now. But a newly married man had only so much patience, and she would have to accept that.

She stood shivering on the rug before the hearth, where the fire he'd tended late last night had died down to a few embers. He could see her hesitation, knew she wanted to dress, but did not want to do so before him. And he was not about to help her with that dilemma.

She hugged herself and rubbed her arms. "Why were you absent so long yesterday?"

She didn't even know if he would discuss what some men would consider falling within a man's domain, but his smile faded and he frowned as he began to speak.

"We received word from a courier that Thornton Manor was 'attacked' by a contingent of Scots."

"Oh my." She went still in sudden fear. What would happen to her and her people should a war break out, when they now had an "enemy" as their lord?

His expression eased. "Fear not, lass. It wasna an invasion, but a half-dozen poor Scots chasing their cattle and not realizing how close ta the border they were. They crossed inadvertently."

She closed her eyes with relief at the news he'd brought, thankful that an invasion had not taken place.

"I wasna meant ta be summoned, of course. The courier didn't realize he wasna supposed ta alert everyone in the area. My arrival almost made things worse, as if I were in collusion with these other Scots. We were lucky that Thurstan de Marlé was not at home ta be summoned. Your stepfather has a cool head about him, and my da's joviality helped everyone stay calm. The Scots were freed at last ta return home."

She sank down on the edge of the bed, her face in her hands. "This will never end, will it?" She felt his hand on her back, and when she stiffened, it dropped away.

"Ye mean this distrust of my people?"

Not just that, but her distrust of him, of the fact that his being a Scot would forever put him at odds with her people. When would he have to side against her? When would this supposed loyalty of a wife to a husband be tested?

"Abrielle?"

She gave a start, then stood up briskly and went to busy herself by choosing her garments for the day. "Do you think you'll be called away often, especially by your king?"

"I dinna ken. Now that I must care for property in both countries, I willna have as much time ta devote ta the king. He will understand this."

Abrielle glanced at him with surprise, for truly there were many things about her husband's life of which she was not yet aware. "I did not know you had other property."

"Ye've never asked me," he said drily. "I have land adjoining my da's in the highlands, and someday his land will be mine as well."

She nodded thoughtfully and, although she was curious, did not ask him more for fear of being misunderstood. She believed that if he wanted to tell her about his home, he would do so, but since he'd not seen fit to mention it till now, and had been so eager to acquire her property, she suspected his own was modest. She did not care overly about his holdings, as they were not her concern. "Will we be . . . visiting?"

"Aye, I want ta show ye everything that's now yours, too."

Nodding, she stood indecisive, her hand smoothing

over her garments. She told herself that more than once she'd moved away from the only home she'd known, what with her mother's marriage to Vachel and then her own betrothal to Desmond. She would accept whatever she had to, and remain strong.

Hesitantly, she began, "I . . . don't suppose you would be leaving the chamber anytime soon."

"Nay, I am still too tired from a long, tense day."

When she glanced over her shoulder at him, he was stretching languidly, and she watched wide-eyed at the way his muscles seemed to ripple over his bones. She had never seen him with a day's growth of beard, and it made him seem like a rakish scoundrel, one who took his pleasure in bed whenever he wanted to, and from what she'd felt before she left the bed, he wanted to now.

She felt somewhat confused, for he had just willingly shared a military matter with her, and she had not expected him to so easily confide in her, as if he truly trusted her. He had his own property, and surely he'd been well compensated by his king. She wondered if he could actually desire her more than her wealth, but didn't know what to think.

She could not remain in her nightgown all day. Thank heavens she had bathed yesterday evening, for she could not imagine doing that in front of him. It was bad enough when she had to turn her back and pull the nightgown over her head. She fumbled with frantic fingers for her shift, knowing she was naked, waiting with dread for him to approach her from behind and demand her submission once again.

But at last the shift covered her, and she felt a little less frightened as she donned her kirtle and the braided belt that hung low about her waist. Only when she was settling a veil over her hair did she hear his approach. She stiffened and glanced over her shoulder.

He put his hands in her hair, drawing it across her shoulders, smoothing it. She shivered.

"Must ye cover such beauty?" he murmured, and to her surprise, he put his face against it and inhaled. "The smell of ye makes me long ta be in your bed, in your arms. I thought about it all day."

Even his words made something inside her shift uncertainly. "I . . . I must wear a veil. I am a married woman now. You've seen to that."

And there was the conflict between them, what she had to force herself to remember—he had made this marriage happen, giving her no choice about accepting him as her husband. He ignored her challenging words, whispering, "Then don't braid your hair beneath the veil. Let me imagine touching it all day long." His nudity and his sweet words were far too confusing. She hastily put on the veil and secured it with a band about her forehead before fleeing the bedchamber.

ABRIELLE FOUND HERSELF wishing that another emergency would call Raven away for the day, because he seemed to be everywhere she went. When she visited the serfs' village, they hastened to tell her that her new husband had been coming by every day, and that she'd just missed him, and what a good man he was. When Abrielle went to speak to the laundry maids in the courtyard, she saw children gathered around Raven as he examined the horses. One little boy, so thin, but moving about with vigor, took to following Raven for the rest of the day like a little shadow. Never once did her husband show his impatience. In fact, when she came upon them unawares, she heard Raven tell the boy that he could be Raven's second squire, and could begin his training on the morrow.

At supper, even her mother sang Raven's praises. Abrielle felt like she was being assaulted on all sides. Vachel, Cedric, and Raven were hefting tankards to one another, toasting whatever success they'd had that day, while several knights approached by ones and twos as if tempted to join in. Married not two days, and Raven was winning over everyone—but her, she insisted to herself, deciding to retire to bed early and feign sleep.

Raven watched Abrielle's quiet departure, and although he continued to respond to his father, his mind was much on his young wife. He had allowed her to escape their bed this morn, and now she was in full retreat, as if she hoped he wouldn't notice her. Did she not yet know that he noticed everything about her? It took all his will to concentrate on his duties, when he wanted to follow her about all day like a lovesick swain. Her gentleness with the abused serfs moved him, her loyalty to her stepfather and her willingness to aid him though it might have cost her her sanity, astounded Raven. Falling in love with her had happened so easily, so completely, that he could not imagine his life without her. He wanted her to feel the same way toward him. But her fears and doubts and mistrusts were strong, and he knew it would take much to overcome them. She would consider his love a burden, so he chose not to tell her.

It took all of his control to allow Abrielle time to settle into bed. Then he set down his tankard and rose to his feet, yawning quite deliberately.

Vachel eyed him with amusement, but it was Cedric

who said, "Lad, ye must be exhausted. 'Twas a dreadful, tiring day seeing ta the horses and chickens."

Several men openly laughed, and Raven took that as sign that they were beginning to accept him. "Well, Da, someone had ta see ta keeping ye housed and fed. Have a good night, all."

There was much good-natured laughter as Raven left the hall, and he was in a cheerful mood when he finally approached his rooms. In the antechamber, candles had been left lit to guide him, and he blew them out one at a time as he went through. In the bedchamber, he closed the door quickly to keep in the heat. There was a deep feeling of satisfaction as he stood there and looked on his sleeping wife, buried beneath quilts, with the firelight flickering over her. He removed his garments quickly, folding and setting them aside. When he lifted the bedclothes and slid beneath, the warmth and the scent were all hers, and if possible, he wanted her even more, with a painful need.

She didn't move, but he sensed a faint tension in her, and he guessed she did not sleep. Gently he moved against her, his hand reaching. He encountered the curve of her lower back, and realized that she lay facedown, as if protecting herself. He began to pull her nightgown up her body, wondering how long her pretense would last.

Abrielle kept her eyes clenched shut, her face turned away, concentrating with every fiber of her being to keep relaxed, as if she slept. But that didn't seem to matter to Raven. His body was hot, pressed to her side, and she knew he was naked. She felt her nightgown slide up, gritted her teeth to keep from yanking it down and betraying her wakefulness. Surely he would give up, if only she could last long enough.

And then Raven slid down beneath the quilts, and she bit her lip against crying out. The bed moved up and down as he crawled. To her horror, she felt his mouth on the back of her knee, and the shock and excitement almost made her jerk. But nay, she held on to her control, even when the moist wetness of his mouth slid up the back of her thigh, to the base of her buttocks. How could she continue to make herself lie still if he was going to—

His mouth left her, but her absolute relief was short-lived, for she felt his kisses move up her other leg, and begin to climb up the hills of her body. A squirm of mortification and languid heat escaped her now, and she felt his low laughter where his face was pressed to her back.

And then he slid on top of her, his loins cradled against her buttocks, his face buried in her hair. She should have been smothered by the heaviness of him, but he held himself gently against her.

"Ah, ye left your hair unbraided for me," he murmured.

Curse it all, in her haste to feign sleep, she'd forgotten.

And then he was moving against her, rubbing slowly, easing one hand beneath her to capture her breast. The sensual haze that descended on her made her forget why she even fought him. All she could comprehend was how gentle he was, how loving, and when at last he eased her onto her back and kissed her, there was nothing she could do but kiss him back, clinging to him, opening her thighs to him, groaning when he made them one by thrusting home. Again, he gave her a woman's ultimate pleasure and took his own.

But afterward, when he eased from her and she was

left with the cold reality of what she'd done, she found herself crying again. She wanted him, but she was too afraid to trust him, to trust that he would stay with her as husband even when Scotland called him. And where that mistrust had once led her only to anger and resentment, it now made her heart ache in a way she had not known was possible. My God, could she be falling in love with him, she wondered, then firmly told herself no, and right after that repeated it to herself for good measure. No, she absolutely was not falling in love with her husband, and firmly refused to do so. He might be able to woo her body to surrender, but she would never willingly give him her heart, and at that she cried even harder.

CHAPTER 19

Raven would not peacefully abide the tears of a weeping woman. He sat up in bed, flung the covers aside, got to his feet, and stood over his wife.

"Abrielle, this cannot continue," he said sternly. "I canna longer seduce ye by force. I willna take ye again like this. 'Tis time for ye ta come ta me."

His easy assumption of his domineering role in her life did more than put Abrielle into a high temper, it caused her tears to dry up as quickly as they'd come. She flung the quilts back from her side and jumped to her feet, facing him across the bed.

"You'll be waiting a long time, Raven Seabern. You may have taken my wealth, but you won't have my heart and soul to crush when you leave."

"Why . . ." He hesitated, momentarily distracted and captivated by the sight of her bunched nightgown sliding over her curves, then he blinked and frowned. "Why would I leave?"

But she would say nothing more, only flounced back into bed and refused to face him. Raven wanted to spin her around and make her tell him exactly what she meant, and he wanted to scoop her into his arms and back into bed, no matter that he'd barely finished making his pledge not to take her again until she came to him, or that he'd thought himself sated from their lovemaking. Gazing at her barely hidden curves, he feared he would never be completely sated. He was a fool to let her flummox him this way, but not enough of a fool to storm off as he was sorely tempted to do at that moment. He would not give his infuriating bride that satisfaction. Nor would he deny himself the pleasure of sleeping near her body, even if he couldn't touch it thanks to his damn pledge. Aye, a fool to be sure, he thought as he too got into bed, folding his arms behind his head to keep from reaching out to her and staring at the ceiling.

ALTHOUGH THERE WAS tension in the new Seabern household, there came a growing strife in the rest of England. Never before had so many heralds been sent out at one time to deliver dispatches to various parts of the realm. The news they bore was grave indeed. Having gone to his castle at Lyons-la-Forêt with every intention of hunting in the surrounding forest, Henry I, youngest son of William the Conqueror, had fallen ill and within a week had died. His death ushered in not only a time of grievous mourning but also a harrowing and lengthy epoch for the whole of the late monarch's realm.

Henry's first queen had been a Scotswoman, sister of King David himself, and their daughter, Maud, was his choice to succeed him on the throne. He had won concessions years before from all his noblemen that they would support her when he died. Although the noblemen found it difficult to generate enthusiasm for Maud, they feared if they bound themselves by fealty and oath to the late king's nephew, Stephen, they'd lose whatever they had managed to gain throughout Henry's rule, whether ill-gotten or justly deserved.

Had not the king been at odds with his daughter and her husband at the time of his death, Maud might have been wont to hasten to her parent's bedside and claim her rightful inheritance before anyone could usurp it. Instead, within a matter of days, Stephen had managed to impose himself as king within the minds of the nobles and was soon aggressively defying anyone who might have found fault with that idea. Although Stephen would not be officially crowned for several weeks, Maud's continued absence from England seemed to solidify his authority. In the ensuing days, it became apparent that the kingly domain was being plunged into the darkest form of strife, a far cry from the peaceful rule that Henry had managed to maintain throughout his years on the throne.

ON THE SIXTH day of their marriage, Raven was called away to confer with King David on Scotland's newly strained relationship with England. Abrielle stood in the chill air of the courtyard beside her mother and watched Raven speaking with his father as he awaited the arrival of his squire and the three other men-at-arms who'd come with them from Scotland.

Elspeth put her arm around Abrielle. "You will be sorry to see him leave, I am sure."

Abrielle nodded, surprised at the veracity of her mother's words in spite of the fact that she and Raven continued to be at odds over the state of their marriage.

The last several nights had been spent in the same bed, but they were separated by a chasm of misunderstandings and anger.

"Perhaps . . ." Elspeth continued slowly, watching her daughter, "the time away will allow you both to see your marriage more clearly."

Abrielle turned to gaze at her mother, sarcasm quirking the corner of her mouth. "And you are so certain that we have things to sort out between us?"

"I see my daughter's pain. I want you to be happy, Abrielle."

Abrielle pulled her cloak closer about her throat and turned cool eyes back to her husband, who was now leading his horse through the courtyard toward her. "Mama, you assume that two countries are not about to come between us. You assume that Raven prizes our wedding over his obligations to his king."

Elspeth opened her mouth, but then could say nothing, for Raven had arrived. He stood before Abrielle, looking down at her solemnly. She looked beautiful and proud and aloof, all part of the contradictions that made up his wife.

Softly, she said, "Farewell, Raven. Come back unharmed."

He leaned down and kissed her cheek, inhaling the sweet scent of her. He hadn't wanted to leave without the final comfort of her embrace, but wouldn't force her hand.

"I shall return soon," he said, then turned away and mounted Xerxes, his loyal stallion. With a nod to his father and her parents, he rode out of the courtyard and headed north.

In the days and weeks that followed, a grim harvest of death, violence, and thievery was rampantly reaped by those seeking to benefit themselves in whatever dreadful form their unbridled maliciousness and greed chose to be exhibited. Pillaging became commonplace throughout both Normandy and England, to the degree that no man was safe from aggression or butchery even in his own home. It seemed especially rampant upon the roads, where innocents were now being frequently set upon by those bent on thievery and other grievous acts of violence.

Abrielle sheltered and healed more than one victim, and she thought often of Raven traveling such dangerous roads between two countries. He was her husband, and for that reason alone it was natural for her to want him to come home safely. Yet she also bore him tender feelings from her woman's heart, feelings that were growing steadily stronger even as they were battered by sadness and regret and confusion. Was this to be her life, always watching Raven ride away, always wondering who might kill him because of the country of his birth? Or would he have to fight with Scotland against Abrielle's own people? There was a time when she'd vowed never to open herself up to the pain of falling in love with him; now increasingly she wondered if she had any more choice in the matter than she had in marrying him.

IT DIDN'T SEEM to matter whether one was loyal to Stephen or to Maud, there were many who were intent upon reaping, either by arbitration or by force, whatever benefit or profit they could garner from the discord now raging within the kingdom. The knights and men whom Vachel had once commanded came riding again to his defense, splitting their forces between

Vachel's home and Abrielle's. These knights as well as the foot soldiers and the families that belonged to each accepted Vachel's invitation to take up permanent residence within the protective stone walls surrounding the keep. Many already living there were wont to agree that the knights' presence calmed some of their fears, for beyond the gates, it now seemed apparent that neighbor was turning viciously against neighbor and kith against kin in this turnabout world whence all reason had been vanquished.

It was to this very same keep that the three Graysons and several of their loyal knights fled in haste during the dark of night. Like the knights and foot soldiers who had fled from the terror encompassing their land, the Graysons came seeking shelter, bringing their most costly possessions as well as trunks filled with clothing and basic essentials. Their flight, however, was not without incident, for a miscreant's arrow had pierced Lord Grayson's shoulder while he was helping the servants load his small family into the conveyance. It was only after they had thrown several valuable items from one of the carts that the rapacious scoundrels flew upon the spoils and began to squabble over them, in their greed allowing the family to escape their murderous intent.

Upon their arrival, servants helped Reginald into the keep, followed by Isolde and Cordelia. Already alerted, Abrielle and Elspeth were in the process of turning down a bed and spreading clean but older linens over the sheets already covering the mattress when the servants bore Reginald into the chambers. Isolde and Cordelia were clearly distraught over the wounding of their loved one, but were encouraged when Vachel assured them that his lordship possessed a hearty stamina and was not one to be easily undone by a culprit's arrow. The women were then urged to return to the antechamber, where they would remain until the arrow could be extracted. Abrielle sent a servant to bring mulled wine for the women, hoping it would suffice to soothe many of their qualms and perhaps help to relax them as they kept vigil together. But Abrielle herself went into Reginald's bedchamber. She had never removed an arrow, unlike Cedric, so she was going to assist him as needed.

With the further assistance of copious tankards of strong ale for the patient, Cedric was able to remove the arrow and then sear the wound with a red-hot poker iron. Afterward, a bleary Reginald gratefully offered him a tankard of ale. By the time Elspeth, Cordelia, and Isolde entered the chamber, Cedric and Reginald were chortling together as if they had just shared some wildly humorous tale.

Cordelia's gaze seemed naturally inclined to meet the vivid blue eyes of the elder Scotsman, and in response he gave her a wink and a lopsided, white-toothed grin, readily bringing a blush to her cheeks. "'Tis certain I am that the stars have come out ta shine upon me this eventide," he avowed with a deep chuckle. "If na, then it must be the radiance of m'lady's smile I'm seeing afore me."

"To be sure, sir." Cordelia gave a winsome dip of her head. "You likely saved my father's life, and for that I will always be grateful. Indeed, I should like to commend you for your proficient removal of the arrow, as well as Abrielle for her capable assistance."

"My humble gratitude for your generous praise, m'lady," Cedric replied, inclining his head briefly in appreciation.

Abrielle simply squeezed her friend's hand, happy

beyond words to have her companionship in such dreadful, trying times.

Isolde slipped her hand within her husband's as she asked in wifely concern, "How are you feeling?"

His lordship grinned up at her. "Rather mellow now with the worst of it behind me. 'Twas to my great benefit that Laird Cedric was here to tend me. I've suffered worse from physicians who've tended simpler wounds. The laird is certainly a good man to have around."

Cedric swept her a clipped bow. "I'll be leaving ye in Abrielle's capable hands. My new daughter by marriage is a fine healer. Now I must be off. There's still training ta be doing on the tiltyard this day."

"Be careful!" Cordelia urged as he hastened through the door. "We would see you again soon."

Casting a glance over his shoulder, he gave the young beauty a wink. "I'll be coming back, m'lady, mark my words."

As Isolde and Elspeth began to fuss over a drowsy Reginald, Abrielle left them with crushed herbs to use in a poultice, before Cordelia drew her into the antechamber.

The two friends hugged each other for a long moment, until at last Cordelia backed up a step, gripping her friend's arms as she examined her face. "You don't look all that different now that you're Raven's bride."

Abrielle sighed. "Oh, Cordelia, it did not feel like a true wedding without you."

"I trust it was a true wedding night," Cordelia offered with a sly grin.

Abrielle groaned and turned away. "Even friends should not discuss such intimate things."

Cordelia pulled her back to face her, her own smile dying. "Abrielle? When I last left, you were treating

Raven as just another suitor, one you'd already asked to leave the castle. The next letter I received was the awkward announcement of your wedding, without any good details."

"I . . . wished you to have the news with haste, so I did not take the time to write more."

"He is a 'bonny lad,' as a Scot would say. So why do I see shadows in your eyes when you talk about him? And do not say that you're simply worried about him in his absence, for I shan't believe it."

Abrielle had never withheld anything from her friend, so she briefly sketched the details, from their discovery alone together to the wedding.

"So 'twas not a joyful ceremony, I take it," Cordelia said drily. "But surely he's a far better man than Desmond de Marlé."

"Who could hurt me far worse than Desmond ever could have if I allow myself to become vulnerable," Abrielle whispered, hugging herself. "You know that from the start I have not been able to trust his motives where his courtship of me is concerned."

"Abrielle, you are a wondrous woman whom any man would be glad to marry for herself alone. Raven is lucky to have won you, regardless of the manner, and I am sure he knows it."

"I wish I could believe that," Abrielle replied. "But even if I did, it is so much more complicated than that. He's a Scot, Cordelia. If we go to war with them . . ."

"Has he demanded that you change your allegiance?"

"Well . . . nay, but—"

"Then you and he will work it out. Countries may be fighting, but husband and wife do not need to."

So torn about her emotions was Abrielle that tears stung her eyes. " 'Tis not that simple. If I let myself love him, and he has to leave me over a coming war, how will I bear it?"

"Abrielle, none of us can predict the future. If we all base our deeds on things that might happen, we would cower in our beds without any decision being made. You just have to allow love into your heart."

"I know not if I can," Abrielle whispered at last.

CONSIDERING THE CARNAGE and aggression now occurring throughout the kingdom, it was not at all surprising when Thurstan de Marlé realized that he had found the perfect tool to use against Raven Seabern. The Scot had taken what was Thurstan's from the beginning—the de Marlé keep and the wealth that went along with it. It was time for Thurstan to send the Scot back where he came from—or even to the very grave itself. But first he would take the castle itself, while its new lord was away.

It was easy enough for him to visit the various lords of the region, to take advantage of their worries about the peace and safety of their homes situated so close to Scotland. Thurstan encouraged all to besiege Raven's new base of power, telling them that they could "hold" it for England rather than Scotland. The Scotsmen should not be allowed to gain any more English territory.

And with their insecurity and fear, the northern lords listened, allowing Thurstan, kin to Weldon de Marlé, who had been so respected, to lead them. Thurstan, in turn, was compelled to allow Desmond's half sister, Mordea, to ride at his side. He was still holding her fast, urging her on in her hatred, waiting for the day he might need her evil skills.

With no warning, Thurstan and a large contingent of noblemen, knights, and mounted men-at-arms came thundering across the land on horseback, sending the serfs fleeing in fear for their lives toward the safety of the stone fortification. Riding on a shaggy steed beside Thurstan was Mordea, with her long, frizzy hair flowing out wildly behind her. A large gray wolf's pelt had been wrapped about her darkly cloaked shoulders, beneath which she wore a breastplate that protected her stout chest.

Upon letting the frightened serfs into the courtyard, Vachel ordered the drawbridge to be lifted behind them to forestall the entrance of the rabble following on their heels. He then selected several of the best riders from among the serfs and bade them to arm themselves with swords and pikes before leading the group through the lower passageway to the postern portal whence Abrielle and Nedda had previously been abducted. Since that occasion, the lower depths had undergone beneficial changes, part of which included a stable wherein a few of their fastest horses were kept in stalls near the outer door, allowing the keep's inhabitants to promptly give chase should miscreants attempt another abduction. From there, Vachel sent several mounted riders racing off in different directions with the hope that they would be able to alert their allies and persuade them to come in haste and lend their assistance in defeating the unprovoked aggressors who now sought to take possession of the keep. But most of the northern lords had long memories, and they would most likely believe that the Scots should be swept from England.

Holding a flag of truce, Thurstan rode forward alone, garbed entirely in black except for a metal breastplate covering his chest. He reined in his horse within hearing range of the men on the battlements.

"For most of you within the castle, we have no quarrel. If you surrender yourselves, you will not be harmed. But the lords of Northumberland will not allow Scotland this incursion into our land. We mean to hold this castle for England."

Vachel stood with his legs wide, his hands braced on his hips, and shouted, "I speak for Lady Abrielle, the rightful lady of this castle, as you well know. Though its lord may be a Scot, the castle and lands are for England, and Lady Abrielle stands firm on this matter. Cease this violence at once, before innocent men are killed."

Thurstan rode away, lowering his flag, having made his attempt at peace. Uneasily he told himself he would have been content with their surrender, but some deep part of him relished the thought of earning his prize, fighting for what he believed was his. And with the modest army he had amassed with the help of his neighbors, the siege would be a glorious one.

On the battlements, Vachel and Cedric stood side by side, watching Thurstan depart.

"Keeping it for England, is he?" Cedric said darkly.

"He cannot possibly think we believe such nonsense," Vachel replied, "although apparently the rest of Abrielle's neighbors do."

"Do ye believe the castle is ready?"

"We could have used more time, but Raven has been

diligent in seeing to the preparations. No doubt he sensed the coming unrest."

"Or at least the animosity of these border lords," Cedric added, shaking his head. "How go the women?"

"Well. Elspeth and Abrielle have assigned everyone tasks to keep them busy—less chance for an outbreak of panic to spread. They're readying arrows, preparing for injuries, and of course seeing to food and drink for weary men." Vachel hesitated. "Think you that Raven will return in the middle of this? I rather hope he stays away until it is over and we are victorious."

"I know not what King David has planned for him," Cedric answered. "But I know my son, and if he has heard of Thurstan's attack, he will come. But until then, we know what we have ta do."

"My thanks for your help," Vachel said.

"This is a battle that affects your family and mine." Cedric clapped his shoulder.

Cedric selected the best archers from those same ranks and positioned them within the battlements for the purpose of dissuading the soldiers who were seeking to lay floating bridges across the stream. In a matter of moments, arrows began raining down upon the intruders, who promptly dove behind whatever tree, rock, or barrier offered protection.

Cedric strode behind the serfs, urging them to aim true and make every arrow count. He was quick to praise their skills, buoying their resolve to defeat the aggressors perhaps even more than their disdain for Thurstan could. Though such deeds would be in defense of the keep, killing a freeman set the serfs a-jitter, knowing they could suffer various degrees of punishment for that offense. They were wont to look to Cedric for guidance. His soothing brogue calmed many, assuring them that their new lord, Raven Seabern, would expect them to protect their lands and families. His assurances did indeed result in a truer sighting, for in a matter of moments, there were many within the enemy's camp who had either been killed or seriously wounded beneath the unrelenting onslaught of arrows.

Upon espying Thurstan's soldiers laying out reinforced planks for the purpose of crossing the moat, Vachel recognized the need to discourage them. He directed the serfs to prepare hot cauldrons of rendered fat to be dumped upon those who would soon be making an effort to scale the stone walls. Leaving the Scotsman to carry on with such tasks, Vachel began directing other defensive measures for the security of the keep, of the sort that he had ofttimes used during the Crusades. He also called for a pair of recently constructed catapults to be loaded with large stones should there come a need.

Even while those within the edifice were involved in preparing their defenses, the enemy was wont to evidence their confidence that they'd be there for some time by setting up camp beneath the protection of the trees just beyond the clearing. At the fore of the moat, they brought up battering rams which they obviously meant to utilize in their assault upon the drawbridge. Thurstan could be seen directing those who had ridden in with him. He swept an arm about as he motioned for his men to bring up one of a pair of wooden bridges to the fore. Upon standing the first half on end on the far shore, they allowed it to fall into the stream. Buoyed by the many animal bladders filled with air, the piece barely dipped beneath the surface of the water.

A volley of arrows rained down upon the intruders from the archers occupying the battlements, wounding a goodly number of the enemy before they managed to raise the shields that had been slung over their backs. In a few moments, another group of men, bearing another section of the bridge, scampered to the far end of the first, whence they allowed the piece to fall into place across the remaining half of the moat, only a step or two away from the narrow spit of land that remained in evidence beneath the raised drawbridge. The original bridge was of such heavy and enduring quality that it was almost impervious to axes and such weapons. Nevertheless, men bearing large bundles of dried reeds and other flammable plants began rushing across the two sections in a quest to pile up what they bore onto the section of earth showing beneath the raised drawbridge.

Their intentions were obvious. Since the original drawbridge was too heavy and sturdy to hack asunder in any reasonable length of time, they were obviously going to attempt to burn it down to gain entrance into the keep. Several of Thurstan's men were already being supplied with lighted torches in preparation.

Vachel sent a half-dozen serfs scurrying in haste to the kitchen to bring back cauldrons of scalding water. By the time they returned to the battlements, the brigands were already igniting the dried bundles that had been heaped up against the bottom of the drawbridge. The contents of the huge pots, borne on sturdy poles by pairs of serfs, were promptly dumped onto the burning bundles as well as upon those bearing the torches. Upon being drenched with scalding-hot water, the brigands ran screaming in agony across the makeshift bridges even as more cauldrons of water were being dumped on the burning reeds.

Inside the keep, Abrielle, Elspeth, Isolde, Cordelia,

and the women who normally worked in the kitchen continued to fill huge cauldrons, this time with rendered fat. The fire beneath the cauldrons was nearly roaring with the intense heat they had created, but it hastened the melting of the lard until the latter began to bubble and spit. Slightly smaller kettles were then filled and borne by strapping serfs to the battlements. The contents were dumped forthwith upon those in the process of scaling the ladders. Agonized screams readily accompanied the descent of those drenched by the scalding oil, and though others sought to take their places, recurring waves of fat cascaded down upon anyone who tried. Only by diving into the moat could the aggressors find any relief from the agony of their seared flesh, but some were so badly burned that they were unable to pull themselves onto dry land or attempt to tread water. Many slipped beneath the surface of the water without notice.

Long poles with cross-planks affixed to the ends served to provide the serfs with some degree of safety as they pushed the ladders away from the niches into which they had been temporarily lodged. Maidservants also scurried to throw bucketfuls of water onto flaming arrows that had lodged in wooden areas of the keep. The miscreants obviously saw nothing to fear from the women's efforts until they began to feel the searing pain of boiling liquids soaking into their own clothing. The burns caused many to fall away from their makeshift ladders, screaming in pain. The water in the moat proved almost as effective as the scalding liquid that had been thrown down upon them, for the chilled winds that buffeted them quickly penetrated their soaked clothing as they sought to drag themselves from the moat.

Soon another flurry of flaming arrows began to assault the battlements and the walkway around the keep, obviously with the hope that they would prove successful in setting afire some of the oil their adversaries were wont to throw down upon them. Wave after wave of arrows bombarded the battlements as well as the defenses that had quickly been erected to ensure the safety of those taking shelter within the edifice. In spite of the relentless urgings and demands that Thurstan made on his men, the serfs fighting for the keep proved even more tenacious. Under the capable direction of Vachel and Cedric, they were wont to believe there was a good chance they'd be able to defeat the foe and send Thurstan off with his tail tucked between his legs. They were well motivated to fight on to the death if need be. Better to battle valiantly and die trying to protect themselves than to be subjected to whatever cruelty Thurstan and Mordea intended to lay upon their hides should they seize the keep.

At last night fell, and darkness forced a suspension of hostilities. Both sides saw to their wounded and rearmed themselves. Inside the castle, optimism reigned, for few had been seriously hurt; supplies could last for many weeks, if not months. Three more days passed in much the same way, Thurstan's forces attacking, Vachel and Cedric leading the defense.

On the fourth evening, Abrielle's optimism had become merely a show for her people, who had been fed and calmed. She herself could not contemplate sleep, as it was becoming more and more difficult to fight her sense of fear and sadness. She went out into the courtyard and climbed up into the battlements above the curtain walls. There the stars were pinpricks of light across the sky, and the moon hung low like a white grin laughing at them.

Vachel was patrolling the walkways with the soldiers, bolstering spirits, keeping a grim eye on the enemy encamped some distance away. When he espied Abrielle, he came to her and swept his own cloak about her. She had not even realized that she was cold until she was enfolded in comforting warmth.

"You should be resting, my dear," Vachel said.

"As should you." She allowed him to put his arm about her, to pull her against him, but his presence could not ease the pain in her heart. "Innocent men on both sides are dying because of me," she whispered, her throat raw, her eyes surprisingly close to tears.

"Nay, that is not true, daughter. Men are dying because of the greed of one man, who has swayed many fools to a false cause. They cannot see beyond their fear."

She leaned near the embrasure to see out over the dark countryside. Dozens of campfires dotted the horizon. "How long do you think this will go on?"

He shrugged. "Until the northern lords come to their senses and see Thurstan for his true motives."

At night, with the sound of battle a distant memory, there was a deceptive peace over the land. All Abrielle could hear was the murmur of male voices carried on the wind, the babble of the stream below—and the faint clash of weapons.

She stiffened at the same moment as her stepfather. "What was that?" she asked.

"Battle," he said grimly. "But at night? And it is not near our walls. Does someone attack our enemies?"

One by one, soldiers came to stand against the

battlements, to peer into the distance, to speculate with cautious voices. Abrielle's eyes hurt from the strain of trying to see, but she thought the sounds were getting closer. More than once, she saw fire glint off metal, heard several shouts.

And then came the thunder of a horses' hooves, and the shout of a man's voice as he neared the castle.

Abrielle did not need to see who had shouted to know in her heart who it was moving through the darkness and danger to reach her side, and she cried out, "Raven!"

CHAPTER 20

Not an hour before, Raven had worked himself through the lines of his enemies. He had crept by stealth, past campfire after campfire, and patrols that were looking toward the dark horizon rather than to the earth itself. And through it all he kept his mind sternly focused on the moment at hand, never letting his thoughts stray from his next footstep, his next hand-hold, not daring to think of the one thing he wanted to think of most, his very reason for being there, lest it cause him even a second of delay.

He had come ahead of the regiment he'd summoned, men loyal to Stephen, 'tis true, but willing to fight an injustice and settle the uneasy countryside. Raven had left his own men-at-arms a league distant, knowing he could get through the enemy lines more easily and quickly alone.

Get through he must, and would, no matter who stood in his way, for on the other side of the wall that was now in sight lay what mattered to him most in the world, more than he'd known was possible, and a million times more than she was willing to believe . . . Abrielle. He would not see her harmed, nor any of those she loved. And it angered him enough to make him even more dangerous than his reputation just to think of what this siege had already put her through.

When he was within sight of the castle walls lit by torches, he heard the first shout of warning, and then the echoing cries of alarm. He had been discovered. He jumped to his feet, unsheathing his claymore as he ran, cutting down the first guard without even breaking his stride. Several more came at him, swords raised, but there was fear in their eyes, too, as if they thought him dangerous because of what he dared. He veered toward the hobbled horses, cut a line, and then vaulted onto the animal bareback, urging him into a gallop toward the castle.

His plan to approach the walls and be let in secretly at the postern gate was no more. He was leading too many enemies for the guards to risk opening the door. If he had to ride away, he would fail Abrielle, which he would not accept.

Just as the castle walls rose above him, a man ran out of the darkness, startling the horse, which reared wildly. Raven was already tumbling backward to the ground as he heard a woman scream. After landing heavily, he rolled to his feet, claymore still clutched in his hand.

Thurstan de Marlé was alone before him, sword held with purpose and skill. "Raven Seabern, you must win your way past me to enter this keep. We claim it for King Stephen."

"'Tis obvious my wife disagrees with ye on the ownership of the castle," Raven said. He could hear soldiers gathering around him, noises and shadows in the dark. "So ye'll attack me in force, will ye?"

"Nay, right now let this be between you and me," Thurstan said, then raised his voice. "The rest of you stay back."

"And if I win, do I receive the dubious award of their swords in my back?"

"You can have free passage into the keep. Agreed?"

"Agreed."

And with that, Thurstan attacked. His advance was immediately met with a deft stroke of the claymore that left a deep cut across his arm. It did indeed unsettle his firm conviction that he was the better swordsman. Soon it was all he could do to hold ground against the Scotsman's unrelenting advance. Rising cuts from the back guard continued to propel him ever backward in a desperate attempt to avoid the menacing strokes of the claymore. In turning the hilt and bringing the point in a position to strike again, Raven left his adversary astonished out of measure by the skill he displayed. Even when Thurstan sought a more aggressive approach with a hanging guard, he found himself again amazed by the deftness with which the Scotsman parried his attack. Beads of sweat were now dappling his brow as he strove to halt the other's blade and keep it from snuffing out his life. His own sword seemed no less than paltry in comparison, and yet, with each passing moment, his arm grew increasingly weary from its weight. He could only wonder how the Scotsman had the strength and stamina to wield the much heavier weapon with unyielding proficiency.

Raven felt almost calm, each stroke of the claymore springing forth from strength born of long hours of practice. He felt a nick to his wrist between his mail and the gauntlet he wore on his hand, but it was not a serious wound. He took a hard hit to the mail chausses covering his thighs, and knew he'd be well bruised. Cheers and cries of encouragement or dismay rang through the air. Up on the battlements, more torches had been brought, lighting the sky as if it were the birth of dawn. From up there, he knew Abrielle was watching. After endless weeks of tedious meetings or long, boring, cold journeys across two countries, at last he was almost with her again. He had to end the battle, to make his wife safe from this fool.

In the next instant, a downward stroke of the claymore evoked a loud, tortured scream from Thurstan, who lifted what remained of his left arm and, in growing horror, stared at the bloody stump. Knowing he would soon die if something weren't done to stem his copious loss of blood, he stumbled in agony toward the fire. Another bloodcurdling scream was wrenched from him as he thrust the stump into the flames and held it there until the wound was seared black and the loss of blood had been adequately stemmed.

The sudden silence was eerie, and was followed by the sound of the claymore, cleaned on moss, sliding home into its scabbard.

"We are done," Raven said in a cold, calm voice. "You can no longer hold a shield. Do you guarantee my reward?"

Mordea came forward, teeth gnashing, arm raised, but Thurstan grabbed her before she could get past him.

"Aye, you . . . have won," Thurstan said, breath coming in gasps, eyes stinging with sweat, "but only this battle. Enter the keep. We shall . . . see how long it lasts before falling . . . to our siege."

The soldiers ringing the battlements began to cheer, but they also readied their arrows as the drawbridge was lowered, in case of treachery. Raven suddenly whistled, and from the darkness came three of his mounted men bearing a flag of truce, and leading Raven's stallion. All four clattered over the drawbridge, and it was slowly lifted closed again.

Only when Raven was safe within the curtain walls did Abrielle sag against the embrasure, where she had stood to watch the battle. To see him risk his life for her, and for her family, left her weak, and it unleashed an avalanche of questions and second thoughts, so many it would take her a week to sort them all. For now, one rang out clearly above the rest, the one that mattered most of all. If all Raven cared about was wealth, as she had been so certain was the truth, he could have waited in Scotland while the castle was besieged, but he had not done so, he had not abandoned her. Nay, he had acted as honorably as any husband could, and suddenly Abrielle could not bear to wait another moment to be by his side.

Vachel put his arm around Abrielle, and although she protested that she was fine, he supported her down the narrow stairs leading to the courtyard. Knights and serfs and castle residents were all streaming into the courtyard, surrounding Raven and his men, throwing question after question at him.

Abrielle pushed her way through. "Enough!" she cried with force.

All around her, people fell silent. Raven focused that intense gaze on her. She saw flecks of blood on the cote over his hauberk, dirt smeared across his face, and a coolness in his features that she was not used to seeing. But still, his blue eyes were hot as they took in the length of her body. It took her some moments before she could compose herself enough to say, "Husband, you need tending. All else can await the morrow."

Raven did not hesitate, but rather with haste pushed past all others to take her hand and lead her through the castle to their bedchamber. Thanks to Nedda, the bed was turned down, linens were laid out, and water heated over the fire. Even the bathing tub had been set up, and a line of servants arrived with steaming buckets of water. Abrielle watched the grateful looks they gave Raven, and though he be a Scot, he had already proven a far superior master than Desmond. They obviously did not care what country he came from as long as he treated them well and fairly.

When they were alone again, Abrielle helped Raven remove his mail and gambeson, and she was relieved to see that the blood did not seem excessive. His breeches, bloodstained shirt, and braies came next, and she still found herself averting her gaze as he sank into the tub and began to soap a cloth.

"Wash your wounds well," she said, sorting through her medicines. She had to keep busy, for it was far too easy to be swayed by the tension between them. They had parted weeks ago, leaving her to feel awkward and worried about their marriage. Now there was an energy and excitement moving through her, and she tried to tell herself it was only because he was safe and because he was here to help rescue her family and her people.

She glanced at him over her shoulder and felt a strange tenderness to see his big body crammed into that tub, shoulders out of the water, his head tilted back awkwardly against the rim as if he were almost asleep out of weariness. Through slitted eyes, he watched her warily as she soaped his face and took a blade to his many days' growth of beard. She pushed his shoul-

ders forward to bare his wide, strong back, and then
began to scrub diligently with a soapy cloth, for she
didn't know when he'd last had the luxury of anything
more than an icy stream. He groaned softly, his head
dangling forward. She put her soapy hands in his hair
and started to rub.

"Let me rinse your hair," Abrielle said at last.

"Bring me the bucket, and I'll rinse everything at
once."

With a splash, he rose to his feet, holding out his
hand for the bucket. She delayed a moment, simply
watching the soapy water run down his glistening, nude
body. At last she put the handle of the bucket into his
grip, and he lifted it over his head to pour. Steam rose
from him, and he gave a big sigh as he stepped from
the tub. She held out a linen for him, and he took it,
beginning to dry his body.

"Your wounds," she began.

He interrupted. "They're na worth bothering about."

To her shock, he went to the bed and fell into it, rolling onto his back as he closed his eyes. She came to
stand over him, his glorious nudity a threat to her con-
centration as she tended to him. There was a slice near
his wrist that still oozed blood, and a dark bruise at his
thigh with raw scrapes where the chain mail had abraded
his skin through several layers of garments. While he
slept the deep sleep of one exhausted, she used her
herbs to cleanse his wounds and speed the healing.

After blowing out the candles and leaving only the
fire in the hearth, she changed into her nightgown and
crawled into bed. He rolled onto his side, and she was
able to draw the quilts up over him. Then, without giving it much thought, she curled against him, her thighs

tucked behind his, her arm around his waist, and she soon fell into a peaceful sleep.

RAVEN AWOKE IN the gray before dawn to a luxurious warmth he thought he'd forgotten how to feel. Cold nights spent on dangerous roads faded away. And then he realized that he felt his wife's curving form against his side. He opened his eyes and found her head pillowed on his shoulder, her long auburn lashes blinking the sleep away. She rose up on one arm, and her hair slid forward over her shoulders to drape across his arm. He shuddered.

And then she slid her nightgown over her head and came down on him, her mouth taking his, her slender hands exploring his chest. Raven groaned and gathered her against him, cupping her buttocks as he pulled her over him.

"I'm starved for ye, lass," he murmured between deep kisses.

"And I for you, my husband. My husband," she said again, the word delicious on her tongue. She put her hands on both sides of his face. "You cannot know how good it feels to freely admit it."

He grinned and rolled to press her into the mattress. "Ye canna know how good it feels ta hear it. Nearly as good, in fact, as . . ." His hands wandered boldly, his purpose clear and arousing. He kissed every part of her as if relearning her body, making her skin flush, setting her limbs atremble. In his arms, Abrielle felt truly a wife at last and she gloried in it, and when he came into her, she gasped at the very rightness of his possession.

"Oh, Raven," she whispered, arching her back, offering her tender breasts to his greedy mouth.

With his lips and tongue he aroused her, with his

manhood he stroked deep inside her, until the passion that always existed between them burst in her mind and through her body—and in her heart.

AT DAWN, THE household gathered in the great hall to break their fast and plan their counter to the siege. But first they had to hear Raven's report on the doings of those who called themselves royal.

"Betwixt Maud and Stephen," he began, "there's na much ta be greatly admired. Maud has her prideful temper, and when the occasion has mattered, Stephen has never proven himself a skilled warrior or an arbitrator. Ta be sure, his failures have taken precedence over his victories, and yet, in his eagerness ta be king, he has enforced his will upon noble and priest alike, as if the lot of them are but lowly serfs meant only ta do his bidding."

"Then to whom should we give our allegiance?" Abrielle queried worriedly. "To be sure, I care no more for Maud than I do for Stephen."

"As a Scot, my allegiance must be ta King David. As for ye"—his gaze took in all of his new English friends and kin—"ye must choose the one ye prefer, whoever that may be, but my advice is ta keep your thoughts a secret from those who can do ye harm. Far too many have died already in this struggle betwixt Maud and Stephen after foolishly admitting where their allegiance lies."

Abrielle shook her head sadly as she thought of the injustices now being invoked upon those seeking to fulfill Henry's wishes in the succession of royals. In her opinion, Maud was just as guilty as Stephen, for the woman could have easily complied with her father's wishes and taken the throne as empress of the realm. Perhaps Maud had expected the nobles to hasten to her side and entreat her to comply . . . in spite of her contentious temper. As it was, her willful disposition had likely cost her the crown. It had definitely left the country reeling from the uncertainty of what the morrow would bring.

Vachel nodded solemnly. "We shall take your suggestion to heart and keep our preferences private except when we're amongst those we can trust." He looked around the table at Elspeth and Abrielle, the Graysons and the Seaberns. Nodding, he said, "Like our good friends and family gathered here."

"I was able ta tell Stephen of the trouble caused ta ye by the northern lords," Raven said. "He sent a regiment of soldiers with me, for he doesna want problems on the Scottish border. This morn, I will tell Thurstan and the rest of your neighbors that we will soon have assistance. They shall soon be fighting a battle on two fronts."

Cedric's face was hard with satisfaction. "We'll see how eager they are ta 'hold' this land for England. As if me and mine would try ta take what isna ours and use it against them."

Although Abrielle said nothing, surely Cedric had to realize that Raven now owned English land, and that was part of what was causing problems.

"This turmoil that's erupted may be only a smattering of the trouble yet brewing," Raven said. "Ta be sure, the violence may continue ta menace us for months, if not years to come. The safety of all is my greatest concern. We must depart for Scotland the moment the siege lifts. Should any of ye here choose ta join us, my da has a fortress there nearly as grand as this. We can house anyone of a mind ta make the journey north. But we cannot make the assumption that we'll remain safe here while this madness rules the countryside."

"Your offer is generous," Vachel said soberly. "Let us discuss how it would work."

As Abrielle listened to the men absently, her own thoughts circled about in confusion. If she was honest with herself, she had known that whoever she married would not want to linger forever in the de Marlé keep. A lord with more than one property must travel every few months, seeing to each castle, and eating through its stores before rot set in. She was not foolish enough to refuse to live part of the year in her husband's home. But "nearly as grand" as Weldon de Marlé's keep? She had a difficult time imagining such a thing.

"Abrielle?"

She gave a start, and realized that her mother had come beside her and touched her elbow. She gave Elspeth a smile. "Aye, Mama?"

"Come speak with me a moment, daughter."

They walked to the hearth and sat on a bench before it, enjoying the warmth of the fire.

"Abrielle, what thoughts give your expression such sadness?" Elspeth asked. "You and I will not be parted right away. For reasons of safety, we will journey with you and take up temporary residence in Scotland."

"Oh, Mama, glad I am for such tidings. And I know that Vachel and Raven will make certain that our homes are well protected while we're gone, but . . ." Suddenly she was speaking past a lump in her throat. "I feel caught between these misguided Englishmen and my loyalty to my husband. Just when my people have begun to accept him, we journey to his household, where I will be a Saxon in Scotland, my place with Raven now in reverse."

"Such is the lot of a wife, my dear. Ever we must move with our husbands, learning to fit in among his people. Think you that it was easy for me, a Saxon widow, to marry a Norman?"

"Nay, I know it was not. Your behavior has surely been a guide for me."

"Then trust that you have learned well. I believe in you. It is obvious this morn that there is a new understanding between you and your husband."

Abrielle tried not to blush. "'Tis true, Mama. I am learning to accept this marriage."

"And appreciate it—and him?"

Now Abrielle's face was truly hot, and she could only stammer. Elspeth smiled.

Suddenly they heard the sound of a horn being blown from the courtyard. Raven threw open the double doors to the great hall and went outside. Several minutes later, he returned to say, "'Tis a royal courier. He has been granted passage through the siege lines. The soldiers are lowering the drawbridge ta allow him entrance. I will escort him inside." He turned and disappeared through the doorway.

"Whatever could it be?" Elspeth asked, her hand protectively over her belly. "Will the new king help us?"

"Raven did say that royal soldiers were not too distant," Abrielle offered.

A moment later, Raven escorted a somberly dressed man into the great hall. To everyone's surprise, Raven pointed out Vachel, and the courier approached him.

"Sir Vachel de Gerard," the courier said, and held out a leather-bound missive. "I come bearing an important dispatch for you from His Majesty King Stephen. Should I await a reply?"

"Perhaps you should, since I have no idea what this is all about," Vachel acknowledged.

Isolde drew the man away to offer him food, then

swiftly returned to gather around with everyone else.

Vachel unrolled the parchment and began to read the contents silently as Elspeth looked on with growing apprehension. Raven watched the couple curiously, and then happened to glance aside at his young wife, whose smile seemed unusually radiant and hopeful. He canted his head inquisitively in an effort to claim her attention, but she was far too busy watching the astounding wonder that soon swept over her stepfather's face.

"What is it, Vachel?" Elspeth asked with a hopeful smile, unable to mistake her husband's mounting elation.

Vachel's lips widened into a grin as he met her gaze. "'Twould seem, my dear, that His Majesty has decided to bestow a title of some rank upon me and to grant me lands of my own for my loyal service to his country as well as my efforts during the Crusades. Upon the receipt of such an honor, I shall be known as the Earl de Venn." He swept into a low bow before his wife. "And you, my dearest Elspeth, will soon be known as the Countess de Venn, a most fair and wondrous lady of the peerage."

"Oh, my!" Elspeth's smile could not have been any brighter as she clasped her slender hands to her rosy cheeks. "But what in the world brought about this honor?"

Vachel flicked the back of his fingers lightly against the parchment as he replied, "According to this decree, His Majesty was recently reminded of my loyal service to the crown by none other than Abrielle." Fixing his smiling gaze upon the younger woman, he raised a brow questioningly. "What I'm now wondering is how you managed to accomplish such a feat without leaving the keep prior to being kidnapped?"

Grinning back at her stepfather, Abrielle shrugged nonchalantly. "I merely wrote a missive to His Majesty pointing out that your gallant service during the Crusades had been overlooked, then I asked Raven to see to its delivery. Obviously, King Stephen received it after Henry's death and understood the need to honor a good man whom his predecessor had overlooked."

"Or he sees the need to woo more men to his side during this battle with Maud," Vachel said drily. "But I care not why. 'Tis obvious that I would never have received such an honor if not for your efforts, Abrielle," he replied humbly. "And if my new title can aid us in this desperate siege, then it will not only be myself who owes you a debt of gratitude."

He put an arm around her shoulders and kissed her forehead, and then suddenly Reginald Grayson lifted his tankard with a cheer. The hall rang with glad cries, so much so that men outside the castle were wont to stare at one another in wonder. What did these besieged people have to celebrate?

But soon the attackers saw that the spirit of celebration also extended to bold confidence, for under a flag of truce, Raven Seabern, with two knights at his side, rode out to speak with the new leaders of the siege.

Several of the northern lords met him.

"I didna have the opportunity ta speak with ye last evening," Raven said drily. "But I wish ta inform ye that I have come from Stephen's court. He is displeased with this unrest ye've caused here in the north. He sent a regiment of knights and mounted men-at-arms, and they follow a day behind me. I traveled more swiftly, for I didna take well the thought of my wife in danger. The king's men will arrive by the end of the day. Ye may send your scurriers ta see that I speak the truth."

The lords looked askance at one another, but before one could speak, Raven continued, "You may have noticed the royal courier arriving today."

"And did we not allow him to see you?" one man said angrily.

"Aye, ye did, and 'tis a good thing, for he bore timely news. My father by marriage, Vachel de Gerard, has become the Earl de Venn, courtesy of His Majesty."

The noblemen were fidgeting now, looking at one another with obvious uncertainty.

"Say what you want, Scotsman," said Baron Gravesend, who only weeks before had challenged Raven to nothing more serious than a game of tables. "But the king does not comprehend our life on the border. We must protect ourselves."

"The king has chosen ta protect my wife and her family," Raven answered coldly. "I suggest ye think on that before ye're foolish enough ta waste more lives attacking me and mine. Abandon this siege and return ta your homes before worse happens ta ye."

And then Raven guided his horse in a circle and rode back toward the lowered drawbridge without even a glance over his shoulder. Though many of them would have longed to bury a dagger in his back, none would risk it now.

Not two hours later, they began to withdraw, already planning how they could return with more men. From his pallet, Thurstan railed against them, urged on by Mordea's lust for vengeance, but no longer was anyone listening. This falling from power ate away at him, clouding his judgment and making stronger the hatred he felt for Abrielle, her husband, and the families cherished by them both.

CHAPTER 21

By the next day, a royal regiment one hundred men strong gathered in the courtyard and clustered in the great hall, straining the capacity of the keep. But Raven could not yet send them away, for word came from his scurriers that the northern lords did indeed think to defy the king, beginning to gather a larger army in their quest to expel the Scottish presence in Northumberland.

Preparations began for the great journey to Scotland, and notice was sent to the surrounding lords that Raven and his family were departing. Since most of Vachel's knights and their families were unwilling to venture to the highlands of Scotland, both Abrielle's and Vachel's castles would remain under their protection. But Raven did not assume that Thurstan had forgotten his vengeance. He sent men to keep watch on Thurstan's manor, and instructed them to send word if his small army moved out in force.

Thurstan, slow to recover, used that time to try to persuade his allies to yet take the castle and keep it

from Raven Seabern. But the men he had assumed
shared his vision of revenge now insisted that all they'd
ever wanted was Raven's departure. With the Scottish
presence no more, Thurstan's allies went back to protect their own homes in this uneasy time. Thurstan,
without enough men to attack, now looked upon the de
Marlé castle as a mocking prize he could not win, a
sign of his failure. In pain and frustration, his sanity
began to slip, and in his need for revenge, he hatched a
plan to follow the Seabern caravan, and if unable to attack it, travel to the very heart of the Seabern strong-
hold to complete his revenge. He enlisted the aid of
Mordea, and together they prepared for the long journey through Scotland. But his wounds grew inflamed,
and a fever took hold, delaying their departure.

At the de Marlé castle, a caravan of horse-drawn
conveyances was outfitted to take the families north-
ward. A number of serfs who had readily affirmed that
they were willing to accompany the northbound group
were wont to drive the carts and wagons and take care
of the animals. Other serfs whose talents lay in cooking tasty dishes scouted out edibles evident along the
trail in order to add flavor to the dishes they created. At
night, huge bonfires warded off the cold. Guards were
posted and urged to be wary of anyone who might be
wont to approach their encampment.

Once the Scottish border had been crossed, peace
seemed to reign in every dale and hillock they passed,
but it was deceptive. Certainly, in comparison to the
strife presently taking place in England, it did seem a
blissful haven in which they could take refuge. But Raven was well aware of the danger that could yet be following somewhere behind, and he spent each day
riding the length of the caravan, looking for signs of

pursuit. A fortnight into the journey, his courier caught up to report that after a week's delay for Thurstan's recovery, his small army was on the move, but no one knew if more men and supplies would be joining him. Cedric sent another courier to discover the current size of the force.

During this time, Abrielle watched the tenderness and care Vachel showed toward Elspeth, and reflected on the obvious fact that their allegiances to either Norman or Saxon never interfered in their marriage. Seeing them together gave her confidence that she and Raven could do the same and helped quell her fears over a Scottish and Saxon union. Other fears—most, she could see now, of her own making—faded as well. Where once she might have thought herself undesirable, now she knew that Raven wanted an equal partner in marriage, a woman grown, not a girl full of frustrated fantasies of what marriage should be. Nay, her married life was no fantasy, not with men constantly on guard all day, or taking turns patrolling their encampment each night. Her precious moments alone with Raven occurred only when he snatched a few hours' sleep in between guard duties. Surely if they could survive this, they could bear whatever lay ahead for them in the scores of years she hoped they would have together.

Finally Raven announced that they were nearing his home. He and his father pushed the caravan hard that final day, exhausting the horses in a last effort to reach the Seabern estate before Thurstan could arrive. The enemy's scurriers had been spotted moving through the trees, so his force could not be far behind.

To Abrielle, the revelation of the Seaberns' keep was humbling, and more than sufficient to prevent her from ever jumping to conclusions about her husband again. It was a massive fortress with numerous towers, and high walls for protection. If anything, the structure was even more impressive than the one that Lord Weldon had designed and built for himself. Abrielle stared at her husband's home—her home, and what a magnificent home it would be for their family. Mortified, she remembered how she'd once thought he needed her wealth. Though she felt a fool for doubting him, she reminded herself that he'd given her every reason to suspect his motives. But now all she saw was a man devoted to his family, who kept them safe on a many-week journey.

Moments later, he drew the conveyance to a halt before the drawbridge and, upon alighting, briskly lifted her down. "Welcome ta our humble keep, my lady." Though his words were an attempt at lightheartedness, she could see his cold eyes scanning the forest several hundred yards distant, as if any moment soldiers waving swords would swarm at them.

"I never dreamt your ancestral home would be so grand," Abrielle said, trying to be as brave as her husband. "Why didn't you tell me how beautiful this valley was?"

He gave her a tight smile, pleased at his wife's reaction to his family's home despite the tension felt by them both. "Come see the interior, lass."

She looked over her shoulder, into the dark of the forest they'd just left. "Of course," she replied, knowing he wanted them all inside as quickly as possible. Up on the battlements, soldiers patrolled, and off in the distance, she saw dozens of serfs moving across fields and lanes toward the keep, carrying baskets and sacks.

Raven saw where she was looking. "I sent word ahead for the last of our people ta gather in the castle before we seal the gates."

She nodded, trying not to think of the fear those poor people must be feeling. She had brought this on them, she thought with despair. If she and Raven hadn't married, Thurstan would not be bringing his evil into this peaceful valley.

The villagers themselves herded their children before them, ignorant of the cause of their summoning, but understanding that Laird Seabern would keep them safe, whatever they had to face. Cloaked against the chill breeze, no one noticed a hooded figure slipping among them when they passed a wooded copse. The person carried a basket like all the others, and patiently waited in line to pass through the postern gate, before stepping into the dark shadows of an unlit corridor to disappear.

Inside the great hall, Raven and Cedric were the recipients of greetings from various knights and castle servants. Bows and curtsies were offered with wishes of good fortune for the marriage of Abrielle and Raven. The head cook promised a feast the bridal couple wouldn't soon forget; but all understood that such celebrations would have to wait.

When at last Abrielle had a moment, she gaped at her surroundings, the intricately carved mantel over the hearth and the many fine tapestries keeping out the drafts. Shields and portraits of ancestors lined several walls of the great room, evidencing a fine lineage of handsome men and women of extraordinary beauty. Her gaze seemed naturally drawn to a painting of a fairly regal, auburn-haired beauty that hung in a place of distinction beside a painting of a young man who looked very much like her own husband.

"My father and mother," Raven said, coming up behind her and putting his hands on her shoulders, his voice full of both love and pride.

"It could be a portrait of you," Abrielle replied, awed by the close resemblance he bore to the man in the painting. "Your mother was a rare beauty, to be sure."

"My da loved her as he has no other. 'Tis only been of late that I've seen a warm sparkle come inta his eye for another, but of course he's wont ta think she's much too young for an old man."

"If you mean Cordelia," Abrielle replied, "he probably has more of a chance at winning her heart than any suitor half his age. If you haven't noticed by now, Cordelia has a mind of her own. I would take her seriously, for she has never shown much interest or patience with suitors closer to her own age. Indeed, for an elder, your father is very fit and handsome."

Raven chuckled as he dipped his head in agreement. "He's been known ta best me more than a time or two. But what de ye think Lord Reginald would be saying ta such a match?"

"He seems to enjoy having Cedric around, especially after his injury. I think if your father were to wed Cordelia, it would serve only to deepen the amity between the two men."

"Ye think so?" he asked dubiously.

"Have I ever given you cause to doubt me?" she asked with feigned innocence.

His smile was slow in coming, but as it did, she thought surely the sun had come out from behind the darkest clouds. For one brief moment, she did not see his burden of responsibility and command, but sober knowledge settled into his gaze once again.

DARKNESS FELL BEFORE Thurstan's men could reveal themselves, and although the castle residents and guests knew that they might find themselves surrounded come morning, for now they shared a simple meal together in thanksgiving for their safe arrival. Conversations were subdued, and people ate in haste, needing to gather their families close in the night.

After Cedric and Raven toured the castle grounds one last time, Cedric rested before the hearth to clean his battle-ax.

Lord Reginald Grayson approached him and cleared his throat. "Laird Cedric—"

"'Laird Cedric'?" the Scotsman interrupted. "Reggie, havena the two of us progressed beyond the use of titles these past months? Ye've called me Cedric almost from the time we met."

Feeling a rising warmth in his cheeks, Reginald offered an awkward smile. "Aye, I suppose I have, Cedric. In all truth, it was my wife who urged me to approach you, and although now may not be the time, we know not what the future holds. 'Tis about . . . our daughter."

Cedric grew even more baffled. "I admire the Lady Cordelia as much as any lass alive. If she has mayhap taken offense with my teasing, then I'll surely mend my ways."

"She has not been offended," Reginald stated. "On the contrary, she has been much heartened."

Cedric nodded slowly, thinking he understood what his friend was trying to tell him. "Well, she is a comely

lass, but I shall make every attempt ta be more respectful in her presence so ye and the Lady Isolde willna be
offended. Ta be sure, the Lady Cordelia makes my very
heart sing, and I'm supposing I've gone a wee bit beyond the behavior of more dignified men in my wont ta
sing her praises."

"Please be assured that none of my family has been
offended," Reginald replied.

Now utterly confused, Cedric set aside his ax. "Then
what in all creation are ye trying ta say, Reggie?"

"We . . . ah . . . that is, Isolde and I have been wondering if you are truly interested in having our daughter to wife?"

Cedric harrumphed. "Well, ta be honest, I dinna
consider the fires of my youth ta be entirely quenched
yet . . . not that I'd ever be supposing something more
could come of my friendship with the Lady Cordelia.
Were I a score of years younger, I'd set my heart firmly
on having the lass for my very own."

"And that is exactly why I've come to you, to assure
you that Isolde and I wouldn't think ill of you if you
were to court our daughter," Reginald explained in a
rush.

Cedric canted his head as he peered at the man more
intently. "And such a thing would be ta the Lady Cordelia's liking as well?"

"Actually, she was the one who brought the matter
to our attention by asking if we'd be amenable to such
an idea. I think the danger of our journey made her
contemplate her future. I've yet to find a suitor for my
daughter who is more pleasing to me. Isolde and I both
want to be able to enjoy our grandchildren ere we depart this life."

"I canna lie. Merely the idea of taking ta wife so

bonny a lass makes me feel young again. Even so, there are a vast number of years separating the lass and me. I'm wont ta worry that I'd be doing the Lady Cordelia a disservice by marrying her. Many a young man would be overjoyed ta court the lass, so she may come ta rue our marriage should we be too hasty. As much as I'd be delighted ta have such an honor, the lass may need more time ta consider the notion." He paused. "Did she know beforehand that ye'd be conferring with me?"

"Nay, after voicing the question to Isolde, I hadn't the heart to approach Cordelia until I had spoken with you. If you should decide against taking my daughter to wife, nothing more will be said of it. Please be assured that our friendship will continue on as before."

Nodding his head, Cedric clasped Reginald's hand in a firm grip. "Then we'll be leaving it here till I've thought on this matter more and am satisfied the lass wants no other man but me for her husband."

THAT NIGHT, IN an ornately constructed prayer closet that had once belonged to Raven's mother, Abrielle pleaded fervently for the protection of those who had remained behind to watch over the keep. In a world that now seemed in total disarray, there were no guarantees that life would ever return to the way it was when Henry reigned. Although of human origin, many ravenous wolves were still prowling about drooling for want of blood and plunder.

When Raven still did not come to her, Abrielle went in search of him, accepting the assistance of the captain of the guard, who guided her up the narrow stairs to the battlements. The shock of the wind whipped her cloak about her legs, and she clutched the warm cloth to her neck. The moon had risen, and between that and the pools of torchlight, she saw Raven standing alone, looking out into the darkness. The captain of the guard ensured her safety as she walked the length of the battlements, until she had Raven's arm about her, and his warm smile to cheer her.

When they were alone, he said, "My wife isna content in her new chambers?"

"You know that they are beautiful," she murmured, snuggling against him, her head tucked beneath his chin. "All of our guests and family are settled, and though you need rest, still I find you here."

He shrugged. "I canna help it."

His soothing voice rumbled deep inside her whenever they touched.

"I trust my people implicitly," he continued, "and I ken that all is done as Da and I wish, yet . . . de Marlé is out there somewhere, waiting, choosing his time."

"Would he be foolish enough to attack at night?"

"Nay, 'twould na benefit him with castle walls ta protect us."

"Then come to bed."

It took every shred of his willpower to look away from the temptation she presented simply by breathing and peer at the dark countryside. "Soon."

She hesitated. "I had not thought to have this talk in such a strange place, but perhaps you need to hear it now. What if I were to tell you that I'm with child?"

He gave a start, then took her by the arms and stared down at her face as if everything he ever needed or wanted to know was to be found in her gentle eyes. For a moment he did not trust himself to speak around the swelling in his throat. "A bairn," he said softly. "My bairn."

"Then you are happy?"

He laughed and kissed her swiftly and then enfolded her in his embrace. "Happy? Aye, ye've made me that, sweet Abrielle."

"Then welcome home," she whispered.

He laid his large hand on her stomach, and she sighed. Feeling a new hopefulness, she was inclined to think of the joy their children would bring to them. She told herself that her marriage would not always be filled with the tension of sieges and attacks. She and Raven had to live for the future—and the infant growing inside her.

BEFORE DAWN, A horn sounded to alert the household, all of whom were already up preparing for the grim day. Those not in the courtyard rushed outside, only to see soldiers running at them, waving them back, their faces harsh with fear.

The first volley of fiery arrows lit the sky, rivaling the coming sunrise, raining down on the courtyard from where Abrielle and the women had just fled.

Chapter 22

Under a dark sky that the sun didn't pierce, the sight of flames flying in the sky made one stare in horror. The terrible screams of frightened people jolted Abrielle back to life, her heart lurching painfully. Although the women were urged back inside, and Isolde dragged Elspeth within the keep, Abrielle could not go. Most of the burning arrows landed harmlessly in the dirt of the courtyard, but several hit the roof of the stables and the barracks, and men were forced to climb up, passing buckets to one another to douse the blaze.

A lone shriek made her whirl around, and she saw a child staggering, waving her burning sleeve in fear. Abrielle ran to her and used her own skirt to smother the flames. She handed the dazed child to her sobbing mother, and then ran about the courtyard, stamping flames wherever she saw them on the ground.

In minutes the fires were extinguished, and she waited in shock, wondering when the next volley would be launched.

"What is happening?" she demanded of Raven's

captain of the guard as he rushed past her. "Why have they stopped?"

The man turned briefly. "They don't have the men or equipment to force their entrance, so they are using your fear against you, my lady. They want you to wonder when the next attack will come."

There were sudden shouts from the soldiers on the battlements only moments before another volley of flaming arrows cleared the curtain wall.

"We're trained in this, my lady," the captain called as he began to run toward the barracks. "Our own archers even now fire constantly on the enemy, who must dodge or hold their shields above their heads. Fear not!"

At least the children were now safe inside, Abrielle thought, glad she didn't have to hear such a piercing scream again, one that had frozen the very marrow in her bones. She was not the only woman to remain in the courtyard, smothering flames with blankets, shouting and pointing when a fire started where they couldn't reach. Men were stationed at the wells, constantly bringing up water and filling buckets.

Overhead, the clouds roiled, but no rain fell to aid them. The air was oppressive with the hesitation of the storm, and the heat of the flames that sometimes resisted death. An hour later, there was a larger gap between the launching of the arrows, and Abrielle had a moment to stare about her. The dovecote had gone up in flames, and no one had been able to save the poor birds. A pile of hay near the stables still smoldered. Women and men sagged wearily wherever they could sit during a moment's respite. Faces were blackened, garments charred, and hair singed.

"Abrielle!"

She heard her husband's stern voice.

"What are ye doing?" he demanded fiercely. "Go inside at once!"

"I will not! I am doing nothing more strenuous than stamping on flames."

"I demand that ye—"

"This is my home now, is it not?" she cried. "I will protect it, too!"

Raven had never felt such fear in his life as when he espied his wife—the woman he loved more than life and who was carrying his child—darting from the path of flaming arrows. Inside him a surge of tenderness warred with his need to see her safe.

"I'll care for her!"

Raven and Abrielle turned to see Cordelia marching toward them. Wisps of blond hair stood out from her dirty face, and she dragged a singed cloth behind her that she'd obviously been using to fight the flames.

"Can you take her inside?" Raven demanded.

"I shall try," Cordelia said firmly. "Now go do what you need to."

With a nod, Raven loped away toward the stairs leading to the battlements.

Abrielle folded her arms across her chest. "I shall not go."

"I know," Cordelia said wearily. "But promise me you'll take care, and you'll stay near me at all times."

"I promise," Abrielle said, looking up at the sky with dread. After a moment she said softly, "How long can this continue?"

"Until they run out of arrows." Cordelia leaned against an empty horse trough. "But if they planned this all along, then they came prepared."

"Do not say that." Abrielle stared up at the clouds, her anger flaring. "Why does it not rain?"

To her horror, more arrows streamed out of the sky, a trail of flames behind them. Her vow to stay with Cordelia came to naught when they both scattered to put out fires. Abrielle beat at flames with the small rug she'd taken from inside, coughing when she inhaled a blast of smoke. But she had a moment's clarity in which she realized that there were fewer arrows than when they'd first begun. Raven's archers were surely hitting their targets. All the keep had to do was outlast Thurstan's supply of men, and then it would be over.

"The roof!" a soldier shouted from the battlements.

All eyes looked up in shock and fear, but those on the ground could not see the top of the keep. Yet Abrielle realized that only the roof on fire could motivate such tired men, who suddenly ran across the walkways overhead connecting the battlements to the keep. Abrielle had never prayed so hard in her life.

But she could not continue to watch the sky when she heard a familiar voice scream. She stared wildly around her, only to see Cordelia frantically beating at her own skirt, where flames licked along the hem and rose higher. Abrielle started to run, but before she could even take two steps, Cedric appeared through the haze of smoke and knocked Cordelia to the ground, smothering the flames with his own body. Abrielle swayed and sat down on a bench near the garden.

Weeping, Cordelia clung to Cedric, letting him rock her, before at last she straightened and wiped at her wet, dirty face.

To Cedric, she had never looked more beautiful. "Lass, are ye well? Are there burns?"

"Nay, you saved me in time," Cordelia said, hiccuping on a sob as she gave him a wobbly smile.

"What a brave, fine lass ye are," he said, grinning. "Now take Abrielle and go inside. Surely there will soon be wounded who need your attention."

"The roof—"

"Is being attended ta even as we speak," he said. "Now go."

Although there was a somberness in his manner that boded ill, Cordelia gulped and nodded, meeting Abrielle's exhausted gaze.

Abrielle forced herself to her feet, knowing that she was so tired, she might do more harm than good in the courtyard. "I will go."

Leaning on each other, the two good friends slowly trudged up the stairs and into the great hall. To their surprise, there were only a few servants about. Elspeth came out of the kitchens and, on seeing them, hurried over.

"Where is everyone?" Abrielle asked.

"Oh, dear, are you hurt?" her mother demanded.

"Nay, I am sure I look far worse than I feel."

"Isolde has led women up into the sewing room to look for heavy cloth to put out fires," Elspeth interrupted, looking askance at Cordelia. "She fears for you."

"I shall go to her. Abrielle, you will remain here?"

"Aye, I will, and this time I mean my promise."

Cordelia nodded and hurried away.

"And the servants?" Abrielle said.

"Most are trying to help in one way or another. Would you assist me in setting out bread trenchers for the stew?"

"But, Mama, surely I can be of more use to the injured."

"The Seaberns have their own healer. Even now, she has set up her medicines in the chapel, but thankfully, there are only a few injuries so far." Elspeth stared into her daughter's eyes. "But you, my dear, need to rest and eat."

Abrielle frowned at the way her mother was hovering over her. And then the truth dawned. "You know, do you not?"

"About the babe? Aye, I guessed. I imagine a man like Raven would not need long to give his seed life."

Abrielle sighed. "We wanted to tell you all in a special moment, where we could celebrate."

"And celebrate we shall, for 'tis a joyous event. I shall be a grandmother at the same time I become a mother all over again."

Abrielle felt a smile tug at her lips.

"Vachel will become a father and grandfather all at once!"

Shaking her head, Abrielle groaned with a faint amusement.

"Now you are feeling better," Elspeth said. "Now come, the trenchers are near the kitchen. Help me set them at the tables."

Two other women emerged from the kitchen to help as Abrielle took a stack of bread and began to walk to a far table. For a moment she could almost forget that outside the sky rained fire, and that people battled to save her new home. The few women working with her did not speak, concentrating on their tasks with the dull lethargy of exhaustion.

And then an unholy scream echoed through the hall, the sound like a demon from hell. Abrielle whirled and had only a moment to see a heavy woman rushing at her, wild black hair fanning back from her distorted face. The witch, Mordea, Desmond's sister, had come for her vengeance.

OUTSIDE THE KEEP, Thurstan de Marlé broke in two the shaft of an arrow that protruded from his chest, distantly surprised that he didn't feel any pain. He watched the flames on the roof spew higher, and waited for the cries of lament to begin over the death of Abrielle Seabern. His revenge was so close at hand that he could taste its bitter sweetness.

ABRIELLE ONLY HAD a moment to fling up her hands, but her meager defense was useless against Mordea's insane strength. Her taloned fingers closed about Abrielle's neck, cutting off the very air she needed to breathe. Abrielle clawed desperately at the woman's hands, but could not pry them off.

Mordea shook her like a dog. "Ye won't give birth ta another heir, not when my Thurstan deserves all ye stole from him!"

Women screamed and fled for help, but not Elspeth. Seeing her daughter in the grip of a madwoman focused her mind, replacing terror with grim determination. No fear could exist for long in a mother's heart when her child was in danger. Snatching up a pitcher, she ran at Mordea from behind, lifted the pitcher high, and brought it down on the woman's head, shattering the vessel into a thousand pieces. Mordea staggered and fell, taking Abrielle with her.

Raven burst through the great double doors just as

Abrielle rolled clear of Mordea's slack arms and came to her knees, coughing violently. Elspeth started to sob, pulling at her daughter as if to get her far away from such a source of evil. But Mordea did not move.

Raven swept Abrielle into his arms, lifting her right off the floor in his need to hold her close to him. He felt the frantic thudding of her heart . . . and his own. "Are ye all right, my love?"

She nodded, her coughing finally fading, her hand at her sore throat. "I'll be bruised, but none the worse for wear, thanks to my mother. Please put me down so I can go to her."

Elspeth stood alone, hugging herself, crying, and the two women fell into each other's arms and sobbed loudly. More and more people streamed from the doorways leading down corridors, gathering around and whispering.

Raven rolled Mordea onto her back and saw her sightless eyes staring at the ceiling. "She's dead."

With a gasp, Elspeth lifted her head from Abrielle's shoulder. "But I didn't mean to kill her!"

"Mama, you were saving me! Her death was an accident, yet she was an evil woman who was bent on destroying anyone she could."

Elspeth nodded several times, her tears slowing until she heard her husband's voice. Then she sank into Vachel's arms and cried again.

"How did Mordea enter the keep?" Abrielle asked hoarsely.

Raven rose to his feet and put his arm around her, speaking with grim certainty. "The serfs entered just before we closed the gates. 'Twould have been easy enough for her ta disguise herself, especially with the cloak she's wearing. I blame myself. Thurstan's forces hadna yet arrived, so I assumed that he had no one near enough ta pose a threat." He closed his eyes for a brief moment. "I could have cost ye your life, Abrielle."

"Nay, think no more of it," she said firmly. "This siege is not yet finished."

"They send in fewer and fewer arrows. Their stores are surely depleted, and more men lie on the ground than yet stand, the victims of our archers. I say that we tell de Marlé that his plan didna work and see what he does."

"We could offer him her body," Abrielle said, glancing with a shudder at the dead woman. "She was almost an aunt to him. And I'm coming with you."

"Abrielle—"

"How can I be in more danger at your side than I've already experienced here?"

And he could not disagree with that.

On the battlements, Abrielle received her first view of the countryside spread out below the castle walls. She felt sick upon seeing the several dozen men lying in heaps, only a few barely stirring. But when she turned and caught her first sight of the castle roof, a corner of it still ablaze as men worked frantically, she could no longer pity the brigands who were foolish enough to follow Thurstan's cause.

Only a dozen men stood upright below, dipping arrows into fires built for that purpose. She looked up at the dark sky, black clouds threatening. Rain might be their only hope for stopping the whole roof from going up in flames, which would take the entire keep with it. If the flames spread any farther, they would soon have to abandon the building.

"Thurstan de Marlé!" Raven shouted.

Down below, the soldiers paused, and Raven could

see the man they turned to. Thurstan stood in the fore-
front of his men, his shield hanging awkwardly at his
side, no longer protecting him. Raven realized that he
had been hit with an arrow, and only remained standing
out of sheer determination.

"I see your roof in flames," Thurstan called back,
obscene laughter threatening in his voice. "It will not
be long now, Seabern."

" 'Twill be longer than ye think, de Marlé. Your men
are dwindling, and my men will soon have the fire under control."

Abrielle glanced back at the roof, and wondered if
her husband only bluffed.

"I offer the body of the woman ye considered an aunt,
the woman ye sent in alone ta do your work for ye."

Thurstan let the point of his sword lower into the
earth, and he almost staggered as he leaned against it.
"She failed?"

"She did!" Abrielle cried indignantly. "I am here,
Thurstan, and I yet thrive!"

His head hung for a moment, all of his plans falling
into ruin around him. But he gathered the last of his
strength and shouted, "You're a traitor, Abrielle of Harrington!"

His refusal to use her married name made her flinch.

"You'll never be able to return to the country of your
birth," he added savagely, falling heavily to his knees.

"Your words mean nothing to me!" she cried. "Raven is my husband, and by the blessings of God and
king and my own woman's heart, to him I'm bound."

As she looked into Raven's beloved face, rain began
to fall, dripping down his skin like tears of joy. In the
distance, she heard the cheers of their tired people.

"I will honor my own heart," she continued, still letting her voice rise in ringing tones, "because not only are nations at stake in these terrible times, but families. I owe my husband the honor of my loyalty."

Raven put his hands on her waist, pulling her against him. "I love ye, Abrielle," he said, his voice husky with emotion. "I've loved ye from the moment I first saw ye standing so poised and brave at the king's court. I love ye enough ta trust that together we can solve whatever life offers us. Ye have my heart, lass, and I can only pray ye trust me with your own, to keep and cherish it forever."

With a glad cry, she threw her arms around his neck and clung, lifting her face to the heavens, letting the rain mix with her tears. "I do love you, Raven, my husband. I love you for your honor and your courage—and your persistence, for I did not make it easy on you. I am so sorry it took me so long to know and understand the man you truly are."

They kissed deeply and smiled at each other and kissed some more, and with each meeting of their lips gave a fresh promise to each other for a lifetime of happiness.

The rain quenched the fires, and as Thurstan breathed his last, the rest of his men deserted him to flee into the forest. The threat was over, and the Seabern family could begin anew.

That night, when the wounded had been treated and the roof temporarily repaired, Raven and Abrielle shared the precious news of their unborn baby. Both families congratulated each other and were wont to toast the young couple. But Raven and Abrielle saw little of this, for they were staring into each other's eyes and seeing the wondrous future.

Epilogue

Neighbors from far and wide were invited to Laird Seabern's keep to enjoy a hearty feast and meet his numerous guests, all in celebration of his son's marriage. Several young Scotsmen closely eyed the only available maiden among the visitors and could not easily ignore the effervescent joy that seemed to radiate from the beauty. Her parents were especially amiable as well, but as much as the hopeful bachelors sought to make the lady's acquaintance and impress her with stories of their own derring-do, much to their amazement, she seemed more inclined to linger in the presence of the elderly laird and listen to his stories.

Little more than a month later, these same Scotsmen were wont to shake their heads in utter bemusement over the nuptials taking place between the comely young lass and the elderly laird within the wee church in the glen. Why, the elder was more than twice their own age, they were wont to whisper among themselves in amazement. If this had been an arranged match, surely when she repeated her wedding vows her elation would have been greatly dimmed by the morose circumstances surrounding her marriage. But they saw no hint of the possibility that she was enduring any dismay or regret. If anything, the lass seemed unusually elated and, for the better part of the evening, disinclined to be separated from the aging, yet still very handsome laird. As for the groom, he proved vigorous enough dancing to the pipes that many of the younger lads who sought to leave him gasping for breath had difficulty keeping stride with him.

Reginald evidenced his own delight over his daughter's marriage by presenting a dowry that staggered the imagination of the younger Scots who attended the wedding. They were just as amazed by the dower the groom gave his lordship, a piece of land adjoining the laird's holdings, large enough to suffice for the building of a grand manor.

"Should ye ever consider becoming my neighbor in the not-too-distant future," Cedric announced with a chuckle.

A wide grin stretched across Reginald's lips as he inclined his head in appreciation. "Isolde will now be content, having the beginnings of a home wherein she can nurture our grandchildren."

The hearty laughter of the two older men filled the hall as the younger bachelors glanced at one another in growing bemusement. The latter group was more inclined to think the elder Scot incapable of siring offspring. After all, he had only produced one son in all the years he had been married to his first wife.

"Our first will bear the name Reginald," Cedric declared, raising a tankard in toast to his friend. "And if mayhap it be a girl, then I'll be giving the honors ta the Lady Isolde."

All lifted their drinks in toast.

In a quiet corner of the great hall, Abrielle and Raven rested from the dancing, content to sit together and watch quietly. Vachel and Elspeth sat with them, and all were in a good humor, at peace with the world.

Elspeth smiled fondly at her daughter. "Your happiness pleases me, my dear. I prayed for this for so long."

To his wife, Vachel said, "Then when we have to return home in the coming months, can I trust that your heart will not break over parting with your daughter, however briefly?"

"You cannot be discussing leaving," Abrielle said, squeezing her mother's hand. "We have only just arrived, and you promised you would not leave until the babe was born and it was safe to travel."

"And we will keep that vow, of course," Vachel replied. "And we might have to remain to see our own grandchild born."

The women grinned at each other.

Then Vachel glanced at Raven and cleared his throat. "Daughter, we'll need to discuss the management of your estate while you're in Scotland."

Abrielle waved a hand. "You may discuss that with my husband, and don't think that will bother me. I trust him to see to it."

Raven frowned and slightly shook his head at Vachel, but Abrielle, focused on her husband, noticed immediately.

"And what was that for?" she asked, looking between them.

Vachel gave a deep sigh. "Now, Raven, there's no keeping this from her."

"What?" she demanded, her nerves growing taut.

"See, you'll upset her by withholding the truth,"

Vachel continued. When Raven only shook his head in surrender, Vachel turned to his stepdaughter. "My dear, it is you who must make the decisions about the de Marlé keep. You are its owner."

"But surely it was the only dowry I could offer to Raven."

"And he refused it," Vachel said.

She stared up at Raven, soft lips parted in surprise and growing embarrassment. "But . . . I thought . . . Raven, every man should have a dowry from his bride."

"But I didna need one," he answered. "If I'd have taken it, ye'd always have had a suspicion that 'twas why I married ye."

She bowed her head. "Oh, Raven, I feel like a fool."

"Nay, my love. Just talk ta your stepfather and tell him what's ta be done with your estate."

She took a deep breath. "Vachel, as long as you will see that the serfs are taught skills to benefit the keep as well as themselves, then I gladly yield that task to you, along with the bulk of my fortune, until I need it for my own family. In the interim, I shall expect a full accounting at least four times a year. Of the profit, you may take a suitable portion as payment for your services. Are you agreeable?"

Vachel and Raven glanced at each other in surprise at the knowledge Abrielle displayed, but Elspeth was unsurprised, and she could not resist a smug smile at her husband.

Vachel had done as much with the wealth he had given to his father and had reaped nothing in return, since the fortune had been bestowed in its entirety upon his older brother after the elder's death. "Five of every hundred that I manage to earn above your present total would be adequate."

"Ten would be better," Abrielle replied forthwith, seeking to assure him that he could expect her to be fairer than his own kin.

After clearing the hard knot of emotion that had formed in his throat, Vachel said, "You are being far too generous, Abrielle, and I'm honored by your trust. I shan't disappoint you."

Abrielle looked at Raven, feeling so happy and full of peace. Their most serious mistakes concerning each other were behind them—not that there would be no disagreements in the future between two such stubborn people.

She was gazing into his eyes, letting her love show, when Raven said, "Come with me to our chambers, my love. I have something to show you."

Blushing, she excused herself to her amused parents and, after waving to a blissful Cordelia, followed Raven. Once inside their chambers, she came to a stop, seeing a small wooden cradle before the hearth.

She inhaled swiftly, feeling tears trembling on her lashes. "Oh, Raven," she whispered, hurrying forward to touch the smooth wood, see the intricate carvings of sun and moon and stars on the headboard.

"I've been making it in secret for our child," he said softly, his hand on her shoulder. "I wanted it ta be a surprise. But now I can bring it inta the light of day, just like ye've brought my love, where it's flourishing. I canna imagine my life without ye, lass."

Her smile was tremulous. Together they knelt beside the cradle, the fire glowing on them softly, and thought about the babe in her womb and the love with which they'd bring it into the world.